The Contest

a novel

Ben Easton

Dedicated to my mother,
Elisabeth S. "Ziggy" Easton.
She always believed in me.

Prologue

TIAGO DÍAZ CLIMBED through an open window of a recently vacated apartment and dropped to the floor. He peered back through the opening and, in pidgin Portuguese typical of the Brazilian underclass, gave the go-ahead to Abílio.

"Come on, nobody has moved in yet ... too much blood."

"Wait! I am not as tall as you."

The boys silently scanned the abandoned space. Even though two of the four walls of the small apartment were spattered with blood, they dared not give too much significance to the grisly scene. To cope with life in the *favela*, they had learned to hold the awareness of violence and injustice at arm's length. With a shrug, the cousins agreed there was nothing of value for them to claim, and they left the apartment to continue their rounds.

"Where are we meeting the others?" Abílio asked.

"Usual place—the cemetery," said Tiago in a low voice as he led the way through an adjacent alley.

Their destination was a flat grassy area at the crest of a nearby hill, which is where they planned to meet the other three members of their little club. Paces away from this spot stood two poorly constructed crosses, suggesting that at least two graves lay nearby. Because nobody else ever seemed to go there, the boys would gather at this unofficial cemetery for the chance to show off their booty in private.

Moving away from the closely packed buildings as inconspicuously as they could, the boys made their way to a stand of trees where they would take the trail to their rendezvous. As they did so, their perspective gradually changed. With distance, the squalor of the favela was diminished, and this somehow gave it a reassuring wholeness. The colorful shanties seemed to have a symbiotic relationship with the subtropical hills on which they were so precariously built. Several kilometers beyond and lower in altitude, sprawled the hub of the city.

Far below them, spread across 180 degrees of their panoramic view of Rio de Janeiro, lay Guanabara Bay, Jobim International Airport, Sugarloaf Mountain, and Copacabana Beach. It was an exotic view, but one which they had only experienced from a distance.

Tiago loved the weather in the late springtime. He especially liked the heady fragrances that wafted up the hillsides on the ocean breeze. He would soon turn ten, and he felt the promise of life floating to meet him, like the morning fog that transformed into the soft clouds that welcomed visitors to this stretch of the Brazilian coast in the summer months.

He felt a heightened sense of importance as summer approached—and Christmas, for that was his birthday. Sharing a birthday with the Christ was an important distinction, and Tiago seemed blessed by this influence. And, because he was both happy-go-lucky and focused, his friends granted him leadership in their little association.

Silvio and Ronaldo stood waiting as Tiago and Abílio raced the final fifty meters to the little plateau, huffing and puffing gleefully.

"Slow pokes ... Come on!" yelled Silvio, the tallest and hairiest of their group. Ronaldo grinned and said nothing.

"What is the hurry? We are not last!" called Abílio.

The four boys then directed their teasing at João, who dodged and darted from a slightly different direction, still half a kilometer down the mountain. The oldest at eleven and a half, he was the best collector among them.

"What do you bring, João?" asked Tiago as their friend stepped onto the grass from the last rise.

"You will see," he said. The others let him catch his breath while they repositioned themselves around an old wooden crate that was placed upside down in the middle of the small clearing. This was the table on which the boys would determine if anything of value could be sold, traded, or used to improve their sanctuary—a tree house with a retractable ladder.

"Look what I found," said Ronaldo excitedly. He reached into his baggy cargo shorts and pulled out a slightly scuffed Motorola cell phone.

"Does it work?" asked Abílio.

"I haven't tried it yet. A Vaquero left it on a table at Fat Man's ... on the patio."

"Shit, Ronaldo!" said João.

"Don't worry—nobody saw me. They had already left the bar. I was looking for my little sister."

"How do you know it was a Vaquero?" Tiago asked.

"It was on the table in the corner, the one with the marks carved in it," explained Ronaldo. "Nobody else will sit there."

Tiago and Abílio exchanged a quick look and shuddered, for they had seen the Vaqueros' sign on the floor of the vacant apartment. It had been written in blood.

"*Dios mío!*" Silvio whispered, mirroring the others' thoughts.

"That will be hard to beat," said Tiago, breaking the spell. He placed a portable cosmetic case, enclosed in faux leather, on the crate. Unzipping it, he showed off the shiny contents: tweezers, scissors, file, and a rectangular mirror held in place by Velcro.

"Not bad, Togo," Silvio said. "All I brought is a bottle of juice."

"Brilliant!" Ronaldo poked him. "After we drink it, you can pee in the bottle!"

The boys laughed.

"What I found is not much better," said Abílio as he emptied his pockets of an oddball collection of construction fasteners.

"Those might come in handy. We just need some tools," said Tiago.

"Okay, João, your turn," said Silvio. "Can you top mine?"

They all laughed again.

"I don't know," said João with a mock grimace. He opened a plastic grocery bag and withdrew a dark red mechanic's rag which he unrolled carefully.

About a dozen AA batteries clattered onto the weathered crate, some of them falling to the ground.

Ronaldo picked them up and brushed them off. "These will fit in our radio!"

"Uh-huh," said João, beaming. He had come up with a portable radio months before, but the batteries had long since run down. They kept it wrapped in plastic to protect it from the rain, hidden with several other items under a nearby bush.

"What is that?" Tiago pointed to the other pile of odds and ends that remained in the plastic bag.

"A coil of wire and some rope."

"What did you do, rob a hardware store?" asked Abílio.

João grinned. "My secret."

After checking the perimeter for unwelcome visitors, including the occasional trespass by younger siblings or wannabes from the neighborhood, the boys moved the meeting to their treehouse, a hundred meters away. While Ronaldo grabbed the stowed cache of valuables, Tiago climbed the tree and lowered the ladder. After scrambling up like sailors ascending to the crow's nest of a pirate ship, each boy settled into his own personalized niche.

João pried open the back of the radio and inserted four new batteries, and they all cheered when a familiar station came in loud and clear. The cheap transistor radio was their window to the larger world. Beyond their ramshackle village, beyond the city, beyond the people and goods that flowed through the airport and the shipyards, magical possibilities existed.

Tiago moved to his favorite perch, a gentle bend in one of the lower boughs of the tree. Through an opening in the lush canopy, he gazed out on the distant waves of the South Atlantic. His daydreams bypassed the city and the beaches below as he catapulted himself to invisible lands beyond the far horizon.

Chapter 1

MINERVA BENNETT DOODLED in the margin of the newspaper as she pondered the next definition. In her all-caps script, she inserted a long string of letters for 24-ACROSS and then two vertical words that became obvious as a result. While she considered the next word, she resumed the network of lines, curves, and shaded figures that gradually filled the space surrounding the crossword puzzle.

Glancing at the clock sitting on a nearby sideboard and noticing that the minute hand of the porcelain dial indicated that it was a quarter past the hour, she reached for the intercom. The 1970s device still functioned perfectly and had never lost its prominent position on her Louis XV writing desk. Her computer, meanwhile, was relegated to the corner of the work space, away from the stack of newspapers, magazines, the mechanical Rolodex, and an early push-button model telephone.

"Isabel, are my guests here yet?" she asked.

"Except for Mr. Proctor, yes. I'll inform you the moment he arrives, Mrs. Bennett."

"Thank you, Isabel."

Her irritation quelled for the moment, Minerva searched her memory for a 9-letter word meaning "early form of communication."

Ah-hah! SEMAPHORE, she thought. *I yearn for those simpler days.*

As she inserted the letters of the antiquated term, she smiled. She continued her internal monologue, thinking about the group she would meet with shortly. *These youngsters don't even know what that is. The world they've created for themselves runs on a different clock … But there's still such a thing as being on time!*

Minerva rested her pale, slightly quivering hand, with its exquisite topography of veins, on the heel of her palm as she carefully thickened a line to give three-dimensionality to one of her shapes. *Not bad for an old gal like—*

"Mrs. Bennett," interrupted Isabel softly from the door of the sitting room, "your guests are all here. They're in the study."

Isabel, the housekeeper for Minerva Bennett for over twelve years, was fiftyish and slim. Trained to communicate concisely, she was fluent at reading her mistress's thoughts and moods.

Minerva replaced the top of her pen with a satisfying click and set it on top of *The New York Times* puzzle. She stood up carefully, smoothed her skirt and blouse, and repositioned her shawl. As far as she was concerned, there was never a good reason not to look presentable. She walked the length of the main corridor of her penthouse, gathering her thoughts as she moved from her private rooms, past the dining room and living room, to the library.

Her heart jumped a little as she considered her agenda. She wondered what they—her advisory staff—would say when she informed them of her vision. She imagined that she could already hear their protests.

Minerva entered through the heavy door of the study, and her five guests rose. Stewart Maxwell, principal legal counsel for the Koyne Foundation, bowed his head and smiled.

"Minerva, my dear, you look wonderful." He was the only one of her many subordinates who had managed to attain a first-name relationship with her. She allowed it, perhaps because he was the nephew of one of her friends and only twenty years her junior.

"Thank you, Stewart. You're looking sharp. I especially like your tie. It brings out the gray in your temples." She spoke as she moved to her reserved chair by the fireplace, next to a side table with a water pitcher, reading glasses, tissue box, and intercom. She sat down and then gestured to her guests to take their seats.

Next to her sat Catherine Myers, her executive assistant for five years. To her right was Brooks Mecom, the head fund manager and portfolio specialist.

Minerva turned and smiled at the youngest member of their team, Libby Armstrong. She had been lured to New York from San Francisco a year and a half earlier, initially to become vice president of development. After performing admirably, she was fast-tracked to replace the former president, who had, herself, been lured away by a marriage proposal. Libby brought a fresh west coast outlook and poise to the executive staff.

"I'm sorry I was late, Mrs. Bennett," said Galen Proctor, fidgeting. "Crosstown traffic took me by surprise."

"Well, none the worse for wear," said Minerva with a hint of agitation.

Galen Proctor, a quiet man in his early fifties, was her accountant. He had never been comfortable in his employer's presence.

Minerva had called this meeting in a more abrupt manner than usual, via a brief e-mail. The subject line had been vague: *Strategic Discussion*. No agenda had been included.

Since returning from almost two months of travels, including time in Italy and Greece, a week in Paris, and then a gala benefit and family reunion in Texas, she had been subtly different to those who knew her well—more impulsive, more imperious.

At eighty-seven, Minerva Bennett was in remarkable shape. But she had been on edge in recent weeks. This led some of her staff to accuse her, behind her back, of being unreasonable, even bitchy. Their simple diagnosis was that age was finally taking its toll.

Her closest friends, however, knew this was not the case. Beset by fears and doubts she had been grappling with for several years, Minerva was caught in a tempest of moodiness and introspection. For a woman who was at the peak of her reign, this was unsettling.

Two days earlier, just before 5:00 AM, her typical waking hour, Minerva had sat bolt upright. She had had a vivid dream and had remembered just enough of it to identify a connection to what had been haunting her. She had donned her housecoat and slippers and had padded into the library to search for a book—three books, it turned out. These had appeared in the cross-sensory strangeness typical to dreams, but there appeared to have been a common theme that tied into the fantasy. Chasing, but not catching, she had been frustrated and maddened. The prey had then turned and chased her, the fright of which had awakened her.

The chasers had been an amalgam of beasts, dolls, and phantoms. But what kept these from rattling her too badly was the appearance of story book characters, each of which had profoundly affected her as a child. These characters had called out to her across time and space, and Minerva presumed there was some urgent message, if only she could piece it together.

After several minutes of scanning and poking about in her library, she spied a group of faintly familiar bindings on an upper shelf. These, she hoped, were the books that had been featured in her dream. They were among her oldest possessions.

Cover illustrations jumbled in her mind as half-remembered scenes echoed in her memory. Sitting in her favorite wingback chair, she recalled how her older sister Helen and she would sit up in bed and read stories aloud to one another. It was Helen who had taught her to read, even before she attended kindergarten in the neighborhood school.

As she sifted through the books, Minerva smiled at the happy little train on the cover of *The Little Engine That Could*. When she came across a vintage edition of *Alice's Adventures in Wonderland*, she briefly considered canceling her appointments for the day to read it again. She set it aside, though, and kept searching for the ones that had called to her in her sleep.

When she picked up a first edition of *The Water Babies*, by Charles Kingsley, she realized that it was one of the ones from her dream. She felt as if she were holding a sacred object; it had been in their family for almost one hundred years. Minerva couldn't recall the plot, but she somehow felt the magical spell it had cast eighty years before.

Then she came across *Anne of Green Gables*, by Lucy Maud Montgomery, and hugged it close to her breast. She opened it and smelled the pages, savoring the rich mixture of memories and emotions. Basically satisfied and prepared to give up her search for any more titles, Minerva noticed another stack of books on an even higher shelf. Though she was too old to go climbing up the rolling ladder, she decided to make a go of it. Halfway up its fifteen-foot span, she grasped a book that looked familiar and then carefully descended to the polished floor.

The moment she glimpsed the cover, she knew that it too had been featured in her dream. The reaction she experienced as she placed it on the table was out of all proportion. *A Little Princess*, by Frances Hodgson Burnett, took her breath away. Her eyes stung with tears that gushed in from nowhere. She pursed her lips, ashamed at losing control.

In a flash of insight, the significance of her dream became clear—it was about the power of ideas. But it was more than that, she thought. It had to do with the portrayal of the undiluted optimism that she had acquired as a young child. This outlook, she suddenly realized, had been presented and reinforced by these books, forgotten for most of her adult life.

The distant irritation Minerva had been experiencing for months suddenly came into sharp relief in that moment of rediscovery. She felt as if the ground had fallen away and the sky had opened up. *What am I to do now?* she asked herself as the weight of the books on her lap disappeared in a flash of excitement. She wanted to run through the park like a child, shouting with joy.

The rapid replaying of that revelation two days prior now braced Minerva Bennett in the present of this meeting.

"I imagine you're wondering why I summoned you this morning," she said, but then immediately paused. She looked around, giving herself one final chance to back away from the precipice ... to shift back into the usual, the comfortable—the normal.

"For several years now, I've been wondering about things that we old people tend to wonder about. Specifically: what have *I* done to make the world a better place? This is a question that most of us think about at some point, since we all hope to leave the world better than we found it.

"This is the mission of the Koyne Foundation, of course, and I'm pleased with the help you have each contributed. For some time, though, I've wondered if we're really doing all we can. I read the newspapers every day. I watch the news on TV ... and I wonder if *anything* is getting through.

"In short, I've been reflecting on our purpose. Yes, I know we give to worthy groups and organizations, all of which do good work. But ..." she paused—not for effect, but out of fear— "... I want to change our approach. I have a rough idea of what I want us to do, but I need your help in formulating it and making it work."

As her senior advisor, Stewart Maxwell responded. "Minerva, I think I can speak for the others by saying how proud we are of the work we do, and ... there's always room for improvement."

Nodding, she continued. "Problems abound in the world, and they seem to be stacking up faster than ever. Solutions, however, seem to be lacking. We seem to bathe in our problems, and we love to imagine that we're open to solutions. It is only recently that I've begun to see through this delusion.

"During my recent travels, I had an opportunity to observe a certain segment of the population that does not hide behind this façade—namely *children*. Of course, children don't necessarily understand the full extent of our problems, but they naturally hold them to be temporary. They imagine and assume that solutions, even to the biggest problems, are high on everybody's list of priorities, and that we adults are actively involved in making things better."

Sideways glances told Minerva that she had lost some of them on what was, perhaps, a strange tangent. Nevertheless, she forged ahead.

"It occurs to me that my money, my contributions, all the efforts of the Koyne Foundation, haven't really changed *anything*. I'm beginning to see my role as a philanthropist and patron of the arts as a subtle lie, as if—"

"Mrs. Bennett, I know I'm still pretty new to the organization," interrupted Libby Armstrong, "but, from what I've experienced thus far, this foundation enjoys the highest reputation in the industry. I don't think I would have joi—"

"Yes, my dear. I know." Minerva cut her off gently. "I have no doubt that our reputation is solid, but I can't ignore my recent revelation. Let me share some of the changes I'm considering."

For the next several minutes, she painted a deliriously bright landscape of harmony, peace, prosperity, and hope. She became animated and enthusiastic;

the bitter edginess that had colored her personality in recent months disappeared entirely.

Her guests sat—frozen, captivated, even amused. As their chairman summarized her proposed objectives and the implied sweeping changes in the fundamental scope of the foundation, the mood in the room shifted awkwardly. Only her secretary maintained a neutral composure as she typed away at her notes. The others, perhaps because they were directly beholden to the Koyne Foundation in varying degrees, now looked at Minerva as if she had, in the space of half an hour, leapfrogged senility and lapsed directly into a sort of benign dementia.

Stewart Maxwell, who was originally hired to explicitly counterbalance all the "yes" men that would naturally surround the likes of Minerva Bennett, cleared his throat discreetly.

"I don't know quite where to start, but I'll begin by acknowledging that your vision is truly childlike in its purity and optimism. I guess my first question is: what sort of changes are you imagining? I dare say that the Koyne Foundation is already doing a fine job of honoring the ideals of which you just spoke."

"I was thinking the same thing, Mrs. Bennett," added Brooks Mecom. "You talked about bringing the innocence of children into the process of problem solving, of giving young people a voice at the table ... fostering competition for solutions. What does that actually look like?"

"Regarding investment in education," added Libby Armstrong, "especially elementary education, we could certainly adjust our annual giving to include more independent schools, charter schools, things of that sort."

Then it was Galen Proctor's turn. "Mrs. Bennett, you said you wanted to distribute a substantial portion of the principal in lump sums to 'deserving leaders or winners.' For one thing, this would contradict our charter. Furthermore, I can only speculate as to the horrendous tax implications."

Minerva nodded, as if to say, *Yes, you heard me,* but she stayed silent for the moment.

Maxwell spoke again. "I'm not quite sure why, but you're being very hard on yourself, Minerva. It's as if you're getting impatient to see the final outcome of all of your efforts, but that's not realistic. And now you want to wave lots of money in the air for a bunch of strangers by holding a touchy-feely problem-solving competition."

"Almost like a contest to save the world," Brooks Mecom said sarcastically.

After several seconds of awkward silence, Minerva laughed. It was neither bitter nor resentful, but simple and melodious.

"I don't blame any of you for being skeptical," she responded. "Over the last couple of days, I've wondered myself if I've just gone batty. I know that I'm talking about a bold break from our present course." All eyes were on her to see if this were a softening of her stance.

Minerva continued, "But you heard me correctly. I *am* talking about giving away our money in a whole new way. I *do* want to somehow involve children. And, Brooks, I love your description of my idea—*a contest to save the world!*"

Relative to the canons of mainstream charitable giving, the rest of the meeting was surreal. As Minerva affirmed that her idea was not a temporary flight of fancy, the looks of disbelief that flashed subtly back and forth among her staff hinted that they regarded her proposal to be nothing less than a renunciation of philanthropic sensibility altogether.

She confirmed her intention to use the foundation's assets for some sort of global competition of ideals, and then she gave them a simple assignment: identify obstacles to such a shift and prepare to offer counter measures. She finished with a warning.

"In light of the unusual nature of my proposal, and the changes under consideration, I want to remind each of you that, because we're a private foundation, our proceedings are secret and confidential. Not only would such changes affect each of us here in this room, they would have ramifications far and wide. If any of this gets out to the investment community or to any of our annual recipients, there will be serious *personal* fallout." She paused and looked each of them in the eye to ensure that her meaning was clear.

"As you gather the facts and figures I've asked for, you'll need to show your hand to a degree. Nevertheless, I expect you to conceal your inquiries and cover your tracks. Be as discreet as possible."

As her guests gathered their belongings and made their way to the elevator, Minerva wondered darkly at the nature of this new course. *What have I done?*

⋯►═◉ ◉═◄⋯

Minerva put on her overcoat and gloves so she could endure the crisp December air. Her Central Park penthouse offered one of the finest views in the hemisphere, and she liked to stand on the terrace and gaze upon the city.

She stepped carefully onto the tiled patio, slid the door shut, and weaved through the groupings of patio furniture and potted plants toward the open space. Some of the plants had been covered in plastic for the coming freezes; the more fragile ones had been moved indoors, to the alcove next to the sunroom.

Standing near the center of her terrace, she scanned the entire city. It was fantastic and beautiful. She could see a hundred buildings: the grand and gothic nestled with the simple and prismatic, all positioned in an elegantly simple grid. She liked them all. Their skyscraping edges flaunted space itself, and their exhalations of vented exhaust, pure white against the deep blue of the sky, brought them to life as familiar giants.

Hearing the muffled traffic below, Minerva was comforted by the faint sounds of acceleration and the staccato punctuation of honking. As she looked skyward, the cacophony was softened by the silence of several airliners, miles above, tracing the sky with their contrails.

She fell into a brief rapture, inspired by the direct perception of a transcendent order and harmony, of which she felt an integral part. The doubt that had burrowed into her mind began to dissolve, and she breathed a sigh of relief.

"Thank you, Lord," she whispered solemnly. She liked the numbing sensation of the cold wind on the tears in the corners of her eyes. Hands in her pockets, she made no attempt to wipe away her tears. They helped her feel alive.

As she liked to do in solitary moments such as this, especially when overcome with gratitude, Minerva took an inventory of the angels in her life:

friends, loved ones, teachers ... some passed on, some still alive. Any lingering loneliness evaporated as she recalled the tender smile of her sister Helen, the powerful gaze of her first husband Bill Fielding, and the friendly confiding embrace of her second husband JB.

Other faces flashed through her mind, mostly from her generation— Gladys, Louisa, Father Ellison, but suddenly a young man's face eclipsed the others, plunging her into a vivid reminiscence of the recent events that had precipitated her altered outlook.

Chapter 2

TWO AND A half weeks earlier, Minerva Bennett had flown to Houston to visit her nephew Robert Godfrey, the eldest son of her late sister Helen. Bob, as most of his friends called him, was the most business savvy of all her relatives; he had done very well for himself in several sectors of the Texas economy. He insisted, as he always did, that she stay with him and his wife Leigh at their house in River Oaks. Minerva liked Leigh, whom she found witty and charming, generally able to keep her husband from getting too one-tracked and belligerent.

Bob and Leigh had invited a small group of family and friends to dine with Minerva. Other than Bob and Leigh, both of whom Minerva knew well, there was only a faint familiarity with the rest of the family. She had only met the Godfrey children, a thirty-something crowd, three or four times previously, but thank goodness for iPads and photo-sharing. During the limo ride from the airport, Catherine Myers briefed Minerva on the flood of faces she would see that evening.

The evening began with cocktails and small talk. Leigh introduced Minerva to her daughter, Marian; then, she led her over to her three sons, huddled together in typical fashion. The boys had remained close into young adulthood and were often found teasing and joking, telling stories about one another. As the matriarch, Minerva could see family resemblances to distant branches of the family tree.

"I know it's been a good while since you may have seen any of the boys, Minerva, so I'll introduce them in chronological order. This is Blake, Henry, and Allister—the baby, though you wouldn't know it, since he's the tallest and has the deepest voice."

While Bob prepared the fish that he and the boys had caught, Minerva chatted briefly with her grandnephews before being introduced to the other guests. After another round of cocktails, the gathering moved to the dining room.

As she often did in such settings, Minerva sat back and listened. She asked a leading question here and there and then enjoyed watching the conversation jump about. Between the boys' banter and Leigh's expert steering of the conversation, dinner was entertaining.

After dessert and coffee, they moved back into the living room where Minerva made a point to chat with the younger generation for at least a few minutes each. Her most engaging conversation had been with Henry, the middle son. He had first caught her attention during dinner when she observed him standing his ground and challenging his father in a conversation over party politics. Just as it was becoming over-heated and ugly, Bob had waved his son off with a dismissive hand.

In that awkward moment, she experienced a strange empathy, feeling the rebuke almost as a slap on her own face. Minerva had always considered herself in the same ideological camp as her nephew, but she was startled to realize she had been pulling for Henry, and that it was more than just rooting for the underdog. Some long-accepted premise seemed to crack under the weight of a fresh perspective.

Two new conversations had sprung up to replace the one that had been squelched, making it difficult for Minerva to reflect on the antagonism between father and son. She resolved, therefore, to approach Henry and find out more about him.

"Henry, your mother tells me you're a teacher."

"Yes, ma'am. I teach middle school math. I also do some coaching."

"At what school?"

"Aegis Academy," Henry answered.

"Aegis ... that's an interesting name," she said distractedly. The name reminded her of something, but she couldn't put her finger on it.

"I think it means *under protection*. The school is considered progressive, even though it's based on the ancient concept of the gymnasium. It's basically a prep school."

"I see," said Minerva, nodding ever so slightly. "I'm intrigued by the viewpoint you defended at dinner. Does that have anything to do with this school, or your teaching?"

"Not directly, other than the fact that it's a private school—a *free market* school. I was saying that government, especially the federal government, has no proper authority in certain aspects of modern life, including education."

"Where did you come across these ideas? Some of them are, quite frankly, extreme." She had purposely worded her statement in alignment with his father's point of view, to test Henry's reaction, but he remained calm.

"I agree. In fact, I like to refer to my views as *radical*, but in the original sense of the word. It means 'fundamental'—pertaining to the root or origin of an idea ... and that does have to do with my school, now that I think about it. We urge our students to question everything."

"Tell me, then, about your chosen subject matter. Why mathematics? It seems that you might be more suited for history or civics, or even debate."

His face lit up. "Well, I've always loved numbers. They're so clean, so definite. This is the one subject where there is always a clear and correct answer. As long as the rules are honored, the answers are indisputable."

"That's well and good, but problems in the real world can't always be solved by numbers and equations. What then?"

"That's true," responded Henry, "but the rules underlying even the most complex issues are based on the principles of reality. If a situation can't be quantified, it can still be treated objectively and analyzed logically."

"It looks like we have an idealist in the family." Minerva stated this almost coldly, as a challenge.

"That's what I am. At least ... that's what I try to be."

Seeing that he embraced a label that, in her world, was often used as an insult, she softened her tone. "I'm sorry, Henry. I didn't mean to be derogatory. In fact," she said, turning toward him in a more intimate and confiding posture, "I have a bit of that within me. I guess that's why I wanted to talk with you. You see, I was once a teacher."

"*Really?*" Henry sat up. "What did you teach?"

"It's been years since I spoke to anybody about that chapter of my life ... it was so long ago. Several years before I met my first husband, I was just an Irish girl fresh out of St. Joseph's College for Women, in Brooklyn. I taught for three years, in the neighborhood elementary school.

"I can't remember anything specific ... not even the number of the school. Nevertheless, I have fond memories of my time in the classroom. I'd like to think the children learned something from me, that I helped them on their—"

Overcome with emotion, Minerva halted abruptly and turned away. She pulled a wadded tissue from her pocket and dabbed at her tears.

"Pardon me, Henry. I'm a sentimental woman," she said, trying to regain her armor of gruff formality, but failing.

He nodded. "Believe it or not, I sometimes have to stop myself in the middle of a lesson." He held his fist up to his mouth, briefly demonstrating one of his own masking techniques. "I guess I'm sentimental, too."

"Oh?" she said, genuinely surprised. "Nothing against numbers, but I always thought mathematics to be a fairly dry subject." She winked, and then dabbed her eyes dramatically.

"It can be, but I use lots of metaphors and analogies. I make up stories—most of them silly and absurd—about problems and solutions. I get all dramatic about heroic victories and such, and of course the numbers are the heroes. The kids love it!" He smiled broadly, obviously recollecting some recent interaction.

"That I'd like to see," Minerva said.

"Maybe you can. I imagine you're pretty booked up, but, if you have a few extra hours, I'd love for you to come visit my school. Our students have been getting ready for Grandparents' Day, which is Wednesday. Tomorrow is Tuesday, though, and that would be the perfect time to come look around. No crowds, no hoopla."

"That's kind of you, Henry, but you're right," she had said, rising. "My staff keeps me very busy on trips like this, even when family is involved."

⋯⟫⊚ ⊚⟪⋯

Catherine Myers, who had accompanied Minerva on the trip to Texas, arrived at the Godfreys' house the next morning, ready to escort her boss to the airport and back to New York. A few minutes from the house, Minerva abruptly instructed their driver to make a detour. When Catherine asked the reason, Minerva waved her off and looked out the window, obviously agitated.

Fifteen minutes later, the limousine turned into the parking lot of Aegis Academy, and the driver eased up to the front entrance. Minerva, who routinely spoke to high-level personalities and powerful boards and committees and whose decisions influenced thousands of lives, sat motionless. Frozen in a fear that made no sense to her, she gazed at the front entrance to the school and wondered why she felt compelled to visit. She replayed her conversation with Henry, recalling that she had thanked him for his invitation and had committed to nothing.

Minerva knew that this impromptu tour would be no worse than countless other visits she had endured—to museums, hospitals, and schools. Yet, she felt a knot of fear in her chest. On the verge of instructing the driver to exit the parking lot and proceed to the airport where her jet awaited, she glanced once more at the entrance. She noticed the coat of arms above the door with the name of the school inscribed below it.

Suddenly she made the connection that had eluded her the evening before, when Henry had mentioned the name of the school. Her fear subsided and a shiver of insight emerged in its place.

"Park the car."

As she and Catherine walked through the doors, Minerva felt a strange sense of familiarity despite never having set foot on the campus. The evening before, her grandnephew had only mentioned the modern meaning of "aegis." She had decided to look it up before going to bed and found that, in ancient

Greece, the *Aegis* referred to the breastplate or shield of Athena or Zeus. She must have been too tired to see it then, but now it was clear. Minerva, her very own mythological namesake, was the Roman incarnation of Athena, goddess of wisdom, courage, law and justice. Henry's school, then, if she were to claim a little poetic license, was a sanctuary under her protection.

Despite the surge of confidence brought about by a symbolic connection with the school, Minerva noticed her relief that the students were in class, and that the hallways were quiet and empty. Peering ahead and seeing a sign that read "Administration," she took a deep breath, exhaled with determination, and walked forward. Catherine flanked her silently. They entered the office, and Minerva felt the quiet industriousness of an administrative staff conducting the nuts and bolts business of a school.

"Good morning. My name is Minerva Bennett. I am here to visit my grandnephew's classroom."

The receptionist looked up from her computer. "I'm sorry, ma'am, but I'm afraid you've arrived one day early. Grandparents' Day is *tomorrow.*"

"Yes, I'm aware of that. My grandnephew is actually a math teacher ... Henry Godfrey. I'm visiting from New York City, and he assured me I would be welcome to visit today—before your rush of guests tomorrow."

This explanation satisfied the receptionist, and she typed up two visitor name tags. As the women clipped these to their lapels, a slender middle-aged man with too much energy bounded into the office and surveyed the situation. He wore grey flannel pants, a white oxford shirt, a blue blazer, and a striped tie—just what one might expect of an administrator in a prep school on the affluent side of town.

"Good morning, ladies. Welcome to Aegis Academy. I'm Gordon Hooper, the middle school principal." He seemed to have put two and two together even before walking into the office, and he continued as if the meeting had been on the schedule for weeks. "I understand you are here to visit Henry Godfrey's classroom, and, time permitting, to look around."

"Evidently ... I see my nephew has tipped you off. Does his confidence get in the way of his teaching?" She smiled wryly at the principal and then turned to Catherine. "What did I tell you?"

"Don't be too hard on him," said Hooper. "Henry knows I'm a huge fan of classical music. He heard me going on and on the other day about Dallas's new music hall. He bragged about how you were the driving force behind that, and that you happened to be his great aunt." Minerva nodded, suppressing a smile.

"Henry drew me aside just after our morning assembly and told me there was an outside chance that you might grace us with a visit before returning to New York. I'm glad you decided to take him up on his invitation."

With that, the three of them entered the main corridor and headed toward the classrooms. Hooper explained that the students were either in class or in study hall, and that they had twenty minutes before the halls would fill rapidly with middle school children. Minerva paused in front of a glass-covered presentation case in which student art work was displayed. In an adjacent case, there were athletic and academic trophies and plaques.

"How old is the school, Mr. Hooper?" Catherine Myers asked.

"In the fall, we celebrated our 21st Anniversary. In the first year, there were only three levels—pre-K, kindergarten, and first grade."

"How high does it go now?" asked Minerva, squinting at some of the plaques. Donning her reading glasses, she read the names on several national mathematics awards.

"We now run from pre-K through the twelfth grade."

The women followed Hooper as he took them by the middle school library, the computer lab, and the commons, a room for large assemblies. As they approached a broad stairwell, Hooper veered to offer them the elevator. Exiting into an open area on the second floor, the guests observed more student work in display cases and grade-level bulletin boards.

While Catherine was admiring clay artwork and science projects, Minerva became absorbed in some history essays written by eighth graders. She could hardly believe the maturity and the level of presentation. *How can these fourteen-year-olds grasp such serious topics? How can their teachers elicit such responses?*

A short time later, the bell rang and students flooded the hallways. The plan was to wait safely out of the flow and to enter Henry's classroom before the next rush of students. Though unsettled by the untamed rambunctiousness of the students, Minerva was invigorated by their spontaneity.

She watched the drama of a crowd of sixth graders, super-charged and buoyant, enter the classroom. As they made their way to their assigned seats, the students carried out high-speed conversations via high fives, pokes, and the faintest hint of future hugs.

Minerva and Catherine, seated in the back corner, studied the room. High on the walls, just below the ceiling panels, tacked around the entire room, was the longest poster they had ever seen. It displayed a list of seemingly random digits. Placards dangled from numerous hooks embedded in the ceiling panels with long abstract words printed on them—some of which were mathematical terms, some of which were philosophical. Minerva was intrigued by the fact that there were several words she had never seen.

Meanwhile, the students appeared anxious for the grown-ups to see what they were up to, and they exuded a sense of proud ownership in the classroom.

"Hey, everybody, get in your seats. Here comes Mr. Godfrey!" called out a girl who didn't mind showing off some responsibility to her classmates.

"Good morning!" greeted Henry Godfrey as he entered and pulled the door to. The bells rang throughout the building, and he let out a mock sigh, "Whew, made it ... just in time!"

Suddenly noticing the small gathering of familiar faces in the back, he smiled and called out, "Holy cow—we have honored guests!" The kids laughed.

Henry walked over, greeted the visitors, and turned to his students.

"Allow me, mathematical wonders of Aegis Academy, to introduce to you my great aunt, Mrs. Minerva Bennett, from New York City." He motioned with a dramatic sweep of his hand. "And this is Ms. Catherine Myers, her colleague and partner in adventure." Another broad sweep of his hand evoked a spontaneous smile from Myers, surprised by the attention.

Standing next to the chalkboard, Henry looked out on his students and grinned. "Let's begin with a few pages from the sacred text." He reached for a battered hardbound edition of *The Hitchhiker's Guide to the Galaxy*, faded Post-it notes protruding from every direction to mark his favorite passages, and started to read. The kids giggled with delight, and a few of them glanced back at the adults to see what they might think of this unusual warm up.

Minerva allowed herself not to be too concerned that she didn't understand what an "infinite improbability drive" was, or that she didn't get the importance of "always knowing where your towel is." The children were obviously entranced with the story, however, and that further endeared her grandnephew to Minerva.

After about five minutes, Henry closed the book and whispered, *"Don't panic!"* It must have been a private joke because the students laughed.

"Okay, now that we've had a little metaphysical diversion, let's wake up our calculators. Let's do some mental math and show our visitors what we can do without picking up pencil and paper." Most of the kids eagerly sat up, and some of them grasped their desks for focus.

"53 ... reverse the digits ... divide by 7 ... cube it ... add the digits ... take the cube root." Henry paused, and half the class waved their hands in the air.

"Corinna?"

"Two," she answered confidently.

"Excellent," he said, and then to the others, "Who else got it?" Most of the kids kept their hands up. "Way to go. Okay, let's turn it up a bit. Ready?

"1 ... plus 2 ... divided by 3 ... minus 4 ... times 5 ... square it ... multiply the digits ... raise it to the fourth power ... add the digits." Fewer hands, but several squirmed with confidence.

"Bradley?"

"Seven," he answered.

"Very good! That one was tricky." After two more, Henry moved on to the main lesson, which involved proportions and percents.

With fifteen minutes remaining in the period, Minerva considered heading back to her limo. She was about to leave when Henry transitioned once again, inviting a couple of students to read aloud. The class had been assigned to write a two-page story about a favorite number, and to give this number a personality within a community of living numbers.

"Mimi, would you like to read yours?" The girl nodded and walked up to the front of the room, nervous but willing.

"If I were a number," she began, "I would be One Million. One Million is a powerful and important number because it's a power of ten, and everybody knows that our whole civilization is based on ten. The prime factorization is 2 to the 6th power times 5 to the 6th power. You can see it has strong doubling power with those 2s. It also has a heavy dose of the artistic energy and personal strength of 5.

"As One Million, I would be the head of the Pentagon or maybe the President. With one followed by six zeroes, I demonstrate leadership and strength. Zero is powerful since it can annihilate any other number, and I have a team of these right next to me. They will do what I tell them to do."

Mimi continued to the second page. When she finished, everybody clapped. Minerva was floored. Something had shifted. She now looked at the classroom, the students, the teacher differently—as if she had just tuned into a frequency she didn't know existed.

It was a clever lesson, and this twelve-year-old girl had knocked it out of the park. Minerva stared off in the distance as she struggled with a memory ... a myth. She looked up distractedly and realized the girl had sat down and that another student had been invited to read.

"If I were a number," a boy named Steven began, "I would be Pi. Pi is a very special number that helps people calculate things that have to do with circles. It is the ratio of a circle's circumference to its diameter. My number allows scientists and engineers to build and send spacecraft to the Moon and to Outer Space. I am also helpful in measuring round objects like stadiums and towers and circular parts of engines.

"All through history, people have been trying to calculate me with more and more accuracy. The Bible says that I am roughly equal to 3, and the ancient Greeks thought that I was equal to 3 1/8. But philosophers and mathematicians were surprised to find out that I can never be described exactly in decimal form. I have infinite digits after the 3 and the decimal point, but most people use a handy approximation of 3.14 or 22/7."

As Steven read, Minerva reflected on the characteristics that defined the boy's point of view, in fact the point of view of the students in general. While children could of course be silly and foolish, in other words childish, they could also be playful, hopeful, and wondrous.

Walking the hallways, meeting a few teachers, and visiting this classroom had thrust her backward in time to the early days of her own journey of understanding. But something bothered her. Annoyance turned to anxiety, and she imagined the uncomfortable chairs were to blame. It was time to go.

Nodding to Catherine, Minerva made it clear that she had had enough. Hooper helped her rise from her chair, and the three moved toward the door. Henry paused the reader, and he walked over and said goodbye to his great aunt.

Rather than backtrack to the main entrance, Gordon Hooper led them toward the lower school building. Aware that they were taking a different route, Minerva met Hooper's eyes in a direct and unambiguous manner. This was not her first hayride.

"Mr. Hooper, I see that my tour is being extended. I know your reasons— I'm used to it."

"Guilty as charged, Mrs. Bennett," he acknowledged as he came to a halt. "I shouldn't have presumed to continue the show, so to speak. My apologies." Extending his hand back toward the administration offices, he invited them to reverse their direction in order to return directly to the limousine.

"Hold on," she said. "Let's proceed to your targets, but I must warn you. I have about twenty minutes before my attention will lapse altogether."

"Understood," he said, inclining his head. "My targets, as you so aptly called them, are the classrooms of two of our brightest and most gifted teachers in the lower school. Henry and his middle school colleagues are able to work their magic due largely to the efforts of the elementary teachers who set the kids on paths that are, by generally accepted standards, impossible."

They walked in silence as they exited the middle school building, along a covered walk, to an older building. Hooper explained that the children were at lunch and recess, which is why the third-grade pod was empty and quiet.

Although the classrooms were well furnished with smart boards and computers, Minerva wondered what outstanding results might be observed without actually seeing the teachers and students in action. Nevertheless, she browsed the desks and scanned the bulletin boards, which were covered with student work. Catherine Myers did the same.

Principal Hooper added bits of commentary here and there about integrated curricula and vertical development from one grade level to the next, but Minerva listened distantly. She was unconsciously edging back toward her default belief that she would find nothing extraordinary.

She stood in front of a wall covered, presumably, with examples of the students' best work: short stories, summaries, poems, illustrations. Some were typed. Some were written in pencil.

One paper caught Minerva's eye. It was a book report.

"I liked *Charlotte's Web*," it began, "because a cuddly pig and a clever spider show how animals can live together. The setting is an old-fashioned American farm, and it was fun to meet different barnyard animals.

"Charlotte is wise, but the big animals ignore her. They think she is ugly. Wilbur is a spring pig, and he is lonely for his mother. He likes Charlotte because she is nice to him. They treat each other with respect. They taught the rest of the animals lessons: like how to be kind, how they are all lucky to be alive, and how they can help each other.

"Sometimes people make fun of me. Charlotte taught me how I can ignore mean people and be friendly anyway. I want to be an author like E. B. White when I grow up."

A sudden constriction in her chest took Minerva by surprise. Her breathing stopped, and her vision narrowed. Tears welled up, and she shut her eyes. A face beckoned from the past.

Overcome by a confusing mix of emotions, she reached for a tissue in her purse and opened her eyes slowly. The stinging of salty tears and the quivering of her lips embarrassed her, yet she longed for the discomfort to continue. She had stumbled into an unexpected communion with her late sister, her closest and dearest friend for most of her life.

As Minerva dried her tears, her vision cleared and she stared at the student's name at the bottom of the notebook paper: Helen. Barely believing in coincidences or miracles, she couldn't deny that this was a powerful omen. Like a spear through her heart, this had reopened a wound that she never admitted to having in the first place, and she suddenly knew it was connected to her earlier agitation. There was a message in this child's writing, beyond the classroom, beyond the moral of that particular story, something bigger and more profound than she could wrap her mind around in the moment.

Minerva turned solemnly and began walking out the door. She sought the open air in order to start breathing again, in order to allow herself time to come back to the present in which she would be expected to converse again. For a few more minutes, though, she held tightly to the treasure that had been given her: a heart connection to her sister ... and her spirit.

-→}══◉ ◉══{←-

During the drive to the airport and their flight back to New York, Minerva said very little. By the time her plane landed at Kennedy Airport, she felt as if she had returned from another planet. It was as if her head had been split in two, her brain removed and rotated 180 degrees, and then replaced and reactivated, so implausible were some of her fleeting thoughts.

Over the next twenty-four hours, she struggled to focus and regain a sense of normalcy. But because she didn't understand the implications of many of her projections, or the volcanic shifting of her emotions, Minerva found herself unwilling to confide in those around her. Who would understand? It was no surprise, then, that she finally found solace by way of her lifelong habit of correspondence.

It had been several months since she had written Gladys Atchley, her oldest living friend. Gladys and her husband Gene, suffering from Alzheimer's, lived near Phoenix in an assisted-living facility. Minerva and she had known one another in their Bronx neighborhood three quarters of a century past. They had not seen one another in over twenty years, yet were as close as ever through their regular exchange of letters, cards, and annual birthday phone calls.

Gladys will understand what is happening to me, thought Minerva as she sat down at her writing desk and reached for some stationery. In a three-page missive, she revealed as best she could the self-doubts and awkward fantasies erupting in her once tidy mental landscape. She followed with two similar letters—one to Peter Ellison, a priest whom she had befriended decades earlier when she and her first husband lived briefly in Chicago, and one to Louisa Tourangeau, the widowed wife of one of her second husband's European partners.

Wednesday afternoon, as the late November sun dipped below the skyline, Minerva addressed the envelopes and applied the postage, taking care to check the rate for Geneva, Switzerland, where Louisa lived. She called Isabel and instructed her to mail the letters right away, though she was unmindful that the Thanksgiving postal holiday was in effect.

Chapter 3

BROOKS MECOM THOUGHT that he had left Minerva's apartment relaxed and calm. But now, standing in close proximity with Maxwell and Proctor as they rode the elevator down to the lobby, the kinship he felt with them in the study slipped away. A sense of being alone in a crowd washed over him. He found himself at the mercy of a line of thinking that he had dismissed during the meeting as inconsequential. Seeing his two colleagues bracing themselves for their own solitary scavenger hunts embedded in him a deeper sense of reality than all the discussion in the preceding hour.

Perhaps it was the physical action of descending from the penthouse summit to the ground floor that put him on guard. Mental images flashed and judgments registered as he stood with the other men, stoically, digging for gloves in overcoat pockets and preparing to make their individual ways upon arrival at the street level. The alarm going off in his mind bore the headline: *Koyne Foundation Investment Strategy Slated for the Scrapheap.*

Nine months before, prior to joining the Koyne Foundation, he had imagined himself as a captain on a battle ship, serving under the fleet admiral of one of the larger Wall Street navies. He had acquired the ins and outs of maritime battle, trained to navigate the turbulent seas of the world economy, taught to handle intense pressure. He had imagined that joining the Koyne Foundation would be almost like retiring to civilian life. He would be able to kick back as he took the helm of one of the largest and most advanced luxury liners in the nonprofit sector.

Now he recalled this metaphor, but with an obscene new twist. Instead of exploring a course around Cape Horn or across the South Pacific, he is told by the owner of the line to make for the shore and to direct all passengers to the lifeboats. Somebody hands out bogus treasure maps and boxes of candy as the owner shouts through a bullhorn: "Hold hands, everybody—listen to your hearts!" He, the captain, is ordered to weigh anchor on the mostly empty ship and to confine himself to the harbor. *Madness!* he thought.

As the elevator doors parted, Mecom's deepest urge was to jump ship. He had expected and been prepared for adjustments, so he thought, when he joined the Koyne Foundation. He had wondered what the trade-off might be from the high-pressure stakes of the global stock exchanges to the subtler demands of slow motion, high-profile investing. And he had been surprised at how much he liked the mellower pace.

But now everything had changed.

Exiting into the foyer on the ground floor, street activity and bright reflections assaulted his senses. For a moment, his crazy vision of lifeboats scattered amidst shark-infested waters and his own identity crisis overlapped and intermixed. He desperately wanted alliance with his new colleagues, but he found himself standing alone. Unable to muster any thoughts of loyalty, his mind strained to grasp something familiar. Reaching for his sunglasses, he thought, *I didn't sign up for this shit!*

He watched Galen Proctor exit the building and turn uptown on foot. Briefly, he considered joining him to dig for a bit of perspective on the old lady. Then he watched Stewart Maxwell walk to his waiting taxi, and he berated himself for his hesitation.

Since joining Minerva's staff, Mecom had been accustomed to making top-level portfolio decisions and acting decisively, almost unilaterally, but it now seemed that those days were numbered. It wasn't as if the ability to pore over a mass of financial data and discern profitable trends had suddenly become obsolete, but he seriously resented the prospect of switching his employment credentials again so soon.

After checking his cell phone for messages, he walked into the noonday sun and looked about distractedly. His personal demons aside, he was momentarily struck by the loveliness of the weather. The deep blue sky dissolved his idea of hitting the nearest bar to get drunk. He thought of trying a midday workout, and maybe sweating through his mental clutter. Neither appealed to him, and he stood looking about.

He felt a strange, almost alien, urge to pray. He was not a man of faith, though he sometimes accompanied his wife to church. No, he wanted practical guidance. He had left the fold of his Wall Street brotherhood, but now he was acutely aware of the absence of what he had once taken for granted—camaraderie and esprit de corps.

Should he call up his old boss at Goldman Sachs? Tell him about the crazy blue hair intent on dissolving her fortune? This was precisely the kind of insider information that could be parlayed into tens of millions of dollars. "Personal fallout" took on a new gravity.

His wife was usually happy to listen to stories of his workplace dramas, but she was neither qualified to understand his present dilemma nor likely to keep it to herself. He searched his mind for other names, other faces—anybody with whom he could confide his hostile, almost macabre thoughts, and he was discouraged further by the fact that not one person came to mind.

He stepped off the sidewalk and dodged a bicycle courier to cross the street, to put more distance between himself and the folly he now imagined was inevitable. Something caught his eye as he made it to the far sidewalk. A small, official-looking sign and a sudden whiff of something strange shook him back to the immediate present, and Brooks Mecom laughed out loud.

With nobody to call on, fate had placed in his path the next best place to find a suitable confessor: The Central Park Zoo. The mix of improbability and absurdity instantly appealed to him, and he quickened his pace. He couldn't wait to rip open a bag of peanuts and share them with some monkeys.

⊷═◉ ◉═⊷

Stewart Maxwell gave the taxi driver directions to the Club. His mind was such a jumble of doubts that he knew he needed a familiar setting to remind him of his reality. He respected Minerva Bennett deeply and had always been impressed with her sense of mission and purity. Now, though, he became aware of a deeper allegiance—to tradition, to prudence. He had the distinct sense that he was suddenly on the wrong side of a looming battle.

As he walked into the dining room, making his way to the back corner, he wondered how well he would be able to disguise his inquiries. If some of the usual cronies showed up for lunch, he had a serious challenge ahead of himself. A round table for eight was informally reserved for their little group, one of the most powerful cadres of business and social gatherings in the city. Most of them had known one another for decades. They attended the same Ivy League schools, and some attended the same boarding schools before that. Maxwell waved to his friends from across the room, and one of the waiters met him at his preferred seat to take his order.

Sam Minton, one of his best friends, who happened to be on the Koyne Foundation Board, wasn't there, but as one of the regulars he was liable to show up on any given day. As CEO of Solarus Entertainment, a media and content consortium, he was as plugged in to current events as anyone. A life-long news junkie, he was known to monitor the stock exchanges from three continents, the global weather forecasts, and the results in a dozen professional sports. The club's rule against electronic devices, except for doctors on call, irked Minton. Taking away his electronics was dangerous though, for Minton would invariably listen even more acutely. He was known to launch whole investment schemes on the basis of a single conversation. And he was rarely wrong.

This suddenly worried Maxwell as he saw his friend heading straight toward their table.

"Gentlemen!" greeted Minton.

"Sam," said several at once.

"Minty," said Maxwell, shaking hands with his friend.

With an even bigger appetite for information than food, as well as his inability to go for long without it, he began with his trademark: "Tell me what's new." He settled into his chair and took off his wristwatch; he laid it on the table as if it were a stopwatch.

"Pretty flat sales these days," said Greer Johnson, owner of a national chain of office equipment stores, "but you already knew that. We had a strong Black Friday, though, and we're hoping the holiday shoppers will stay interested in cameras."

"What kind of cameras?"

"You've heard of nanny cams, right? They're still popular, but we've got some of the new spot-cams, miniature versions of the nanny cams. Oh, and have you seen those new programmable bugs? They're amazing! The kids are buying them up as fast as we can stock the shelves. Unfortunately, we're back ordered, probably due to the Chinese embargo."

"I'll bet," nodded Sam Minton, who then looked around the table, eager for more.

"Can't compete with that, Minty. Business as usual at the Koyne Foundation," lied Maxwell.

"Come on, Stew, you can think of something. What's on old lady Bennett's mind these days?"

"I've just come from a staff meeting, in fact. Straightforward ... progress reports, projections, proposals for next year. I know you're not really a fan of classical music, but Dallas just got a new chamber music hall. She was down there two weeks ago for the grand opening."

"Aren't fairy godmothers wonderful?"

"Yes, indeed," agreed Maxwell. He took a bite of his sandwich.

Turning to the others, Minton launched off in a new direction, "Who's got the line on the midterm elections? Chris, is the GOP going to hold their majority?" The interview had shifted to Christopher Lachance, a staunch Republican and a major fundraiser for the party.

"God, I hope so," he began. "The Democrats continue to wreak havoc though, and the dollar is at its all-time low, even with the worsening Asian Recession. The Chinese are convinced we're the culprits, that we've dragged them down. They blame the Indians too. They've renewed their threat to dump the dollar and peg on a mix of currencies, for real this time. The Saudis and the Japs are siding with the Chinese."

"What's stopping them?" asked Maxwell, genuinely interested. He had rarely heard so much come out of Lachance's mouth, and was glad that Minton had shifted the conversation. They all perked up since this topic would affect everybody's pocket book one way or another.

"Fear of the unknown," answered Lachance. "Hell, it's common knowledge that we've been destroying our credit—and credibility—for decades, but our momentum has been so enormous that we've been able to pressure our trading partners to stick by us. For more than a couple of years now, we've dangled by mere threads, pretty much on China's hopes that we'd stabilize the dollar by trimming the deficit ... but that's just not happening. Smoke and mirrors work for only so long. The only thing holding China or India, or Europe for that matter, from ditching is fear. The key question of course is, what will replace the almighty dollar?"

Ed Nance had remained quiet, which, despite a generally outgoing nature, was his typical dynamic at the club. As the lone Democrat in their circle, he knew his friends wouldn't let him get away with too much soap-boxing. While he appreciated their perspectives and areas of expertise, he generally disagreed with them come election time.

"Come on, Chris," Nance said, "don't be so quick to shift the blame. You know damn well that your side, with its own brand of fiscal irresponsibility, has contributed just as much to the deficit. I think we can all agree that it's an inside-the-Belt phenomenon."

"Perhaps, but your candidates are so busy proposing new programs, or expanding existing ones, that more and more people think fiscal restraint is a bad idea ... that it somehow implies discrimination—or racism, for God's sake! Meanwhile, the Fed can't get a grip on its easing strategies, and that, more than anything, has caused the Asians to draw back from the table."

While the conversation proceeded, Maxwell concentrated on his lunch and keeping his cool. He wanted to ask about investor confidence and tuning investment portfolios amidst a currency devaluation, but he wasn't quite sure whether these were his biggest concerns. Besides, Mecom and Proctor would be overseeing those scenarios. He was in charge of legal issues—finding out the ramifications of fundamentally altering the Foundation's charter and thus shifting money away from longstanding recipients.

"I don't think the Chinese are going to wait for next year's election—their minds have been made up," interrupted Minton. The others turned to him in surprise.

"Minty, you know something we don't?" Maxwell asked.

"Maybe, maybe not," he admitted. "But I see a pattern. I've been analyzing the way they craft their press releases."

"Sam, what the hell are you talkin' about?" asked Greer Johnson.

"I'm talking about how the Chinese officials have shown their hand. They've danced around the truth for a year now. I can feel it. They're going to dump the dollar any day. I won't be surprised if it happens over the holidays. They know we'll be distracted."

Minton sat back and glanced at his watch. The others looked at him doubtfully.

"I agree, Sam," said Lachance, "but I'm not as confident about the timing. I'm thinking late spring or summer."

Before it could deteriorate into a sport bet, Maxwell voiced his concern. "What's this mean for our holdings? Will it only affect our economy, or will it have a more global impact?"

"You asking for yourself, Stew, or for the Foundation?" Minton asked.

"It's all the same, isn't it?"

"Pretty much," Nance offered. "We're going to have to brace for a broad devaluation, one way or the other."

"Again?" asked Greer. "Jesus, life's been one ongoing devaluation since I can remember!"

"Don't look so glum," chirped Sam Minton. "All this means is that we have some new opportunities. Remember: *knowledge is power.*"

The lunch gang scattered twenty minutes later, and Maxwell headed back to his office. As the senior staff member and head counsel for the Foundation, he felt the lion's share of the burden that Minerva Bennett had laid at their feet that morning. He was responsible for charting the way—either forward, along the odd course their Chairman requested, or backward—backward to the *status quo* that, until a few hours ago, seemed so normal and beyond question.

⋅⊱⊰⊱⊰⋅

Upon leaving Minerva Bennett's apartment, Galen Proctor decided to forgo a taxi so he could walk back to the Foundation offices. His cross-town errand earlier that morning, the appointment which had caused him to be late, had been an annual check-up. He was peeved that his doctor had told him, for the third year in a row, to quit avoiding exercise. A man of considerable habits, he was apt to make it four years in a row.

Heading north along the sidewalk, he thought about the staff meeting. The sensation that he was an outsider had been particularly acute that morning. Walking into that space, in which his colleagues seemed so at home, intimidated the hell out of him.

Now, the irritation that he had spent all morning swallowing began to bubble up, and he was glad he was on foot. He quickened his pace. What had, for a fleeting moment, been a prescription for a rejuvenating walk and some fresh air, had now become, in the space of just a block and a half, a determined march to root out the source of his rage at the world.

Barely noticing the other pedestrians as he strode ahead, replaying not just the morning's proceedings but his entire life, he had unknowingly resumed his oldest habit: looking for somebody to blame for his unhappiness. What made this inward trek even more maddening was that he knew it was hopeless. But he couldn't stop.

By most standards, Proctor had one of the best jobs on the planet. He worked for one of the most prestigious private foundations in existence. He was responsible, to the degree that accounting decisions could sometimes afford advantage, for much of its soundness and growth. He lived in a lovely well-furnished apartment, and he had, at the age of fifty-two, already built himself an enviable retirement account. But happiness eluded him.

Unearthing ancient resentments and bundling them with a handful of fresh ones, Proctor dwelt on the injustice of his powerlessness.

"Those cocky bastards!" he mouthed angrily as he leaned into the chilly breeze that had come up. His grim expression parted the mass of oncoming pedestrians as if the symbol for radioactive waste were tattooed on his forehead.

Twenty blocks into his walk, having condemned Minerva Bennett for being a pampered and spoiled bitch, Stewart Maxwell for being an ass-kissing Ivy League prick, and Brooks Mecom for being an arrogant jerk with a borrowed reputation, he realized that his insulin pump was empty. *That figures*, he thought, tossing that final resentment on top of his impressive pile of reasons to embrace his sense of impending doom and to flaunt it at the city around him.

The realization that there was some logical trigger to his tirade helped Proctor apply the brakes on the runaway train of self-loathing. He realized that he had not been on one of these expresses for some time, and he was relieved that he could now begin to trim this particularly nasty mood swing. *Just a few more blocks to go*, he thought. He passed the Guggenheim Museum and turned away from Central Park.

It was high noon, and the shadows on the sidewalks and streets were at their shortest and sharpest. Anticipating a fresh cartridge of insulin, he gathered his wits. Two more blocks and an elevator ride delivered him to his office on the sixth floor of the Fielding Building. It housed several non-profits and a prominent think tank, but the Koyne Foundation was the main tenant.

He walked straight to the small refrigerator next to his desk and grabbed the packet of hermetically sealed cylinders. Feeling under his shirt, he removed the spent cartridge and inserted a new one. Within thirty seconds, Proctor felt his manic edge fade as the compound restored balance to his endocrine system. He buzzed his assistant and ordered a sandwich.

After checking e-mails and glancing at his calendar, he shifted his attention to the assignment issued by Mrs. Bennett and reflected on his mood. Though his insulin had kicked in, he still felt like ripping somebody's head off.

He woke up his computer and accessed the internal network. A few clicks, and he was looking at the raw financial data of the Koyne Foundation. As he scanned file headings for summary documents, a remnant of his tantrum spilled over.

Is that crazy bitch going to waste all my efforts of the last decade? Is she going to just toss everything to the wind and hope that a bunch of brats are going to make things better?!

Feeling his blood pressure rise, Galen Proctor closed his eyes and tried to relax. Opening and then narrowing his eyes, he took on a look of grim determination.

I'll just have to prove that it can't be done!

Chapter 4

THE NUMBNESS OF her nose inspired Minerva to retreat inside, and she exited the frigid terrace. She felt the warmth begin to thaw her as she waved to the maids, who were busy cleaning.

Minerva knew better than to get in their way. She flagged down her butler, Felix, who was chattering with them in high-speed Spanish, and told him to have Vincent make her a tuna salad and send it to the library.

After her lunch, which she ate slowly and methodically, she looked through the tray full of mail and memos that Felix had brought in with her lunch. When she finished reviewing the bills, initialing the ones that Catherine Myers was to pay, she turned to the personal items and reached for a letter with foreign postage. It had been stamped with the traditional *par avion*, which tickled Minerva.

It was from Louisa Tourangeau, the wife of one of JB's European partners. They carried on like sisters from the moment when they first met—in France in the mid-1980s. Louisa settled in Geneva after the death of her husband Philipe, in a vacation home that seemed more suited to her in terms of climate and culture than their former residence in Paris. A wanderlust, her letters to Minerva often bulged with photographs, tour maps, and even souvenir keychains.

They had seen one another only two months before, on the *Tesseract*, Minerva's 180-foot yacht. Louisa had been her "date" for that trip to the Aegean Sea, and they had enjoyed ten days of early autumn weather among the mythical region that had served as the womb of western civilization. Her little jaunts often included family members, to the extent that they could extract themselves from their routines and meet her on the tarmac at Kennedy Airport by the appointed hour. Bob and Leigh Godfrey had done just that in order to accompany Minerva and her friend on the cruise.

Gently sliding the familiar stationery from the faded blue envelope, Minerva saw that there were a couple of photographs amid the handwritten content. Adjusting her blanket to cover her stocking feet, she smiled in anticipation.

My Dear Minerva,

What a delight it was to receive your recent note regarding your reflections on life and legacy. How it mirrors some of my own thoughts—we are truly soul sisters! Before I address that subject though, I wanted to point out that I am still savoring the glorious time we had on your "little boat." I have enclosed a photograph of you with your nephew and his charming wife, and one of us.

Now to your conundrum. You are doubting whether you have made a difference in your life, particularly through your philanthropic efforts. You should know that your foundation is famous, even over here, for its scope and excellence. In short, I think you ought to relax and, as they say, "cut yourself some slack."

Your conflicting thoughts about whether or not to shift the whole program of your giving were understandably vague. You mentioned that you are considering giving to a much younger population ... "all at once." Would that imply the dissolution of the Koyne Foundation. Isn't that a scary thought?!

Whatever the specifics, I support you in your efforts. Have you shared this vision with any of your colleagues? What have they to say about this new perspective? I would imagine that some of them might be resistant to such change.

Louisa, with her trans-Atlantic objectivity, had hit the nail on the head. Though caught in an eddy of self-doubt, Minerva smiled at the healing nature of a long and genuine friendship. Her friend knew the kind of world she occupied—how her inherited wealth, paradoxically, had its own costs.

Harkening back to their deck-top conversations, Minerva imagined that she could still hear Louisa's laughter.

Keep me informed, Minerva. Best wishes with whatever you decide. It all sounds terribly exciting, and I look forward to hearing from you regarding our next rendezvous. The Maldives? The Canary Islands and Morocco?

All My Best,
Louisa

When she arrived at the last paragraph, nodding in agreement to both of her friend's suggestions for their next trip, Minerva laughed giddily at that which had flashed by her earlier, too quick to grasp: the identification of a genuine "tesseract." Suddenly, after more than twenty years of owning one of the more beautiful motor yachts in the world, she could fully embrace its name.

She had chosen it during a whimsy of conversation with JB when he first showed her a Polaroid of the yacht. It was during a candlelit dinner in New York, at one of their favorite Italian restaurants. On a good day, Joseph Bennett was as romantic as he was financially savvy; he scored a perfect ten on their 20th anniversary.

"According to the encyclopedia, china is the suggestion for number twenty," he had said. "And since we already have plenty of plates and bowls, I reckon we oughta go on a trip." He would resurrect his Texan accent for such theatrics, which had always made her smile.

Minerva recalled her excitement when JB had opened a fancy travel folder with Chinese characters all over it, along with pictures of Hong Kong, Beijing, the Forbidden City, and the Great Wall. Then, he reached into his coat pocket and casually flipped a grainy photograph of the boat next to her salad plate.

"I bought this so we could be comfortable on the way," was all he had said. She could still remember her reaction: eyes moist, smiling and crying at the same time.

Now, in the present, as if she were using a tesseract to fold space and time in order to jump from one world to another—like Mrs. Witch in *A Wrinkle In Time*—Minerva sighed. She let the pages and the envelope slip to the floor, but she continued looking at one of the photographs Louisa had included. She smiled at the image of them leaning against the teak railing, a Greek island hovering in the distance.

After a while, she reached for a large manila envelope from the pile of mail and noted the return address: Aegis Academy, Houston, Texas. That was unexpected. As she drew the contents out, she wondered if it would be some communication from her nephew, or perhaps an official program of Grandparents Day, which, in a sense, she had previewed. Would it be some thinly veiled tug on the Koyne Foundation's purse strings—one more request for a contribution?

Ignoring for the moment an official-looking cover letter, she pored over the other documents. These had been scanned into a high-resolution printer and reproduced with care. The colors were accurate, and every little smudge and artifact were captured and frozen for posterity.

At the top of the first page was a carefully rendered heading, dictated no doubt by a quirky sixth-grade math teacher. The title of the paper was "One in a Million," and the name at the top left was Mimi Peterson. A flood of memories rushed to Minerva as she recalled her visit. *I'll be damned*, she thought. *The principal took my request seriously.* She shuffled the small bunch of papers to see what else he had included. It was another math essay, this one by Steven Jacobs: "My Name is Pi."

Shuffling to the next page, she noted the much larger and loopier handwriting. This was the work of a third grader. The content was significantly simpler than the previous works, and the layout was very basic. Glancing to the bottom of the page, Minerva noted the cute little drawing that had first attracted her. It was a pink pig shaking hands with a grayish spider, unrealistically large in comparison.

Minerva let the page fall from her fingers as tears stung her yet again.

◦▸▦◉ ◉▦◂◦

Stewart Maxwell rubbed his eyes, wishing he could take them out and drop them in a bath of ice water. He had been reading and scrolling, clicking and reading and scrolling most of the day, for the second day in a row. It wasn't as if he'd been digging ditches, but he felt exhausted nevertheless. He straightened up, stretched, and looked around for sympathy. There was none to be had—he was alone.

Missed the dinner bell again, he thought.

His computer was equipped with one of the new concave monitors, which he doubted was worth the hype. It offered a compelling light in his otherwise dimly lit office. He had neglected to turn on any other lights since he had missed the decline into full darkness outside the curtained windows. The approach of the winter solstice, one week away, meant they were soon to experience the shortest days of December. He turned and leaned backward, careful to dodge several stacks of papers and files, and reached for the lamp on his credenza.

Daylight's loss was nighttime's gain. The city outside was already alive with its overdrive of neon signs and LED billboards. For several weeks, these had been augmented by a kaleidoscope of holiday lights, wreaths, ribbons, and stars. Scattered pockets of Christian culture held firm to the origin of the seasonal decorations as celebrations of Christmas, while in the background the mainstream media continued its long-running campaign to subvert this truth. It was difficult to say whether the media were influenced by Madison Avenue and City Hall, or vice versa, but the co-opting of Christmas spirit in order to sell more products was undeniable.

One of the few isolated pockets of traditional Christendom was the twelve-story Fielding Building. Several years before, Minerva Bennett, in one of her trademark moods of reactionary intransigence, had ordered that the entire Fielding Building, interior and exterior, as well as all Foundation shared space, would be uniformly decorated in old-fashioned Christmas decorations.

Every year at this time, Maxwell would flash on the still vivid memory of helping Minerva to compose "the letter," spontaneously dictated to him in her Mercedes Benz as the two of them were being driven to some long-forgotten appointment. They had passed by a freshly neutered department store entrance, a former holdout for the Christmas spirit. Stripped of all symbols related to the Christ, it was festooned with crass images concocted by social scientists and advertisers, and Minerva had become red-faced with contempt. He still remembered the look in her eyes when she had whirled toward him and ordered: "Take this down, Stewart—*verbatim!*"

In the sharp, clipped words that followed, she took a written stand, an unauthorized excerpt of which eventually found its way into the op-ed page of the *New York Times*. She proclaimed the right of citizens to enjoy the trappings of their spiritual, cultural, and religious traditions and heritages, and that hers were unabashedly Christian. She declared that, while the city might be justified in secularizing seasonal decorations in government buildings, she was not about to let this dilution take place in her private world, which, "thanks to the providence of the Lord God Almighty, I have been privileged to receive and enjoy in great abundance."

Although he didn't share the depth of her religious devotion, he had fully supported her, then and even now. He had delighted in disseminating her memorandum to the full roster of employees of the Koyne Foundation, its Board of Trustees, and all other tenants of the Fielding Building. He had laughed aloud many times following the mention of her letter in the *Times*. The vast majority of opinions and comments, even from non-Christians, were enthusiastically supportive of Minerva Bennett's declaration. *Thank God for the private sector!*

Maybe that was why he was willing to stay late and bend over backwards for this woman. He honestly liked her and deeply respected her standards and her commitment to them. He appreciated her fierce independence of spirit. And yet, he found himself torn. He was split between his allegiance to a world-class philanthropist and to an employer who had, he hated to admit it, perhaps gone off her rocker.

Opening a new tab on his browser, Maxwell googled a term with which he was already very familiar, and yet on which he hoped for fresh insight. It was one of those legal terms that gets tossed about from time to time, and he suddenly hated himself for calling it up. His integrity demanded it though, for it was going to be a weapon wielded by one side or the other. Due diligence required him to address this issue—the final bullet point on the report he would submit at the staff meeting the following morning.

Non compos mentis.

Did he really think Minerva had cracked? Had she lost control of her mental faculties? No, he didn't think so. But it was a possibility that she was moving in that direction. He knew the odds were strong that this accusation would be leveled at Minerva if and when she disclosed her new program to the Board, or to the public at large.

Had she moderated? Had she reconsidered? Was she really ready to break up one of the largest, finest, most established service entities in the world? *Non compos mentis.*

Not of sound mind. If he were a witness called to the stand, to give his input, to offer his experience of a woman who had been like a surrogate mother for much of his adult life, and a boss going on twenty years, could he condemn her with this seemingly innocuous Latin phrase?

"It depends," he said aloud, surprising himself. His words echoed off the opposite wall—covered with gilt-framed diplomas, certificates, and awards, as well as numerous framed photographs of Foundation gatherings, Presidential Commissions, and family reunions—before being absorbed by the massive antique Chesterfield suite of leather furniture. *Yes,* he thought, *it depends ... on whether it's true or not.*

On virtually all computer screens, the time is displayed in the corner, but Stewart Maxwell, raised in the pre-digital age, ignored that resource. He extended his right arm and shook his cuff free to glance at his wristwatch, an antique Patek Philippe in white gold with an alligator skin band. Its Roman numerals indicated that it was a quarter to eight. He wanted to finish his report and print it out to review at home. He wondered if he dared share it with Doris, his wife. If he didn't hurry up, though, she would be gone to bed anyway.

Placing the cursor at the bottom of his one page report, he typed: *Non Compos Mentis*—Potential Adverse Reception by the Board of Trustees and Foundation Partners. He kept this last entry brief, for the heading pretty much said it all. A legal challenge on one's mental status was a subtle and intangible toxin. Once introduced, whether it was validated or not, the potential for a lingering doubt to be established—in friends, as well as foes—was inordinately high. Illegitimate uses of this charge had been well documented through the ages.

Even a hint that one's mental faculties have been compromised is a deadly serious proposition. Could an 87-year-old woman, even of Minerva Bennett's stature and popularity, withstand the intense scrutiny such an accusation would warrant? Maxwell shuddered.

Here's a woman on top of the world, in first place as it were, who for some strange reason, about to win the Indianapolis 500, suddenly puts out her arm, signals a left turn, and exits into pit lane. Dissatisfied with that metaphor, Maxwell tried another ... Minerva, in the Kentucky Derby, decides to jump off one horse onto another—right before the finish line.

Now I'm losing my *mind,* he thought. He grabbed his overcoat, clicked off the lamp, and headed out the door.

Chapter 5

"GOOD MORNING," MINERVA said to her advisors. "Thank you for coming. I can't wait to hear what each of you has to report." She crossed to her chair and made herself comfortable.

Catherine Myers distributed the folders that she'd prepared, each containing the agenda and a copy of each member's report. In the background, the fire hissed soothingly. The heat radiated just enough to balance out the slightly frigid temperature in the study, and to offset the mood suggested by the overcast skies beyond the window.

"Okay, let's get to it," Minerva began. "Last week, I dropped a bit of a bombshell. I heard your initial reactions, and then I asked you to gather some information. I asked you to remain open-minded. Let's see how you did." She looked around and smiled, hoping to put them all a little more at ease. "By the way, since I haven't heard anything in the news about some crazy old lady wanting to throw away lots of money, I want to congratulate you for keeping this affair confidential. I know that wasn't easy."

"I'll go first," volunteered Libby Armstrong. "Since we all have a copy of the reports, I won't bother to read directly. I'll just highlight what I consider the main points.

"I already knew, and my research confirmed, that private foundations are constantly going through shifts in their strategies. This happens for many reasons: personal priorities change, scientific research changes ... new opportunities come into existence, etc. So, the prospect of the Koyne Foundation's shifting the target of its giving is nothing new.

"What is new, radical even, is the way this might happen. Keeping the numbers simple, we have approximately $60 billion of principal, and this yields an average annual distribution of $3 billion. I've shown the full list of recipients here: foundations, organizations, universities, and so forth ... along with their gifts and percentages. These funds will cease to exist if and when a shift takes place according to Mrs. Bennett's plan.

"The timing and the extent of this proposed shift are, of course, unknown as yet, but I've taken the liberty of presenting three potential scenarios, along with advantages and disadvantages of each case.

"Option A: Divert a relatively small percentage of the portfolio, perhaps 10%, to the new cause, a global search for independent ideas on how to solve world problems. The advantage is this would lead to only a minor shift in the rest of the Foundation's operations.

"Option B: Divert 50% of the portfolio. This would lead to a serious recalculation of our entire program. Of course, that could simply mean that all present recipients take a 50% cut in their annual distribution, or that we would filter out all but the most important projects and maintain these at current levels of giving. Advantage is that some recipients might still be served at current levels. Disadvantage is that some recipients, and the causes they represent, might get dropped altogether. Disadvantage to the Foundation is that the new structure would cause fundamental modifications in design and human resources, as well as the public profile via media and branding.

"Option C: Divert 100% of the portfolio. This would represent a profound change to the Foundation's recipients. Some organizations would be catastrophically affected, given that a large portion of their operating expenses derive from the annual distributions we fund. An advantage of this move might be the massive simplification of our present administration, although the replacement of this by the proposed new program could require such significant hands-on daily attention that the overall change in Koyne Foundation administrative needs might actually increase, at least in the short run." Libby looked up from her folder, having taken a few notes as she went. "Questions?"

There were none. The others seemed to gather that so much was still speculation, and that to scrutinize any one scenario at this stage would be pointless.

"Thank you, Libby. That was a good opening report," commented Minerva. "Who's next?"

"I'll go," said Brooks Mecom. He had been subdued since his arrival, and he looked pale. "Truth be told, I'm nervous. You'll probably consider my report critical, but I couldn't figure a way around that."

"Go ahead," she said.

"Although I imagined several lesser scenarios, similar to Libby's three options, I took you at your word, Mrs. Bennett: 'to imagine and illustrate a total shift in our methodology.'

"I'm in the camp of those who believe that if it ain't broke, don't fix it. To be fair, I suppose it's possible to improve on a winning strategy. This is usually done by fine-tuning existing programs. Wholesale rejection of successful formulas and strategies—for a completely unknown set of methods—is, by its very nature, risky in the extreme.

"To prepare a complete liquidation of the Koyne Foundation portfolio, in order to make available cash distributions on some date in the near future, whether that be six months from now or 30 months from now, will be enormously complex and challenging. The main challenge is that a huge portion of the holdings are bound up in long-term assets, which for the normal operation of a private foundation is standard practice for maximizing dividends and taking advantage of tax-exempt instruments. This would all change.

"Furthermore, given the substantial holdings we have in several prominent stocks and mutual funds, our exit could signal a larger sell-off. In other words, the Koyne Foundation is so large and is such a major player in several markets that a wholesale exit would hurt us.

"The way I see it, the demands on those of us in the asset management division will be higher than ever in the near term, up to the point of liquidation, at which point we will become obsolete.

"In the meantime, disbursements to our present grantees could still occur, as we wind down the current approach. Alterations would occur in stages.

Even after the new program is announced, regardless of what it is called, it would take at least twelve months to extract Foundation monies from certain investments. During that time, I would recommend a staged phase out. This would pacify at least some of the present recipients, giving them lead time to find new sources of funding."

Mecom sat back, exhausted, having strained to maintain a neutral tone. By the lack of raised eyebrows and the sober nods of agreement around the room, he could consider himself successful. He reached for his handkerchief to intercept a bead of sweat that was trickling down his forehead.

"Thank you, Brooks," said Minerva. "I appreciate your frankness."

Minerva gazed into the fire, noting flashes of green and blue amidst the yellow and orange flames.

"I'll go next," said Galen Proctor, sitting forward in his chair. "In terms of dollars, Libby's figures were slightly high. At the close of the markets on Friday, the total valuation of Koyne Foundation assets was down slightly—approximately $57.4 billion.

"Our tax-exempt status is a fundamental element of this organization, and it requires all recipients to be, likewise, tax exempt entities with charitable or socially beneficial profiles. Much of my effort is in coordination with Brooks's department—management of portfolio assets and distribution to grantees. When we do our job well, there is little to no loss of value as the monies are transferred from one entity to another.

"The fundamental problem of the proposed change is that Foundation money will go directly to individuals, many of them citizens of other countries. As I said last week, this will have horrendous tax implications. By virtue of the latest revisions of our tax code, all gifts are now taxable at 65%. This implies a tragic loss of wealth redirected to the U. S. Government, as well as foreign governments of eligible contestants."

Proctor paused, as if expecting Minerva to interject. When she didn't, he continued.

"I estimate that at least half of the Foundation's assets, perhaps as much as three quarters, would be siphoned off to host governments. This catastrophic loss of value could be rationalized, I suppose, by the belief in the benevolence of governments—that they efficiently transform tax revenues into social benefits across a wide spectrum of needs. But this goes against everything the Koyne Foundation, as a charitable institution, has done since its inception. The explicit justification for the existence of tax-exempt organizations is that these can identify vital and emerging social needs, and then address them more efficiently and more quickly than government.

"In summary, the Koyne Foundation would no longer distribute tax-free proceeds to socially conscious organizations but would instead make one-time gifts to individuals who would retain, as I've said, only a tragically small portion after taxes."

"Thank you for that sobering input," said Minerva, frowning.

"I suppose it's my turn," said Stewart Maxwell. "I'm afraid that I must also be the bearer of critical feedback.

"Legally, there is nothing prohibiting a sudden or major shift in our giving policy, as Libby pointed out earlier. The Foundation has the right to tailor its giving to fit its mission statement, and this can be amended to change present recipients and bring into focus a whole new set of beneficiaries, as long as these fit into the broad description of positive social change. The Board of Trustees, according to our bylaws, is the only official body able to amend the mission and its subsidiary policies, and it, therefore, poses the most significant legal obstacle to your proposal.

"Mrs. Bennett, you are the source of all the original assets of the Foundation, and you embody its spirit and its mission. From the beginning, you and the Koyne Foundation have been practically synonymous, so congruent has your personal vision been with the stated mission of the Foundation. You have engendered almost perfect and total loyalty in your employees, your staff, and certainly all the organizations that have benefitted from your generosity." Maxwell paused, in order to let the "but" go unstated. Minerva already anticipated it though, for he had addressed her as "Mrs. Bennett."

"Trust and loyalty are not impervious to life's vicissitudes. The changing tides of social priorities, shifting technology, and the integrity of leadership have an effect on the attitudes of a community, an organization ... a private foundation." Another pause.

"A proposal to the Board to dramatically alter the mission in the way you outlined last week—especially given the unstable economy—will likely precipitate unprecedented animosity and dissension. And, as head counsel, I am obliged to identify the possibility of this distasteful scenario.

"Frankly, argument wouldn't be the worst part of such a controversy. I believe the worst aspect would be the damage to you, personally ... your leadership, your reputation. Although the odds are slight, I had to include the possibility that even your personal judgment would come under scrutiny.

"There is a legal concept that, if invoked, would have very unpleasant consequences. I refer to this in the last item of my report."

When Maxwell stopped, Minerva looked around the room. The others were flipping the pages of their folders and scanning for this bullet point. A deeper silence and several grimaces told Minerva that her attorney had managed to darken the horizon. As if to underline this point, the overcast skies, visible through the tall study window, let loose with a sudden and dramatic shower. The distant buildings became invisible due to the sheets of rain and spattering of wind-driven drops as the expected winter storm arrived in Manhattan. Well insulated and protected from the elements, the buffeting of the wind against the window was nevertheless a symbol of the resistance that Minerva faced.

Nobody dared to say anything. During the silence, the drumming on the window turned sharper. The rain turned to sleet.

"Stewart, you still have the touch I was privileged to witness in the courtroom many years ago," Minerva said, managing to smile ever-so-faintly. "I guess I shouldn't be surprised that you managed to gain the cooperation of the weather to make your case so dramatically."

They all laughed.

"So, Catherine, what about you?" Minerva asked. "I didn't really request a report from you, but would you like to add anything? To this torrent of optimism?"

Catherine set her laptop aside and looked around the room before answering.

"Mrs. Bennett, I suppose if I were to give you any feedback, I would address the changes to your personal life."

"*Oh*—interesting perspective. Go on."

"Your public presence is confined to the rarified atmosphere of philanthropic circles, and your voice in the media is crafted and filtered internally. You get to present the image you want to present, and you have the prerogative of standing clear of the general public by virtue of running a private foundation." Minerva nodded, anticipating now where her secretary was headed.

"If the Koyne Foundation begins to adopt these changes, regardless of the legal status as a private foundation, you'll be thrust into the spotlight. The media will put you and the Foundation under the microscope and probe for details beyond anything that any of us has ever experienced. Even if most of the attention is positive, some is bound to be critical.

"I would worry about you, Mrs. Bennett. As healthy as you are, I'm not sure you could take it." Her voice diminished in volume as she struggled to finish the last sentence. "I'm not sure if *I* could take it."

Minerva nodded introspectively. "Thank you, my dear. I hadn't considered things from that angle."

The tapered strikes of the sleet on the window had softened, not because the storm had passed but, because the sleet now turned to snow. As if taking the meteorological cue as a softening of the resistance in her own team, Minerva continued.

"This past week," continued Minerva, "I shared my new vision with several old friends who, perhaps because they aren't the knowledgeable insiders you are, actually encouraged me to explore my ideas further. Nevertheless, as I lay out my tentative plan, I want you to know that I do so in the context of your sobering feedback."

Chapter 6

Bob Godfrey followed the wise counsel of his wife Leigh to wait for the right time to approach Minerva with his concerns, and to do so privately. In the meanwhile, he relaxed into the luxurious suspension of reality for which the Owl's Nest seemed perfectly designed.

Minerva's ranch in Colorado, sandwiched between the San Juan and the Uncompahgre National Forests, was the equivalent of a small resort and spa. Guests could avail themselves of drivers to take them to the ski lifts, snowmobiles for open country explorations, horses for quiet walks, or Nordic skis for those inclined toward cross country skiing.

The main house was a destination in itself. The great stone fireplace at the center of the house could be enjoyed from either side of the hearth; the free-standing chimney extended up to and through the vaulted ceiling, which was supported by immense pine beams. It was the radiant centerpiece of life in the snow-banked compound.

Godfrey finally got his opportunity to broach the subject with his aunt. An afternoon sleigh ride had attracted the entire contingent of guests, and the house would be otherwise empty. A team of horses would pull an antique sleigh across the snow to the south ridge lookout, at which point the foreman would serve hot cider and cocktails.

Knowing that Minerva had already indicated that she was not up to the exposure, Bob declined as well. He settled into a chair near Minerva's chaise, wondering how best to begin. She beat him to the punch.

"What's on your mind, Bob? We both know it's not a business proposal."

"Did Leigh tip you off?"

"No, although her body language helped me to understand yours. Because you waited all week until you could have me alone, I believe I know what it must be." He looked at her openly, skeptical of her powers of divination and yet, somehow, intuiting that she was right.

"Okay," he said, playing along, "tell me what's on my mind."

"Julian called you and told you about the proposal I'll be making to the Board next week. He thinks my ideas are unrealistic, and he even questions my sanity."

"Well, that may be overstating matters, but he certainly is concerned. And, after hearing his version of the conversation you two had over Christmas, I'm intrigued. How in the world did all this start? Julian seems to think it had something to do with your trip to Houston."

"I'll be happy to tell you, Bob, but I want you to listen with an open mind. You sound as if your mind is already made up."

"I don't know about that—I need more information. But I admit I'm skeptical. I don't see any point in launching off on some fanciful quest, especially when what we're doing—what *you're* doing, through the Foundation—is in alignment with perfectly acceptable standards and practices."

Minerva remained silent, so he continued.

"I've been on the Board for fifteen years, and I'm intimately familiar with the efforts made by the Foundation during that period and the results it has produced. As you well know, its reputation is impeccable. I'm proud of that, and I believe you are too. I can't imagine what could have inspired you to consider dissolving the Foundation.

"Julian said you're going to propose that the Board adopt a scheme—some sort of global giveaway ... Apparently, everything is to be liquidated and then handed over to God knows how many amateur philosophers ... including a bunch of damn kids!

"Minerva, *please* tell me that I've misunderstood your son."

"It seems that Julian communicated the basics facts, but he probably omitted the key ingredient, which is my motivation. You see, I've come to question a basic premise—a belief—taken as gospel by our Board and, no doubt, our beneficiaries. I'm the first to admit that I've always considered it beyond question. Until recently, I couldn't imagine not taking it as an absolute."

"What premise?"

"That our annual distributions are benefitting mankind."

"*What?* That's *absurd!* Of course they're benefitting mankind. We give huge sums to—"

"Hold on, Bob. Let me speak. I'll explain what I mean." He'd sprung forward in his chair, and she waited for him to settle back before continuing.

"I created the Koyne Foundation almost fifty years ago with the money I inherited from my parents. Since that modest beginning, its mission has been clear ... and very traditional, by the way. It would distribute sums of money to various organizations that would, over time, produce positive humanitarian results.

"For a very long time, the principle grew, the number of beneficiaries grew, the annual distributions grew. Everybody was pleased. Everybody was happy. Everybody was proud. Myself included.

"Regarding your assertion that these distributions *are* benefitting mankind, I've recently come to the conclusion that this just isn't so." She saw Godfrey lurch forward, ready to object again, and she held up her hand.

"Hear me out. *Some* people are benefitting by our work, but not enough. Since first considering this idea, I'm more convinced with every story in the newspaper, every editorial, and every conversation I have that the trickle-down benefits that I imagined, since the very beginning, don't exist ... at least not enough to warrant our present course.

"Even if I take into account the small number of scientists we fund who've actually made discoveries in various fields, I'm no longer convinced that the overall effect of our giving is doing what it ought to be doing."

Godfrey couldn't hold back. "Do you know what you're saying? That tens of thousands of people are deluded into thinking that they're making a difference in the world? How can that be? What do you expect?!"

"I expect the world to be better off. I expect there to be hope for mankind." He stared at her blankly, sensing a gulf wider than he thought possible between them. He got up abruptly and walked to the bar. "I must be in need of a drink, Minerva, 'cause I'm missing your point. Can I get you anything?"

"No, thank you," she answered, pausing until he returned to his seat.

"Bob, I don't expect the world of problems to suddenly go away, but it occurs to me that not only are our problems not going away, I believe they're actually getting worse. Furthermore, people from all walks of life seem to be sinking deeper and deeper into a malaise that frames the difficulties and challenges that life presents as inevitable tragedies. The sense of life that I knew as a girl was one of hope and optimism. Sure, problems existed—*big problems!*

"We had wars, famines, droughts. We had dictators and evil empires. We had Hitler, for God's sake! We met each crisis with uncertainty, but that was followed by hope. Our faith served us through thick and thin. We expected to reach the other side, and we usually did.

"But somehow the tables have turned. It seems that Society has taken a wrong turn—several of them really, and we've lost our way. Instead of meeting the big problems of life with a 'can do' attitude, most people react with pessimism and futility. We meet each crisis with resignation and despair. We give up before we even get started.

"My point is that our work through the Foundation has had little to no effect on this. By the way, Bob, I don't regret the contributions we've made. If anything, we've helped stem the tide of the decay."

She sipped her water and sat back.

"Does it occur to you that this malaise you're referring to is an artifact of civilization itself?" Bob asked. "I agree with your general point—people do seem to have a harder and harder time holding their heads up against the onslaught of challenges and crises, but that doesn't mean that the Koyne Foundation should be dismantled and scattered to the wind! Frankly, Minerva, it sounds like you're advocating for a new breed of public servant. The trends you've named are way beyond what any charitable organization can hope to influence."

"Possibly," replied Minerva, "but I still believe it's my duty—*our* duty— to try. Whatever you may be thinking, don't accuse me of giving up on the influence we hold. I know that we have a special kind of leverage that goes far beyond the value of our monetary assets. That's why I'm excited to see how these can be deployed in a new way."

"How do you propose to refocus the Foundation's assets? And why do you imagine that this big giveaway would accomplish anything more than what we've already accomplished—again, what *you've* already accomplished—in all these years of selective distribution?"

"Interestingly enough, I have your son Henry to thank for one insight. He and I spo—"

"*Henry?!* What in the hell could he possibly contribute to this discussion?"

"Listen to you, Bob! *That's* the kind of closed-minded stubbornness that's underlying this whole picture. Have you ever seen your son teach? Do you know what kind of magic he performs every day in his classroom?"

Godfrey was stupefied. For several seconds, he just stared at his aunt.

"You're losing me, Minerva. What does Henry's teaching have to do with *any* of this?"

"Your son is on the front lines of the only battle worth fighting. He guides children to discover their dreams, to explore them, to embrace them. Teachers in classrooms everywhere are producing a key ingredient that has been left out of the committee rooms, board rooms, and halls of Congress."

"And what is that?" Bob asked, not bothering to hide his sarcasm.

"Hope."

"*Hope?!*"

"You heard me. I said it was a key ingredient, but there are obviously others. Some people, especially teachers, emphasize and explore these too. Beauty, safety, fair play ... truth."

"Come on, Minerva. Now you're lapsing into fantasy. Nobody has said those aren't perfectly wonderful ideals, but I still don't get the connection. Did my son somehow fill you full of his particularly idiotic version of naiveté? Have you somehow been swayed by his utopian politics? Give me a *break!*"

Godfrey rose again, walked toward the window, and looked out on the snowy expanse. He turned abruptly to add something, but stopped himself, agitated beyond all reason. Minerva continued.

"In fact, Henry knows nothing of this. He has no idea what I took away from my visit to his school. He has no idea what conversations I had with his colleagues and administrators." Her eyes followed Godfrey as he paced. "Don't you dare make your son the scapegoat for your own jaded views."

"Good God! Somehow, you've lost sight of the fact that the world just doesn't work the way he and his heroes see it. It never has."

"Oh, and *you* know how it works?! Buckle down, put up the walls, mistrust everyone, and scramble to defend what you've scraped together?" She watched him fidget with the curtains. "You're afraid of something, Bob, and you cover it up with anger. What is it that you can't accept about your son?"

Turning back toward the center of the room, Godfrey walked down the gently tiered hardwood floors, passed Minerva in her chaise, and stepped onto the stone tiles by the hearth.

"How in the world did we get off on this tangent? I stayed in this afternoon to speak to you about a vision you apparently have of how things need to change for the Foundation. Now, we're talking about idealists, and fear, and ... Minerva, I don't know *what* you're talking about."

"I believe you do, Bob. You just don't want to admit it. Why did you get so upset earlier when you believed that Henry had somehow influenced me on this issue?"

"Because he's a simple-minded fool, *that's why!* He skips along in a never-never land of his own wishful thinking. He has no idea what's really important—or how hard life really is."

"You blame yourself, don't you? You think you failed him?"

"*What?!*"

"Look, I've seen you with Henry, and despite your occasional harsh judgments to the contrary, I know you love him. I know you're proud of him. Yet, you're critical and angry that he chose a different course than the one you wanted for him. And, you blame yourself."

Godfrey stood with his arms crossed and his jaw set, unable to respond.

"Believe it or not, Bob, this conversation is a metaphor for the ominous challenges facing the world."

For a long moment, they just glared at one another. Minerva finally looked away, angry with herself for losing control and wondering if she had had any in the first place.

With a sigh of exasperation, she said in a strained, but calmer, voice, "I'd like to sit quietly and be with my thoughts, if that's okay with you. I'm going to consider your points, and I hope you'll do the same."

Chapter 7

At 9:00 AM on the second Wednesday of January, Minerva entered the board-room of the Koyne Foundation. Catherine Myers, her personal secretary and executive assistant, was the only non-trustee in attendance.

Board members—half of whom represented different branches of the Koyne family, half of whom were recruited from the business world—greeted one another and took their seats around the long oval table. After procedural formalities and a quick review of some old business, they moved to new business. Minerva stood up.

"Please excuse my cryptic description of item one. I've done my best to keep this proposal confidential until now because the changes, if approved, would signal a fundamental shift in the course of the Koyne Foundation. My staff worked hard to help me shape this presentation. Two board members, namely Julian Fielding and Bob Godfrey, were approached as well for their input and feedback."

Catherine Myers dimmed the lights and initiated the sequence of slides, the first one of which showed the title: *A New Approach*. Minerva began mechanically, but after several minutes her shaky start gave way to her usual confident manner. In the darkened room the trustees seemed attentive and neutral, the planes of their faces, pale in the bluish light, were directed at the large viewing screen at the end of the room.

Ten minutes later, Part One of her slideshow was complete. The lights came back up as the screen retracted into the ceiling. She had recapped the history of the Koyne Foundation, highlighting achievements with upward-trending graphs that represented annual growth figures of the principal assets, the distributions, the administrative costs, and more. Hoping to create a context against which she could pivot, she had set the Board at ease with the known, the familiar ... the positive.

Her last two slides identified the current assets, their growth in the previous calendar year, and then projections for the coming year within the context of the gloomy economic outlook predicted by their in-house analysts. There was some spontaneous chatter about the fluctuations in the markets and exchanges, and glances went to their academic representative, Dr. Kazuhiro Hisakawa, a professor of economics at Columbia University, as well as to Sam Minton, both respected for their media savvy and grasp of economic trends.

Before stepping into Part Two of her presentation, Minerva suddenly recalled a scene from her early days as a fundraiser. On a tour of museums and hospitals in the Midwest, she had observed a councilman in a small township give a pitch to a hostile gathering of citizens intent on denouncing any and all moves to raise taxes or approve a bond initiative. Despite the considerable cuts made by a frugal city council, and despite the fact that the expansion of a superannuated auditorium would significantly improve the ability of the town to attract new business, the constituency was adamantly opposed.

The man had stepped out in front of this crowd, fearless, and had proceeded to give them what he knew they needed: reassurance. Then he delivered some sobering news, laying out exactly how much debt the city would be carrying and for how long. The councilman ended with how wonderful it would be when they paid off the bond fifteen years hence, and how, in the meantime, they would enjoy a superior facility and a heightened civic reputation in their region. The boos turned to applause, and the whole debate shifted as a result.

Minerva, in her early forties at the time, had approached the man after his speech. He was a stocky man in his fifties, with the wandering eye of a traveling salesman. Ignoring her wedding band, not to mention his own, he had winked at her brusquely after giving her the once-over.

"It's all how you frame your message, honey. You gotta give it to 'em in a way they won't mind ... the bad news wrapped in somethin' familiar and palatable." He had leaned forward and whispered, no doubt for effect, "My father called it a shit sandwich." She never forgot how the man had been able to shift from friendly councilman to crude chauvinist in a matter of seconds. More importantly, she never forgot his lesson.

Recalling that story now, Minerva wondered if she had toasted and buttered the bread enough to serve up her real message. And in a brief flash of shame, she chastised herself inwardly for applying such an ugly analogy to her lofty new vision of salvation. She took a sip of water to hide her momentary grin, and then she continued.

"By all accounts, you and I have done great work at the helm of the Koyne Foundation. Why then, you might ask, am I proposing a *new approach*—a new direction? The simple answer is that I believe our work, which is putting money and resources into the hands of organizations committed to serving specific needs for specific sectors of society, has reached what economists call a point of diminishing returns.

"Many years ago, I set out to serve a higher purpose and to be of benefit to my community, my nation, and even mankind. I followed the paradigm that others had long since set in motion. Invest in causes that yield solutions and positive change. Who could argue with that?"

Shaking her head simply, she answered her own question, "*I* couldn't. I set up the Koyne Foundation according to this time-tested formula and acted accordingly. The results, I was sure, were clear." She paused and took a sip of water. Panning the room, she looked each trustee in the eye and then addressed them all in a tone that was oddly inscrutable, "But are they?"

Because of her preliminary conversations with Julian and Bob, she knew the other trustees wouldn't be won over easily, if at all. She proceeded cautiously.

"Through a series of recent realizations, I've come to a startling conclusion ... for me at least. It is this: the results of our work are *not* clear. What we have taken as evidence of our good works for such a long time is *not* conclusive. In fact, the more I consider things from my new perspective, the more the evidence seems to support my hypothesis that we're actually contributing to the problems of the world, rather than solving them."

She expected some sort of outcry at this point, but the trustees remained silent. Group dynamics had always fascinated her, and she wondered what might be holding the tide back. The seven trustees on her left and the seven on her right looked at her with expressions ranging from mild interest to cautious skepticism. It was as if the leather-bound folders in front of each person soothed them into a state of trust, so perfectly were the crisp, colorful documents presented that one couldn't imagine that they contained anything apocryphal. She continued.

"For many years, we have come to the aid of certain populations via our ongoing relationships with our beneficiary organizations, with the best of intentions, of course. It is my belief now, though, that we have lapsed into a dysfunctional symbiosis with those we had targeted for aid. Rather than imparting solutions to people, and helping them to bridge a myriad of difficulties, we have created dependencies and institutionalized their problems.

"Aunt Minerva, what are you saying?" cried Brenda Koyne-Hollingsworth, looking quickly from side to side. "*Dysfunctional symbiosis? Institutionalizing the problems?* That's out*rageous!*"

"Yes, Brenda, it is," said Minerva tersely.

The others looked at Brenda with a mixture of sympathy and stern reproach. What remained was a room full of raised eyebrows, and attention shifted back to Minerva.

"This is the reasoning behind my proposal, which is in two parts. One: that the Koyne Foundation rewrite its mission statement to the effect that it end its perennial distribution of funds to the current beneficiaries. And, two: that the new mission authorize the one-time distribution of our entire holdings to organizations that will compete broadly for our support. In this process of sunsetting the Foundation, assets would be spread among a completely new set of initiatives."

"Minerva," ventured Bob Godfrey in his most diplomatic tone, "if I may?" She nodded.

"What you've laid out so far is pretty startling and catches most of the Board completely off guard. As you noted earlier, I was given a preview of your ideas, but, even with that lead time, I'm still finding it difficult to wrap my mind around your proposal. Perhaps you could explain what results you're talking about. In other words, on what are you basing your opinion that the Koyne Foundation has not succeeded in its stated mission?"

"Mother, I'm with Bob on this," added Julian. "We need evidence before we could even begin to take your proposal seriously?"

"Fair enough," Minerva responded evenly.

"I read the same newspapers as the rest of you, watch the same evening news on TV. The evidence is everywhere ... it seems to be implied in practically everything I see nowadays. The general mood that pervades the culture is one of hopelessness and resignation. Yes, small victories are claimed in isolated battles, here and there, but these are swallowed up within days or weeks. The course of the war is unchanged: humanity is losing.

"I suppose we can be proud that we've helped win some of these small victories. We've given hundreds of millions of dollars over the years to the American Cancer Society, the Red Cross, numerous universities and research institutes ... and many others. But I ask you to consider for a moment: what is the overall effect? Have we altered the path of Society? Have we changed the way humans approach the big issues confronting us?" She paused, hoping to see a glimmer of recognition, if not agreement. Seeing only blank stares, she continued.

"I must admit, the newness of my vision, and the counter-intuitive nature of it, still intrigues me. I suppose I shouldn't be surprised by your skepticism.

"Consider, if you will, that Society is like an ailing patient who's been in the hospital for far too long. The patient has been content to follow the advice of a team of doctors, all of whom have fought to give this patient their favorite drugs and treatments, some of which work at cross purposes. The patient has grown accustomed to this attention and resorted to a regimen of pain-killing drugs on which he is now dependent. What the patient really needs is fresh air and exercise."

Elizabeth Clarke, the President of Bank of America, spoke for the first time, "Mrs. Bennett, I think I get what you're driving at, but I don't believe this is a condemnation of our work. Nobody blames the Foundation for not providing society with a way to turn the whole world around. Without our contributions to all those key organizations, which we have striven to hand pick by the way, the world would certainly be worse off."

The others around the oval table nodded at one another with a sense of conciliatory smugness, suggesting that, at least among themselves, a consensus had been reached that Minerva's proposal ought to be tabled.

Sam Minton raised his hand.

"Mrs. Bennett, I know you're speaking metaphorically. Nevertheless, you seem to be suggesting that, by divesting the entire portfolio of assets in a final grand distribution, we could begin to solve, in wholesale fashion, the problems confronting us all over the world. Am I missing something?"

"No, Sam, you're right on track. I like the way you put that, too ... that we can '*begin* to solve ... the problems confronting us.' There's one point I haven't made and won't make—that we can solve things overnight. We can't. What we can do is admit that the present approach is not working and then be willing to commit to a new approach, which will necessarily be a bold departure. If we don't, society will keep on getting what it's been getting, which, from my experience, is gloomier and uglier and more tragic each year."

"I can't argue with that," Minton stated amiably, leaning forward slightly with curiosity. "Can you describe this 'bold departure'?"

"I'd be happy to," Minerva replied, immediately realizing that this wasn't exactly true. Even if Minton were mildly receptive, the others appeared to be consolidating their resistance, and she was beginning to doubt the value of continuing.

"There's an ingredient that's missing, even in discussions like this. We're here to solve problems, build towards a brighter future, but too often we leave out the sense of hope that can fuel us past tough times ... and I believe the best source for this is children."

"*Children?!*" blurted Stanley Koyne, another nephew. Roused from his mild stupor, he looked about for confederates to share his derision. He was hung over.

Minerva ignored him. "The natural perspective of youth is one of unbridled optimism; children expect to grow up and live in a society that embraces a grand vision. If you consider the way things have gone for some time, you will agree, perhaps, that some of the core beliefs that have comprised our grand vision are given lip service at best.

"Our standards have been overshadowed or overturned by factional infighting, deception, greed, and confusion. Ideals have fallen by the wayside. They've become unfashionable. Instead, we live in a world that seems to be running on opinions, boasts, and threats. In the mainstream media, the only tools we hear mentioned are the pragmatics of corporations and the politics of consensus. The answer to every argument, we are told, is either dependent on the short-sighted delivery of a bottom line, commonly known as the quarterly report, or the latest poll, administered by special interest groups.

"The fact that our institutions have lost their moral compasses is what concerns me most. When I was a child, I saw no conflict of interest between security, prosperity, and charity. I still don't.

"Why is it, then, that our political parties and our mainstream media do see a conflict here? Perhaps they create this conflict where none exists, in order to cash in on the antagonism and the inevitable infighting, to make a buck on both sides of an issue that doesn't, in reality, even exist. We all suffer for this approach, even those who believe they have a private pipeline to the profits and the privilege."

She took a sip of water, pleased to be feeling a surge of passion and confidence, and glad that it was displacing the self-doubt that had lingered until that moment.

"Mrs. Bennett," Minton asked, "you were saying something about youth and children?"

Realizing that her soap boxing was something she could ill afford at the moment, she nodded at Minton and smiled.

"Yes, they are central to my proposal. I believe we must harness the playful approach that children naturally assume if we're to have a chance at turning things around. I'd like to see the Koyne Foundation provide an opportunity by which we enable and encourage children—and youthful thinkers in general— to join in the big conversations. The naiveté they bring can combine with the experience and expertise of older voices to create a revitalizing force in what would otherwise be stagnant and pointless discussions. I see this platform as a competition—a contest that calls forth ideas from the best and brightest around the world regarding the basic question of how we're to live together peacefully and abundantly."

"Mrs. Bennett, are you talking about holding a philosophical contest? And then presenting the assets of the Foundation to the *winners*?" asked Belinda Dalton, president of Atlantis Rising, a consortium of service and volunteer organizations in North America and Europe.

"That's precisely what I'm talking about."

"That's ... that's incredible. You're proposing to award $60 billion to the winners of a *contest?*" Dalton was dumbfounded. The look on her face was mirrored by at least half in attendance.

"Yes."

Daniel Bennett, the middle child of her late husband JB, cleared his throat. "Minerva, I've only been on the Board for a couple of years, but I'm proud of the work we do. I have nothing but admiration for your leadership and the mission of this foundation.

"If you sense that, for whatever reason, it's time to move in a new direction, even if that new direction holds some kind of expiration date, I'm here to listen. I must say, though, that holding a contest in order to give away a fortune seems extreme. Wouldn't it make more sense to just make enormous one-time donations to the beneficiaries with whom we already have relationships, along with perhaps another ten or twenty hand-picked special projects?"

"That's an excellent point, Daniel." Minerva's glance of pride at her stepson was genuine. "If I were simply proposing that we dissolve the Foundation, that would be the perfect approach to take. But that's not my purpose today. I'm here to advocate for a new mission—to raise a clarion call to put *ideas* back on the front burner. I want to take fear and misguided pragmatism off the agenda and to replace these with hope and, if you will, intelligent idealism.

"As I was suggesting earlier, Society is sick and growing sicker every day, resigned to living in fear and mistrust, like an alcoholic who must have his gin ... or a hypochondriac who can't imagine a life without dependence on her doctors and medications. People in these predicaments have only one chance at regaining health—some kind of spiritual transformation. And *we* are in a position, by virtue of our reputation and our wealth, to facilitate that. I am proposing that we take advantage of this before too many more calamities push us to the point of full withdrawal and chaos."

"Mrs. Bennett, that's an interesting take on the state of things," Minton said, "but, as they say, talk is cheap. Analogies are great for conversation and storytelling, but they don't necessarily guide us in specific action. Can you give us more detail on this contest approach? Who would be eligible to enter? What would be the specific objective?"

"Yes, well ... please realize this is a broad vision so far. If we were to embark on such a vast enterprise, it would require serious planning and a great deal of intricate coordination. I believe I have the seed of a worthy idea, but it needs to be fleshed out in far greater detail. The general idea is this: teams from around the world would compete to produce a written document—you can think of it as a manifesto or a treatise—that addresses the challenge of solving major world problems with a comprehensive plan."

"Hmm ..." Minton nodded. "How many teams are you talking about, and how would they be comprised? On what basis would we decide who wins?"

Minerva looked at each of the trustees around the table. "If the Board were to get behind this idea, we could hold a planet-wide contest with perhaps one thousand teams. This number would be trimmed through numerous rounds of judging by a panel of experts.

"Each team would be gender-balanced and consist of a broad age range. And, to insure the positive attitude I think is missing in so many endeavors, we'd require that at least two members be children."

Mocking glances and raised eyebrows flashed around the table in a not-so-subtle fashion. These were the silent equivalent of: *You've got to be kidding!*

Minton, who appeared to still have a modicum of respectful neutrality, continued with his questioning. "Once most of the teams are eliminated, how many would remain? How much would the winners receive?"

"Given the level of our assets, one scenario I've imagined would yield twenty top teams, with each one winning a substantial sum ... ranging from one to five billion dollars. The winnings could also include individual prizes, taxable in the same manner as the Nobel Prize, but the main awards would be on a team basis. The finalists would be required to set up tax-exempt foundations so that any disbursements from the Foundation would be on the same basis as our present grants."

"Mother, I think we've heard enough," said Julian in a petulant tone. "It pains me that you've lost faith in the ability of the Foundation—that *you* created—to perform the good works that have always been so important to you. Everybody here has learned from your example, and it just seems incomprehensible that you are willing to jettison your legacy.

"You propose to dissolve the Koyne Foundation in order to fund ten or twenty, or *fifty*, no-name foundations around the world, consisting of amateurs and kids? I don't get it. *What* has gotten into you?!"

Of all the dissension, Julian's explicit condemnation hurt the most. Minerva realized that her presentation was finished. Not only would the projections and scenarios that she and her staff had prepared be premature, they would now appear laughable to the gathering. She glanced at Catherine and shook her head.

"That's the sixty-four-dollar question, isn't it?" she said, more to herself than to the trustees. She closed her eyes and sighed, her passion all but extinguished.

"Julian, you seem to be voicing the consensus of the Board. It would be pointless for me to restate my motion. Even if somebody were willing to second it, the results of a vote would be obvious. So ... I'm done."

The finality of her last statement caused the trustees to shift uneasily in their seats. They had been perfectly comfortable in their demonstration of scorn during her proposal, but they now seemed to recall that Minerva Bennett was still their leader and that, with perhaps this one startling exception, she had been a paragon of sensibility.

"Given the gulf that now looms between my vision and the ongoing mission of the Foundation, I think it only appropriate that I make a bold departure of a different sort. Thus, I hereby step down as Chairman."

The faint sound in the Board room was not so much a gasp as it was the sudden and uniform intake of breath. Nobody saw this coming, and the look on Minerva's own face revealed that she was as surprised as the rest.

"Minerva," interjected Bob Godfrey, who was the next most senior member of the Board, "I think you're overreacting to the skepticism and the criti—"

"It's okay, Bob," Minerva interrupted. "Thank you for that gesture, but I believe this is the perfect opportunity to announce a change of this sort. I've led this organization for long enough. Putting things in terms that I myself advocated earlier, it's time to pass the mantle ... to the *youth* of the Board." The bitterness and disappointment she felt were replaced by a sudden relief and wave of humility. She smiled with a weary nod of resoluteness that made it clear that her mind was made up.

Time seemed to stand still as the trustees stared at their long-time leader. They were now presented the opportunity to witness Minerva's ability to admit defeat in her final campaign, as well as the alacrity with which she reacted to the swift currents of shifting influence. Whatever they thought of her just minutes before was now replaced by the recognition that she was, indeed, a gracious woman.

"I don't know what to say," Godfrey said. "Wouldn't you like to think about this?"

"I have," she said. "Perhaps this is what my vision was telling me all along—that it was time for *me* to step aside." She panned the room quickly, making eye contact with each trustee.

"Please accept this as my formal resignation as Chairman. It's been my honor and deep pleasure to serve with each of you. I will, if necessary, remain a sitting trustee until I am replaced, but I think it's appropriate to make my exit now."

"Mother, are you thinking of departing right this minute—before the end of the meeting?!" asked Julian.

"Yes. Don't worry, you still have a solid quorum for all official business." She stood up, straightening her papers as she did so, and she gave the room one final look.

"Please don't feel as if you've chased me off. This morning's events have helped me to gain a fuller perspective on many things, and I think it's all come out for the best."

The trustees stood solemnly as she walked out the door, Catherine Myers in her wake.

Chapter 8

CATHERINE MYERS, SITTING at her desk in her apartment, glanced at her e-mail inbox one last time, anxious to close her laptop computer and make it to bed. It was a few minutes after midnight, and her screen calendar indicated that it was now Monday, February 29.

"LEAP DAY"... that's appropriate, she thought.

Tomorrow morning—later today, she realized—she and her colleagues would initiate the grand scheme that until now had remained private, and there would be no turning back. Not that this was a possibility. Not since her boss had forged ahead with such an uncanny resolve.

Catherine thought back over the last six weeks and mentally reviewed the manner in which Minerva Bennett's world had been turned upside down and, somehow, in the last couple of days, seemed to have righted itself. In the next twenty-four hours, they would launch a media blitz the likes of which the world had never seen. The overwhelming surge of new files, new contacts, and new accounts she had entered, along with new distribution lists and calendar events ... these were her visual proof that this new enterprise was real.

She recalled the aftermath of the board meeting back in January. Minerva gathered the other members of her core staff immediately after the aborted proposal and informed them of her resignation. Then she had given them the rest of the day off.

As the heart and soul of the Koyne Foundation, but no longer the head, Minerva had retreated to her penthouse in a cloud of unanswered questions. She had informed them that she would be back in the office on the following

Monday, at which time they would sort out whatever changes might be needed in the chain of command.

It wasn't long before Minerva jumped the gun on her own self-imposed break, and Catherine recalled the e-mail she had received the very next day. In bold language, the former chairman made it clear that she intended to pursue her new vision independently.

In a separate e-mail, Minerva had requested Catherine's assistance in preparing a short list of realtors, art dealers, and estate managers who could help her liquidate some of her more substantial individually held assets. Obviously determined, she had committed herself to implementing the plan that had, only a day before, been summarily rejected.

Catherine had experienced a surge of pride upon realizing that she was the only recipient of Minerva Bennett's inaugural declaration, and she revisited that now. It was an official touchstone of her own destiny, by virtue of designating her as a pivotal player—a midwife—in this unusual campaign to reverse the decline of modern culture.

Although she knew her employer intimately, she never imagined that the woman was prepared to go the distance with her pet project after such a poignant rebuff. By the time she had finished reading Mrs. Bennett's brief note, Catherine had cheered out loud. The sense of that exclamation continued to resonate, only as a slightly more subdued: *You go, girl!*

Within twenty-four hours of Catherine's quiet inquiries, word of Minerva Bennett's plans to liquidate long-held assets had come to the attention of her more senior relatives, several of whom felt that they knew better than their matriarch that sudden liquidation of one's property was neither sound nor responsible. At no small cost to her own dignity and serenity, she had braved a family fight that almost broke out in the Arts, Style, and Business sections of *The New York Times*.

The non-family members of the Koyne Foundation Board had been able, barely, to exert pressure with their own media connections to keep a scandal, which included a dubious court-ordered battery of psychological testing, out of the news. Stewart Maxwell's dark prediction had come true, and it had been ironic that his testimony, given by deposition, had been instrumental in giving the judge the confidence to denounce the suit brought by two of her heirs as unfounded and frivolous.

Catherine and Maxwell had marveled at the lack of animosity that Minerva had shown to her relatives, both doubting that they could have been so forgiving. Immediately after that legal victory, which might have taken months but which, through some Archimedean ingenuity that nobody could explain, took only one week, Minerva created a new foundation.

During that interlude, the Koyne Foundation underwent several alterations. The first major change came one week after Minerva Bennett's resignation when the Foundation's president, Libby Armstrong, followed suit. Catherine had related to her friend how their leader had been treated by her own flesh and blood. It was a vivid picture of generational antagonism and an incredible lack of gratitude. Libby had spent several days reading between the lines of some memos originating from the new chairman, Julian Fielding, and she had decided to make her own exit.

Catherine had informed Minerva of this news, and Minerva, she found out later, had invited Libby to lunch. Minerva inquired as to her plans and prospects, and she expressed appreciation for Libby's implied loyalty.

"Mrs. Bennett, don't worry about me. There're several organizations I intend to approach. I've already done some networking, and I expect an opportunity will present itself in the near future."

"I'm not going to let that happen," Minerva told her.

"Excuse me?"

"I don't want you to receive any offers, or to entertain the possibility of working for any such people."

"*Why not?*"

"Because I want to hire you right back again, and I won't take no for an answer."

Now, as Catherine recalled Libby's story, she looked back on all that had transpired in the intervening weeks. She had a sense that they had missed something big and obvious, but all her checklists seemed to be in order.

It had been three weeks since they moved into their new offices, a few blocks from the Fielding Building. It was not as posh as their former headquarters, but *Minerva*, which is how she had requested they all address her from now on, loved it. Her new burst of enthusiasm was infectious.

Catherine considered another positive development: they had hired Brockman, Solomon, and Vogel to run their public relations. It was an outfit that had built quite a reputation in the last three years, and they seemed genuinely inspired by the prospect of handling Minerva's fledgling foundation and its unique mission.

Just as she turned out her desk lamp and yawned deeply, Catherine glanced at the logo highlighted in the document that was still open on her computer monitor. It was the fourth version that their graphic design firm had submitted, and they had finally gotten it right. Minerva had approved it late Friday afternoon, just in time to be inserted into the newly created website, as well as their print advertising and letterheads.

Catherine got in bed, pulled the quilted comforter up to her neck, and turned out the light. Hoping and praying that she hadn't forgotten something on her endless list of to-dos, she let out a great sigh. She closed her eyes and pictured the logo: a stylized ancient Greek warship. Somebody in the office, one of the new guys, actually knew that it was called a *trireme*. As the cottony wisps of unconsciousness tugged her toward slumber, she couldn't remember where this image had come from ... something from Minerva's world.

Her last thoughts were of a long, sleek sailing vessel, surging forward in a blue green sea. Rows of oars reached in a choreographed motion as they struck the water and sent spray into the Mediterranean, during a battle against an unknown foe in a distant age. A warrior stood, sword extended toward the prow, with a billowing sail adding to the thrust of the oars.

⊷═◉ ◉═⊷

In contrast to the stately and substantial profile of the Koyne Foundation, with its recently affirmed tenure of perpetuity, Minerva's new brainchild was designed to be an explosive burst of activity that would crescendo and dissolve in two years. While they wouldn't need five floors, it was expected that the project would eventually expand its administrative needs and occupy at least one more floor, perhaps two, of the mid-century brick building that had just become their new headquarters.

Libby Armstrong stepped out of the elevator at 6:30 AM, imagining that she would be the first one to arrive. She noted the newly etched glass door, installed over the weekend, and gave a nod of approval to the empty hallway. VOX STELLARUM was etched artfully across the frosted white upper panel of the heavy wooden door. Underneath, in smaller figures, was the newly adopted motto: *Remis Velisque.* She'd forgotten the exact meaning of the Latin phrase but knew it was related to the logo.

The translucent door revealed lights inside, and she wondered if the building manager had forgotten to secure the space after the glass installer had finished, sometime over the weekend. She swiped her key card and entered, immediately hearing some faint music from one of the offices to her left. One of her colleagues had been even more eager than she to get a jump on the day.

She gave a soft hello, so as not to startle anybody, and walked toward the source of the music. Bobby Jabari, an encryption specialist and hypertext programmer, looked up from his spread of monitors, hard drives, and keyboards. The door to his small office was wide open, revealing the Spartan needs of a modern Internet warrior. For a desk, he used a scuffed white plastic folding table, the kind that hotels and convention centers keep by the hundreds in their vast storage areas. He'd been given two vertical filing cabinets, but they were unopened and unused, relegated to the far corner to gather dust for lack of relevance. Content to augment his desk space with the four packing boxes in which he'd transported his hardware, Jabari used them to support his auxiliary gear and his beat-up boom box. Libby could now tell that it was the source of the sound—some kind of world music—picked up against all odds on a bent antenna slanted toward the window.

When he saw her in the doorway, he smiled broadly. His dark skin and pure white teeth reminded her of the keys on a piano. Her impression was confirmed by the lyrical, almost musical, way he spoke.

"Good morning!"

"Hi, Bobby. You're here early."

"Actually ... I'm here rather late," he said, flashing his smile.

"You've been here all *night?* You must be exhausted."

"I'm fine. This is the way I work. Sometimes I'll go twenty-four hours straight and then sleep for twelve hours." Libby looked at him closely, but he brushed away her concern. "Don't worry. I feel good. I'm way too excited to rest or fall asleep."

Libby walked down the hall to her office and found herself wondering how old he was. With his shaved head and slender build, Jabari could pass for a thirty-something, but his bearing hinted that he might be fifty. Maybe it was his old-fashioned manners, or the hint of his foreign upbringing.

During the next hour, the rest of the hand-picked members of the new foundation made their way into the suite of offices, and the energy was charged with anticipation. Quick hellos punctuated the intensity as the staff delved back into their work, getting ready for the onslaught of activity. Nervous energy crackled in every conversation.

Shortly before 8:00 AM, Minerva arrived. She poked her head into each office and each cubicle, greeting each person before heading to her office to prepare for the day. At 9:00 AM, the entire group gathered in the conference room for a full staff meeting.

Seated around the table in no particular order were fifteen men and women poised to implement the project that had been but a nebulous vision only three months before. Some were hired for their organizational skills, some for their knowledge of public relations and media image, and some were recruited purely for their desire to be part of a global competition of ideals.

Among the new faces were a linguist, fluent in six languages, an expert on world religions and cultural trends, a mathematician with a doctorate on game theory and statistics, and a social media expert who was a regular contributor to the *Daily Beast*, *Rolling Stone*, and *Forbes*.

Minerva took her seat at the head of the table, marveling at the staff that Libby and Catherine had assembled in such a short period. She'd given her lieutenants unbridled authority to create the team that would breathe life into her vision.

"Good morning, everybody! I'm going to say just a few words and then turn the meeting over to Libby. To put it simply, I am impressed, and proud, and excited. Impressed by the incredible intelligence and drive that each of you has already demonstrated, proud that my vision has attracted such a wonderful assortment of people, and excited by the grand challenge we're about to unleash. We're going to make history tomorrow, one way or the other, and I want you to know I'm confident in you.

"Perhaps you noticed the new sign at the entrance: *Vox Stellarum*. We, collectively, are the lens that will focus and magnify hope to a world much in need. We will supply the microphones and the speakers by which 'the voice of the stars' will be heard."

She nodded solemnly at the opposite end of the table, and Libby Armstrong proceeded.

"Here's what needs to happen in the next two hours. By 11:00 AM, final proofs are due at our targeted media sources. As you know, we're going to depend on word of mouth and free news coverage once the announcements are made. The initial framing is critical, and we want to influence the reception we'll get as much as possible." She paused and pointed at the stack of large off-white sheets of paper in the middle of the table. "Those are copies of the draft for the first ad, and I want each of you to take one now and spend several minutes looking it over. Several of us have already scrutinized it, but fresh eyes might catch something we missed. All comments are welcome. Although this will be a phased announcement, we want this first glimpse to be unforgettable."

They sat silently and pored over the print. The layout was of a full-page ad that would be posted on the back cover of hundreds of newspapers around the world.

Joshua Starkman, the comptroller, raised his hand. "This looks great in English, but do we have any idea how this announcement will be received overseas?"

"Good question. I'll let Bill speak to this." Libby nodded at Bill Finch, a dapper man with a carefully trimmed beard and mustache.

"Translation is an art. Even with fluency, some readers will raise an eyebrow at the connotation and layout of a given advertisement or announcement. Nevertheless, I've taken great care to translate these announcements in the languages that I know firsthand, and I've recruited some colleagues from the United Nations to handle those that I don't. The tone we're striving for is somewhere between colloquial and strict formal." He paused to see if anybody would get his joke, and then continued when it was clear that his humor was too dry for the room.

"I think we're in good shape. Even if we make a few idiomatic *faux pas* in some of the more obscure tongues, our main intent will be clear."

"Of course," Libby interjected, "many of those whom we want to reach don't bother to read newspapers anymore, but our announcement will be posted in over one hundred on-line sources, besides the web versions of the newspapers themselves. Wanda and Bobby have been hard at work to prepare the Vox Stellarum website for the initial influx of traffic." Libby glanced at them for details, but they only nodded and grinned.

"Okay then ... we may be done. Catherine, do you have anything to add?"

"Yes. As you all know by now," she said, rising from her chair, "Minerva's vision is big and bold. As much as we clearly embrace it, we need to realize that many people won't.

"An awful lot of people just aren't ready for the revolution that we're forging. Tomorrow, when they see our announcement, there will be skepticism and doubt ... even ridicule. Minerva saw this firsthand from some of her own family members.

"My point is this—we're a private foundation that is getting ready to go very, very public. Say goodbye to privacy, for a while at least. As the public spokespersons, Minerva and Libby will be especially vulnerable, but don't be surprised if you are approached and challenged. I don't think it's stretching things to say that, tomorrow morning, we march into battle. Let's be prepared."

⤜⟩⟨⤛

Bits of chatter floated down the short hallway, from behind a closed door. It would have gone unnoticed but for the high-pitched giggles and spirited exclamations that periodically punctuated the relative calm in the living room. The three adults seemed largely unaware as they conducted their own conversation. When a loud thump and bang occurred, followed by a moment of silence, and then another burst of laughter, Margrit Hoowij, rolled her eyes and shrugged. Her husband, Joost, ignored it altogether, though he may have simply been engrossed in their friend's story.

Johannes Driessen, a friend of the family and frequent visitor, had come over to share exploits of his recent travels. The principal buyer for his family's import-export business, he had just returned from a trip to the Middle East and Italy.

A tall distinguished man in his late-fifties, Driessen looked every bit the world traveler that he, in fact, was. One could easily imagine him in a French drawing room, in a Russian art auction, or in a street bazaar in Calcutta, haggling with the locals. Full of nervous energy, he paced the room. He stood at a window and looked out on the city as he spoke, his eyes resting momentarily on a bridge across the inner-city canal below. The light traffic reflected the tail end of rush hour; it would remain quiet for another hour or two before the streets would resound with the movement of the night life crowd, in search of restaurants and cabarets. He lifted his gaze to the distant sectors of the city and then turned back to the warmly lit room and his friends.

Joost and Margrit were accustomed to his frenetic manner, knowing he would gradually relax as he related his adventures. A trader through and through, he would bring news of faraway places in exchange for the grounding hospitality of his friends. They had met Driessen at an art opening years before, when their daughter was only three. He had been attracted to the couple for their quietly cosmopolitan personalities. From that first conversation, he had been impressed with their ability to listen without envy. They would occasionally cross paths, and this evolved from a cordial acquaintance to an almost familial bond. When he met their child, she took to him as if he were an uncle or a godfather.

Margrit was a dancer turned choreographer with the Swearingen-Osterhoudt Dansgroep, one of the few Dutch dance troupes that drew consistently good audiences despite their avant-garde repertoire. Joost played viola for the Royal Concertgebouw Orchestra, one of the world's great music ensembles. These vocations afforded the couple an enviable lifestyle in the heart of one of the centers of European culture and commerce that was Amsterdam.

Despite their rarified positions in the world of art and culture, the couple managed to remain down to earth. Perhaps that was why Driessen, who had an extensive network of friends and associates, chose to insert himself into their lives.

An hour earlier, when her husband announced that Johannes was on his way over, Margrit had brewed a pot of coffee. Though it was eight o'clock in the evening, she knew this was his preferred cocktail, somehow permitting him to unwind.

Driessen paced about, gesticulating, searching for the words to describe the colorful scenes still etched in his memory. He crossed the room without skipping a beat, glanced at an abstract water color, and then returned again to the window. His ability to relate details of his adventures, even as he appeared to engage in the particulars of the present, was astonishing. Finally, he walked to the upright piano across from the kitchen and sat on the edge of the bench; half leaning, half standing, he cupped his coffee mug between his hands and took a sip.

Their guest was in a good mood—even more animated than usual. He spoke Dutch, but he lapsed into French or German as he lost himself in the places he was describing. Joost would occasionally have to slow him down, "Hold on ... go back." This kept his storytelling mostly on track, for Driessen tended to ricochet, shifting suddenly from one city, one culture, to another.

"Are you still in Cairo?" asked Margrit.

"No, sorry ... Istanbul." He put down his coffee and gestured directions with his hands, imagining that his friends could tell that he had zipped across the eastern Mediterranean, had crossed Asia Minor, and was now in the ancient city that straddled two continents. They hadn't, of course, but they nodded politely.

"I had decided to visit the Akmerkez, a collection of shops near the center of the city, on the European side. I was there fifteen years ago, which is when it opened. It's lost some of its luster, but it's still very impressive. Totally different than the Grand Bazaar, much more modern. One of my contacts gave me a tip on where to find some vases that we're going to feature—blown glass, exotic glazing, that sort of thing. You would love it.

"On the outskirts of the city, which is enormous by the way, I found the glass blower he told me about, but then, down the street, I found one I *really* liked. It worked out perfectly. The old man is going to design fifty pieces for our gallery, all original. His price was a bit high, but they'll sell like mad!"

"How much?" Joost asked idly.

"Pretty pricey I'm afraid. I don't think you'll be able to afford them: 3000 euros ... each."

"We'll take two," teased Margrit. Driessen hopped up and poured himself another cup of coffee.

"Did you go to the Grand Bazaar?" asked Joost. "I've heard you can buy pretty much anything there."

"I did, but it's too crowded. I was disappointed by the number of booths that are now filled with electronic gadgets. The old world still rules, but the new wave is influencing more and more the way they operate. Many of these people don't even haggle properly. They put price tags on everything and sell their goods like an American supermarket.

"Nevertheless, I found some very nice chests and wardrobes, very handsome and well crafted. I also met with a rug dealer I'd done business with a couple of times before. We cut a deal for a shipment of Persian prayer rugs. Exquisite detail ... the colors are incredible."

"Prayer rugs?" asked Margrit. "*Muslim* prayer rugs?"

"Yes. I have a few loyal Muslim clients, but these pieces have a universal appeal. Some are wool, some silk. The quality is superior. My supplier has a good sense of what attracts Europeans and Americans."

"Speaking of Muslims, how were the Turkish women dressed?" asked Margrit. "Were they wearing burkas?" Johannes saw the contempt on her face.

"Some, but most seemed to wear the hijab, so their faces were mostly visible. Certainly, they were very modest by our standards. Some were quite beautiful."

"The women? Or their shawls?" asked Joost, smiling. Margrit shuddered.

"Margrit, my dear, you have some strong judgments around this practice?" Johannes asked.

"Yes. I'm sorry. It's horrible—the abuse that those women must endure, the least of which is having to wear those straitjackets. I can't imagine never being able to dance ... to move freely. And that's just the tip of the iceberg. There's female genital mutilation, physical abuse, prohibition of education, lack of freedom to marry the man of their choosing ..." She closed her eyes and shook her head. "It's ghastly."

"Hmm. Yes. I agree. Fortunately, I saw no evidence of this in the market place. It's run mostly by men, of course, but I did see some women. They appeared reasonably content and engaged."

"Did you notice any civil unrest? Any protests?" Joost asked.

"No. Interesting that you should ask. Now that I think about it, though, there were soldiers everywhere in Cairo, or at least men with automatic weapons. There was a constant tension there that I didn't notice in Turkey. I got used to it, I guess.

"The Egyptian women were much more covered up, which was a good thing." He winked at Joost.

"*Now* who's got the strong judgments?" asked Margrit, grinning. She knew of their friend's preference for fair-haired women.

"Didn't you tell us you were going to Beirut?" asked Joost.

"I had to cancel. With the rise of ISIS, the Syrian government is in turmoil and the unrest has spilled over into Lebanon. I decided it wasn't worth the risk."

"So ... after Istanbul?" asked Margrit.

"Rome. What a city! I don't know how the Italians do it. No matter how many times I get fed up with their delays and their cancellations, and all their goddamn strikes, I can't stay away. It still seems worth the hassle."

"What do you mean?"

"You've heard about the Mexicans and their philosophy of *mañana*? Well, the Italians do this too, but they're subtler. They're masters at giving plausible reasons for why you can't have what you've already paid for. 'Signore, we had to back order some parts.' 'Signore, our inventory was damaged *en route*.' 'Signore, the factory workers are on strike.' Then, they just toss you a 'Ciao' and smile. What's really maddening is that they don't care if you cancel your order or not. It's just business as usual to them.

"But I love their city. The food, the people, the hospitality. The women!" Driessen winked this time at Margrit.

"Did you find any bargains?" asked Joost.

"That remains to be seen. Like I was saying, if my purchases are delivered as ordered, which they rarely are, I'll make a decent profit. But even if they aren't, I should do okay. I found some very nice pieces."

"It *is* a lovely city," remarked Margrit. "We took our dance company to Rome a couple of years ago, on a southern tour. The Italians were very friendly. I don't remember too much ... there was Campo Marzio—Oh, and the Via Condotti. *Gadverdamme, what prices!*"

Nodding, Driessen responded. "It's considered by some to offer the best shopping in Europe, but I think it's overrated. Too crowded and overpriced. I stuck to the Via Margutta, which is where some very good artists can be found, and the Via dei Sediari ... for chairs and household objects and such. Speaking of which, I have a little something for Pem."

"You spoil her, Johannes," said Joost.

"We'll call her out in a minute to say hello," said Margrit, glancing at her watch. "It's time for her friend to leave anyway. They're obviously not getting much homework done."

"I found something for you two as well, but you'll have to wait. It will be mixed in with one of the shipments. It might be two or three months, but I'm sure you'll like it."

"*Oh!* You spoil us, too, but that's different," said Margrit, smiling. She rose and walked to her daughter's room. She emerged several minutes later, shaking her head in mock terror.

"How can two girls make such a mess?! In two hours, the place is a disaster area." She sat down and sighed, a faint smile on her face reflecting that she may have practiced some of the same mischief when she was twelve. "When they clean up that pigsty, they will come say hello."

Johannes had finally migrated to one of the large leather chairs next to the space heater, which emitted a pleasing hum. He listened to Joost tell about the concert series for which they were preparing.

"And you, Margrit? When is your next show?"

"We're actually in the middle of a three-week run. You might not like it—it's a bit carnal."

Before he could find out just what, exactly, warranted that intriguing description, Pem and her friend emerged from her bedroom.

"Come around and say hello, girls," directed Joost, pointing at the space on the couch next to Margrit.

"Hello, Oom Jan!" Pem said as she sat down.

"Very good to see you, Pem. It sounds like you and your friend were having a *smashing* good time back there!" She blushed, but managed to smile.

"Johannes, this is Katrien van Leeuwen," said Margrit. "She and Pem are inseparable these days. Her family lives downstairs, second floor."

"Hi, Katrien. I believe we've met. Aren't you the one who plays the piano so brilliantly?"

"Uh-huh," was all she managed to say, also blushing.

"Girls, Mr. Driessen has just returned from one of his international buying trips, for his import-export business." Joost had said this with the intention of inspiring some sort of reasonable conversation, perhaps a question or two. The girls sat there looking uncomfortable, probably wondering if they could be excused already.

"Pem, dear, Oom Jan was telling us about how he came across some of his finds. It's quite fascinating. He said he brought you back a little something." With this, Pem sat up and looked at her mother, then at Driessen.

"Did you really?" she asked, her shyness evaporating.

"Well, I may have. It's hard to remember. Oh well, you're not interested in travel and international bazaars, things of that sort." Driessen knew how to bait and trap his friends' daughter. They had teased one another many times. Pem knew what was coming.

"I am. I am," she assured Oom Jan—her "Uncle" Johannes.

"Let's find out ... Do you know where Cairo is?"

"Of course! It's in Egypt. Did you get me something from Egypt?"

"How about Istanbul?"

"You mean: where *is* it?" she asked, glancing at her friend for support.

"Yes."

"Romania? No, wait ... Turkey?"

"Very good," he said. "Okay, one more question. What was the city called before it became known as Istanbul?"

"How would I know—that's not fair!" she objected, crossing her arms in protest.

Driessen saw a sparkle in her friend's eyes. "Do you know?" Katrien nodded. "Go ahead."

"Constantinople ... and before that it was called Byzantium."

"Goodness, dear. How on *Earth* did you know that?!" Margrit exclaimed. Pem looked at her friend with a comical scowl.

"Correct! Okay, here's another one. What—"

"That's not fair! She got the right answer," protested Pem. "Does she get something too?"

"Perhaps, but I only brought *one* 'little something' with me. I tell you what ... Just for fun, if she gets one more, I will order one for her." They nodded reluctantly. "What is the name of the body of water that divides the city?" Katrien turned to her friend with a searching look.

"Don't look at me," said Pem. "I have *no* idea!"

"That's alright, my dear. I just wanted to—"

"*Wait!* I know it ... it's ... it's the Bosphorus Strait. It connects the Black Sea and the Sea of Marmara."

"Oh my!" gasped Joost.

"Then it flows through the Dardanelles Strait to the Aegean Sea ... and the Mediterranean."

"*Show off!*" Pem said, miffed by her friend's grand standing.

"Very impressive, young lady," said Driessen, laughing softly. "You win!"

Pem looked at her Oom Jan plaintively. "We *both* get something then?"

"Yes, Pem, fair is fair," he said. Both girls smiled. "Let's see ... where did I put it?" He walked over to the door where he had left a bag against the wall.

"When I was in Rome, which was my last stop, I saw all the young people buzzing around the city on their Vespas, and many of them were wearing these." He pulled out something wrapped in crinkly tissue paper and handed it to Pem. It was a sleek leather satchel. "These are the latest fashion statement for young people on the go."

Pem quickly showed it to Kat and then jumped up to hug Driessen. "I *love* it! Thank you, Oom Jan."

"That's enough excitement for tonight, girls. It's a school night, and it's time for Kat to go home. Pem, you need to finish your homework, and then it's time for bed." Margrit ushered the girls out the door and down the hall, respectively.

"It's a school night for me too, so I'd better be on my way." Driessen grabbed his empty bag and headed to the door. He turned back to his friends. "How does that girl know such things?"

"When she's not goofing off with Pem, she's either practicing the piano or reading," explained Margrit. "Pem tells me she's the smartest student in the class."

"I guess I walked into that one. When you see her again, please tell her I ordered a shoulder bag for her as well." Still grinning, he walked out the door. "Ciao!"

Chapter 9

ON MARCH 1, newspapers were delivered as usual. Some were tossed in the age-old fashion, onto lawns, sidewalks, and bushes by the armies of pre-dawn deliverers. But most were loaded into newsstands and stacked on shelves in coffee shops, grocery stores, airport shops, and railway stations around the world. There was no rush to buy them, but devoted aficionados of the printed page picked them up and perused them as part of their daily routines. After the usual fare of train wrecks, murders, bank defaults, sport scores, and political ramblings, readers happened across the unusual, but not unheard of, instance of a full-page advertisement on the back cover of the main section.

In Malta, South Korea, Finland, Chile, Dubai, Niger, New Zealand, and over one hundred fifty other nations, an organization was introduced to the world: *Vox Stellarum*. In forty-three languages and dialects, a message was de-livered to those who bothered to pause and read the announcement. A contest was being held that invited all who were interested to participate in a process that would "change the world for the better" by shifting the daily conversa-tions and individual attitudes from tragedy, despair, and resignation to hope, cooperation, and solution.

To give legitimacy to the enterprise, a woman's name was mentioned. Most had never heard of her, even though it was stated that she had been the founder of one of the largest private foundations in the world and that she had run it as chairman for over forty years. This woman had just donated the bulk of her personal fortune as the source from which eight team awards would be granted. Near the bottom of the page, above the address of the official contest website, was the portion that even the barely literate understood.

- No application fees.
- Eligibility: Any person (age 9+) as of March 31.
- Prizes: $5,000,000,000 to be distributed among the Top 8 Teams.
- Team Awards: $300,000,000 – $2,000,000,000.
- Individual Awards: $1,000,000 – $2,000,000.
- Registration limited to the first 1,000 teams that satisfy all guidelines.

At 1:15 PM EST, the Vox Stellarum servers crashed. The tidal wave of hits constituted the greatest volume and density of traffic to a single website in the history of the Internet.

◦→═◉ ◉═←◦

"Yikes!" exclaimed Wanda Freeman as she watched the website traffic, which had built rapidly during the day, finally spike and redline. "Bobby, the servers are down! We have *way* underestimated the numbers. We need to address this immediately."

"I'm on it, but this is *fantastic!* I've never seen anything like it. We're going to be down until people start to go to sleep, at least in Asia. That's the source of our heaviest traffic."

Bobby Jabari kept his cool, typing furiously even as he spoke a rapid-fire blur of jargon at somebody through his headset. Catherine Myers was practically knocked over in the hallway by Wanda, who had gone to inform her of the issue. Catherine immediately did an about-face to inform Minerva. On top of this news, Libby had told her of Jabari's penchant for working around the clock, and she realized that she would need to keep a close eye on him as this crisis would certainly require another all-nighter.

Meanwhile, Libby and her new assistant, Rowan Detering, had been fielding calls almost nonstop since 7:30 that morning. Requests for interviews had come from media outlets that were not even open yet. Scores of late-night, scoop-hungry journalists—monitoring their social media accounts—were the first responders to the tidal wave of hits before they ever went to bed.

At 3:00 PM, Minerva called for an impromptu meeting, ordering everybody off their land lines, computers, and smart phones. The team had swelled to seventeen since the day before, as two secretaries had been hired to answer inquiries and to take up administrative slack. They were happy to rest their ears. Half the staff wheeled their chairs into the central open space, while a few opted to stand near the catering tables and graze.

"Thank you for gathering so quickly," Minerva announced. "I think it's safe to say that the world knows who we are. The response is, to put it mildly, off the charts. Bobby and Wanda watched the statistics showing Internet activity on our new website go through the roof until the server boxes—or whatever they're called—shut down. We've just made arrangements to quadruple our capacity, and I'm told we should be back on line by midnight.

"This morning, Catherine and Libby have been in touch with producers from all the major TV affiliates; requests for interviews and appearances have been pouring in non-stop. Tomorrow night, Libby and I will be guests on 'The Tonight Show.' I am also booked Friday to appear on the CBS 'Late Show with Tucker Middleton.'

"Bobby tells me that the activity to our website, just as the system went down, was over ten times the previous record. This is beyond comprehension, and these figures have been confirmed by numerous sources. This is real. And it's only the beginning.

"Irina, our mathematician, predicted a large initial spike in interest, and then a gradual fall-off over a period of two to four weeks. That will mark the beginning of Phase Two. Meanwhile, we must survive Phase One, and I think it's going to remain a roller coaster all week.

"We've already issued tomorrow's announcement. We go into more detail and begin to lay out some ground rules and a little statement of our vision and our goals. Those who haven't heard of Vox Stellarum and The Contest by tonight will get another opportunity tomorrow.

"So, I just wanted to give you an update. In short, we're on the map. Great work!"

⋆⋅►◉ ◉◄⋅⋆

"Mrs. Bennett?" Isabel called softly from the entrance to Minerva's library.

"Yes, Isabel?" Minerva opened her eyes, but remained very still.

"Please excuse me. I know you gave orders not to be disturbed, but there's a long-distance call from Madame Tourangeau. Would you like me to take a message?"

Shortly after her mid-afternoon update to the staff, Minerva had called for her driver to pick her up and return her to her apartment. She had retreated to the comfort of her chaise, exhausted. The stress and excitement of their first day in the limelight had drained her more than she was willing to admit. It was a sudden source of joy for her to hear her friend's name mentioned in the aftermath of the day's events.

"Transfer her to my phone here. Thank you."

She sat up and turned her side table lamp on low.

"Louisa, what a nice surprise," she said, slightly groggy.

"Minerva, darling, you're *famous!* I'm a little amazed that you let me get through. I imagined you'd be in the middle of interviews and press conferences and such."

"Thankfully, I avoided that today. Tomorrow will be another story. Where are you?"

"In Geneva. It's quite late, but I couldn't get to sleep. I was so excited about your ... your adventure. I knew you were moving ahead with your plans, my dear, but it's suddenly very real now that I've seen you on the evening news."

"Oh my! I haven't had the chance to watch any coverage yet. It's been a hectic day. The ad campaign must be working, though, because so many people visited our website that the system overloaded and shut down."

"Good grief, I hope they fix it. So, how are *you* holding up?"

"I was exhausted earlier, but I'm better now. It's so nice to hear your voice, and to speak to somebody who knows me beyond all this ... this business. Things have changed in the last three months, and I can barely believe my own eyes sometimes. Did you get my letter?"

"Yes, and I should have written you back. Oh well, no excuse. I'm sorry your family and your trustees didn't embrace your ideas as you had hoped."

"Well, looking back, I'm beginning to understand it a little bit more. Nevertheless, my decision to move forward on my own, with my own money, has caused a ... how should I say, a *rift* between my family and me. I'm seeing them in a new light, and I don't necessarily like what I see."

"Mmm ... I could tell from your letter that it was bothering you. I wish I could say something to make it better."

"But you are, Louisa! This call is exactly what the doctor ordered. You always know what to say and how to listen."

"When are we going to see one another again? I imagine you're busier than ever. Does this mean you're going to be traveling less?"

"I don't know, but somebody will be doing lots of traveling. After all, this is a global affair. We're in the process of hiring field scouts who will go to various regions to check on the progress of the teams. I suppose I'll get away here and there, to be a spokesman for the cause ... and to go shopping with my best friend."

"That's my girl!" Louisa cheered. "By the way, tell me about the motto."

"Do you like it?"

"I do ... very esoteric."

"It's a naval expression, from the time of the ancient Greeks and Romans. After he left the navy and went into business, Bill would use it occasionally to inspire his employees to go the extra mile. He had his factory managers make these huge placards with inspirational sayings, mostly in English, but some were in Latin. *Remis velisque* was one of them. The literal translation is 'with oars and sails.' It means row hard, but use the wind too."

"I love it."

"Thank you, Louisa. Now listen, I can hear that you're getting sleepy, and you should get to bed. It's time for me to go eat my dinner and then do the same."

"Okay, Minerva. Good luck tomorrow. Oars and sails!"

⇢⇛ ⇚⇠

At the dinner table, Minerva reviewed the agenda that Catherine handed her before she left the office. It contained the scheduled meetings for the next day, and she had added her own list of reminders and action items.

In her new incarnation as chairman of Vox Stellarum, Minerva had been busier and less social than she had been in years. She couldn't say yet whether it suited her, but she was happy to be following through with a plan that felt right. She no longer felt the predictable currents of a broad river with well-defined banks. Her recent experience was more like the swift and erratic torrents of white water in a narrow canyon. While she was exhilarated, she wondered if the water would rise and move too swiftly for her to keep up.

She switched on the TV to see what the evening news might have to say about their efforts. Eight commercials in a row finally gave way to some coverage of the top stories. Minerva was disappointed. There was no mention of a global contest or a record-setting media campaign. She paid only cursory attention to the squad of announcers and on-the-scene reporters that delivered the news in the usual dizzying fashion about the sludge of negative developments.

"Thank you, Kris, and now back to Nicki Cho."

"We are live from Sacramento, California—I'm standing in front of the capitol where the state's budget crisis worsens daily. The governor announced this morning that the spending cuts passed by the Democratically controlled House back in Decem—"

Minerva tried a different channel.

"... cyclone has ravaged more than 600 square kilometers of South East Asia—"

Click.

"London's Stock Exchange went off-line for forty-five minutes earlier today due to a glitch in the software. It's unknown whether this was the cause for the late afternoon sell-off in which the composite index plunged by more than ten per—"

Click.

"... the lone gunman has been cornered in a warehouse near The French Quarter, one of the main tourist destinations in New Orleans. A male Caucasian in his mid-thirties is reported to be well armed and prepared for a siege. Three fatalities have been confirmed, and a dozen or more wounded are being treated in nearby hospitals ..."

This was exactly the kind of muck that she hoped her new foundation would eventually displace. It wasn't as if there were no good news; it was that the mainstream media were convinced that mayhem and tragedy were the topics most valued by the public. It was this paradigm that she was devoted to overthrowing and replacing with something else.

Click.

Minerva sat up abruptly.

"... closing out our evening broadcast, we bring you a story that should lift your spirits. This morning, around the world, an announcement was made that apparently struck a chord of hope in the hearts of millions. A private foundation with the enigmatic name of Vox Stellarum, which I am told means 'voice of the stars,' declared its intention to hold a world-wide contest that will distribute several billion dollars to the top teams. Exactly what these teams will be doing to compete for these prizes is not at all clear, but there is a website that one can go to for information.

"The problem is that just after one o'clock Eastern Standard Time, the unprecedented web traffic gushing in from six continents knocked out the servers of this newly established foundation. A representative at their New York office assured us that they were working on the issue and that they would be back on line as soon as possible. She also hinted that more information would be forthcoming, in the same manner as the initial announcement. By the way, the Internet traffic to the Vox Stellarum website wasn't the only world record achieved by this outfit. The blitz of full-page advertisements in the top 200 newspapers around the world was the most intense and expensive in the history of the printed page, shattering the previous mark. We'll be keeping a close watch on this story ..."

Minerva switched off the TV. Somehow, the enormity of what she had created began to register for her in a way that, until that moment, hadn't been fully real.

It's vaguely like getting married, she thought. Months of engagement parties, a roomful of gifts, engraved wedding invitations sent to hundreds of guests ... these were nothing compared to the simple act of standing at the altar and giving one's vows. A cold sweat and dizziness overcame her as she thought, *I've just said "I do" to a billion people.*

⋯⋙◉ ◉⋘⋯

Forty-eight hours later, the Foundation's announcements had finished the third day of the media blitz that was every bit the story as the competition it promoted. Three billion people now knew at least two words of Latin: *vox stellarum.* Minerva Bennett, the chairman of the new media darling, and its president, Libby Armstrong, were instant celebrities. And, as if cued by Irina Turchin's predictive computer models, the backlash was poised to counter the sudden surge of positive energy.

While lone naysayers had emerged after the first day of news reports, they had been massively outweighed by the positive, or at least neutral, reporting by every dimension of the news media. Friday morning in Asia, Europe, and Africa, the absence of a fourth consecutive day of announcements was met with a sudden question: What's next for Vox Stellarum? What ultimately was the purpose for the stunt? Is the foundation legitimate? Do they really intend to administer this gigantic project, spread over an impossibly large scope to a world population that is diverse beyond comprehension?

⋯⋙◉ ◉⋘⋯

"Of course. I agree ... Unprecedented? That's putting it mildly ... 50 million? No, I'd say closer to a hundred ... Hmm ... Yes, that's a good point ... So far, I'd say the effect has been negligible, but this is just the edge of the wave front ... No ... No ... *Black swan*? Possibly, but even if it isn't, it's a wildcard. I'm devoting significant bandwidth on this ... How long? Until we identify the inflection point ... Okay, I don't have a problem with that, but you should know I've put a man on this ... New York to begin with ... I agree, sharing identities is unnecessary at this point."

A subtle tap of a button on the recessed panel in the arm of the man's chair disconnected the call. He continued his agenda of running protocols and assessing this latest phenomenon.

The Watcher's monitors displayed news feeds on stock exchanges around the world and the top hits of the day on the Web, including custom filters on ten influential social media sites. Lighting a cigarette, he zoomed in on the top five stories and wasn't surprised to see that the Vox Stellarum event, in one form or fashion, was mentioned in four of them. This confirmed his judgment that an independent probe had been warranted.

Exhaling a stream of smoke, he clicked on a video that caught his eye. Posted in France that morning on YouTube, it showed a lively discussion among patrons of a café. A young woman held up a copy of *Le Monde*, while a gray-haired man held up a copy of *Le Parisien*. The Watcher didn't speak French, but he caught the gist of the exchanges: they were excited about The Contest.

Are these the kind of people Bennett intends to enlist to solve the world's problems? he asked himself. *What a clusterfuck!*

As if in sync with his internal assessment, he clicked on another video, posted within the last hour on a blog in one of his RSS feeds. The blogger was an Irishman, if his bio could be trusted, which was a big if. Inquisitor, whose on-line avatar was a cartoonish agent of the Spanish Inquisition, had already posted several rants against Vox Stellarum. He used ambiguous concepts and colorfully derogatory epithets, usually summarizing his posts with quotes lifted from the pantheon of Europe's leftist heroes.

Indeed, the darling of the philanthropic world had her detractors. Most of the responses to Inquisitor's rants were sympathetic, but there was one who pointed out that the American was at least egalitarian in her "capitalistic charade." The man stubbed out his cigarette and sat back, taking in the full array of screens. He relaxed and allowed his vision to blur slightly.

After several minutes of gazing at his digital kaleidoscope, nothing obvious presented itself. The Watcher leaned forward and entered several lines of code, deciding to go with timeline overlays. He activated a program that displayed selected sets of data graphically while allowing him to manipulate variables. He searched for patterns.

Patterns imply predictability, which implies profit, which implies power. Power, in turn, implies more predictability. This closed-loop feedback system was his idol, his religion. He and his cadre considered threats to this mechanism to be profane. Their categorical imperative was to cultivate the *status quo* and harvest it.

⊷⊨⊚ ⊚⊨⊷

It was Friday morning, and Henry Godfrey was at his desk in Room 216, grading papers. Midway through the first stack, he was startled by the telephone. It wasn't his classroom land line; it was his cell phone. The caller ID said "BLOCKED."

"Hello," he said curiously.

"Henry, this is Minerva Bennett. Did I catch you in the middle of class?" she asked apologetically.

"*Aunt Minerva?* Wow, what a surprise!" He put down his pen and sat up straighter, marshaling his undivided attention. "No, I'm on a break, grading tests ... but I'm free to talk."

"Marvelous. How are you? How is the world of mathematics? Are your students learning their lessons?"

"A few are struggling, as always, but I'm pleased. Gosh ... what an unexpected pleasure."

"I agree, Henry. It's nice to hear your voice again. As you may be aware, I've been busy in recent days, with a rather all-consuming adventure of sorts."

"No kidding ... *Congratulations!* Several of my students brought in their newspapers and showed me your advertisement, and they wanted to know all about Vox Stellarum. Yesterday, in fact, they pretty much held me hostage." He laughed. "We spent the entire period, for all four classes, discussing the purpose of philanthropy and the objective of The Contest. We even had a mini-lesson on Latin phrases and mottoes. They were terribly impressed, especially the group that you met the day of your visit. You've inspired the topic of essays in several of my colleagues' classrooms as well." He paused to give his great aunt a chance to address her real purpose. The line was quiet.

"Aunt Minerva?" Henry heard the muffled sound of a woman blowing her nose gently.

"Yes, I'm here. Excuse me ... my emotions run away from me at times." She paused again, and Henry waited. "I'm flattered. However, I didn't call you to fish for compliments or any such thing as that. Henry, you probably have no idea what part you have played in all this ... in these events that have now spilled onto the world stage. Well, let me just say that it is you who inspired me. The invitation to visit your school last November, among other things, set into motion a reawakening that is still in process.

"I promise to tell you, when we have the time, the full story about how my attitudes and priorities have shifted over the past year ... why I stepped down from the Koyne Foundation to go off in this new direction. My visit to your school was a divine tap on the shoulder, so to speak, like the whispering of an angel to set me on a truer path than any I had known. So much has happened over the last several months that I've barely had time to catch my breath. I've been meaning to contact you for some time." She paused and waited for a reaction, but Henry was stupefied and couldn't speak. Minerva continued.

"I'm calling to thank you, finally, for the pivotal part you played. And, I'm calling to make you an offer." Still frozen in disbelief, he remained silent.

"Henry? Are you there?"

"Yes," he gulped.

"Good. I want you to listen with both ears to what I have to say, and you don't need to give me an answer right away. We're still building our team. Vox Stellarum is not nearly as big as the Koyne Foundation, but due to its unique mission, it actually requires a far greater number of staff and employees. We're in need of somebody who is knowledgeable about education and children ... what makes them tick. I thought of you, my dear. You would be perfect for the position I have in mind." She stopped to let her words sink in.

"Aunt Minerva, I don't ... I don't know what ... Now it's my turn to be flattered. I really appreciate what you're telling me, but ... gosh, I'm no expert. I don't even have a degree in education—I majored in philosophy. And I've only been teaching for five years."

"I thought you might say something like that, which is all the proof I need. You are the perfect choice for this role, which requires flexibility and open-mindedness ... and humility. I realize my call may have caught you off guard, but I want to give you some pertinent details that might inform your decision.

"Firstly, you'd be able to finish out your school year, as long as you could relocate here in New York immediately afterwards. Secondly, I imagine your school compensates you reasonably well, but I'm in a position to offer you a raise—a *substantial* raise. Thirdly, this is a position that, along with the entire foundation, will dissolve in approximately two years. If your heart calls you back to teaching, you can return, having been a part of a grand adventure."

"Gosh, I don't—"

"Henry? I mean it. Don't answer me right now. Just think about it."

"I don't know what to say, except—yes, I will think about it. It's just that I'm blown away ... I wonder if your faith in me is ... I mean, are you—"

"You must give me credit for my judgment and experience. One can tell a great deal by watching human interactions, especially in a complex and sometimes chaotic environment such as a classroom. My call today is based on an interview that, at the time, neither you nor I realized was being conducted. I'm here to tell you that, in hindsight, you passed with flying colors."

"Thank you," he said huskily, barely getting the words out. He gazed over the rows of empty desks at the opposite wall, unsettled by his sudden tears and quivering lips.

"Let's talk in a week or two, and we'll see where you stand. Goodbye, Henry."

"Bye, Aunt Minerva."

He put down his phone and looked at his hands. They were shaking. When the bell rang a few minutes later, jarring him back to his senses, it took him a second to realize that, even after it stopped, his body continued to vibrate.

Chapter 10

Lieutenant Steven Pace lay back in his beach chair, glad to have his upper body in the shadow of the wide umbrella, the pole of which pierced the sand just behind him. At the southern tip of Africa, it was early March, and the intensity of the late summer sun was unattenuated by a generous sprinkling of small cumulus clouds. He watched his best friend play in the waves like a kid—boogie boarding—catching several of the towering waves that had just begun to roll in with the rising tide.

Major Rory Davis had been like a brother to him for the last three years, since he had first gone through boot camp and then Special Forces training with the South African army. The two soldiers had converged via separate tracks within the reconnaissance division and had served together on numerous missions. They had each lost more friends than they cared to remember.

As he struggled to reposition his body, Steven was mindful of the obvious—that he might never walk again. His left leg was in a tension brace from his toes to his hip, with twenty titanium-alloy pins holding his bones and tendons in place. He couldn't remember the explosion that had almost claimed his life; the concussion had spared him the horror by way of traumatic amnesia. He was told three days after the fact, upon regaining consciousness, that he was lucky to be alive.

Rory, with whom he shared an apartment in Durban, had driven him to the military base hospital earlier that morning for a check-up.

"Good news, Lieutenant," the doctor had said. "For the first time, I'm confident that you'll get to keep your leg. The question now is how much utility you'll regain. The femur has accepted the bone grafts from your pelvis, but the shrapnel above your ankle is almost indistinguishable from what remains of your tibia. Head up, man. You've come a long way since they wheeled you in two months ago."

That had been good news, of course, but now he had a decision to make. What next? Though he was finally ready to admit that this chapter of his life was at an end, he was unable to imagine his next step.

After surviving clandestine night missions in Eritrea, the demilitarized zone between the Democratic Republic of Congo and Angola, conflicts on the Zambian and Zimbabwean border, and even riot control in Johannesburg, it was ironic that he had almost died in a peacetime assignment that he was video-ing for training purposes. Using a modified technique for defusing explosives on a new type of detonator, he made an error in judgment. It hadn't been determined whether it was due to substandard circuitry, or if he had simply misread the pattern and cut the wrong wire. And, of course, he couldn't remember.

The commandant had personally ordered the surgeons to spare no effort in putting the lieutenant back together: "My nephew is to make a full recovery, or somebody will have hell to pay!"

Now, gazing out on the vast expanse of the westernmost reach of the Indian Ocean, Steven looked past his friend on the boogie board, past a cluster of surfers farther out, and he noticed a few specks on the horizon. He wondered idly whether these were ships, or sailboats, or drilling rigs. He did his best to let his mind float along with the gulls and the terns that wheeled and soared in the onshore breeze, opening himself to new possibilities that were still just beyond his reach. While feeling cared for and provided for in a way that he had never expected to call upon, he began to look out, cautiously, into his own future, into several possible futures that seemed to lay before somebody in his predicament.

What good is my commitment to honor and service, he asked himself, *if I can't put it into action?* There was a part of him, a part of every soldier he suspected, that had to come to terms with the next question he put to himself. *When I leave the battlefield, what code will I live by?*

He was accustomed to setting fear aside in order to perform deadly tasks surrounded by combatants in faraway places, but he reeled with the sudden realization that he was afraid to bring up these issues with his best friend. Would Rory, two years his senior, sympathize with his questions and doubts? Or would he dismiss them as lapses in courage—cowardly invitations to self-pity and psychic weakness unbecoming of a *recce*?

For weeks, he had been wondering if he could trust his objectivity, directed inwardly at this problem that no training could ever really address, and he desperately wanted somebody to guide him through this mental minefield. Assuming that he regained at least fair mobility, he would have only a mild chance at remaining in the corps, as an analyst or administrator. With more than twenty successful missions and several decorations to his credit, he could request and probably receive a desk position. But after being part of the spearhead of military intelligence and technology for six years and having experienced the rarified glory of life as a green beret, he cringed at the thought of a desk job.

He wondered if his friend, closer to him than his own brother, could really listen at this level. There, in the noonday sun, was an elite warrior who spoke the language of invulnerability, distilled in him by the most arduous training regimen on the continent.

But will he understand me when I speak the language of mortality?

One hundred meters distant, Rory exited the surf and carried his board under his arm, the salt water dripping off his lean body as if he were a leopard or a gazelle. Cockiness dripped off him as well, as evidenced by the shit-eating grin on his face. It reflected the discipline and focus that all green berets had been selected and trained to exude.

"Nice 360s," Steven commented as his friend threw the board on the sand and grabbed a beach towel. "That last set was monstrous. I wish I had a camera."

"Thanks, Stevie." Rory plopped down in his chair and looked at his friend. "You doin' okay? Can I get you anything?"

"I'm good, unless you want to round up some company for lunch." He pointed down the beach. "The blonde that walked by a few minutes ago was hot. What a goddess! And her friend was checking you out."

"Sweet."

Rory reached for the cooler, grabbed two beers, and extended one to Steven. "It's almost noon. Cheers!"

"Thanks. And thanks again for schlepping me to the doc. I really appreciate it." They sipped their beers and listened to the waves. Rory sat back, stretched his legs, and dug his toes into the sand. Steven watched his friend and realized that his doing this, in the sight of a friend who couldn't, was not insensitivity, but a sign of loyalty to a friend who would recoil at pity. This simple gesture convinced him to finally share what was on his mind.

"Rory ..." His friend turned and looked directly at him, sensing the seriousness of the quiet tone. "I have something to tell you, and I've been afraid to bring it up. I guess I didn't trust you to understand ... but I think you can."

"Stevie, you can talk to me about anything." He paused, knowing that his friend was deadly earnest about something. "We're brothers—no walls, no limits," he said softly.

"Yes," was all Steven could say as his voice grew husky with emotion. He leaned forward and carefully picked up his cast and repositioned it a few inches toward the center of the shaded area and then turned his upper body a little more directly toward his friend. Rory took a deep breath and then released it slowly to demonstrate that he was fully present. Steven continued.

"Since early high school, I've known what I wanted to do: become a marine and then a recce. I knew it was how I could live the fullest and most exciting life I could imagine. I'll never forget the time I was visiting my uncle—he wasn't the commandant yet—when Jake Patterson showed up at the base. The grounds were busy ... platoons were marching all over the campus, and this maniac comes tearing down the main drive—"

"*Dude,*" Rory interrupted, laughing, "I was *there*. A couple of us had to dive into the ditch!"

"*Really?!* ... So, you know what I'm talking about. I never imagined anybody could get away with a stunt like that, and still have generals eating out of his hands. It was *un-fucking-believable*." Rory grinned and nodded. "After scattering 200 men in uniform, this guy screeches to a halt in the sweetest sports car I'd ever seen and hops out as if he owned the place. He had long hair, blue jeans, sunglasses!"

"I remember," Rory said, smiling wistfully.

"So ... my uncle was talking to one of his officers, and I was standing nearby. We were, I don't know, fifty meters from the main building. The guy hops out of his car and walks into the headquarters without even bothering to look back at the drill instructors that he'd almost run over. I felt like I'd just seen the god of thunder land on the front lawn.

"I asked Uncle Harry, 'Who *is* that?' I'll never forget what he said. With a look of awe that I've only seen him show a few times in my life, he said, '*That* is a green beret.'

"It was then and there that I knew what I wanted to be."

Steven paused and looked off beyond the waves. Rory waited patiently.

"The rest is history," Steven continued. "Boot camp, basic training, marine specialist training, 'the Walk.' There aren't many who know of the suffering we had to endure. Well, it was that vision of Jake Patterson that inspired me through my hell.

"My year, only nine of us finished ... and were selected. It took me a long time to see beyond the physical torture and realize that, ultimately, it was all mental."

Rory nodded and remained silent.

"That training served me well ... through dangers I couldn't imagine. But that's all changed. Even if I regain the use of my leg, I'm through with the army."

Rory couldn't hold back. "That's not true, Stevie. You know there's a place for you, even if it's just as an instructor or a specialist. You're *brilliant*, man! You can do whatever you put your mind to."

"Thanks, but what I've been afraid to tell you is ... it's time for me to move on. I've been afraid that you and the other guys would think I'm pussing out. And I guess I'm a little afraid of leaving the unit. Who's gonna back me up when I'm ... you know, going solo?"

"Stevie, you won't be alone. I will *always* help you, no matter what." Rory looked at him with that piercing look he rarely demonstrated, a look of naked loyalty and love. "We've saved each other more times than we can count. It might seem I take it for granted, but I want you to know ... I *don't.*"

Steven started to say something, but his emotions prevented him. He nodded solemnly.

"What will you do?" Rory asked.

"I'm not sure. I suppose my next assignment, or job, whatever it is, will have to be more mental than physical, maybe something creative."

"The time will come," said Rory, "when I'll want to strike out on a new path myself. You're just beating me to the punch on this one. As much as I love what I do, I know there's more out there." He looked out over the waves, and Steven followed his gaze. He wondered what his friend's sense of future possibilities looked like.

Rory continued. "You're a smart fucker, Stevie. You're good at music, computers, maths ... engineering. Any ideas?"

"Nothing specific. One thing I'll miss," said Steven, "is the intensity and excitement—the sense that any given day could be my last. I don't know how I'm gonna manage civilian life. I just hope I don't get bored to death!"

Rory laughed.

"It's against your nature to play small, Stevie. You'll find your way to center stage ... the only question is where."

⇥☉ ☉⇤

Julian Fielding had only spoken to his mother a few times since she made her exit from the Koyne Foundation. Their conversations had been polite and cordial, but a tension underlay their words. The distance that had grown between them had not been bridged, and lately he worried that it might never be. She had congratulated him on his appointment as chairman, and she had offered to help him if he should want it.

In his turn, Julian had questioned his mother about the progress of her new venture, but his curiosity was superficial. He still would not believe that his mother had the wherewithal, or the support, to carry out the plan that he and the other trustees had rejected. Stewart Maxwell, with whom he had maintained a working relationship, and still respected as a neutral party within the maelstrom that had divided his family, had discreetly informed him of the steps his mother had taken to form her new foundation.

In terms of professional allegiance, Maxwell had chosen to resign his position as head counsel at the Koyne Foundation and to join Minerva's new staff. Even though Maxwell gave Minerva "long odds on succeeding," he had told Julian that serving as an agent in a risky new enterprise would be more engaging than remaining with an empire that, for the most part, ran on automatic.

It was that smooth automaticity and predictability, however, that allowed Julian Fielding, who had remained a full faculty member of the Cornell School of Architecture, to schedule one or two monthly visits to Manhattan and make an appearance at the Koyne Foundation offices. He resented the six-hour drives, but he consoled himself with the fact that, besides stepping into the leadership role of a world-class charitable operation, his destination was a building that he had designed.

Sitting in his mother's former office, he glanced at the wood-paneled walls, sheathed in pictures, portraits, certificates, and awards. His mother had neglected to take her mementos, and he hadn't bothered to remove them. These were proclamations of an illustrious career, of good acts, of real charity rendered to thousands of people over decades. *These prove we were right, don't they?*

This, however, was not the heart of the agitation that ate at him. He could point to many of these documents and photographs and claim at least a small piece of the recognition and the gratitude, for he was part of the whole. It was something deeper. Was it about loyalty? If so, he racked his brain to figure out who had been disloyal to whom. It was as if his mother's desertion of an edifice she had built was an affront to the rest of them who remained.

Had she denounced it, or them? No, that was too simplistic. Julian wondered if the others felt as he did—those who had aligned with him in what amounted to a vote of no confidence. Even if he had been convinced of the value of her vision, how could he have been justified in voting to approve his mother's proposal? Wouldn't that have been a betrayal to the original mission, which, by the praise within the glass-framed tributes surrounding him, has undoubtedly been such a magnificent success? He shook his head in exasperation, wishing there were an easy solution to this riddle.

Julian reached for the phone and dialed Bob Godfrey's number. The two of them had spoken more in the last two months than they had in the previous two years. Upon Minerva's abrupt resignation, they were the only ones nominated to replace her. There was no tradition stating that a Koyne family member needed to sit in the chairman's seat, but it was a monolithic fact that one had done so since its inception. When that suddenly changed, it was presumed to be the rule, and the board had reacted accordingly.

It was conceded, even by Julian, that Bob Godfrey was probably the better choice, in terms of leadership and administrative skill. But he lived in Houston. After some discussion, the trustees decided to go with Julian, who certainly possessed considerable analytical skills and social savvy. He lived in Ithaca, but the Big Apple was his home town. He could make visits as needed.

"Bob, it's Julian."

"Jules, good morning! Are you in New York?"

"Yeah, I drove in early yesterday. This wasn't really a scheduled visit, but given the hype surrounding my mother, I wanted to be here to run interference if necessary."

"Have you gotten any calls? Any reporters?"

"A few, but no requests for interviews or anything like that."

"You sound a little disappointed."

"I suppose I am," Julian admitted. "Her new foundation has attracted all the press, and that's left the rest of us sidelined, like a bunch of beached fish. I've been wondering if it's just a temporary displacement of media attention, or whether this is a permanent downgrading of our perceived relevance."

"I've been wondering the same thing."

Julian remained silent.

"Something else bothering you?" prodded Godfrey.

"I'm reluctant to admit it, but yes ..."

"Talk to me," urged Godfrey gently.

"I can't help it, Bob. I know this is going to sound selfish ... I mean, I feel like a spoiled brat for even thinking about it ..." Godfrey waited.

"It's the *money*," admitted Julian. "*Jesus!* I can't believe I'm telling you this ... it's the *money!* My mother seems hell-bent on liquidating her personal fortune and blowing it on this crazy contest. I mean, it was bad enough when she wanted to dissolve the Foundation, but it's ... it's a fucking outrage." The last few words were not so much spoken as hissed.

Godfrey's only response was a long sigh. It somehow communicated the depth of sympathy Julian needed, and his own sigh of weary resignation dissipated some of his anger.

He continued. "Oh well ... easy come, easy go."

"Mm-hmm," agreed Godfrey before changing the subject. "So, any updates?"

"I met with the full staff yesterday. We discussed changes in responsibilities and adjusted our projections. Mecom is worried about the upcoming G10 Summit in Japan, the weak euro, the weak dollar, yada, yada.

"Meanwhile, the entire office is streaming news stories and podcasts on their computers—trying to stay up on all the buzz surrounding Mother's contest."

"She's made quite a splash, hasn't she? I didn't believe she had it in her to follow through with this thing until I saw the ad in the *Wall Street Journal*."

Julian knew his cousin well enough to see through the Texas drawl. Bob's tone was heavy with scorn. "Yeah, but I keep thinking of the price tag for this show she's putting on."

"Speaking of which, what's the status on her garage sale?" asked Godfrey. "I can't imagine her parting with the Hudson property, or the ranch for that matter. Are they still on the market?"

"I don't know," Julian said bitterly. "Neither Stewart nor Catherine will tell me specifics. Meanwhile, Mother's put a good chunk of her holdings into global hedge funds and gold."

"Gold? You're *kidding!*"

"No. Sam Minton told me as much. He has a crystal ball apparently, and he helped her buy a substantial stake when the spot price dipped back in early

February. That was a month ago, and the price has already rebounded—up by ten percent."

Godfrey let out a low whistle. "Damn! Maybe she'll reel some of those properties back in. It's none of my business, but I sure do enjoy the family reunions. The cotton doesn't grow any taller." This struck a dark chord with Julian, and he sensed that Bob's intention was to probe a little deeper into the family dynamics they both knew were strained.

"To be honest, Bob, I'm worried that our family gatherings are a thing of the past."

"Me too," said Godfrey, mirroring Julian's downbeat tone. "Some sort of rift has split wide open at our feet. We still speak the same language, but it's as if your mother's speaking in some new dialect. It reminds me of those people back in the '60s that used to go off looking for nirvana. They'd return after six months and give all their money to some barefoot monk."

"Exactly! And if we could just figure out who sent her down this crazy path ..."

Chapter 11

AN ATTRACTIVE WOMAN, divorced but financially independent with two children in college, Catherine Myers was a prime candidate for the dating scene, or so her close friends told her. They were constantly trying to set her up, which gave her the semblance of an active social life. None of the men seemed to fit the bill though, and she rarely granted any of them a second date, much less a third. She felt as if she were caught between two worlds: the plush and privileged sphere of art patronage, in which she was a mere employee, and the arena of urban singles struggling at self-improvement and one-upmanship. Professionally comfortable in the one, she seemed destined to be socially confined to the other.

While her athletic and toned body was that of a thirty-five-year-old, with smooth facial features to match, her eyes and hair hinted that she was a youthful forty. Only one or two friends knew that she had, in fact, just turned fifty-three.

Friday afternoon at 5:00, Catherine was exhilarated and exhausted. As far as she could tell, they had pulled off the impossible. They had launched the largest media assault of its kind. The word on the street, and on-line, was positive. The turbulent and frantic pace the Vox Stellarum team had maintained for several weeks was behind her, for a day or two at least, and she was ready for a break. She yearned for a quiet evening at home to relax and recharge, but she was still in overdrive.

She shooed the stragglers out of the office at 6:00 and headed for the gym. It had been five days since she'd worked out—for her, an eternity. A full round of weights and thirty minutes in the pool revived her, and then she hurried home to change.

Libby and Scott Armstrong had invited some friends to dinner, and Catherine was included. Libby, who was just as exhausted as Catherine, had decided on the brilliant option of ordering takeout. The main course, though, would be "The Late Show with Tucker Middleton."

A faint aroma of soy sauce and wasabi wafted above the curve of chairs and couches directed at the wall-mounted TV, and everybody settled back to watch the show. The dining room table in the adjoining room of the high-rise apartment was littered with the stiff white paper containers universally preferred by Asian restaurants, along with empty bottles of mineral water, wine, and sake. High ceilings and eclectic decor somehow gave the place warmth, but this was no doubt augmented by the free flow of alcohol and anticipation of the interview.

"Okay, here we go," said Scott, aiming the remote at the set and turning up the volume. Middleton's broad smile flashed, and his eyes sparkled behind his designer eyeglasses.

"Ladies and gentlemen, my first guest this evening is somebody who, a week ago, I would bet most of you never heard of. I would also bet that, tonight, there is not a single person out there who hasn't heard of her. She may be my wealthiest guest yet, although I'd have to check the archives. That's incidental to her meteoric rise to fame, though, and I'm delighted to introduce to you Mrs. Minerva Bennett!" The studio audience erupted with applause as the grand dame made her way onto the stage. Wearing a Chanel design and minimal jewelry, she exuded grace and quiet confidence.

In Libby and Scott's living room, everybody cheered as well, and Catherine swelled with pride at seeing her boss looking like a movie star.

Minerva settled into the guest's chair, proving that a woman who was barely five feet tall could, by sitting upright and demonstrating good posture, somehow appear on the same level with a man who was six-foot-two.

"So, Minerva ... may I call you Minerva by the way?"

"Of course," she nodded and smiled.

"Thank you. I love that name. It's a Greek name, isn't it?" Middleton asked.

"It's Etruscan actually—*Roman*. It's the equivalent of Athena, the Greek goddess of—"

"Of wisdom, right? And according to my notes, Minerva was also the goddess of poetry and medicine ... and she invented music. Those are pretty solid credentials," he quipped. "Does any of that fit your personality?"

"Well, I certainly approve of those, and I appreciate anybody who is accomplished in the arts," she answered earnestly. "Did you know that she was also the goddess of warriors? In fact, she was often depicted in armor, carrying a spear." Minerva turned to the audience as if to say: *Let's see what he does with that!*

"Ooh! Is that a warning? Is there something you need to tell us?" Laughter.

"No, not really. I'm just reminding you that every rose has its thorns."

"Okay," Middleton said, raising his eyebrows and adjusting his glasses. "So, please tell us about your background, how you got to be in the position you're in, and how you entered the world of philanthropy."

"I've had a very good life, Tucker. Rarely does a woman marry the man of her dreams, but I did it twice. At the age of twenty-three, I married William Fielding. Bill and I were very happy—work, family, success ... unfortunately, he died of a heart attack just after our 22nd anniversary. Several years after he died, I met another wonderful man, Joseph Bennett. He was from Texas but lived here in New York. We were married for almost thirty years. JB died about ten years ago. They were both self-made men, and I've been blessed with a privileged lifestyle through their hard work and financial success."

After a couple of more warm-up questions, Middleton gestured with his index finger.

"So now, for the big question that everybody's been waiting for. What do you really hope to accomplish with this campaign? You've already spent a huge amount of money on advertising, and this contest, which hasn't even officially begun, is going to cost a small fortune ... scratch that, a big one. What is the objective?"

Having set Minerva up for a nice fall, he sat back to see how good his guest's balance was.

"Maybe the objective is so simple that people think there has to be more to it. Well guess what ... it *is* as simple as we explained in our newspaper ads and on the website—which is back up, by the way. We've had far more Internet traffic than we anticipated, and we've quadrupled our capacity."

"That's good. It sounds like you're going to need it."

"Yes. So ... the goal is simple. Each team will compose a manifesto that demonstrates a comprehensive approach to the major problems confronting us all.

"Tucker, the world's in trouble. I don't think that's news to anybody. I've obviously got some life experience to draw on, and I want to tell you that, with a few minor exceptions, life on Earth has gotten more fouled up each year I've been alive. While my personal life has been pretty insulated from difficulty and squalor, the conditions on this planet have gotten bleaker. It seems that, as we use more advanced technologies to solve the next wave of problems, we do more and more damage to the environment and to one another.

"It's like the parable about the village that brings in cats to get rid of the mice, only to be overrun with cats. Then they bring in dogs ... then lions, elephants, and so on. Only, the story of mankind isn't nearly so cute. The remedies we throw at our problems are almost always worse than the original problems, and this is madness. How can we stop this merry-go-round? Well, that's what my vision is about. It's time to start over—to go back to the drawing board.

"Consider the contest to be a brainstorming session, and everybody's invited. There are so many brilliant people around the world, but we need to get these people to jump out of their institutional boxes and throw off their prejudices ... their dogmas. The contest is a way to allow us to look at the whole problem—the human condition—village by village, nation by nation, and propose ways for us to proceed that doesn't put us all at odds."

"And once the teams create their manifestos, your judges will decide which are the best and which must fall by the wayside?"

"Yes," Minerva said simply. "After all, it's a contest. They require standards, rules, and—in this case—a panel of judges. Because *I* don't have the answers. If there's anything clever about what I'm doing, it is simply that I'm inviting people all over the world to help me—to help *us*—find solutions."

Middleton leaned forward, elbows on his desk, hands clasped.

"I would imagine," he said, glancing toward the studio audience and then back at Minerva, "that all the English and philosophy professors out there are probably cringing, trying to imagine how hard it would be to grade and rank 1000 term papers, and then to come up with the top eight. How long will this take?"

"Approximately eighteen months."

"That's a *long* time. Can you keep your people on track 'til then? I was kinda hoping we'd get a winner by Labor Day." They laughed.

"It is a long time, and, yes, we can do it. We've put together an excellent team that knows how to make this happen. We intend to do a thorough and professional job, and it's important that we take our time between each round of elimination. This is not a lottery; we won't just be picking names out of a hat. The judges will be taking their time to carefully apply the standards we've generated."

"And you believe that your global competition is going to find the answers we need and show us all what to do?"

"That's a good question. Do I hope that some great new ideas will surface? Of course. Do I expect this to happen in a smooth, Hollywood choreographed fashion? No. Despite what a lot of critics are saying, I am not *that* naive."

"Then what results do you actually expect?"

"To get people excited, like they haven't been in a very long time. I know you weren't even born yet, Tucker, but consider the '60s. It was a turbulent and unforgettable decade. A lot of crazy things happened during those years: Vietnam, race riots, broken families, social upheaval ... but there were also some wonderful things. One of these was the landing on the Moon.

"I mention this because those of us who were alive remember the concerted effort and pride we Americans took in that astounding milestone. In less than ten years, a nation focused its might on a goal that was literally considered to be impossible only decades before. It is that kind of hope and optimism that we at Vox Stellarum want to reintroduce, not just to the United States, but to the whole world."

Hope and excitement ignited in one of the oldest forms of socially acceptable behavior: the audience erupted in applause, whistles, and cheers.

"I think you're onto something," Middleton said, smiling. He waited for the audience to settle down before continuing. "If your contest can harness the enthusiasm that just blasted through here, we're in for quite a ride." While not an endorsement, his spontaneous reaction was genuine, and Minerva inclined her head and smiled in return.

"Thank you, Tucker. I'd like to say one more thing. On Sunday, you'll see the last of our newspaper ads. Thereafter, our website will be the place to register and to get details on the official rules and guidelines, and where to go to eventually follow progress of your team or those of your friends and family members. This thing is just beginning. It's more than a party or a parade. It's a global competition, and you are *all* invited."

Applause and more cheering erupted as Tucker Middleton stood and hugged Minerva. He escorted her off the stage to an ovation that lasted until his next guest arrived.

⋅→⫘◉ ◉⫘←⋅

Monday was a busy day at the Vox Stellarum headquarters. The registration page of the website was to become active at noon. Catherine's first order of business was to assign several groups in the office to sign on and process a test team; they needed to make sure the instructions were clear and that the forms loaded properly before they opened the flood gates.

Wanda Freeman, who designed the website, and Bobby Jabari, who built it, decided to clean up some of the language and expand several fields. Then, Bill Finch, the linguist, proceeded to input several teams in alternate languages. By mid-morning, a dozen test cases had been entered without a hitch. The Contest was ready to go live.

They had estimated traffic would be light at first, and that it would steadily increase until the 1000-team limit had been reached. By the close of business, a low-level anxiety hung in the air. Not a single team had registered.

"I guess we should have anticipated this," Wanda said to several colleagues that lingered around the table in the lunch room. "It's relatively easy for one person to spontaneously commit to this sort of thing, but finding eleven suitable teammates is another matter."

"Yes," agreed Catherine. "I heard Irina talking with Joshua, and she said as much. She thinks it might be four or five days before any teams are entered."

Catherine and Libby spent the afternoon in one meeting after another. Now, sitting with Minerva and a few other senior staff, they listened to the new man in charge of certification, James Ruhle. Having run quality assurance for Coca Cola, he was hired to handle verification logistics.

"The scope of this project is so vast that it may be necessary to take a statistical approach to certification, at least in the beginning," Ruhle explained. "This is basically a sample and test process that is standard in all facets of manufacturing and production. Instead of sampling one out of every ten thousand or one hundred thousand units, we'll be able to significantly increase that ratio to, say, one or two out of ten. Would this be acceptable?"

"I'm open to that approach, in the beginning," Minerva answered. "Once we've gone through several rounds of elimination, and our numbers are more manageable, we'll want to be on the ground with practically every single team."

"James, what's your estimate of the number of scouts we'll need to cover the bases?" asked Libby. "Maybe just a range at first, with areas of coverage that could be handled in a reasonably cost-effective manner."

"Having only one scout would be as absurd as having one thousand," he explained, "and the place I like to begin in such analyses is the geometric mean—which, for 1000 teams, is roughly 32—and then to reduce that number if possible.

"I believe we should take a regional approach. Of the six inhabited continents, three might possibly be handled by one person: Australia, Africa, and South America. Europe needs two, Asia three or four, and North America three. Without quibbling about the exact boundaries here, I think we'll need at least 12 to 15 scouts. And I believe this number should be doubled. The scouts should work in pairs, for safety. Some of these people will be going into some real backwater spots."

Minerva said, "I need to hear more about the timing. For instance, at what point do you see us switching from statistical sampling to actual team-by-team verification?"

"Good question. I think it may be possible to hold off on the team-by-team verification until we've trimmed way down from the initial number, which we're assuming will be one thousand."

"I think that's a pretty solid number," interjected Libby. "Even if no teams register for several more days, we're confident that once they start to log on and register, the numbers will grow quickly and max out a week before the deadline. In fact, Rowan even suggested that we accept a little over the limit due to washouts and disqualifications."

"I like that idea," said James. "Such teams could be notified upon submitting their registrations that they have been wait-listed." He nodded at Rowan.

"Regardless, the most important factor in keeping contestants in line is *fear*—fear that this opportunity will be withdrawn at the slightest hint of non-compliance to the rules and guidelines. The carrot dangling in front of those who are, at this very minute, lobbying their friends and neighbors to form teams is too fantastic for the members to take lightly.

"If we make an example out of just one team that breaks the rules, that will inspire five hundred teams to banish any thoughts of taking shortcuts. And that will make our job far easier and less costly."

"Yes, but I will *not* have us taking a guilty-until-proven-innocent approach," said Minerva.

James nodded. "Of course. From the outset, we must come across as calm, neutral, fact gatherers. We'll go on location to sample and check, and only if infractions are discovered and confirmed should we consider disqualification. If an example presents itself, though, we must take advantage and leverage the negative consequences of non-compliance."

"Agreed," said Libby, "but conducting ourselves ethically is an absolute. Nothing would damage our image and our goals faster than crooked judges or biased scouts."

"James, I like your approach," said Minerva. "Here's what I want then. Prepare a strategy and create a budget. Bindiya and Rowan will help you gather geographical and cultural data and calculate travel expenses. I think a core of six pairs of scouts could get us started. These will become our senior scouts as things get busier and our numbers increase."

"Minerva, do you have any strong opinions as to what the makeup of the scout pairs should be?" James asked. "Male? Female? Co-ed?"

"I hadn't thought of that." She looked around. "What do you people think?"

Bindiya Bhattacharya, hired for her knowledge of world religions and the wide variance of adherence to cultural mores, spoke up. "I think working in pairs is a good idea. In most circumstances, two men would be the safest option. But two women, with proper credentials and with the cooperation of embassies and local authorities, would probably be fine. Now that I think about it, I like the co-ed option. It gives us gender parity." She looked at Minerva to see if her point resonated.

"Go on."

"One of the most popular guidelines regarding team structure is the half-and-half gender requirement. Applying this to the scouts would demonstrate consistency and integrity."

"My first reaction is to agree and consider it settled," said Minerva, "but I've traveled extensively and seen some ugly instances of prejudice against visitors who paraded their so-called enlightened beliefs. Even without physical violence, there are patriarchies that still prohibit free movement by women. Let's all think about this and meet again later in the week."

⊷⊱⊜ ⊜⊰⊶

After the third day of the Vox ad campaign, Umit Burkitbayev, a high school teacher in Atyrau, Kazakhstan, entered the classroom she shared with two other teachers, her book bag rolling behind her. She heard some students speaking the Latin phrase again—the same one she had heard the afternoon before. Having been swamped with paperwork and grading for two days, she was unaware of the hot topic circling the globe.

"Young man, what is this I hear you and some of the others talking about?" The sixteen-year-old boy spoke excitedly, in Kazakh, about how he and his friends were going to win a million dollars.

"Try to explain in English," she urged him, for in her classroom the rule was to think and speak in English.

"Mrs. Burkitbayev, a rich American woman creates competition in world-wide to help fix problems of society. There is *big* prize for team which can solve problems in best way."

That evening, upon logging on to the Internet, she came across dozens of articles related to The Contest. Interest turned to enthusiasm as she let loose her imagination.

Umit and her husband, an assistant manager for a food processing plant, spent the next day, Saturday, brainstorming ideas and making a list of friends and colleagues who might be approached to form a team. Each of them read and reread the official contest guidelines concerning eligibility, and they concluded that there was no rule against family members being on the same team.

They held a family meeting about making a commitment to enter the contest. Within twenty-four hours, they had filled nine of the twelve positions, and they came up with several prospects for the three remaining spots.

Their son approached a girl who was two years older than he and was considered one of the brightest in his school. She immediately agreed to join. Their daughter asked a boy that she knew from her gymnastics academy. "He's more mature than the other ten-year-olds."

Umit had only to hear back from a young professor whom she had first met at a language symposium a couple of years before. They corresponded occasionally, and she always enjoyed their conversations about Russia, the trans-Caucasus region, the future of Kazakhstan, and opportunities for educators like themselves. She knew the man to be progressive and slightly rebellious, which she quietly admired. She had good reason to believe he was in the 29 – 44 age range, which was the last slot they needed filled.

Now, on March 10, Umit Burkitbayev was excited. Checking her e-mail as she ate her lunch in the school cafeteria, she immediately spotted Marat Kriazhev in her inbox.

< I would like to join your team. Another friend asked me to join *his* team, but he lives in Astana—too far. I look forward to a shot at the big prize. *Thanks!* >

A second e-mail followed that one.

< I forgot to answer your questions. I am 34. I live 15 km from your school—well within range. Let me know when we are official. >

Umit immediately called her husband. "We have 12. We can register tonight!"

Chapter 12

Upon arriving Friday morning, Libby walked straight to Jabari's office. She waited for him to look up.

"Good morning, Bobby. How many teams do we have?" she asked.

"Yesterday, we were at eighteen. Now, we're at fifty-four. Wait, make that fifty-five." He smiled.

"Can you see any trends yet, in terms of geographic distribution?"

"Not really, except that participation is widespread," he said, clicking on an analytics page. Three from Africa, one from Australia, fourteen from Asia, sixteen from Europe, three from South America, and eighteen from North America."

"Huh ... I hope Australia and Africa bump it up. I'd hate to see us resort to regional quotas."

"I agree."

"I take it your figures do not include the test teams we entered?"

"Wanda and I deleted those before we went live."

"How about the counter we talked about? Is it on the home page?"

"Yes. When you log on to the site, a notice gives the current count. We're hoping that anybody sitting on the sidelines will get excited and want to join."

"Excellent. Thanks, Bobby!" she exclaimed as she walked down the hall to her own office.

She threw her purse on her desk, grabbed her laptop, and walked across the open space to Catherine's office. She repeated the numbers that Bobby had quoted her and was surprised to see a subdued look on Catherine's face.

"What's up?"

"Minerva's not coming in today," answered Catherine, from behind her desk. "She called me this morning and sounded real tired. She said she didn't get much sleep last night and that she probably wouldn't be coming in. She wants all her appointments rescheduled for next week."

"Oh, no!" exclaimed Libby. "That's not good."

She turned back toward the door, noticeably flustered. "I'm going to get some coffee. Want one?"

"Sure."

Returning a few minutes later, Libby placed a tray on the coffee table and took a seat on the couch. Catherine rose from her desk and sat in an adjacent armchair. Libby motioned distractedly to the coffee mugs and a plate of pastries, but then immediately sat back as if she no longer wanted anything. She stared at a stack of magazines, as if in a daze.

"Okay, something's going on. What's on *your* mind?" asked Catherine.

"I'm feeling scattered, and I guess it shows. I know you're busy. We all are, but ... I just needed to come in and chat."

"Okay ..."

"Ever get the feeling that, just as things are coming together, they're about to unravel?"

"I suppose so. You mean things here at work?" probed Catherine, sensing that it was something else.

"Yeah, I mean, do you ever wonder if there's some obvious step we forgot to take, and that any minute somebody's going to walk up and point it out?"

"Of course. Welcome to the club! We're in uncharted territory here. My strategy is to stay a couple of days—sometimes just a couple of hours—ahead of the next deadline.

"Look, you're probably just feeling the pressure of all this media attention. I think we all are, but you're the president ... next in line after Minerva. Were you stressed before I told you she wasn't coming in today?"

"Uh-huh," said Libby, finally reaching for her coffee, "but that made it worse. Minerva and I have an interview scheduled for this afternoon, and now

I don't know whether to cancel it or to do it alone, or to reschedule it." She faced Catherine. "That's not what's really bothering me."

Catherine nodded and waited.

"Last night, as I left the office, I found myself wondering if I had any idea what I was getting into. And this morning, I'm still in that same space. What the hell am I doing here? I don't know if I'm cut out for this."

Catherine laughed softly and asked, "Would you like to hear my thoughts?"

"Sure."

"The way I see it, you're as qualified as anybody I know. Remember, I've been with Minerva for almost five years. I've seen her rub shoulders with some of the most powerful and connected people in the world. She's an amazing judge of character and ability, and I'm not too shabby myself. She sees in you a person of insight, integrity, and independence. You have the ability to bring order out of chaos. That's why you're perfect for this job. The fact that maybe you didn't see how wild this adventure would become is no fault of yours. When the shit hits the fan, you're the kind of person who grabs an umbrella as you calmly reach for the power cord and yank it from the wall socket."

"You're sweet," said Libby. She leaned forward and picked up a bran muffin. "You were wondering if it's all work related—my stress, that is." She took a bite and, with her mouth half full, she continued. "It's also about Scott ... and my birthday."

"Your birthday?"

"Uh-huh. It's coming up in a couple of weeks. Scott wants to take me on a little weekend getaway."

"That's great. Is there a problem?"

"Well, there's something he doesn't know, and when I tell him the whole mood's gonna change, and ... everything's gonna change."

"Have, have you been—have you been having an aff—"

"No—nothing like *that!*"

"Well ... what haven't you told him?" Libby took a big breath and then exhaled loudly. She sat up straighter.

"Scott and I have been trying to have children for years—this is confidential, okay? Keep this between us."

Catherine nodded.

"We've seen doctors and specialists from coast to coast. We exhausted our options in San Francisco, and when we moved here almost two years ago, we tried another procedure. *Twice.* It didn't work either. Well, we finally gave up. I'm getting ready to turn forty-four, and we couldn't afford any more treatments. They're really expensive."

"So, what doesn't Scott know?"

"I took a pregnancy test last night and, wouldn't you kno—"

"*Libby, that's fantastic!*" Catherine squealed.

"*Shhh!* This is *not* public knowledge. You have to keep this a secret," she said, but a small smile smoothed her furrowed brow. "I've been pregnant before, but I've never made it to the second trimester. I'm not gonna tell Scott until I've reached that point and things are looking, you know, solid."

"I understand. You can count on me." Catherine reached over and squeezed Libby's hand. "I guess I'm still puzzled though. Why is this sending you into a tailspin?"

"Because it's just one more layer of uncertainty. I mean, I'm happy we have another shot at having a baby, but that comes with its own costs. Not the money, but the fact that it would derail my career."

Catherine said, "If you ask me, this is a blessing. Why don't you just wait and see?"

"I guess that's all I can do."

⊷⊶ ⊙⊷

The story of Minerva Bennett's vision and The Contest had occupied the top story for two weeks, but it was finally toppled by the Chinese government's announcement that they were on schedule to launch a manned mission to the Moon in just over a year. They were positioning themselves to pick up where the Americans left off, and their agenda would culminate in a permanent scientific outpost, much like the international community had accomplished in Antarctica. Practically every article and op-ed piece mentioned the recent failures of NASA to follow through on its promise to leapfrog the lunar agenda with a manned mission to Mars.

Meanwhile, practically every media outlet covered the Vox Stellarum team count. Its recent press release freshened the urgency of would-be competitors to get their teams ironed out and to register. The fact that several celebrities had entered heightened the interest.

Other entrants of note were a family of Mormons from Utah; the entire team lived under one roof. There was a team wholly comprised of students and faculty at the Texas School for the Blind and Visually Impaired. There was a team that lived off the power grid in a shanty town near Rio de Janeiro, Brazil. When a Saudi prince decided to enter a team consisting of his extended family members, he influenced several other royal families in the Middle East to follow suit. A young social media entrepreneur living in the north end of Basil, Switzerland decided to recruit four members each from the neighboring towns—in *France* and *Germany*.

Most of the teams, though, were formed in a more mundane fashion and consisted of friends, colleagues, and neighbors convinced that they could tackle the solutions to the world's problems as well as anybody. The vast majority of the registered teams were selected on the basis of eligibility and the willingness to cooperate over a two-year period.

There were a few teams that were not so much formed as engineered, like an elite team of gymnasts. One such team was gathered by a professor of political science at Harvard University. After a careful reading of Rule 8 in the official contest guidelines, the professor leveraged their credentials to include the maximum of two PhDs, two JDs, and two MDs, and he filled out the remainder of their roster with college, high school, and middle school students, each of whom had straight-A report cards. Similar teams were formed in a dozen metropolises around the world, including Singapore, London, Mumbai, Cairo, Beijing, and Tokyo.

Numerous teams had been brought together based on a wide variety of themes. Their members were like-minded by virtue of a "higher" pursuit—some of them quite reasonable, some of them clearly fanciful. One team seemed to value culinary skill and caloric intake over any other form of intelligence; it included food connoisseurs, chefs, and wine enthusiasts. Another team seemed to hold anarchy in high esteem, and the leader, a multi-media artist in Berlin, recruited its members on their willingness to swear an oath against the establishment.

⊷⟩⟨⊶

Cade Tompkins, one of the senior account managers with Brockman, Solomon & Vogel, hung up the phone with Libby Armstrong, and he glanced at his assistant seated nearby.

"I think we're in for a long weekend." He ran his fingers through his hair, rubbed his face, and sighed. "The good news is that we're billable for the foreseeable future. The bad news is: we've got a tiger by the tail. I don't think they have any idea how rough this roller coaster is going to get."

His assistant, Abby Mitchell, nodded. She sat across the desk, still holding her laptop on her knees. Her notes from the first half of the phone conference were detailed; the last item was just a row of question marks. "Yeah, they seemed pretty scattered and overwhelmed."

"Okay, we have three clear action items, pretty straightforward, and then ..." He trailed off as he looked out the window at the traffic on the street below. Then, suddenly, "*Shit!* How can something so solid crumble in such a short time?"

Abby knew Cade didn't expect an answer, and she waited.

"So ... do you think you can handle the first two items?" he asked. "Fix the press release templates and update the first tier of media outlets?" She nodded. "I'll work on the corporate sponsor issue. I suppose it's good that they want to keep the numbers down. Who knows, maybe it'll help us secure some future business. Jesus, if we could get our foot in the door with Google or Disney ..."

"What about the judging panel?" asked Abby soberly.

"I have no idea. First of all, I can't believe they haven't handled that yet. Libby's a smart girl, but she as much admitted they're still at square one. I don't know what they expect us to do about it. I mean, all we can do is generate a smoke screen ... 'progress being made, details to follow' ... the usual drivel. She must realize they're gonna get hammered with inquiries."

"And what about Minerva Bennett's status? She had to cancel two interviews yesterday, and several scheduled for next week are postponed indefinitely. That can't be good."

"Yeah," sighed Cade. "My instinct is to let that one go for the time being. Let's just hope she gets back on her feet. I consider it good news that Catherine Myers hasn't called. If Bennett's condition were serious, she would have let us know ... I think. In the meanwhile, we need to put the spotlight on one of the others in charge. Until this phone call, I would have said Libby Armstrong, but now I'm not too sure. Something is going on with her."

"The pressure's gotta be pretty intense over there," Abby offered.

"Well, one thing we can do is redirect attention. It's the oldest trick in the book."

"On?"

"The teams! We've got over six hundred to choose from ... soon to be one thousand. I say we pick several that, you know, cover the spectrum. The media are already nibbling at this, so all we have to do is chime in on some of the existing press. We could start with that local team she mentioned—the one billing itself as an intellectual powerhouse, then move to one with some oddball theme. Then, we zoom in on some shaggy underdog. The public will forget about everything else, and that'll buy Minerva Bennett some time to get back on her feet."

"I like it," Abby said, impressed with her boss's ability to turn anxiety into adventure. "If you want, I'll create a list of teams to consider."

"That'd be great, but let's get the other business handled first."

⊷⊶◉ ◉⊷⊶

Minerva opened her eyes to a bedroom lit by a partly cloudy morning sky. She was propped up against several pillows, and her comforter was smoothed neatly under her arms. She vaguely remembered being visited by Catherine Myers the day before, and that she had been unable to hold much of a conversation before falling asleep again. Dr. Forrester had also visited.

"As far as I can tell, Mrs. Bennett, you're suffering from exhaustion. What you need is peace and quiet, and lots of rest."

Catherine had left her an envelope, which, as she slowly maneuvered herself to a sitting position, she could see on her bedside table. With the vague recollection that it did not contain anything urgent, Minerva relaxed and enjoyed the sensation that she was floating. The pressures and obligations she had struggled with for weeks, even months, had dissolved somehow, and she breathed easily for the first time in days.

She had not touched any of the meals urged on her, except for a protein drink with vitamin supplements. Now she was hungry, and she clicked on the intercom.

"Isabel? Isabel, would you come here, please?" Minerva was reaching for the envelope on her table when her housekeeper knocked and entered.

"Good morning, Mrs. Bennett. How are you feeling this morning?"

"Much better, thank you," she said, straining to sit up.

"Here, let me help you." Isabel leaned over and helped her mistress to sit more upright. She repositioned the pillows and grabbed a tray that was leaning against the wall and placed it over Minerva's lap.

"Thank you, Isabel. Would you hand me that packet and my reading glasses?" Isabel did so, and then handed her a glass of water.

"Would you like to try some breakfast?"

"Yes, I'm famished. I'd like Vincent to fix me an omelet and a small bowl of blueberries."

"Vincent is off, but I can start that right away."

"On Saturday?" Minerva asked, puzzled.

"Today is Sunday," Isabel said gently.

"Oh my! I've misplaced an entire day." She held her pale hands to her face, pressing them against her mouth and chin, as if to regain a grip on physical reality. "Was I asleep the whole time?"

"All Friday and most of yesterday. The doctor gave you a mild sedative, but he said it was mostly the exhaustion that knocked you out."

"When did Catherine come by?"

"Thursday evening, Friday afternoon, and then again yesterday afternoon. That's when she left the envelope."

"My, my, ..."

"Would you like the newspapers, and your mail?"

"Yes, please."

Isabel returned a few minutes later with a stack of pre-opened mail and three days of newspapers. She organized them on the unoccupied side of the bed.

Minerva turned to the newspapers first and scanned the headlines before discarding each section on the floor. The front page showed the Vox Stellarum count at the top, even more prominently than the NCAA basketball scores: 803 teams, 197 openings. There was no other mention of The Contest. *Good—it's running smoothly*, she thought.

Catherine's notes were updates and an outline of meetings for the coming week, so Minerva moved on to her mail. The last envelope in her stack was a personal letter, the postmark partially obscuring an Audubon Society stamp. She knew it was from Gladys Atchley. Just as Minerva plucked the pages from the envelope, Isabel returned with her breakfast.

Isabel arranged plates, cups, and silverware on the tray, and then handed Minerva another note. "Mrs. Bennett, here's a list of people who called in the last couple of days." It had about ten names on it. "Your son was about to drive in to see you yesterday, but Catherine told him that you were doing fine, and that you just needed to sleep. He asked that you call him as soon as you wake up. I told the others that you will call when you can."

"Thank you, Isabel."

Minerva glanced at the list and decided to eat before trying to return any calls. Still holding Gladys's letter, she admired her friend's handwriting, an exquisite cursive that reminded her of the Declaration of Independence. She sifted through the letter, counting five pages, and smiled as if she were holding a box of gourmet chocolates.

Gladys congratulated her friend on the miraculous progress with her new foundation and the ambitious contest. She remarked about the conversations she had overheard in the community room at her residential facility—people who had no knowledge of her friendship with Minerva Bennett speaking so enthusiastically. "I am so proud of you, Minnie!"

At the bottom of the first page, the tone changed. Minerva's smile and appetite suddenly vanished. Gladys's husband Gene had passed away.

Minerva's arms went limp. She let her head fall back and her eyes close. She felt a stab of grief and then a sting of tears. *Why didn't you call me?!* she thought.

After a few moments, she lifted her head and read on. As if in response to Minerva's question, Gladys wrote, "I wanted to tell you right away, and more than anything I wanted to reach out to an old friend who could support me, but your announcements had just flooded the news. I couldn't find it in me to intrude on this important time for you."

Darn it, Gladys. You're too considerate for your own good! She wanted to reach for the phone and call her friend that instant, but she decided to finish the letter first. Minerva read on, sadness and remorse slowly becoming gratitude for her friend's distant touch and respect for her inner strength. As much as Minerva felt like she ought to have been the one to support Gladys, she eagerly drank in the accolades served up by her childhood friend who seemed to be reading her mind.

That her friend found the presence of mind and desire to reach out and explain how she, too, had become aware of her own misgivings and regrets, with respect to her own legacy, impressed Minerva. She was entranced at Gladys's explanation of Gene's decline and how that affected her overall attitude and desire to live again.

So, Minnie, don't be too sad for me, or Gene. I love the man he was more than ever, but now I realize how much I had stifled my emotions, how they were tied to long distant memories. Somehow this relates to my joy at seeing you forge ahead with new adventures! You may think I'm avoiding my grief, but I don't think so. Watching you from afar, through the newspapers and the interviews, I am clear about how life is ongoing, or ought to be.

I don't regret being with Gene during his final years. That's what you and I and our generation understand better than anybody. For better and for worse, for richer and for poorer, and—if I may—for the remembered and the forgotten. I watch from a distance, with immense pride, at how you have started afresh. You've thrown out the old program and now you challenge us all to wake up and get busy again, creating a future with hope and excitement.

The more she read, the more Minerva's sadness retreated. By the time she had reached the last page, her mourning had come and gone, and she found she was excited at Gladys's realizations. She couldn't wait to call her friend. Like a salve to her own self-doubts, the letter had delivered a timely transfusion.

An idea occurred to her suddenly, and she beamed. Twenty years apart was an injustice that it was time to remedy. *Like-minded soul sisters ought to be able to share in one another's lives on a regular basis, and I have the power to make that happen,* thought Minerva as she reached for the phone and dialed.

"Gladys? Gladys Atchley, is that you?!" she cried out in a tear-choked voice. "It's Minerva!"

"Minnie? I was just thinking of you! How *are* you?"

"I should ask you that, but I've just read your letter. Oh my goodness— what you have been through! I should say how sorry I am about Gene, but you explained things so well that, incredibly, I'm happy for you. Please don't take that the wrong way."

"How could I? That's precisely what I was hoping you'd appreciate. Life takes us on strange journeys, and the lessons we learn are often beyond our understanding or control."

"Listen to me, Gladys. I have an idea. I think you'll like it ... I *hope* you'll like it."

"What is it?"

"Just listen. Now that your dear husband is gone, you may not have too much reason to stay there in Arizona. Oh, I know you have friends there and all, but it has been entirely too long since we've seen one another in the flesh.

Well, I propose that you pack up your things and come to New York. Come and live with me! I've got more bedrooms than I know what to do with, and I can't think of anything more wonderful than to have you here with me."

Silence.

"Gladys? Are you there?"

"Yes," was all she could say. Minerva waited. "Are you serious?"

"I've never been more serious in my life."

"That's about the sweetest thing anybody has ever offered me. I probably ought to think about it, but I already know I would love nothing more than to come be with you."

"Then it's settled!" cried Minerva. "I'll get my assistant to call you soon, to take care of the details. Hooray!"

Occasionally giggling like schoolgirls, the two friends chatted for twenty more minutes. When Minerva hung up, her transfusion was complete. She felt like a million dollars.

Chapter 13

It was Sunday afternoon, and a small crowd converged in one of several meeting rooms of the M. J. Fowler Public Library in the suburbs of Tulsa, Oklahoma. Peter Talley and Malia Jordan, the organizing pair, sat at the head of a U-shaped arrangement of tables and took roll. In ones and twos, people filed into the carpeted room, musty and stale from lack of use. Several children were escorted by their parents.

"I think that's everybody, Pete," Malia said. "What do you think? Shall we get started?"

He nodded and stood up. "Good afternoon, everybody. It's great to see you all here under one roof, assembled for the first time as Team 489 in The Contest." He looked around silently, making eye contact with every person in the room.

"Some of you know me, and some don't. I'll introduce myself and give you my intention in this adventure. Then, what I'd like us to do, if there're no objections, is to go around the room and have each of us do the same." They nodded at one another, and then all eyes were on him.

"My name is Peter Talley. I'm fifty-seven, father of three—two in college, one in medical school. I'm a pediatrician with over twenty-five years in private practice, specializing in immunological concerns with my patients, mostly around food and environmental allergies.

"I'm fortunate to be living the American Dream. Occasionally, though, I look on the world in dismay, especially if I look at the headlines. I decided to enter when Malia," gesturing to his left, "mother of two of my patients—and a friend—showed me the ad for The Contest. She was very excited and asked me what I thought.

"I checked out the website and was immediately captivated. Thirty minutes later, I called her and said, 'Let's do it!'

"We met the next day and started putting together a list of people that we thought would make a great team and ... here we are." Again, his gaze swept the room. "This is a once-in-a-lifetime opportunity. This is our chance to take our dreams and hopes, perhaps hidden away and kept secret, and put them front and center ... to share them with each other ... and then with the whole world.

"One thing you should know about me, at the beginning of what I hope will be a long working relationship, is that I like to push myself. When I do something, I give it my best. And if it's a competition, I play to win. I don't know what the current number is, but soon enough there'll be 999 other teams out there, around the world, gathering with the same objective. I believe we have a great chance at winning.

"No matter what's going on in your heads right now, whatever fears and doubts may be bubbling up, I hope you realize that you are *here* ... *with us* ... for a special reason. You have been hand-picked.

"One of my mentors in high school was my football coach. He told us to act like winners from the first day of practice onward ... and that this attitude would carry us all the way through to the play-offs. That advice worked then, and it'll work now."

Talley stood there for a few seconds to let his words sink in. Then he sat down. Even after his introduction, and perhaps because of it, the participants didn't know whether to applaud, cheer, or shout "Amen!" It was all too unprecedented. They watched in silence as the next member stood.

"Hello, everybody. I don't know if I can speak as articulately as Dr. Talley, but here goes. My name is Malia Jordan, and I'm a 34-year-old mother of two. My husband is an insurance broker, and he's home with the boys so I can be here. They can't wait to meet everybody.

"I'm an artist, and occasionally I find time after family and parenting duties to paint and sculpt. I've sold a few pieces, but mostly I create for my own enjoyment and peace of mind. I write a little too, mostly poetry. I'm a community activist, and I've been involved with a number of causes over the years. I'm one-eighth Comanche and embrace that heritage when I can. When it's appropriate, I try to honor a native approach to spiritual concepts in my art.

"I'm interested in environmental issues, but I think balance is important. I believe we can hold on to most of our modern technology as long as we be much more mindful and patient.

"In terms of the perspective I bring to our team, I believe common sense shows us what works and what doesn't work. But what we need is a clear sense of how to transition from destructive practices and habits to healthy, constructive ones.

"I'm really honored to be here. And by the way, I agree with Dr. Talley. We can *win* this thing!"

The rest of the members introduced themselves, and one by one a loose association of strangers began to make connections. A bond began to form in a way that was uncommon, even after years of intimacy. In one hour, the small gathering of citizens, ranging in age from nine to seventy-nine, had taken their first steps at becoming a team.

After the last introduction, Talley reached for two grocery bags and took out twelve three-ring binders.

"Malia and I talked about ways to keep ourselves organized, and we came up with these. We included some colored dividers, which might take some of you back to your school days. First, you'll see a team roster with contact information. Assuming we're in agreement with what we hope to accomplish, and that we commit to fulfilling our assignments, this information shouldn't change to any great degree.

"Next, you'll see a rough calendar with proposed meeting times. Before we talk about that, though, let's take a look at the blue section. These are the official rules of The Contest shown on the website. I suspect most of you have checked these out, but it's important that we all read them by our next meeting. Philip and Lindsay, you two may want to get your parents to guide you through this material. Some of the wording is kind of formal, but I think the organization has done a pretty good job of keeping the language plain and simple.

"The main reason we want you to read through the rules and guidelines is so that you realize what's allowed and what isn't. The consequence of even one member of our team not following the basic rules is elimination. I can't emphasize enough how important it is to honor your commitment to the success of the team by making sure that you are absolutely aware of the rules. Are we all clear about this point?" Talley paused and looked around the room.

Malia continued. "We have just a few more items to go over before we adjourn. Notice that the page on the front of the binder is blank. Pete and I figured we ought to have a cool name—something a little catchier than Team 489. Have fun—see what you can come up with.

"Besides that, your main assignment will be to go to the Vox Stellarum website and view the official list of issues we must address. We chose not to include them in your binders because we figured that, by writing them down, you'd get a feeling for certain ones that you think should take priority.

"That's pretty much it. Pete has one final point."

"We need to elect a team leader," said Talley, "and that person will be responsible for official communications with the contest administrators. This is a basic requirement in the guidelines. I have acted as that leader today, but I think nominations and a vote are in order. This can be the first item on the agenda at our next meeting.

"By the way, one of the rules requires that we meet at least once a week while we're on task. My understanding is that this is during those periods when we're actively working on a response to the assignments, whatever they turn out to be. That's going to be difficult. I imagine the people at Vox Stellarum included this to shake out the teams that aren't fully committed.

"That being said, I hope this time and place works for everybody. Let us know if you foresee any serious conflicts." Everybody nodded.

"That's it then. Thank you for stepping forward and making such a huge commitment. See you in one week!"

The sun was low in the sky. Orange light streamed into Minerva's sitting room, adjacent to her bedroom. She sat at her card table, working a puzzle when the phone rang.

"Hello?"

"Mrs. Bennett, this is Ed Forrester. I'm calling to check on your progress. How are you feeling?"

"I'm feeling quite well actually. I'm taking it easy, as you suggested."

"How's your strength?"

"I'm a little weak, but I've eaten well today. I'm moving about reasonably well."

"I imagine you're anxious to return to work in the morning. Nevertheless, I feel obliged to tell you that that's too early. I want you to limit your work time to only a couple of hours, for a few days at least." Expecting an argument, he quickly added, "at least through Wednesday."

"Doctor, I've got to get back. We're falling behind, and there's just ..." She paused. "Is there a problem with me working from home? I can have some of my people come here, if it's traveling that's the issue."

"I don't see a problem with that. The danger is for you to be on your feet and getting your stress level up. If you hold a couple of meetings at your home and make sure you eat your meals on schedule, I'm sure that will be fine. Just don't overdo it."

Minerva hung up and immediately called Catherine Myers. Ten minutes later, satisfied that the important meetings scheduled for the next day could be rerouted to her apartment, she resumed her jigsaw puzzle. After only a few minutes, her focus waned. She decided to follow the doctor's advice by getting in bed earlier than usual.

Isabel was out, so she asked Felix to bring her a piece of pie. With her nightgown on, and the pie on her tray, she turned on the television, hoping to catch up on news and weather.

Flipping channels from evening news to local news to weekend sports highlights, with nothing really catching her attention, she concluded that not much had gone on during her three days off the clock. She switched to the BBC to watch one of her favorite British dramas. It was ten minutes to eight;

she would have to endure the last segment of the international news before her show would air.

"... to round out this evening's broadcast, we recap the day's important events. A Boeing 737 has crashed en route to the Seychelles, a small group of islands in the western Indian Ocean. The charter was carrying 148 passengers and 6 crew members, the majority of which were French and Germans on holiday. There were no survivors. The cause of the mishap is being investigated by authorities.

"Early this morning, an earthquake measuring 6.1 on the Richter scale was detected in the South China Sea, just east of Taiwan. A spokesman for DART, the Deep-ocean Assessment and Reporting of Tsunamis system, has reported that a tidal wave as high as five meters has inundated the coastlines in the region. Estimates of casualties are in the hundreds.

"Anti-government protests in France, the latest to beset western Europe, erupted Friday upon the announcement by Hans Van Dijk, Chancellor of the European Union, of a binding resolution passed by member states to pass strict economic sanctions for any postponements or defaults of repayment to the World Bank. France had announced on March 1 its inability to keep up with its payments due to wide-spread labor strikes and unwillingness of government unions to follow through with recent agreed-upon concessions. The protesters have upset traffic in much of Paris by occupying Place Charles de Gaulle, site of the Arc de Triomphe.

Disturbed by the rash of mishaps and disasters and disgusted by the economic mess in France, Minerva got out of bed and carried her empty plate to the kitchen. *I wonder how our teams will address this madness*, she thought as she padded back to her bedroom and climbed back in bed. When she unmuted the TV, something caught her attention.

"... and is 92 years old, announced she had registered in The Contest, the global competition being administered by the Vox Stellarum foundation. Beate Sirota Gordon, a Ukrainian Jew by heritage, but raised and educated in Japan, is acknowledged as ... She resides in New York City.

"That's it for the evening news. Good night."

A smile crept onto Minerva's face as she lay in bed. A surge of excitement gave her a sense that she could hop right out of bed and start her week at full speed.

It's going to be hard following Forrester's advice. If Beate can jump in at ninety-two, what excuse do I have?

⊷⊨⊙ ⊙⊨⊰⊷

Upon awakening the next morning, Minerva grabbed a notepad and began to outline what she needed to do. Prep for 10:00 AM meeting; scan reports; prep for 1:00 PM meeting; set goals for Task Committee; check with Catherine about the lunch menu; return calls. What else?

She paused in order to think back over the previous days as best she could, and suddenly she recalled the conversation with her son the day before.

"Mother, are you sure you're okay? When I heard that you had collapsed, I imagined the worst."

"I'm *fine!* And I didn't collapse. It was a fainting spell."

"Isabel said Dr. Forrester ordered bed rest, and that he gave you some supplements. Are you following directions? Taking it easy?"

"In fact, I have—I've been in bed or in my chaise all day. Please don't worry. I just overdid things a bit."

"Do you need help with anything? I'm driving in Tuesday afternoon, but I can come earlier."

"That's sweet of you, but I'm fine."

Except for his peremptory insistence that she stick to the doctor's explicit instructions, she reflected that Julian's voice had had the friendly and accepting tone that she hadn't heard from him in quite a while. She was glad they hadn't talked of foundations, or board meetings, or The Contest.

She recalled, too, her conversation with Gladys, and this immediately brought a smile to her face. She added a note for Catherine: arrange Gladys's move! As her to-do list grew bit by bit, she was relieved to note that it was her staff that would be doing most of the leg work.

Several hours later, after dispatching the newspapers and completing the crossword, she dressed and moved to her desk to make her calls. Sam Minton was first on her list.

"Good morning, Sam."

"Minerva, so good to hear your voice! How are you?"

"Very well, thank you. I woke up feeling pretty much my old self, but I'm going to take it at half speed for the next couple of days, work-wise ... doctor's orders."

"I hope your staff can keep up. Half speed for you is like full speed for everybody else." His exuberance came through the phone line and into Minerva's body; it made her feel warm and reassured.

"You're one to talk, Sam. I don't know anybody who can keep up with you."

He chuckled, but then spoke in a quieter tone. "Seriously ... I was relieved to hear that it was exhaustion and nothing more serious."

"Yes, I suppose I was too," she said, not wanting to dwell on darker possibilities. "So, I'm returning phone calls and getting ready for a meeting. My people are coming here for a ten o'clock, and then I'm hosting lunch for everybody before another meeting at one. If you're looking for a free meal, we'd love to have you."

"You're so kind, but I can't. I'm heading to San Francisco in a couple of hours, and I'll be gone for the week."

"What's the occasion?"

"An IT convention—the Predictive Analytics World Conference. Gotta stay ahead of the curve." He laughed. Minerva was well aware of his compulsive adoption of the latest gadgets and techniques.

"Good for you. I'll let you go then."

"Actually, there was another purpose for my call on Friday. Do you have a few more minutes?"

"I do. What's on your mind?"

"I spoke with Catherine Myers last week. She called to discuss the panel of judges. She wanted to know how I would go about selecting them, if it were up to me."

"Okay ..." Minerva said in a tentative voice, wondering what had prompted Catherine to do that. The issue had been frustrating her for several weeks, and hearing Minton bring it up now so unexpectedly had a sobering effect.

"I told her that I first wanted to hear what steps had been taken. She said you were actively gathering names of panelists to approach and asked if I had any suggestions."

"I see ... Did you give her any names?" Minerva asked. Office politics and chain of command aside, she was genuinely curious. Sam was a news hound, and Minerva had to grant that Catherine had chosen a good source; she had no doubt that he would have an extensive network of contacts.

"I was about to, but then she told me that *you* would be approaching them."

"Do you see a problem with that?" she asked, startled by his point.

"Yes, I do. It comes down to separation of duties—checks and balances, if you will. You know me well enough to know a little about how I operate. I like to monitor and watch."

"Yes, I know you're very 'plugged in,' as they say."

"Well, what I'm hearing is a wide variety of opinions, beliefs, and so forth. One of the main threads is this: Minerva Bennett is a nice old lady—she means well, but she has no business jumping into global politics. They admire you and appreciate the positive intent of your competition, but they don't believe you have the expertise or background to judge the outcome, especially given the global scope. In short, there're a lot of critics who say you're in way over your head."

"I'm quite aware of the critics, but I can't let them define who I am ... or let them dictate my actions. When I committed to start a new foundation and to move forward with my vision, despite what my own family was saying, I knew I couldn't afford to dwell on the negative. And I assure you, Sam, I know this contest is a risky business."

"Minerva, remember, I'm on your side. The point I'm getting ready to make is that we need to shield you from the slings and arrows of the pundits and nay-sayers. We need to establish Vox Stellarum as a flexible, neutral, well-oiled machine that's designed and committed to administering the process with absolute objectivity. The public's trust in you will be compromised if you try to work both the starting line and the finish line."

"Hmm ... go on."

"We need to put as much distance between you and the judges as possible. When the finalists are announced, there can't be the slightest hint that it was a *fait accompli*. You must trust the integrity of your own design and let go of the results."

"What does this distance look like exactly?" she asked and then sighed loudly with more than a touch of exasperation.

"I've been thinking about this for the last several days. Obviously, you're still running the show—it's your foundation, your idea. Nobody expects you to take a back seat. What should happen, I think, is that you pick an outsider to select and enlist the judges so that you can devote yourself to maintaining the public profile, which you're already doing, as well as manage the front-end administration."

"Okay, I get your point. Do you have anybody in mind?" she asked and then added, only half jesting, "How about *you*?"

"Hell no, Minerva. I'm practically in the same boat as you. As a member of the Board of Trustees, I would disqualify myself. No, it needs to be somebody we don't even know."

"Now you're getting cryptic. How in the world do we find such a person?"

"We put out a couple of very discreet inquiries, and we hold our cards very close. A minute ago, you asked if I had anybody in mind, and my answer is yes. Not as the panel selector, but as somebody who knows a couple of names for such a task. If you can think of a name or two, and it might be a good idea to ask Julian, and Bob Godfrey, and maybe Libby ... that should give us a half dozen prospects. What do you think about that?"

"I suppose it makes sense, but I think you're being a bit paranoid. I can't imagine, frankly, who would accuse me of playing favorites if I were to select scrupulously independent figures from around the world. Most of the people I have been considering are people I've never even met!"

"You're too trusting, and I think you've missed my point. Even if the vast majority believe as you just stated—that you're objective and fair, there'll still be the potential of a vocal few to make you out as someone who's just pushing her influence around, but on a much vaster scale than before. Such people don't play by your rules or share your integrity. They think nothing of fabricating and slandering for whatever ulterior motives suit them. Trust me on this, Minerva."

"Assume for the moment that I do. Who else have you discussed this with? Have you already spoken to Julian and Bob, or Stewart, for that matter?"

"No. I've kept this to myself. I hinted to Catherine what was on my mind, but she only knows that I think there needs to be a separation of duties."

"Okay, go on."

"Timing is critical. Catherine mentioned that your goal is to announce the panel of judges concurrently with the release of the first task, or very soon after. Is this accurate?"

"Yes."

"Okay. I'm thinking that, by tomorrow afternoon, we need to get you a short list of names. Then, as soon as possible, you and your people can contact them and make a decision. This is pretty urgent—the start date is in only four weeks. But the good news for you is that, once you assign your staff to interview these people, you can step back."

"Easier said than done, Sam. It's difficult to consider letting somebody else take the reins, especially at such a critical juncture."

"I understand," he said with a soft chuckle. "By the way, this has nothing to do with your health. I was prepared to make this recommendation before I knew you were under a doctor's care."

"Okay, Sam, you've made some good points. Let me sit with this. I'll let you know."

Chapter 14

THE AEGIS ACADEMY carpool line was rowdier than usual, especially for a Monday morning, and Henry Godfrey watched several sixth graders exit their parents' cars with extra grocery bags, strange-looking hats, and poster boards. As one girl walked into the main entrance holding a Pyrex dish with a home-made pie, Henry smiled. It was March 14th—Pi Day.

Schools around the nation had taken to celebrating the important mathematical constant on this date due to its mimicking of the first digits: 3.14, and Mr. Godfrey was among the math teachers who took advantage of the opportunity to let the students cut loose. They were assigned to bring pie, homemade if possible, milk, and whipped cream, and they were encouraged to make silly hats and posters. They loved it.

At the beginning of each class, Henry would announce, "Welcome to Pi Day, a time to celebrate all things round and curvy. This is an important and sacred day—a day to be *pi*ous!" He would take an inventory of the pies and then assign slicers and servers. Once the kids had a chance to sample several flavors, he would begin the bonus point challenge. Students had been informed weeks before that they would receive extra credit for every digit to the right of the decimal point they could recite.

A long scroll extended along almost three walls of the classroom: 3.1415926535 ... and the enthusiasm of the students to see who might set a new record was palpable. One year a girl made it past the 75-digit poster, and Henry had to refer to a printed copy of the first 1000 digits to check her accuracy. She flawlessly recited 245 digits as her classmates looked on in disbelief.

A few years later, a boy doubled that by making it to 509 digits before making a mistake.

The students would invariably challenge Mr. Godfrey, imagining that he could somehow divine as many of the infinite digits as he wanted. He would always decline, admitting that he could only name ten digits. "Hey, six-time shuttle astronaut Story Musgrave assured me that ten digits are twice as many as NASA needed to get to the Moon, with orbital precision to spare." They were so impressed by the fact that he knew the astronaut that they forgave his laziness.

All these memories and more crowded his mind as Henry recorded the mnemonic prowess of class after class of students. As much as he loved the parade of digital dictation, the gorging on countless pies, the judging of silly hats and posters, and even the occasional "circular" song or dance, other thoughts kept cropping up to distract him. As he considered the circular and cyclical nature of his own life as a teacher, he wondered how many school years he might be able to bear, teaching the same lessons over and over. He found himself imagining a life with a new direction.

If I accept Aunt Minerva's offer and move to New York, where will I be one year from now? As exciting as the prospect was, he couldn't ignore his gut reaction, which was fear. He couldn't decide what to do.

After his final class of the day, Henry sat on a stool near the chalkboard. Stuffed and coming off his own sugar high, he felt like the desks scattered about the room—flat and sticky. Another Pi Day gone, already indistinguishable from the previous ones.

Armed with a roll of paper towels and cleaning spray, he proceeded to restore order. He felt relief as he straightened row after row of desks, wiping surfaces to an antiseptic shine.

Henry adjusted the desks scrupulously. Starting in one corner, he continued across the room until he was satisfied. At times self-aware to a fault, he wondered about his penchant for order. Some of his colleagues teased him occasionally; he was definitely a neat freak. He would do his best to accept it, even flaunt it, but he wondered if it had a root in some psychic imbalance.

After he put away his cleaning supplies, he perched again on his stool—as on a fence between two worlds. *What should I do? Does it make sense to walk away from this, where I know what I'm doing? What are my chances of success ... out there?*

The story he told himself was that he wanted adventure, but he also knew he often avoided it. The thought of moving to New York scared the hell out of him.

He looked about the classroom, hoping to summon the energy to do some grading. He noticed the compass labels under the long Pi chart. They were in Spanish as well as English: "north" and "norte," "south" and "sur," and so forth, and the juxtaposition reminded him of an encounter with one of his former students over the weekend. The boy, now a junior in high school, had recognized him from across a crowded Mexican restaurant.

Above the din of the restaurant, which served some of the best enchiladas in town, he approached with a "Hey, Mr. Godfrey! Remember me?" After running through his mental Rolodex, he identified the boy who had been, to his recollection, a shy and bookish student. Hormones had transformed him, and he now appeared rather handsome and outgoing.

After introducing the young man to his girlfriend, Suzanne, he expected that to be the end of it. But first Henry had to endure a few compliments.

"Mr. Godfrey was my favorite teacher in sixth grade—we did all kinds of cool stuff. I remember when ... and he even ..."

When Suzanne's eyes began to glaze over, Henry interrupted, hoping to make clear they wanted to get back to their dinner date. "Good to see you, Matthew. Thanks for stopping by."

But the boy lingered. "What I really wanted to tell you is that I'm on a team!"

"Good for you."

Disappointed by Mr. Godfrey's dismissive tone, the young man tried again for positive acknowledgement from an adult whom he admired.

"We're registered in *The Contest* ... you know, the one your grandmother created?"

"*Oh!!*" He had totally missed the cue. "I am so sorry, Matthew. I thought you were talking about baseball or lacrosse or—*Congratulations!* Do I know any of the other members on your team?"

"Probably not. I live in Clear Lake."

"When did you sign up?"

"Last week. We were actually one of the earlier teams to register, and ... you're not going to believe what number we are. I'll give you a hint—it's sacred."

A light went off, and Henry smiled broadly. "*No way!*" he practically yelled.

Suzanne had been content to sit back and watch the dialogue politely, but she suddenly couldn't stand it any longer.

"You *know* what their number is?!" she asked. "Aren't there, like, a thousand teams or something?"

"Uh-huh," the young man said, grinning.

"He's on Team 42," Henry said as casually as he could. Matthew beamed.

"That's *impossible!*" Suzanne declared.

Shortly, the two shook hands again, this time with genuine eye-to-eye contact. When his former student left, Henry turned to face Suzanne, who was still mystified.

"Don't be too impressed, Suze. His hint gave it away. There's a book I sometimes read to my classes—I call it 'The Sacred Text.' In the story, which is pretty far out, there's a giant computer that is programmed to find the answer to the ultimate question of life, the universe, and everything. After running for millions of years, it returns a ridiculous answer: 42."

"What book?" she asked, now more critical than curious.

"*The Hitchhiker's Guide to the Galaxy*, by Douglas Adams."

Back in his classroom, Henry looked at the reflection of trees and clouds in the rectangular array of desktops. It suddenly occurred to him that this chance encounter may have been a sign. Was it time for him to try something new, especially given that, against all odds, the boy's team number had such a personal, if not cosmic, significance?

A definite possibility, he thought as he grabbed his backpack and headed for the door.

⋅⊷⊜ ⊜⊶⋅

Tiago Díaz sat with his mother and his two brothers as Bruna, his sixteen-year-old sister, cleared the table. Cloud cover and a steady rain lent a chill to the evening, and dampness rather than light seemed to reflect off the adjacent structure, less than a meter away. The room was lit by a lone light bulb that dangled precariously above the faded wooden table.

"Tiago, tell us about the meeting. What did you talk about?" prodded his mother, Camila. She was immune to the muffled sounds from above, beside, and below that filtered into their tiny three-room apartment through the thin walls and the ill-fitting window.

"It was exciting, Mamá. We met in a warehouse down the mountain, close to the main road. It's run by the man Tío Jose works for, and he organized it. He let Abílio come too, even though he is not on the team. Señor Martín is the leader. He is very smart. He told us about the rules and what our jobs are."

"What kind of rules?" asked Marcelo, Tiago's six-year-old brother.

"Quiet, niño! Go on," ordered their mother.

"I knew there would be rules for The Contest, but I didn't know there would be so many details."

"Such as?"

"Every team must have twelve people—six girls and six boys. And the members have to be spread out in ages. I am the youngest!" Tiago stated proudly.

"Why did they pick you, hermano?" asked Fernando, his older brother. "Why not me?"

"I don't know. Maybe because I'm smart."

"I'm smarter than you!" exclaimed Fernando, slugging his brother competitively.

"Niños!" his mother yelled and raised her hand mockingly.

"Maybe they picked me because I do odd jobs for everybody. That's what Señora Vereira said. We introduced ourselves, and she spoke up for me. She is very nice."

"Who is she?" asked his mother.

"She works as a cleaning lady, I think, but she is also a waitress at a cafe where businessmen meet."

"How does she know you, my son?"

"Abílio and I, and the others, you know—João, Silvio, Ronaldo—when we're exploring, we sometimes hang out in the alley behind the cafe. She saw us collecting things once—"

"You mean stealing things!" corrected Fernando.

"No! We only take things that have been thrown away. Sometimes the Señora gives us some little treats. She asked us why we collect things, and João told her about our clubhouse. Since then, she trusts us and invites us to come there any time. Sometimes I run errands for her, and she has even paid me a little."

"*Oh?* Why have you kept this secret from your father and me?"

"It's not much, Mamá! Just a few centavos here and there. I am saving to buy some books."

"*Books?*" asked Bruna, who had finished the dishes and cleaned the heating plate. "What would you do with books?"

"I am learning how to read," Tiago answered defiantly.

"Now, now, niños. Okay, go on, my son. What did you talk about after all the people introduced themselves?"

"We talked about the rich lady in the United States who created The Contest. If my team wins, she is going to pay us for helping her."

"How much?" asked Marcelo.

"Millions of dollars!" said Tiago, and his brother's eyes grew big.

"Go on," prodded Camila. She grinned at her daughter, who was rolling her eyes.

"Señor Mendes, an old man with white hair and a mustache, was looking at his computer. He has a laptop! He was reading things from the Internet, and I was amazed. His computer showed all kinds of different things, and then he stopped on a list of big problems—global problems. He said we need to choose some of these and then solve them."

"That's all?" sniffed Bruna, her sarcasm wasted on Tiago's innocence.

"Bruna, be quiet," ordered Camila.

"Señor Mendes gave us homework. We must come up with ideas and be ready to tell the others what we think at our next meeting."

"And when is that going to be?" asked his mother.

"Next Sunday. The rules say we must meet as a team every week."

"How will the rich lady know how often you meet?" asked Fernando.

"We have to take a picture of the whole team standing together, with a newspaper showing the date. Then Señor Mendes will send the photo ... on the Internet."

"How does he do that?" asked Marcelo.

"I don't know. One of the girls got sick and couldn't come. So, we didn't take a picture today. We will take one next week, I hope." Tiago nodded confidently, his hands placed in his lap.

"I'm proud of you, Tiago. Your father and I will help you. Just ask us. Okay?"

"Gracias, Mamá."

⋆⟫⊚ ⊚⟪⋆

To comply with Dr. Forrester's orders, Minerva confined her activity to her apartment for the next couple of days. She invited Catherine Myers to join her Monday morning for breakfast before the staff meeting, in order to review the agendas for the day and the week.

Minerva showed her the short list of names that had come together in the last twenty-four hours. As promised, Minton had forwarded two names, while Bob Godfrey and Julian had each come up with one.

"When I spoke with Sam Minton yesterday, I was a bit uncomfortable with the fact that you had gone to him directly, before consulting with me," Minerva said. "I thought it was understood that you and Libby would keep our conversation last week to yourselves."

"But you said we were to use our resources, discreetly of course, to sniff around for ideas. I'm sorry if I misinterpreted your intention. I figured that, as a trustee, Sam would be a good place to start."

"Quite alright, my dear. You were using your head, and it was actually a smart move. He convinced me that my approach wouldn't have been prudent." Catherine nodded.

Minerva continued, "So, I've decided to go with his recommendation—to recruit an outsider. This has become our top priority. You're welcome to add names to the list if you think of anybody suitable."

"Nobody comes to mind at the moment."

"Okay, let's move on. The others will be here in about half an hour, and we have until 11:00 to handle our business and then shoo them away. Are we all set for the interview?"

"Yes. The reporter and photographer should arrive at 11:30, and Ms. Gordon is due to arrive about then as well."

"Good. Would you like to stay?"

"I'd love to," Catherine said. "I read her bio after you told me about the interview request. You two have quite a bit in common."

"I suppose that's why the reporter contacted us. A couple of old gals involving themselves in the same political arena ... ought to make for a good spectacle. Beate has been at this far longer and more seriously than I have, though. I'm looking forward to seeing her again."

"You know her?"

"Not well, but we've met two or three times over the years. I liked her right away. She has a gleam in her eye, and she's very sharp. I was amazed to hear that she had joined a team. She's older than I am!"

They ate in silence for a minute, and then Catherine asked, "Do you have a sense yet of when you'll be returning to the office?"

"Assuming Dr. Forrester doesn't give me any bad news tomorrow, I think Wednesday."

"Good! Everybody's been asking—they miss you."

Minerva smiled. "That makes me feel good."

Isabel came in to remove their dishes, and Minerva got up to stretch. She walked out on the terrace to take in some fresh air and sunshine. It was a beautiful day, cool, but with a hint of spring in the air. Catherine followed her out.

"I've been taking brief walks out here, and it feels good," said Minerva as she looked off in the distance. Central Park spread before them, an expanse of greens framed by a parade of stately buildings. The Lake, the Turtle Pond, and the Jackie Onassis Reservoir shimmered in varying hues of blue.

"I can't wait to share this with Gladys," Minerva said spontaneously. "Oh, by the way, I've invited my dearest old friend to come live with me. Her husband died recently, and she loves the idea of returning to her old hometown. I need you to contact Gladys Atchley and make the arrangements."

"You told me about that Sunday. In fact, I spoke with her yesterday. She sounded very sweet."

"Oh," Minerva said softly, "good." She looked away, her brow furrowed in dismay. *Why don't I remember that?* She dared not challenge Catherine, lest she learn about other instances of her forgetfulness. She felt a small knot of shame in her chest, and she turned to go back inside.

Shortly, six more staff members filed into the study. At Minerva's request, Libby Armstrong presided over the meeting. She quickly laid out the agenda and the members went around the circle giving updates. After all the basic departments had checked in, Stewart Maxwell spoke about the contract he had drawn up for the corporate sponsors that had committed substantial sums to be associated with the global enterprise.

Then Libby turned to the item that had yet to be handled to anybody's satisfaction.

"Some of you have asked about the makeup of the panel, and you should know that Minerva, Catherine, and I are handling this. No names yet, but one thing I can tell you is that we're going with the 12-person motif—half male, half female. More to follow.

"Let's see ... what else?" Libby wondered aloud as she looked at her list. "Minerva, would you like to add anything?"

Minerva nodded. "I just want to say how pleased I am that you folks are keeping this thing on track in such a professional manner. There are so many variables and so many unknowns to deal with, but you make it look easy, as if you've done this before.

"I don't like being out of circulation, but this has given me a chance to see how well placed my confidence in each of you is."

Minerva looked around the room, regarding each person before she continued.

"It's no secret that I'm getting old. My doctor says I need to take it easy, and that I should cut back on my hours, even once I return to the office. That'll be difficult, but he may be right. I'm feeling well today, though, so keep your fingers crossed." She smiled feebly and shrugged.

The meeting broke earlier than expected, and half the group filed out of the study to return to the headquarters. Minerva walked them to the door and then returned to the study. There, as she had requested, Libby, Maxwell, and Catherine were waiting for her.

"Girls, I want to include Stewart in our conversation, for a couple of reasons. The first one being that he's going to draw up the agreement with whomever we select. The second is that I trust his judgment. He's got a keen eye when it comes to personalities; he sees peoples' weaknesses no matter how hard they try to hide them."

"Of course," said Libby. "We'll take all the help we can get."

Minerva explained the issue to Maxwell, sharing details of her conversation with Sam Minton. She watched his poker face as he listened, wondering whether he'd already been tipped off by his friend.

"So, Stewart, there you have it. We have four names to consider, and—"

"Five," interrupted Libby. "I got an e-mail during the meeting with another name."

"Good ... five then," said Minerva. "Let's take a look."

Libby had already added the new name to her spreadsheet. She connected her laptop to the projection system in the study. Brief biographical profiles appeared on the screen that hung from a slot in the ceiling.

For several minutes, nobody spoke. They studied the names and tried to imagine which ones fit the profile for a pivotal job that had never been done.

"Okay," began Minerva, "tell me what you think. The first issue is whether any of these need to be scratched, before we even bother to contact them. Ones that look promising need to be called as soon as possible—today—this afternoon."

"They all look pretty impressive to me, but number three lacks the international credentials the others have. I recommend we eliminate her," said Libby.

"I agree," said Minerva. "That one came from Julian. I think I met her once—very sharp lady, but you're right. She doesn't have the diverse background the others appear to have."

"Who suggested number two?" asked Maxwell. "That guy looks pretty hardcore. Check out his military background." He paused as they all examined his record, and then continued. "He speaks four languages, which is good, but I wonder if he speaks *cooperation*."

"Where do you get that?" asked Catherine. "He was the undersecretary of two different federal agencies and then worked extensively with a third."

"True, but prior to that he worked for DARPA. You know what that is?" Maxwell asked.

Catherine shook her head.

"I forget what it stands for exactly, but it's the branch of the DOD—Department of Defense—that funnels new technology into the military's arsenal. These guys tend to be right-wing hawks ... and very secretive."

"You may be right, Stewart," said Minerva, "but let's keep him on the list. I'll call him myself. Any other observations?"

They shook their heads.

"So, we have some calls to make," Minerva said.

Chapter 15

EMERGING FROM THE study, Minerva and Catherine found the reporter and photographer waiting in the sunroom; the furniture had been rearranged to provide a more intimate setting. The reporter was a smartly dressed woman, thirty-something. The photographer, who stood nearby, was engrossed by the surroundings. He stared in disbelief at the signatures on two paintings hanging in the corner of the room and then looked up sheepishly.

As Minerva met the reporter, Catherine watched the photographer with a sympathetic fascination. She knew how intimidating it could be to see museum quality artwork placed so matter-of-factly in a private home. She walked over and introduced herself.

Fifteen minutes later, the doorbell rang. They all stood as Minerva's driver, Carson, an athletic man in his late thirties, escorted the other interviewee into the room: a woman with pure white hair and a nimble smile. She moved slowly and carefully, one hand on his arm, one hand on a wooden cane. Almost obscured by the lavender hat she wore at a fashionable slant, her penetrating gaze was the first feature one noticed. Her body, compressed and bowed by a long and active life, was accented by her youthful expression. Her eyes danced curiously about, delighting in the details, like those of a detective. Her old world bearing instantly infused the setting with an exotic presence.

"Hello, Beate. Welcome!" greeted Minerva. "It's been several years, but you have somehow managed to look younger than the last time I saw you."

"Thank you, Minerva. You are too kind. I was so excited to be invited to your home." They shook hands vigorously and beamed at one another.

"Let me introduce you," said Minerva, and she turned to the others. "May I present Mrs. Beate Sirota Gordon. This is Marguerite Kaufman, a reporter with *The New York Times* ... Catherine Myers, Vice President of Vox Stellarum ... Jonathan Wright, also with *The Times*. He's the photographer."

As they made themselves comfortable, Felix wheeled in the refreshment cart.

"Ladies, it's an honor to be granted this opportunity to interview the two of you. I really appreciate your accommodating us," Kaufman said as she motioned to the photographer. "I know you requested that we keep it to one hour or less, and I intend to do just that. Jonathan will be taking some candid photos. Don't worry—he's very discreet."

She placed a small digital recorder on the coffee table and readied her notepad. "Shall we?"

"We're all yours," said Minerva.

For the first ten minutes, the reporter asked only one or two questions. Mostly, she sat and listened, scribbling notes with her pen. Both of her subjects knew from experience to cover general background and highlights. Beate described her experience at the German School and then the American School in Japan, touching on her Jewish background and her Austrian heritage. In order to speak more in depth about her work as a Japanese translator during World War II, she quickly covered her university experience, then her work with the Foreign Broadcast Information Service.

"And this led to your being recruited to help write the post-war Japanese Constitution?" asked Kaufman.

"That is correct. My subcommittee was asked to handle the civil rights portion. Among other considerations, we stressed the legal equality of men and women, and this is what most journalists, and historians I suppose, have highlighted about my past."

"That was almost seventy years ago, and I imagine that your political efforts didn't stop there. We know, for instance, that you've been a very active speaker and lecturer at universities around the world since then. But I wonder ... did you consider yourself a feminist? Or even a communist sympathizer, for which at least one American general accused you at the time?"

Beate responded with a melodious laugh. "I only sought to address the stark inequities between men and women that were a fundamental and long-accepted part of the Japanese culture. I have never advocated that men be penalized or brought down, but that women be elevated to an equal and fair footing. I had a somewhat unique perspective of Japanese life, given that I was an outsider—a European, a Caucasian, but a female too. This gave me a subtle advantage since I wasn't held to the same subservient standards as my native friends.

"When I returned to Japan after the war, I was able to capitalize on my Japanese upbringing and, with my linguistic and cultural fluency, introduce western principles into the dialogue. This has been my message ever since. This same argument applies to ethnic groups, religious groups, and so on. I have always been interested in bringing a level playing field to people regardless of their differences. That's what attracted me to Minerva's program."

"I see," said Kaufman, making a few notes without looking up. "May I get you to pause there? Let's hear from Mrs. Bennett, if that's okay. Don't worry, we'll revisit your point."

Minerva gave a brief summary of her youth, her education, her Calvinist upbringing, her good fortune in the spheres of matrimony and money. As Kaufman paused for a moment to phrase her next question just so, the photographer clicked several pictures.

"Mrs. Bennett, it is well documented that the Koyne Foundation, which you founded and managed until very recently, has been on the front lines of humanitarian efforts for forty-five years. Can you recall how you first became inspired to set off on your philanthropic path? And has your vision changed significantly since those early days?"

Minerva spoke for several minutes, integrating as much as possible all the minor components that led up to her being thrust onto the world stage.

The reporter nodded. "I see. And has your view of this methodology changed over time? As you might guess, my question is predicated on your decision to step down from the chairmanship of the Koyne Foundation in order to create Vox Stellarum."

"Yes, I gathered that." She flashed a quick smile. "It's a good question. I would say yes; my views have changed. In hindsight, I have to say that I agree with the board's stance. A foundation founded on a formula of long-term giving to research institutes and humanitarian entities was not the right vehicle. Because I'd become so attached to my new vision and felt my passion for making a difference come alive again, for the first time in years, I knew I had to create something new."

"Very good," interjected Kaufman. "Mrs. Gordon, is it fair to say that you agree with Mrs. Bennett? After all, joining a team is a pretty clear endorsement. Would you comment on that?" A clock in the dining room sounded, and the sonorous chimes rang twelve times. Kaufman glanced at her watch, impressed by the accuracy of what she imagined was an antique grandfather clock.

"I'd be delighted," Beate said. "First, I must say that I disagree with Minerva about the ultimate extent of the accomplishments for which the Koyne Foundation and similar organizations are responsible. Foundations are special resources. They serve as outlets for change, and they provide critical buffers against encroaching challenges that would overwhelm whole segments of the population were they to disappear. They accomplish much more than just helping society 'tread water.' Without them, society as we know it would have already drowned.

"And ... I love it that she's questioned her motives and opened herself up to creating a new way to spark ideas and solutions. When I first heard about The Contest, I had no idea what inspired it, or what decisions had prompted it to take the form that it took. I just considered it at face value and cheered.

"Here was a bold, fresh idea that had the potential to reach a global audience and inspire the broadest possible conversation. It was a stroke of genius."

"Did you decide to join right away?" asked Kaufman.

"My first reaction was: *How fun!* I can't wait to see what people will come up with. My age, as you may imagine, was the obvious reason why I didn't think of joining—at first, that is. I told myself that I've had my run, I've made my mark. But then I started reading about some of the people who were signing up. I looked more closely at the rules and requirements, and I was impressed on a deeper level. The fact that male and female input was intentionally balanced, and that each team had to draw from a broad age range, was astonishing.

"The team count was more than three quarters complete when I suddenly decided to make some calls. The very next day, I was speaking to a married couple from my synagogue that needed a woman in the oldest age bracket. I joined on the spot, and they went straight home and registered."

"You obviously beat the deadline," said Kaufman. "What number did your team receive?"

"Team 981," Beate answered. "It's my new lucky number!"

"Would you like to make a prediction about the success of the competition," she asked, looking to Minerva, "or about the approach of Team 981?" she asked, looking to Beate.

"As far as I'm concerned, we've made progress every day," began Minerva. "Every time we pass a hurdle in terms of organization, I breathe a little sigh of relief. I'd say the best measure of success is the unprecedented response we've received so far, and the fact that we've registered teams from *six* continents.

"People from every walk of life are talking about The Contest. And the conversations are just beginning. In less than a month, the first task will be called, and then we'll see the real potential that we've tapped into: 1000 communities committed to working out solutions on a grand scale. If even a small fraction come through, this could turn the tide."

"That would be wonderful," said Kaufman.

"I'm not really one to make predictions," Beate said. "Judging from our one meeting so far, my teammates are smart, generous people. We haven't had a chance to develop our strategy yet, but I think we've got as much chance as any at creating ..."

As Beate spoke, Catherine Myers noticed Felix and Carson enter the sunroom from the direction of the study. Felix paused at the doorway, but Carson took a few steps in and waved her over.

"Excuse me," Catherine whispered. She rose from her chair and followed the men around the corner and down the hallway.

"What's the problem?" she asked, peeved, imagining a minor wrinkle in the lunch menu. Carson spoke, struggling to keep his voice steady.

"I'm sorry to interrupt, Ms. Myers, but we have a situation."

"What are you talking about? What's going on?" she asked, suddenly feeling fear in the pit of her stomach.

"There's been a bomb threat," he said gravely.

"*What? Here?!*" she asked, turning instinctively in the direction of the interview.

"No, at the headquarters. The receptionist received a call to the main number at Vox Stellarum. Ms. Armstrong called us a couple of minutes ago and asked me to alert you first. She wants you to call her immediately so she can tell you what measures have been taken. The FBI has been notified, and we're to stay put until we've been told otherwise."

"That's ... that's *outrageous!*" was all Catherine could say. She hugged herself as a shiver ran down her spine. She took her silenced cell phone out of her sweater pocket and turned it on.

"When did this happen?" she asked.

"At noon."

"Do you know any other details?" she asked. Both men shook their heads as she looked at the missed call and voice-mail on her touch screen. Libby had tried to reach her at 12:05, two minutes earlier. She clicked CALL BACK.

"Libby, it's me. *What* is going on?"

"All we know is that a man called. Susan said his voice was garbled or filtered, and she couldn't understand him very clearly. He said something like, 'Beware the Ides of March—the Liberators are watching.' When Susan tried to ask him a question, he silenced her and ordered her to listen to their demands."

"Which *were?*"

"That Vox Stellarum call off it's 'destructive parade of political meddling.'"

Feeling the loathing in Libby's voice, Catherine said, "That's absurd."

"Uh-huh."

"Was there a threat attached?"

"He said, 'You have 48 hours to silence your so-called voice of the stars, or we will do it for you.' Then, according to Susan, he abruptly ended the call."

"*Jesus!*" Catherine said. She stared at the floor.

"Where is Minerva?" asked Libby.

"In the sunroom, still being interviewed. Do you think I should interrupt them?"

"No, let them finish," said Libby. "The FBI agent said that even if it's a credible threat, we're probably not in immediate danger. The bomb squad just arrived here, and they're going to search the building. Another unit is on the way to your location."

"Okay. I'll inform Minerva as soon as they're done."

Catherine turned slowly, as if in a fog, and rejoined the others in the sunroom. When Marguerite Kaufman turned off her recorder, she gave them the news.

⋅⊷⊨◉ ◉⊨⊶⋅

"Message delivered? Excellent ... Probably not. They'll squelch it, but I have some contacts that'll be able to monitor their reaction, and their countermeasures ... I agree, but no need to ramp it up until we see if it has the desired effect ... Uh-huh ... Nothing so far, but he's indicated he's making progress ... Follow through? Not yet. I propose we wait ... Right. I think we all agree with that—a wrench in the works will serve better than a strong-handed approach ... Will do."

The Watcher placed two more calls in quick succession and then lit another cigarette.

⋅⊷⊨◉ ◉⊨⊶⋅

Steven Pace lounged in the apartment, drinking coffee and eating a bagel. Rory, his roommate, had departed for a mission several days earlier, and Steven was acutely aware that his solitude was different than in times past. The friends had been deployed together many times, but it was just as common to receive different assignments in different regions. He had always felt connected though—on the same frequency. Until now.

As he got up to refill his coffee, he considered their shared space. Cluttering the third-floor suite was a grab bag of souvenirs, posters, and various knick-knacks that gave the apartment a certain feel—post-collegiate bachelor pad with a dose of soldier-of-fortune. He'd never given it much thought, but the mix of photos, surf gear, free weights, empty beer bottles, stacks of *Rolling Stone* magazines, and guitars gave him a sudden shot of nostalgia. Late night parties, all-night jam sessions, drinking contests ... poker games. He smiled wistfully.

He returned to his spot on the couch and pushed his empty plate aside, making room for his laptop, its cord snaking across the room. He scrolled through his music library and selected a playlist he hoped would help him shake his melancholy. The mood lingered. He found it strange that his new civilian status struck him as more foreign than all his exotic deployments as a recce.

It had been two weeks since he'd informed his uncle, the base commandant, of his decision to resign his commission and pursue life in the private sector. He recalled his disappointment that his uncle hadn't tried to talk him out of it. For years, their relationship had been primarily professional, both maintaining silence regarding their familial bond. Steven knew his performance had proven his worth many times, but he now felt like he needed something extra, some kind of assurance that he wasn't being put out to pasture.

If anybody could grant him this, it was his uncle, but no such consolation had come. He received the same neutral response from his unit leader. Maybe it was simply a matter of respect, for his integrity and maturity. Neither man had ventured to question his decision, but his doubt remained. Was it the warriors' code in action, defined by a respect for each man's sovereignty? Or was it the fact that his staying would have been perceived as a liability?

Worrying was getting him nowhere. He decided to go for a walk. Getting into action had a broader and more vivid meaning now that his doctor had given him the go ahead to exercise as much as he could handle.

The physical therapist had removed some of the rigid spars in his cast, and this improved his mobility significantly. With the use of his grabber tool, he changed into gym shorts and running shoes. He exited his apartment building and found that the morning traffic was tapering off. Trained to be acutely observant on the battlefield, Steven found himself enjoying the simple act of walking down the street.

Face to face with a neighborhood full of what he had to assume were "friendlies," he had to constantly relax his default mode of vigilance. The game he played with himself was to guess the identities and habits of the passersby. What were their jobs? What were their hobbies? Were they married?

He grinned when he saw his own reflection in a store front window. For a brief instant, he applied his questions to the guy in running shorts—to himself—and decided he must be active, intelligent, capable.

This led Steven to recall a chance encounter he'd had a week earlier. It had triggered a subtle invasion of new thoughts against which he wasn't sure his former self-image could survive.

"Hi, Jess. What's going on? How are you?" She was standing in the produce section of the local market.

"Steven ... Hi! Life is good ... still teaching," Jessie said. She held her hand at waste level and added, "Little ones."

"You must be brave."

She laughed. "They keep me busy. That's for sure." After some small talk, she suddenly asked, "What do you think of this big contest?"

Now, thinking back on their conversation, Steven realized he must have appeared pitifully ignorant. For fifteen minutes, he listened to Jessie speak excitedly about some American woman who was all about changing things for the better. As she went on and on about how great this thing was, he stared at the cabbages, feigning familiarity and interest.

"Why don't you consider joining us?" she asked. "It might be a nice change ... brighten your outlook."

Her playful spontaneity hit him like a ton of bricks. Before he knew what he was doing, he nodded: "I will."

When he returned home, Steven put away the groceries and immediately logged onto the Internet. He saw the deluge of entries on Vox Stellarum, Minerva Bennett, and The Contest.

So that's *what the buzz is all about!* He suddenly realized the extent to which he'd been blocking out news and current events, especially anything that reeked of human interest emotionalism. From his perspective, that was the land of the weak.

He remembered Rory asking him what was so damn interesting—he'd isolated himself in his room for several hours, glued to his computer. He'd scanned the contents of the Vox website and then become engrossed in the editorials from several major newspapers. That same day, just before midnight, Steven phoned Jessie to join the team.

Now, walking distractedly down the street, Steven questioned his decision. Arguments and counter-arguments swirled in his head. The counselor at the Base Hospital had encouraged him to relax and avoid starting anything new.

"You have one priority, Lieutenant—to heal. Take your time. Be patient."

Then he'd gone and signed up for a two-year commitment with a bunch of strangers! He wondered if it was just about getting in her pants.

But there *was* a deeper reason: his research had stirred emotions that had been buried for years. It was as if he'd found a piece to a puzzle that he'd assumed would remain incomplete.

The previous Saturday, Team 765 had held its first meeting. During their introductions, Steven acknowledged he didn't have any grand vision of how things should be—but a very clear vision of how they should *not* be. This prompted the eldest team member, a man in his seventies, to comment.

"The man who can let go of the past holds the keys to the future." At the time, the mystical nuance was lost on him.

Crossing the street to return to his apartment building, it occurred to him that the man had once been a soldier. His insight wasn't based on anything the man had shared, but on the uncanny way he had regarded Steven—with a simple look of understanding, devoid of pity.

He felt relief as he realized he'd begun to loosen his grip on his former life, and he caught a fleeting glimpse of an unknown future.

Chapter 16

THE RENTAL CAR pulled away from the county airport, and Catherine, Libby, and James entered the highway in silence. Within two miles of the simple terminal, they were in the countryside. Catherine realized their conversation had been minimal since earlier in the day, since they had boarded Minerva's jet.

The assignment had come late the day before, on the heels of the bomb threat and a push for heightened security. These new developments, along with the rest of their crowded agendas, wore on them as they drove into a light Appalachian drizzle. Minerva, still recuperating from her exhaustion and no doubt stressed from the security issue, had dispatched them to follow up with one of their prospects for the job of enlisting the panel of judges.

The "promising lead" felt anything but that. Catherine had pressed Minerva for details, and all she got was, "I have a feeling he's the man for the job."

Because limbo on this priority threatened the timeline of the competition, Minerva had abruptly ordered them to drop everything and make arrangements to meet this candidate face to face. Her cryptic details did little to assuage their doubts, and an air of futility permeated the rental car.

"Catherine, you've got the address, right?" Libby asked, sitting in the front passenger seat scowling at the weather.

"For the third time, yes. *Relax!*" said Catherine, from the back seat.

"We need to enter it in the GPS. Call it out." Catherine did so, and Libby typed it in.

"I don't think the weather's going to cooperate," said Catherine, viewing a weather app on her iPad. "This light rain and fog is just the beginning of what looks like a pretty big front."

"Great," said James, who was driving.

Within minutes, large rain drops drummed against the windshield.

"So, what's the deal with this guy?" he asked.

"Minerva told us we needed to follow up on her prospect," said Catherine. The exasperation in her voice matched the look on Libby's face. "She wasn't sold on the others."

"I gathered that," James said, "but why this face-to-face visit? Why didn't she just hire him on the spot or have him come to us?"

"We don't know," said Libby. "He must have put up some kind of resistance—told her he'd think about it. Who knows? It's our job to sign him up."

Catherine pulled up his profile and admired the photo, wondering when it was taken. "He's been retired for six years. Even if he once had connections, it doesn't seem likely he could have maintained them."

"I agree," Libby said, "but Minerva must have picked up on something."

They lapsed into silence again. With only three people and light carry-on items, the car somehow felt crowded. Personal demons hovered, almost tangibly, above the musty velour of the seats and the ugly dashboard of the maroon four-door sedan.

The countryside was gorgeous and wet. A well-defined layer of stratus clouds gave way to smeary tendrils of low clouds as the car moved up a long incline. The weather worsened as they entered the foothills, and it became obvious that their attire—business casual—was miserably ill-suited. Catherine looked at her pantsuit and her leather flats and wished that she could reach into her leather satchel and pull out some gardening overalls and rubber boots.

Other than the rasp of tires slicing through puddles on the highway, the only sounds providing relief against the moody silence came from the GPS: "In one quarter mile, turn left." James did so. It was the left-hand fork of a barely maintained county road. Limited visibility barely gave him time to swerve around potholes as they came into view.

The farther they drove, the more the roadside growth appeared to have the right-of-way. The condition of the road worsened, and returning to the airport suddenly appealed to Catherine. As if to veto that notion, the road narrowed into a one-lane ribbon of mud with no turnouts.

A gap in the underbrush offered a momentary vista, and it appeared they were gliding a hundred feet above a misty ocean of treetops. Any enjoyment was short-lived though, for the right rear wheel suddenly lost traction at the road's edge. The engine revved sickeningly, and Catherine—imagining they were about to plunge over the side—didn't breathe again until James managed to regain control and proceed at least a hundred yards down the road.

"*Jesus!* I feel like I just had a shot of espresso."

"Or two," Libby said with gritted teeth.

"Sorry!" James apologized. "This thing handles more like a boat than a car."

"Just ... don't let it happen again," said Libby. "I'm feeling a bit—"

"You okay?" asked Catherine. Libby, gripping the door handle with her right hand, held her left hand on her tummy.

"I'm okay," she said after taking a few deliberate breaths.

"I'd like to think we're getting closer," said James, "but it feels like we're just getting farther away. Why in the hell would anybody choose to live out here?!"

The Blue Ridge Parkway was somewhere nearby, but the GPS seemed to be zeroed in on archaic designations and state highway numbers that nobody had bothered to post. Libby, who had given up her responsibilities as co-pilot shortly after they left the airport, turned to look at Catherine in the backseat.

"How confident are you of the address? We're in the middle of fucking *nowhere!*"

Catherine smiled at Libby's language; it was a good sign—she was feeling better.

Lost and frustrated, the three had no choice but to listen to the soundtrack of the wheels as they churned and sprayed. Behind them, a twin wake of tire treads whipping through a pancake batter of mud.

"You will reach your destination in one-point-five miles," stated the GPS.

"It's about time!" exclaimed Libby.

With a countdown every quarter of a mile, the robotic voice seemed to grow giddy with its news. Through the drizzle and mist, a guardrail appeared on the right side of the road, hinting that civilization had not receded altogether. In the final half mile, the road leveled out and ended with an old wooden bridge that spanned a swollen creek. A simple rural mailbox and a "Posted: No Trespassing" sign were the only pieces of evidence that they had arrived.

James steered the mud-splattered rental across the bridge, which was constructed of massive wooden beams covered in electric green mold. They were reassured by the sight of a pickup truck parked to the side of a cabin, smoke rising from the chimney.

"Somebody's here. *Thank God!*" said Catherine as she unbuckled her seatbelt.

The three exited the car, slowly, checking their footing amidst the puddles and sprays of grass. They made for the cover of the front porch that ran the length of the cabin.

Several chairs and a coffee table stood well back from the overhang of the tin roof. One chair was obviously preferred, as evidenced by a well-used ottoman and a faded seat cushion. The adjacent side table held an ashtray, a pipe rack, a tin of tobacco, and several books. A couch with dry, but discolored, cushions was against the wall farther down the porch. Next to it were two large stainless steel bowls, both empty, and a third, which was ceramic, full of water.

"He's got dogs," Catherine said, "but I don't hear any barking."

"That's strange," Libby said.

"Judging from the size of those bowls, they're—"

"You people are a little off course, aren't you?"

Catherine jerked so quickly that she slipped and almost fell off the porch into the flower bed. She stared at a man who stood on the end of the porch, instantly recognizing Malcolm Conroy from his profile. He walked slowly toward them, his inscrutable gaze revealing nothing.

"This is my property," he said brusquely, now standing by the front door. "State your business."

He wore a brimmed hat and a dark green waterproof field jacket over a plaid long-sleeved shirt, heavy canvas hunting pants, and camouflaged rubber boots—the perfect outfit for moving about in a rain-soaked forest on a chilly day. He took off his hat and unbuttoned his jacket, but showed no inclination to offer his hand or properly greet them.

Catherine stepped forward. "Mr. Conroy, we had no intention of trespassing. We're here to speak with you. I'm Catherine Myers, from New York City. These are my colleagues from the Vox Stellarum Foun—"

"Ahh ... so she sent you people anyway," he said, dismissing Catherine's niceties. He spoke with a strong, clear voice and had the commanding presence of a man who was used to giving orders. As Catherine's eyes adjusted to the dim light under the porch, she studied his features, suddenly doubting the accuracy of his bio, which listed his age as sixty-seven. Except for the gray of his short-cropped hair, he looked considerably younger.

"When I spoke with Mrs. Bennett yesterday," Conroy said, "I told her I wasn't interested in the job. She offered to send a couple of her senior staff members ... to 'discuss matters.' I told her not to bother."

"That doesn't make any sense," said Libby. "She gave us your name and address, and we were expect—"

Conroy cut her off: "Look—it's clear you're just following orders, but you're wasting your time. I'm retired and prefer to be left alone. Now, if you'll just get back in your car, tell your boss I'm not interested." He pointed toward the road.

Minerva's team stood on the porch, awkwardly, looking back and forth at one another.

Catherine persevered. "Sir, Mrs. Bennett obviously thinks you have some special talents and resources we could benefit from. But even if that's true—that you're in a position to help us, you appear to be invested in staying hidden away. I guess we ought to respect that."

She was speaking from a place of already having failed, and therefore from a place of having nothing to lose.

"The way I see it, there are two options. Either you run us off, which you have almost succeeded in doing, or you can invite us in and hear us out."

She had been looking back and forth at her colleagues, but now she fixed her eyes directly on him, giving him a taste of his own medicine.

"Since you've already made up your mind, you've got nothing to lose by hearing what we have to say. We'll answer any questions you ask and listen to whatever you have to say. Quite frankly, I've got nothing better to do at the moment, and ... if I'm correct ... neither do you."

Conroy held her gaze for a long moment; his stoic countenance softened into a faint smile. He regarded her colleagues and then looked back at Catherine.

"It seems that Mrs. Bennett's persistence has rubbed off on you." He grinned. "And you've given me reason to regret my lack of hospitality, which is one thing, at least, that I can remedy."

Conroy grabbed his hat and escorted them into the cabin. "Make yourselves at home. There's a bathroom down the hall, second door on the left."

Leaving the door ajar, he immediately exited again. Catherine lingered by the window and watched him curiously. He stepped to the edge of the porch and, in a low, clear voice, issued a command, as if to the forest or the clouds. "Apollo, Mercury, come!"

A moment later, from opposite sides of the property, like wraiths from the shadows, two large and powerful dogs trotted silently to a position directly in front of him. They were the most magnificent German shepherds she had ever seen.

With the barest of motions, perhaps a nod or a raised eyebrow, both dogs sat as one. They were still at full attention, eyes locked on their master, posture exquisite. Catherine imagined they were regarding Conroy with respect, even pride. While not a single word had been spoken, man to beast, she had the sense that she had eavesdropped on a private conversation.

Just as she was about to turn to her colleagues and wave them over to witness the bizarre interchange, it was over. With another silent command, Conroy released them. It must have been some equivalent of "At ease, soldiers," and they instantly transformed into a couple of big, friendly dogs. They pranced excitedly on the pathway leading from the driveway, shook the rain from their drenched coats, and then hopped up on the porch behind their master.

Catherine moved away from the window with a touch of embarrassment as Conroy walked back inside with his dogs in tow. The cabin filled with the sounds of paws tapping on the hardwood floor and powerful tails batting against the door.

"*There* they are," exclaimed Libby. "What gorgeous dogs!"

She immediately came forward and knelt down to greet them. Catherine watched in disbelief as the animals, which she now knew were superlatively trained attack dogs, wiggle-waggled their bodies in such a friendly way. One came over, and she scratched it behind the ears. James kept his distance, seated on a barstool next to the kitchen counter.

"Don't you want to pet the dogs?" Catherine asked.

"Hell, no! I don't want slobber and hair all over my clothes."

Conroy took off his jacket and hung it by the door, next to several other pieces of foul weather gear.

"Now that you're here, you might as well get comfortable. You can hang your coats in the closet." He pointed to the far corner of the large, open living area. As the three travelers slipped out of their jackets, Conroy walked toward a nook and opened the louvered doors, revealing a well-stocked wet bar. He grabbed four glasses and set them on the counter.

"First things first. Who would like a drink?" Catherine noticed that, for a man who lived in such seclusion, he was by no means without modern comforts.

The four of them moved to the area around the fireplace and settled onto the matching chairs and sofa. At first, the décor gave the appearance of a bachelor suite, purchased at a Pottery Barn clearance sale. But like other first impressions in this unusual outpost, Catherine began to realize she needed to look a little closer. The Italian hand-sewn leather cushions, which caressed her body in a way that was intoxicating, had been selected by someone with rarified tastes.

Several paintings adorned the walls, muted colors with mostly rural scenes of Americana gave way to hunting themes, and scattered among these were some trophies. A pheasant in flight, a head-mount of an impressive white-tail buck, and a large rainbow trout gave one the sense of a sportsman who valued quality over quantity. Catherine had to admit that, for a reclusive bachelor, Conroy's home felt warm and cozy. Seeing his dogs settle down near the fireplace made her smile.

For several minutes, they engaged in small talk. Catherine found herself enjoying the conversation. She noted the twinkle in Conroy's eyes as he talked about his dogs. When Libby changed the subject to Vox Stellarum, his expression and tone instantly hardened.

"Shall we get down to business, then?" he asked.

As if sensing that his guests were still adapting to the situation, he said, "I have you at a disadvantage. I know more about you than you know about me. As Ms. Myers pointed out, you have little to lose by asking me whatever you want. I'll be as open-minded as I can, given the circumstances." He turned to Catherine. "Well?"

Catherine looked at Libby, deferring to her role as head of their delegation.

"Go ahead," Libby said to Catherine. "You got us in the door."

"Mr. Conroy," Catherine began, "I know very little about you—only what I was able to glean from your on-line bio and a couple of articles about your work in the Defense Department and the State Department. You have an impressive background—military service, Harvard law degree, high-level service in several government agencies just below cabinet level posts ... but then you dropped out of the public eye about six years ago. Is this basically accurate?"

"Yes."

"Your first post with the government was Under Secretary of Defense for Technology ..."

"For Acquisition, Technology, and Logistics," Conroy offered.

"Thank you. Were you recruited for that position?"

"Yes."

"On what basis?" she asked.

"I studied engineering in college and was a member of the ROTC. I enlisted in the Air Force and trained as a fighter pilot."

"What kind of aircraft?" asked James, perking up slightly.

"Fighter jets," he answered.

"How long were you in?" asked Catherine.

"Six years ... just as the Vietnam conflict was ending."

"What did you do after that?"

"I went to work for Raytheon, an aerospace firm with military contracts."

"Did you work on design?"

"No. I was hired to negotiate new contracts with the DOD and the Pentagon."

"I'm going to assume you were successful, Mr. Conroy, so ... why did you leave?"

"I had achieved my objectives."

"Which were?"

"Knowledge, experience ... adventure," he answered.

"What about money?" asked Libby. "Raytheon is known for its lucrative military contracts. Didn't that interest you?"

"Not primarily, though I like to be well compensated."

"What attracted you then?" asked Libby.

"Expertise," Conroy said. He leaned forward and took a sip of his drink.

"What was it, exactly, that you wanted to become expert in?" asked Catherine.

"Ahh, now we're getting somewhere," he said. "I wanted to learn more about the nature of power ... who has it, how to wield it, and so forth."

Libby set her glass down and asked, "You were after *power* then?"

"No," he said simply.

"Then what?"

"What was I *after?*" Catherine wondered if he were intentionally goading her friend, for she was obviously getting more impatient with every exchange. Just as Libby was on the verge of prompting him, Conroy continued.

"If I had to say one thing, I suppose it would be freedom."

"*Freedom?*" asked James. "Do you mean for the *United States?*"

"No. I mean personal freedom."

"Do you mind explaining what you mean by that?" asked Catherine.

"Not at all. Freedom is a function of knowledge—about ability and opportunity. By joining an organization that would prepare me to understand and acquire these, I would put myself in an optimal position to benefit accordingly."

"So, it wasn't the security and freedom of the nation you were after, but your own selfish ends?" pressed Libby.

"Are you implying it must be one or the other?" Conroy asked tersely.

"I'm just trying to understand how you operate. It seems to me you went about your career choices in a very intentional and plotting manner, always looking out for yourself first."

Expecting him to be insulted, Catherine was surprised to see Conroy smile and nod.

"That's correct. If you understand what you just said, then I thank you for the compliment."

Libby and James looked at one another and shrugged. Conroy continued.

"Whether you admit it or not, everybody looks out for number one. The problem is that you seem to believe that this is a vice, whereas I believe it's a virtue. A minute ago, Mr. Ruhle wondered if I were concerned for the freedom of the United States, and, of course, I am. You don't join the armed forces or work for the Department of Defense without holding that as a high priority.

"I believe the nation is served by honoring the interests of its citizens, not the other way around. Unfortunately, my perspective has fallen out of fashion. You three are from a younger generation—one that values the community over the individual. You think in terms of the health of the collective, happy to ignore the rights of the individual when convenient. I see things from the other end. When the freedom and sovereignty of the individual is acknowledged and respected, the community benefits."

"How can you say that?" Libby asked. "We work for a foundation that's all about helping people—people who've been abused, victimized, marginalized—people whose rights have been ignored."

"That's *just* what I mean, Ms. Armstrong. You go after classes of people, trumpeting that we must all endure yet another set of rules to handle the abusive plight of certain special cases. There was a time, though it's hard to believe nowadays, that we were a nation of individuals who supported one another by simply being responsible and accountable."

This last point confounded Catherine. There was something about his views which resonated with her, but his arrogance was offensive. Debating him was pointless, besides the fact that he had an impressive command of certain historical facts and—

It suddenly occurred to her that Conroy had used James's and Libby's last names, even though they hadn't been fully introduced. *What else does this son of a bitch know about us?*

Outside the windows, the rain increased to a full downpour. Distant thunder had drawn much closer, and the hiss of the fire was now drowned out by the sheets of rain.

Catherine continued. "You stayed with the company as long as you felt it worth your while, and then you entered law school. What were you hoping to accomplish with this move?"

"I'd been involved in numerous contract negotiations, and I was always running up against men who seemed to hold the upper hand by virtue of a superior knowledge of the legal system. I reasoned that studying the law would put me on a level playing field with these people."

"What did you focus on?"

"Constitutional law, but then I branched into patent law and intellectual property."

"What drove that decision?"

"Mostly my personal experience and my engineering background. I had a good grasp of technology, especially military applications. I figured that studying the Constitution would help me reintroduce a little justice."

"You were interested in *justice?*" Libby asked in a sarcastic tone.

"Of course. Still am."

Catherine shot a glance at Libby and continued.

"You then practiced law for several years? Who were your clients?"

"Mostly Fortune 500 companies—ones with aerospace and military contracts: 3M, General Dynamics, Lockheed Martin, Dow Chemical."

"I take it you made good money in those years?" Catherine asked.

"Certainly."

"That must have been a pretty sweet arrangement. What motivated you to leave that and join the Department of Defense?"

"Contrary to what Ms. Armstrong seems to be imagining, I was not so fully focused on my personal wealth as to ignore the bigger picture. Of course, I had to deal with politicians and off-the-book lobbyists who did."

"What do you mean?" Libby asked.

"I mean some of those people didn't give a damn about budgets, or taxes, or the prudence of staying within appropriations guidelines. They were after signatures and a share of the deal. I, on the other hand, saw the government take on ridiculous commitments to buy marginal, sometimes even obsolete, technology. Even when the technology was decent, I witnessed how we would routinely—and secretly—pay premiums to the shareholders. I wanted to see if I could clean up the process. There was plenty of money to be made, without the graft and the lies."

"Were you able to make a difference?" asked James.

"In the beginning, I thought so. After a while, I realized I was swimming against the tide. What progress I may have made was diluted by entrenched policy mandates from above."

"If I recall correctly," said Catherine, "you moved to the State Department, as Under Secretary for International Affairs. And then you served as Under Secretary of Commerce?"

She felt herself growing impatient with the interview. She was hoping that something would emerge in the way of leverage, something to grab Conroy's allegiance ... to something bigger. But he seemed cloaked in an air of self-contained superiority, which thinly covered a distant resignation and, she sensed, sadness.

He replied, "That's correct." His tone said: *What's your point?*

"Mr. Conroy, I hope you understand the questions my colleagues and I have been asking have been designed to satisfy our need to know that you really are the man described in those biographical summaries. More to the point, that you are someone who could succeed in the important task for which Mrs. Bennett approached you."

"In fact, I do. And I understand a lot more than that. For instance, I understand that merely confirming I am who I say I am doesn't move me any closer to considering working for your foundation."

"And why is that?" Libby asked, unable to hide her antagonism.

"For several reasons, the most important of which is that I don't believe in your project."

"Mr. Conroy, I find that hard to believe," James said. "How can you not believe in making the world a better place? In finding solutions to major problems?"

"Even if I were to grant you that those were goals worth pursuing, I would say that you people are going about it all wrong. Minerva Bennett's methodology is so pie-in-the-sky and scatter-brained that it won't amount to more than a couple of months of fading headlines. And eventually, a lot of money wasted on random promotion."

"In your *opinion*," Libby interjected.

"Of course, it's my opinion," Conroy said derisively, "but your boss must think pretty highly of it to bother sending you three all this way after being turned down. Look, I've answered your questions, and I've tried to imagine the possibility of reversing my decision and helping you. I'm afraid I just don't see it."

Libby and James looked at one another and sighed, but Catherine wasn't ready to admit defeat. "Mr. Conroy, if there *were* something that we could say, or *do*, that would change your mind, what would it be?"

"Now there's an interesting tactic, Ms. Myers—fold your hand and hope for mercy."

"If you want to put it that way, sure. It's pretty clear that we're not getting through to you, so ... *what the hell!*"

Meanwhile, the storm showed no sign of letting up. Lightning flashed outside the windows. Catherine decided that, despite Conroy's arrogance and smugness, his cabin was shelter from the storm, and she was grudgingly grateful.

For almost a full minute, Conroy looked at his dogs, apparently pondering her question.

"It might be interesting to note," he finally proceeded, "that I never heard that approach in my years with Uncle Sam. The government is a monolithic beast that can't be anything but what it is. I know that now.

"Vox Stellarum, on the other hand, is a private foundation. Minerva Bennett created it to serve her own vision of salvation. The problem is not that I don't agree with her agenda, it is that I don't believe in salvation."

"*Salvation* is your term, Mr. Conroy, not ours," Catherine said. "As far as I'm concerned, The Contest is designed to shift people's thinking, away from tragedy and victimhood toward solution and hope. But whatever you call it, are you saying that you can't imagine being a part of it? Is there anything we embody that you actually oppose? Or is it simply that you see us as naive?"

"That's just for starters, Ms. Myers. It's beyond naive. Your contest is just the latest attempt to promise hope where none exists. At least Minerva Bennett has originality on her side. Beyond that, though, I believe she's playing with forces that she can't fathom. That little incident with the bomb threat is just the beginning."

"Mr. Conroy," said Catherine, looking at him as intensely as she dared, "you don't strike me as somebody who would be scared away by a prank call, which is what the FBI determined it was." She knew her ploy—questioning his courage—was risky, but she gambled that it might push him off the fence to accept their offer.

Conroy stared into his glass of scotch. The others waited for his next pronouncement, but none came. He seemed to be done. Lost in thought, or memory, Conroy's jaw was set.

Did I go too far with that? Catherine wondered, suddenly regretting it.

Conroy's dogs, with their sixth sense of loyalty, must have felt their master's emotional shift and looked up. First one and then the other walked over and placed his head in his master's lap. They looked at him plaintively. Conroy held the dogs tenderly and regarded them with an appreciative smile. His reverie broken, he turned back to his guests.

"I'm sorry if I've wasted your time," he said. "My answer is still no."

Chapter 17

MINERVA STOOD ON her terrace, as if on the rampart of a medieval castle. She desperately wanted to experience the usual infusion of inspiration and pleasure from looking out over the city, but she felt besieged. The bomb threat, delivered so cryptically the day before, had put her in a serious funk.

The wave of recent success and celebrity she had begun to enjoy seemed now to evaporate under the influence of an insidious foe, lurking in the shadows, waiting to inflict mortal harm to her benign domain.

She recalled Sam Minton's words of warning: "Minerva, you're too trusting. Such people don't play by your rules or share your integrity." Though he'd been referring to the relatively harmless crime of slander, she couldn't help but imagine some evil commander issuing orders to his henchman to rape, pillage, defile, and enslave. Such was her flight into an irrational state of hopelessness.

How can we fight this?

Never a fan of westerns, she nevertheless invoked her idealized hero figure—an implacable sheriff walking into the center of a deserted main street, challenging a gang of outlaws to come from their hiding places and face him like men. This reminded her, suddenly, of her late son Alan. He loved John Wayne with a passion, never missing a chance to see one of his movies on TV. With his little brother and neighborhood friends, he would always insist on playing the hero, whatever the Duke's part had been, often combining several roles into one, making himself virtually invincible in his make-believe quest for justice.

Though it was pleasantly warm outside, Minerva hugged herself close against the chill of fear. Seeing Alan's dauntless smile in her mind's eye, she smiled wistfully and asked: *Would you ride out to meet this danger?*

She knew that he would ... that he, in fact, did. But this was no consolation as she stood in the present, looking out over Manhattan. This was a different world than the simple cowboys and Indians morality of 1960's Hollywood dramas.

To shake the bitter taste of her gloomy reverie, she turned to walk back inside. *Stop worrying—get into action!* she scolded herself. She reached for the phone to call Libby and Catherine when she remembered that they were out of the office on their special mission. It occurred to her that she was peeved—they hadn't checked in yet.

⋅◦⟊◉ ◉⟊◦⋅

Libby, Catherine, and James drove across the bridge, disappointment mingling with the anger of having wasted most of their day on a wild goose chase.

The memory of the slippery conditions still fresh in her mind, Catherine sat brooding in the back seat as James eased out of the driveway and along the level portion of the road leading to and from Conroy's property. Within yards of passing the crest of the hill, it became obvious there was almost a complete lack of traction. The car began to slide.

"What are you *doing?!*" yelled Libby. "We're going too fast!"

"No shit!" yelled James. "The brakes aren't working."

The car moved straight downhill, then side-slipped toward the ditch on the right. He whipped the wheel in the opposite direction. This caused them to veer toward the left ditch.

At a speed of twenty miles per hour, the sedan scraped and bounced off the end of a short section of guardrail. The left rear panel was gouged and the fender torn as the car pivoted and spun into the ditch backwards. The vehicle came to an abrupt halt in a spongy mass of undergrowth.

For several seconds, they remained frozen. No windows were broken, no airbags were deployed, but they were obviously stuck. They let out a collective groan.

"Are you guys okay?" James asked after cussing under his breath.

"I think so," answered Catherine. Libby nodded and relaxed her grip on the door handle.

The engine was still running, so James put the car in park and turned off the ignition.

"Great. Just great," said Libby. "Now what?"

"Even if I could maneuver out of the ditch, which I doubt, it would be crazy," James said. "We're not going anywhere." The peaceful solitude of the mountainside seemed to magnify the only sound for miles—the drumming of the rain on the roof and the windshield.

"I'm not getting any signal on my cell phone. We can't even call a tow truck," said Catherine. After a few seconds, she added dejectedly, "You know what that means."

Libby turned around and looked at Catherine in the back seat. The inevitable had occurred to her in the same instant.

"We gotta go back to that bastard's house."

It took them five minutes to convince each other that there was no option but to return to the cabin. They exited the car and stepped into the thick mud, their expletives almost drowned out by the rain. It took Catherine less than one minute to slip and fall in the mud, ruining her umbrella. She threw it in the bushes angrily. It took only a few minutes for Libby and James to follow suit.

By the time they reached the *No Trespassing* sign, they were mud-caked and soaked. They trudged across the wooden bridge and slupped their way up the driveway. From a distance, Catherine saw the dogs peering through the porch windows. They didn't even bother to bark.

Catherine and Libby searched for sticks and patches of grass to scrape off as much mud as they could and to somehow look more presentable than was possible. James sprawled on the ground as he tried to use the grass as a washcloth.

Conroy had seen their approach and opened the door. They didn't notice him until he burst into laughter.

"Good grief!" he cried. "You should see yourselves."

Catherine glared at Conroy, but his lighthearted expression dissolved her anguish, and she found herself grinning.

"I'll give you three chances to guess what happened, and the first two don't count."

Conroy looked them up and down. "Is the car in bad shape?" he asked with a straight face.

"Not too bad," snapped James, "except that it's stuck in a fucking ditch!"

"Why don't you take off your shoes and coats. I'll get you some towels."

Wet to the bone, the stranded trio migrated to the fireplace. Conroy added a few logs and then fetched an armful of towels and some old blankets. Meanwhile, the dogs sniffed curiously at their legs and feet.

"Once you warm up, try to relax. I can put some of your clothes in the dryer if you like, and you can wrap up in a blanket until they're dry."

Conroy's mood was buoyant. He seemed to enjoy being in control and issuing orders. Only when he produced a tray with a teapot and mugs, did the stranded travelers finally sit.

"Thank you," said Catherine softly, grasping a mug with both hands.

Conroy stood by the fire, absentmindedly scratching one of his dogs behind the ears. He looked out the window and noted the color of the sky and the movement of the clouds.

"The rain is letting up ... probably stop within the next hour. I could give you a ride to the airport, and you could call a tow truck to retrieve your rental car tomorrow.

"Would we all fit?" asked Libby. She could see that it was just a two-door pickup, with a bench seat.

"It would be tight, but I think so."

"How well would it handle?" asked James. "Not to doubt your driving ability, Mr. Conroy, but it was pretty scary going down that hill. There was no traction whatever." The women looked at James and nodded, apprehension returning to their faces.

"It would probably be exciting," Conroy acknowledged.

Libby spoke. "Mr. Conroy, your offer is ... I have to say ... I don't ... I don't think I could handle that road again ... in the rain, I mean."

"I see ... Well, it looks like you're my guests for the evening. The road will be much firmer in the morning."

"Thank you, Mr. Conroy," Libby said, obviously relieved. "I'm sorry we've ruined your peace and quiet. I appreciate your hospitality."

"It's quite all right," he said. "We'll just to have to make the best of things. I hope you like venison."

Several hours later, dirty clothes and towels were out of the washer and drier, and the travelers began to look somewhat human again. As Conroy prepared dinner, the guests made phone calls and looked around.

After alerting the pilots of their predicament, Catherine sat by the fireplace and petted the dog with the darker coat, brown with a smoky sheen. He gazed at her and panted, tongue cradled in a set of perfect white teeth.

"He likes you," commented Conroy from the kitchen.

"How can you tell?" she asked.

"He's relaxed. If he didn't like you, he'd close his mouth or growl."

"What's his name?" Catherine had heard him summon them earlier, but she didn't know which was which.

"Apollo."

"And this one?" Libby asked as she walked over to pet the other dog. He was a lighter shade of brown with only hints of the darker overlay.

"Mercury," Conroy answered.

"Interesting names. Greek gods?" Libby asked affably, obviously trying to offset the animosity she had demonstrated earlier.

"Roman actually, but their names are only indirectly related to mythology. I originally acquired three pups from the same litter, but one died. His name was—"

"Gemini?" Catherine guessed suddenly.

"Yes," said Conroy, impressed.

"How in the *hell* did you know that?" asked Libby.

"I'm a bit of a geek. Plus, I noticed a photograph on the shelf," Catherine said, pointing, "signed by all seven of the original astronauts—the Mercury Seven."

Conroy stared at Catherine as if evaluating an opponent. "Hmm ... I'll bet you're good at Trivial Pursuit."

"You definitely wouldn't want to play against me," she said, giving him an *I dare you to take me on* look.

Seeing that Libby was still confused, Conroy explained. "There were three stages of the American manned-flight program at NASA: Mercury, Gemini, and Apollo. Gemini isn't a god, by the way; it's a constellation."

"Castor and Pollux—twins who were mythical warriors," said James, demonstrating his own nerdy bent.

Shortly, the four of them sat down to dinner. The conversation varied widely, and everybody seemed relieved that there was no agenda. Stories flowed as the liquor poured.

Catherine asked Conroy about his property, how long he had lived there, and if he had designed the house. Libby asked him about politicians and celebrities. James asked about military weapons, the space program, and any close scrapes he might have been in.

The more Catherine got to know Malcolm Conroy, the more intrigued she became. She wanted to explore his personal life and find out if he'd ever been married, but James kept asking him about his air force experience.

"What about secret missions in Cambodia or Laos?" asked James.

"Come on, James," Catherine teased. "What's with all the morbid questions? With you men, it's either spaceships and lasers, or death and destruction."

"I don't mind." Conroy smiled. "The answer is no. Those missions took place—it's part of the public record, but they were mostly bombing runs: B-52s. I flew all my sorties against the official enemy, though some of our objectives were questionable."

"Such as?" James asked.

"I'll never know for sure, but there were times when we were given what appeared to be non-military targets: villages for example, controlled by the Viet Cong. That was fine, but there were probably innocent civilians too.

Sometimes we targeted dense forests with no sign of a living soul. I'm glad I never had to see the results close up.

"If I had to do it over, I might approach things differently. Of course, that's impossible ..." He took a sip of his drink, and the visitors waited for him to continue.

"We never really accomplished what most of us were there to do. We were told about communism and the Domino Effect, and how we were putting a stop to it on behalf of the West. I believed it too, for many years.

"Our efforts merely put off the inevitable. No matter what we threw at them, the enemy dug in a little deeper and became even more determined."

"If it was ultimately a waste to get involved in Vietnam," Libby asked, "what do you think about our ongoing military actions?"

"They're all a waste of resources, not to mention lives. Uncle Sam is still running the same program. There's very little anybody can do about it. One thing I've learned, though, it's not about what I think. It's about policy. It's about what the President decides, and what his advisors think ... and what *they* think the constituents want."

"But that can change!" said Catherine. "Eventually the anti-war protesters won the day, and the President ordered the troops home."

Conroy shook his head. "You're talking like an idealist. Times have changed, and the enemy has changed. The President no longer needs Congress's endorsement to send troops into faraway places; he only needs to define a new threat and then declare a state of emergency.

"I've seen how it works, up close, and it's not pretty. The Pentagon makes decisions based on what the administration believes the herd wants. Political scientists call it *groupthink*. But giving it a clever name doesn't make it more palatable." He sipped his drink.

"Policy decisions are driven by financial motives, the lucrative results of which then breed loyal campaign donors, and the cycle repeats. These decisions, which usually have long-term consequences, are based on short-term gains for a select few. The system is corrupt. There's nothing to be done about it ... except maybe take advantage of it."

Catherine suddenly realized why Bob Godfrey had put this man's name on their list: they spoke the same cynical language. She wondered about the extent to which each man had helped enrich the other, and at what expense to everybody else.

"By the way," said Catherine, "I *am* an idealist. What's the alternative? Being a realist? How realistic is it when so many of our policies backfire?"

"Now you're being simplistic. It's much more complicated than you think."

Catherine was enjoying the exchange. She took the bait.

"I know there are dozens of decisions that go into each new piece of foreign policy, but that doesn't mean we can't judge it as a failure, especially when it happens time and time again. I'd say it's unrealistic to commit such a huge part of our budget to fighting wars and attempting all this nation building. Not only do we inevitably fail, as you acknowledged, but we provoke resentment around the world. And we dig ourselves further into debt with every new campaign."

"Ahh ... another sign of the idealist," Conroy said, "... expecting things to be logical. What if things aren't as clear as you make them out to be—in hindsight? Besides, I would venture to say that your facts are incomplete. My experience has been that the public rarely gets the whole story, and what they do get is filtered and watered down. The mainstream media are in bed with the ones pulling the strings. They toe the party line in order to obtain high-level access and to get their press cards punched.

"And for their trouble, they get to help control the flow of information. You know ... it just occurred to me that the media are like the member nations of OPEC. Whenever possible, they regulate the content and the timing of so-called news to keep the viewers hungry for more. It's no wonder they've got the public eating out of their hands. They spin things to get the majority to endorse the next initiative. Classic propaganda.

"Because you're trying to change the way things work, you idealists are always frustrated. You keep overlooking the rules."

"*Rules?* What are you talking about?" asked Libby.

"In law school, I had a professor who used to tell us about what he called the 'rules of the game.' Sometimes he even called them the 'facts of life.' He was a tough son of a bitch. Nobody liked him, but his classes were packed. He kept us on the edge of our seats 'cause he challenged us to think. One of his rules was: If you're smart enough to see the truth, then you're smart enough to take advantage."

"That's a pretty selfish view," Catherine said. "What was the course? *Backstabbing 101?*"

"Cute," Conroy said, grinning at Catherine. He turned to Libby and added, "Another rule was: Don't beat your head against the wall—Walk around it! Of course, these don't make sense unless you apply 'em in the right way. My point is that the government-media alliance is a fact that we're not going to change, no matter how much we want to. The government needs the appearance of approval, and that's what the media supply. It's all smoke and mirrors.

"Drug lords, warlords, overlords ... terrorists, communists, fascists. You name it. The media produce the government-approved cover stories and insert just enough facts to give the appearance of a valid concern. We, the American public, will be safe as long as we write the checks. And the result? The military-industrial complex that Eisenhower warned us about is funded for yet another term.

"Do we close foreign bases? Hell no! We restock the existing ones and open new ones. We keep our carriers parked in the Straits of Hormuz, the Bay of Bengal, the South China Sea. Shit, even the Gulf of Mexico, for crying out loud!"

Catherine realized that Conroy was drunk. She leaned forward and was about to point out that at least half of what he'd just said supported her view, their view, but then decided against it. As she reflected on her antagonism earlier in the day, she decided to invoke his professor's rule: she would walk around the wall of Conroy's obstinacy. She sat back and sighed.

When the conversation eventually played out, Conroy rose to clear the table. Catherine helped while the others retreated to the chairs by the fireplace.

After cleaning up, he led the women to the guest room upstairs; for James, he tossed a pillow and a blanket on the couch.

⋯⊨◉ ◉⊨⋯

The next morning, just as the sun was rising over the Blue Ridge Mountains, they piled into Conroy's pickup. It was a tight fit, but they didn't complain. They were glad to be on their way. The dogs rode in the back.

The truck descended the hill with no problem. The road had firmed up and was no longer an amusement park ride. Conroy drove in silence.

Catherine, pressed up against Conroy, enjoyed the spectacular vistas that the weather had denied them the day before.

"What a gorgeous place," she said as they carved their way around the ridge and descended through a tree-lined lane.

"Yes. It is," said Conroy solemnly.

After twenty minutes, he turned onto the main highway, and they began the long shallow decline to the valley.

Self-conscious of the way she'd been staring at his hands, of the way she'd been stealing glances at his face—his mouth, Catherine suddenly blurted, "How often do you make this drive?"

"Once or twice a week, to run errands and get supplies," he answered evenly.

"Too bad it wasn't this pretty, yesterday," she said, "You would have been spared all this trouble."

"Perhaps, but then I wouldn't have had the pleasure of your company."

"Oh? You've enjoyed our company, have you?" she asked playfully.

"Yes ... much to my surprise." He was relaxed; his face bore no sign of sarcasm.

"I'm glad," Catherine said. "You've been very generous."

"Sometimes I take my self-sufficiency a little too seriously, and I find that a little human contact can work wonders."

"I don't know if I speak for the others," said Catherine, "but I've enjoyed your company. I'm especially grateful for your putting us up for the night ... and putting up with *us*."

Conroy smiled. "You're too kind, Ms. Myers. I'm afraid it was me that you three had to put up with. As I think back on my conversation with your boss, and her insistence on sending somebody to change my mind, I realize how laughable my image was of the sort of people she hired. You three weren't what I expected, although it took me awhile to appreciate the difference."

"Assuming that's a compliment, how had you imagined us?" asked Catherine.

"Oh ... kind of a cross between used car salesmen and new age missionaries ... or maybe tree hugging do-gooders with a chip on their shoulders."

"Oh my!" exclaimed Libby, who'd been listening with interest. They all laughed.

"Our image of you shifted a bit, too, Mr. Conroy," Catherine ventured. "We imagined a hard-headed, arms-dealing insider who treats people like pawns on a chessboard."

He laughed. *"Touché!"*

They turned onto the airport access road, and Libby pointed to the other side of the airfield where the private planes were hangared. Conroy drove up to the security gate and rolled down his window.

"Good morning, Mr. Conroy," greeted the guard and waved them through.

"Why in the world would he know your name?" asked Catherine, astonished.

"I keep my airplanes here," he answered simply.

"Air*planes?* You have more than *one?!*" she asked, wondering if he were putting them on, but quickly realizing that he wasn't.

"Yes," Conroy said, smiling. He drove slowly past the private hangars.

"It didn't occur to me you might still be an active pilot, Mr. Conroy. What do you have?" asked James, not bothering to hide his envy.

"A Cessna and a Learjet. A sailplane too, if you want to count that."

"Sweet!" James exclaimed.

As they made their way onto the tarmac, Catherine spotted Minerva's Gulfstream, boarding ladder extended, glinting in the early morning sun.

"Now *that* is a beautiful aircraft," stated Conroy. "Your boss has excellent taste."

When they pulled up and exited the pickup truck, the copilot descended the ladder to greet them.

"Good morning, Ms. Armstrong. We'll be finished with our pre-flight shortly—ready to go in about fifteen minutes."

"Thank you, Sean," Libby said.

Conroy's dogs stood in the bed of the pickup, wagging their tails vigorously. A small commuter jet began its roll down the runway, and the travelers watched as it took to the air, highlighting the fact that their own departure was imminent.

James and Libby shook hands with Conroy and then boarded the plane, but Catherine remained next to the pickup. With one hand on each of the dogs, she said her goodbyes to them in a mix of baby talk and ear scratches. Then Conroy escorted her over to the ladder and extended his hand.

"It's been a pleasure."

Catherine wiped her hands on her coat. "Dog hair," she laughed. "Sorry!"

"I'm used to it."

Lingering at the stairs, she looked at the plane and then back at Conroy.

"Is it my imagination, or are you getting a little misty-eyed?" she asked, openly teasing him. She was now seeing him in a wholly different light than the day before.

"Just a little," he said, grinning. "We arms dealers are a sentimental bunch, once you get to know us." She smiled and then turned to board the plane. Conroy watched her climb the steps.

"Ms. Myers," he called out, just as she reached the door to the cabin. "Will you deliver a message for me?"

Catherine turned, curious about this last-second request. "Of course."

"Please tell Mrs. Bennett that I've reconsidered."

Chapter 18

It was a gorgeous day in the city, and Minerva decided to move the meeting outside. In a buoyant mood, she seemed to be back to her old self.

She stepped out onto her terrace and walked over to the largest table. There, in the shade of a large umbrella, sat Sam Minton and Malcolm Conroy, chatting away as if they had known one another since high school.

"Gentlemen, now that you've had a chance to get acquainted, let's get down to business. I wanted to keep this gathering informal and off the books, for now."

"The first order of business is to welcome our new member. Mr. Conroy ... Malcolm, that is, has agreed to take on the critical role of which we're all acutely aware. According to Libby's report, there was some playful sparring that took place at his property in Virginia.

"My goal this morning is to come to a meeting of the minds and turn his tentative commitment into a solid agreement. Assuming we accomplish that, he can immediately get to his task." She nodded at Conroy, giving him the floor.

"Thank you, Minerva." He took a breath and looked quickly around. "I want to be clear about what my priorities are ... what my limitations are. And, I need to be clear about the resources at my disposal."

Minerva nodded and then turned to James. "Why don't you start by spelling out what we've published regarding the profile of our panel."

"There are only a few points we've been specific about. Just as there are twelve members on each team, we are assembling a panel of twelve judges. And just as for the contestants, the panel will be gender balanced.

"There will be one pair of judges in each of six global regions, by continents basically. And although each region will have its own resident pair of judges, each will operate independently. Since each judge will be receiving a translation into his/her preferred language of the contestant teams' submissions, he/she will be receiving a random mix drawn from the entire field of contestants at every stage."

"Makes sense," Conroy said.

James continued, reading directly from an internal memo. "The panel of judges shall be comprised of men and women of integrity who have demonstrated a thorough commitment to stewardship of culture, even civilization itself, in the broadest possible terms." He looked up and added, "Somebody suggested that we require a minimum age of fifty, but it wasn't seconded."

Conroy looked off in the distance, perhaps going through a mental list of potential candidates. The others waited.

"Okay. No surprises there. What about political alignment or religious affiliation? Is there an expectation about balancing Christians, Muslims, Jews, and so forth?" he asked. "What about capitalism vs. socialism? What about industrial vs. agrarian?" He paused, and the others turned to Minerva.

"Nobody has suggested that we need a specific mix of beliefs or philosophies. We're all biased, though. Certainly I am. My hope is that you gather people of such caliber that their religious beliefs never come up or are seen as irrelevant. The first thing people should notice about our judges is how transparent they are. What you see is what you get. The attribute they should all have in common, among others, is fair-mindedness."

"Got it," Conroy responded. "Have you compiled a list of prospective candidates?"

"Minerva, if I may?" asked Sam Minton, sitting forward slightly.

"Sure, Sam. Go ahead."

"Malcolm, this is a crucial issue, and it happens to be the reason we sought you out in the first place. As a Vox Stellarum trustee, my duty is to support and encourage Minerva and her staff to run a successful contest. From the start, in direct response to our media campaign, we began to notice some negative press. Some of that was to be expected. There will always be a base level of antagonism, but we want to remain sensitive to any legitimate points that come through. The most critical thread expresses the view that the contest is rigged—that the outcome is preordained. The winners, some have said, will be nothing more than pre-approved delegates for the power elite of the West ... well-dressed, mostly white, Christian clones spouting capitalist, consumer-oriented memes."

"I see," Conroy said.

"As normal as these fears and doubts are," Minton continued, "it is our job to be vigilant and to eliminate anything that would give them credence. The best way to do this is to keep the administration of the tasks separate from the judging. The judges must be seen as independent contractors—several steps removed from Minerva Bennett and her staff."

"It seems I'm on my own then, which is fine. Been there before," he said with a chuckle.

"Malcolm, we need to go over the time line requirements and the salaries," Catherine said, sensing the need to keep things moving forward with specific action items.

"I agree," he said. "Shoot."

"Stewart Maxwell has prepared the contract. It'll be translated into whatever language is preferred by each of your recruits. Each judge will receive a $100,000 signing bonus up front, along with a fee of two million dollars. Half is to be paid after one year, and the balance is to be paid after the final winners have been announced. Each judge will also receive a separate amount for support staff ... to last the duration of the Contest."

Conroy nodded. "That ought to get their attention."

"We spent an entire meeting discussing this issue," added James. "Some of us thought the honor of being asked to sit on the panel would be enough consideration, with maybe a nominal stipend. But it was pointed out that we'll need to offer enough financial incentive to rearrange existing priorities. Those worthy of judging a contest such as ours will tend to be very busy."

"No doubt," said Conroy.

"Regarding the time line," continued Catherine, "you have three weeks to get the job done."

She paused, hoping that her expression wasn't too grim. She tried to imagine accomplishing what Conroy had agreed to do but couldn't. It reminded her of the time she had studied for the LSATs while attending night school and working ten-hour days ... no sleep ... no time to play ... no time to ... She shuddered.

"Don't worry—" Conroy said, gazing directly at her, "I can handle it."

The reassurance he gave Catherine Myers went a long way. They all breathed a little more easily.

"Malcolm, your confidence has put me at ease," said Minerva. "To show my appreciation, as well as to provide a little insurance—time-wise—as you embark on your assignment, you will have unrestricted use of my jet. I know you're a pilot and that you like your independence, but I think you'll find my plane is better suited for the overseas trips."

"That's very generous," Conroy said, genuinely taken aback. For a man who had traveled the world in style, he was obviously affected by this fringe benefit. Even he suddenly breathed more easily.

"When do you think you'll begin?" asked Catherine.

"Immediately," he said. "This afternoon." He looked around the table to see if there were other items on their agenda, but everybody seemed satisfied.

"To be clear then," he continued, turning back to Minerva, one eyebrow cocked slightly, "am I to understand that I don't need your approval, or that of your Board, to sign my prospects? What if my choices don't meet with your expectations?"

Minerva looked at him, unfazed.

"I was wondering when you were going to ask about that?" She narrowed her eyes and pursed her lips slightly. "As I think you know, Malcolm, I've done my homework. I've seen your public record. I've sought the counsel of my staff, in whom I have complete faith, regarding your trustworthiness and character." She paused, looked at the others, and then back to Conroy.

"We have faith in your good judgment, and we expect you to use it. Enjoy your *carte blanche*."

⊶⊷

A fortunate son, born in the heart of Texas, Henry Godfrey grew up with everything he needed and most of what he wanted. Like countless youths before him, he became critical of the environment in which he had been raised—not so much the fruits, but the trees. He acquired the habit of challenging people, particularly his father. His constant initiation of arguments gave him a reputation of being impertinent and combative. By the time he was a sophomore in high school, he realized his attitude toward authority was significantly more aggressive than his peers.

For his first two years at a prominent liberal arts university, he successfully juggled team sports, schoolwork, and fraternity life. But in his junior year, spontaneous road trips and designer drugs took their toll; he was suspended from athletics and placed on academic probation. Only when his father threatened to withhold his entire allowance was Henry inspired to improve his grades and salvage his chances for a diploma.

His first real job was with an insurance company, but, due to a windfall inheritance from a distant relative, that lasted less than a year. Henry decided to take a premature sabbatical. Shortly thereafter, he wandered off the map ... then off the grid.

Three years later, with a string of misadventures in his wake, the prodigal son resurfaced. With the support of his family, he found his way to a drug rehab in Arizona. At the age of twenty-five, Henry Godfrey's life was simultaneously over and just beginning.

As the weeks and months of sobriety accrued, his return to normalcy involved numerous realizations, one of which was that he had set himself up for this self-defeating squeeze play at a very early age. One of his counselors had suggested that the fantasies into which he habitually escaped were proportional to his inborn talent and power. He had originally discounted this as psycho-babble, but it eventually began to make sense.

Now, Henry wondered if he were revisiting this dark mindset again. For the first time in several years, he had a serious urge to call his old dealer and get stoned. He did not actually experience his hands turning the steering wheel, like he had heard about in meetings, but his desire to escape was real. He fought the impulse by thinking through the absurdity of it, the way his sponsor had instructed him, but it was unsettling nevertheless. He recited the Serenity Prayer and rolled down his windows as he drove. *Maybe the wind will blow away my dark mood.*

This is what he thought about on the way to pick up Suzanne. He had invited her to join him for dinner at his parents' house, but he vaguely regretted that now. Their relationship, tenuous in recent months, had been tested the evening before. They had gone to a local saloon with a large patio and live music, and he had run into some of his old buddies. Even though he was sober, and therefore had the edge on guys who had already put down several beers each, Henry was sucked into his old competitive mindset. Working the steps of "the Program" is all fine and good, but character defects like his deep-seated desire to look good had no more been removed by a higher power than had the nose on his face.

When one of his old rivals drove up in a black Porsche convertible, the conversation had devolved into a brag fest about whose upcoming travel plans were the most exotic. He had felt compelled to bring up the possibility that he might soon be moving to New York City to join The Contest as a special assistant. It had been a conversation stopper, and Suzanne had nearly fallen out of her chair.

"You're going to do *what?!*" she had hissed. A noisy patio was hardly the place to explain himself, and for several minutes he had had to swallow his pride as Suzanne gestured angrily.

Yeah, he now thought, *being unattached would be so much easier. I could just show up wherever, by myself, say hello ... take off, whenever ... I could just drive over to Jeff's and pick up a couple of—*

"No!" he said aloud, glancing around to see who might have heard him. Nobody. He was in light traffic, and everybody else had their windows rolled up anyway. *No,* he thought, *that's not the answer. I'll pick her up and face the music.*

As he pulled up to her apartment, Henry hoped that the rift from the night before had been magically mended. He was quickly disappointed by the stiffness of her hug and the parry of his kiss. It seemed ironic to him that, as she pushed him away, he felt more desire for her than he had in a long time, her light cotton dress revealing more than just her suntanned legs.

Coming from the direction of downtown, they turned onto a major boulevard. The dramatic jump in lot sizes and house values signaled that they had entered River Oaks. Having grown up in this enclave of Houston's conservative wealth, Henry felt a dual shot of nostalgia and animosity as they made their way along the parade of houses and gardens lining the quiet streets.

He turned into the familiar circular driveway and parked behind his brothers' cars. As Suzanne and he got out, they were immediately strafed by a mockingbird that was patrolling its territory. This, and the fact that the air was rich with the fragrance of magnolias, seemed to chip away at the iciness that lingered between them.

Henry grabbed his blazer from the back seat and dusted it off. Suzanne grinned as he checked his appearance in the side-view mirror, combing his hair with his hands and straightening his collar.

Leigh Godfrey was preparing dinner in the kitchen, and the others were on the patio. As Henry and Suzanne walked through the French doors to the backyard terrace, their eyes met briefly. He searched her face for a hint of where they stood, and he suddenly smiled. *I've got home court advantage. My family has my back.*

It was hard to stay in a bad mood at the Godfreys'—they were a hospitable and generous family. Conversation was typically upbeat and colorful, and it was practically impossible for anybody to retreat or keep to themselves.

"Henry, Suzanne, you're just in time!" called Bob Godfrey, who was standing next to the outdoor grill, intent on his job of preparing the main course.

"Hey, Dad!"

"Hi, Mr. Godfrey."

They greeted the rest of the family, all of whom were standing or sitting by the pool—Marian and her husband Peter, Blake and his wife Sally, and Allister with his fiancée Maria. On his father's announcement that dinner was ready, they moved to the table under the adjacent gazebo. He placed a platter of bacon-wrapped quail amidst the colorful place mats and silverware. In a practiced choreography, Marian helped her mother carry out the salad, the wild rice, and the dinner rolls.

As he ate, Henry listened to the conversation—predictable and safe, noting it bounce from one approved topic to another. He wondered if he could stay within the confines without getting too irritated. Adhering to dogma and arbitrary guidelines wasn't one of his strong suits. Bound up in all of this was the bottom line at his parents' house: the "golden rule." He who has the gold makes the rules.

His father had recited it to Henry and his siblings many times in their youth, especially as they reached their reactionary adolescent years. When one of them would challenge the old man's authority, Bob Godfrey would remind them who was in charge. When the golden rule wasn't sufficient, he would add his favorite corollary: "If you don't like it, you can pack your toys and leave."

Deep down, Henry loved the black and white clarity of that attitude, even when he was on the other side. He respected his father for laying it out that way, and now, looking back, he felt a shot of pride for having been the only one who had, in fact, taken the challenge. He *had* packed his toys and left, including several times before his post-graduate disappearance.

Henry appreciated his family and was usually happy to play along. Nevertheless, he believed that staying sober need not require compromising his philosophy. He considered it his duty to enlighten his family—especially his father, whom he judged to be politically and socially narrow-minded. That is why he dreaded the subject that he now knew he must broach. Suzanne's reaction the night before, to his secret, made him realize he needed to inform his family about Aunt Minerva's offer.

Henry listened as his mother prodded his brothers about travel, about jobs, and then again about travel, and he waited for his turn. His father was viewing photographs of Marian's children; she was famous for whipping out her iPad to show off her kids. Meanwhile, her husband Peter looked on with detachment.

Suzanne stood behind them, watching and listening. Henry sidled next to her and gave her a gentle bump with his hip. She smiled and poked him back, but continued to keep most of her attention on Marian's narrative.

"Wow," Suzanne said, turning to Henry, "he looks just like you!" She was pointing at a picture of Henry's six-year-old nephew jumping on a trampoline.

"You think?" asked Marian, turning to face Suzanne.

"Definitely—they have the same eyes. And look at the way he's balancing, even in mid-air." She looked at Henry, his face just inches from hers. "Henry can't dance, but he has great balance." He smiled at Suzanne's playful insult, taking it as a good sign the ice was melting.

"Interesting ..." said Marian. "Jeffrey *is* coordinated, but who knows where he gets it. Peter was quite an athlete, and of course all three of my brothers were."

"*Were?*" asked Peter, finally prodded out of his amused silence.

"Yeah—*were?*" challenged Henry as well, playfully shaking his sister by the shoulders.

"You know what I mean," Marian said, laughing. "When y'all were younger, you were way more active. You played all kinds of sports and, you know, you just *did* more."

"Hey, *I'm* still active!" said Allister. Sitting at the middle of the table, he'd been doing his best to monitor conversations at both ends.

"What—golf? And *yoga?!* I'd hardly call that active," said Marian, with exaggerated sarcasm. "At least Henry gets out and hikes and rock cli—"

"Speak for yourself!" Allister said to Marian while looking at his fiancée. "Maria knows how active I am."

"I thought y'all were abstaining from *that* activity!" quipped Sally, Blake's wife.

For a moment, it looked as if her risqué comment sailed by unappreciated, but Bob Godfrey noticed. "Careful, Sally, some of us take our religion seriously." He winked, emphasizing what everybody already knew—that he was *not* talking about himself. He angled the slideshow back toward Marian and rose. "Who needs a refill?"

The sky was a deep navy blue, with a few clouds turning from pink to dark gray. Indirect landscape lights had come on gradually, and these were now hot and bright enough to send faint wisps of steam into the green leaves that framed the backyard. Somebody switched on the pool light, and this gave a gentle glow to the setting.

When he returned, Bob offered cigars to the boys and moved toward the other end of the pool. Blake and Peter accepted, but Henry declined. After a few minutes though, standing amidst all the puffing and exhaling, Henry suddenly reached in his blazer pocket and withdrew a pack of cigarettes.

"I thought you were going to quit," said Blake.

"Yeah, I was," Henry said, "but—"

"He smokes when he's nervous," interrupted Suzanne, who had stationed herself nearby.

"What're you nervous about, Henry?" asked his father. "I thought you were on spring break."

"I am." He turned toward Suzanne, annoyed.

"Is something going on?" asked Blake, looking at his brother, then at Suzanne. "Do you two have an announcement to make?"

"No-o-o," Henry said, half laughing, "nothing like that." They all turned to Suzanne, but she looked back at them with a poker face.

"What she might be referring to," said Henry as he flicked his ash nervously, "is the fact that I've got a decision to make. I got a job offer two weeks ago ... an unusual offer. And I've been wondering whether to accept it."

"Hell, Henry, that's *great!*" exclaimed his father. "At a new school?"

"Why haven't you mentioned this yet?" asked Blake. "What's the big secret?"

"The main reason I've been keeping it to myself," he said, turning to Suzanne, "is that it would involve a change—a big change. For starters, I'd have to move to New York." He now had their undivided attention; they stared and waited.

"It's not a teaching position, although it would involve managing a curriculum ... and testing. Sort of ..."

"What the hell does *that* mean?" his father asked.

"Aunt Minerva offered me a position with her new foundation."

"You're kidding," said Blake.

"Nope."

Remarkably, Bob Godfrey said nothing. His eyes were fixed on the drain at the deep end of the swimming pool. He remained silent as he relit his cigar, which had gone out.

"Come on. You can't stop there," Peter urged. "What are you going to do?"

"That's just it—I'm not sure." Henry was reluctant to give any details. "She called me two weeks ago and told me that her visit to my school, right before Thanksgiving, had been important to her. She said it had helped her begin to see a new way to deal with something that had been bothering her for a long time."

"Something that had been *bothering* her?" echoed Peter under his breath.

"*And?!*" prompted Blake.

"And she told me she was impressed with my teaching ... that, as a math teacher, I was drawing more out of my students than a lot of English teachers. I was flattered, and ..."

Henry stopped to take a drag on his cigarette. The others stared at him impatiently.

"... I thanked her. I was amazed she even called me."

The other family members were sitting too far away to hear any specifics, but they could tell something was going on in the smoking section. Unable to decipher the queer look on her husband's face, Leigh became curious.

"What's goin' on over there?" she asked as neutrally as she could. Her question broke the spell on her husband, and Bob responded.

"It seems that Henry received a job offer—from none other than my Aunt Minerva. We're trying to get details, but he's being a little tight-lipped about it."

"That's wonderful!" Leigh shouted. "Why don't y'all move over here so we can hear all about it?"

Now that she had achieved her objective of bringing Henry's indecision into the open, Suzanne maneuvered herself back to one of the patio chairs.

Henry took a few reluctant steps toward his mother and the others, and then he repeated what he had just related. "... Aunt Minerva didn't give me any details, only that she wanted somebody who's knowledgeable about education and good with children."

"Good with children?" asked Bob, sarcasm in his voice.

"In a classroom setting," Henry said directly to his father. "Obviously, I'm not a parent." Before any animosity could erupt between father and son, Leigh Godfrey intervened.

"For all her eccentricities, your Aunt Minerva is a very astute woman, and she obviously sees great things in you, Henry. I'm so proud of you! Have you decided to take the job?"

"No, I haven't ... one way or the other. I figured I would use my break to consider it in depth." They all looked at him expectantly, as if "in depth" meant *right now*. "Taking the job has points in its favor but remaining here does too."

"You amaze me, Hen," interjected Blake. "I know what I'd do, and it wouldn't take me a month to figure it out!"

"Hush!" their mother scolded. "I imagine Henry's just trying to be responsible and considerate." Her eyes darted toward Suzanne and then quickly away, hinting at her female bias in such matters.

Bob Godfrey noticed his wife's glance, but he took a different tack. "Manhattan's an expensive place to live, Henry. Did she say how much she would pay you?"

"Not exactly ... just that it would be substantially more than I'm making now."

"That's pretty vague. Aunt Minerva can be very generous, but I doubt she's familiar with the cost of living that we mere mortals have to deal with. You need to clear that up. Even then, you can't really compare apples to apples in terms of standards of living. Life in New York City is quite different than it is here. You could at least find out what your peers are making, and see if it's enough."

"That's true," offered Peter. "My cousin—roughly your age, Henry—works for a mortgage bank. He makes 200K but still has to live in a studio apartment."

"Peter!" cried Marian. "Henry, don't let them put you off with those scare tactics. Aunt Minerva wouldn't invite you up there only to have you live in some tiny dump."

"You're probably right," said Bob, "but I'd hate to see Henry go up there with blinders on."

"Dad, I know you think I'm naive, but I'm not an idiot."

His father sidestepped that point and asked, "When are you going up there?"

"I don't know ... that's what I've been saying. I haven't decided."

"I'm talking about going up there to visit, to see what you'd be getting into. Henry, when somebody gets a job offer to relocate, it's standard practice to go there first—on a fact-finding mission. And usually the recruiting employer pays for the visit."

The look on Henry's face betrayed the fact that this hadn't even occurred to him.

"Hmm," was all he managed to say, struggling to mask his shame. Though his father had made a good point, Henry considered that sort of financial negotiation to be inappropriate. He had always been more comfortable making certain decisions intuitively, based on an inner sense of proportion and balance.

This was the real reason he hadn't mentioned this to anybody yet. The right choice hadn't revealed itself to him, and he had told Aunt Minerva that he would give her an answer by the end of his break. While imagining they were supporting him, his family members were really short-circuiting his natural decision-making process. He felt cornered.

Making important decisions under the influence of his immediate family had always been tricky. He had learned this the hard way. The stifling influence of his father's orthodoxy tended to color all conversation when he held court, and Henry had had to make a serious commitment to keep things light and impersonal where his father was concerned.

So why am I angry? Henry asked himself. His father had actually behaved quite well so far. The tension in his jaw, however, informed him that he had a charge against somebody ... perhaps Suzanne for forcing him to show his hand.

What is she after? Why did she push this agenda in front of my family? Am I angry at myself, for not speaking up decisively? Or at Dad? Or at the whole family, for being so—

"Earth to Henry," said Blake. "Earth to Henry!" he repeated as he poked his brother. "Since you're obviously not going to give us any more details, let's switch the subject."

"How about something noncontroversial," said their father, as if on cue, "like sex, politics, or religion?" Even Henry laughed. Though they had heard it a thousand times, his father's segue did the trick. The mood shifted, and Henry was able to step out of the spotlight.

He was in between moods—in between worlds. He couldn't decide whether he was angry at Suzanne for bringing up the topic, or grateful to her for staying out of it. The tension between them lingered as they sat next to one another, listening to the random conversation.

Somebody said something about China's proposed moon mission, and this somehow led to a review of James Bond movies. Allister and Peter argued about which ones included space launches and then which ones had Chinese villains.

Later, when Henry took Suzanne home, he made no effort to be invited in. She hadn't warmed to his advances all evening, and their subtle battle of egos had inserted a wedge between them. Still in between worlds, Henry didn't care whether they broke up or not.

As he drove home, he couldn't help but replay pieces of the evening's conversation, especially the part about his lack of knowledge regarding any details of Aunt Minerva's offer. He was ashamed that he had come off as a fool.

On a deeper level, he was angry at his family's apparent lack of interest in important matters. Nobody had asked the obvious question, the one that really mattered: Do you believe in Aunt Minerva's cause, or not?!

This omission fed his growing resentment. Wasn't it his fault for not bringing it up? Wasn't it his own lack of ambition which had caused him to come off like an indifferent slacker?

Yes and no, he told himself as he parked his car. *Yes and no*, he thought as he walked up the flight of stairs and unlocked the door. *Yes and no*, as he glanced about his condo.

He recalled several questions that his family members *had* asked. They all centered on concerns about his stuff ... his material comfort. On one level, of course, these were important. On another level, though, it was crazy. His family and his friends—hell, the whole country—had a preoccupation with comfort, and he condemned it without fully understanding why.

His contempt for American consumerism expanded anew, like a loaf of bread baking in the oven. The yeast of his aesthetic ideals reacted with the fermenting sugars of his family's provincial mentality to produce a big, fat muffin of rage.

"How can they not get it? *Jesus Christ!*" he yelled. "Is this what they think life is all about? Granite counter tops and fucking flat-screen TVs?!"

Though it was midnight, Henry was wide awake, adrenaline fueling his anger. He reflected on his father's idea of conversation. It had nothing to do with an authentic desire to explore the mysteries of life and reality. It was about setting the stage so he could show up as the director. Henry's anger grew as he paced the floor. All varieties of people and institutions were sucked into the vortex of his resentment—his mother, his siblings, Suzanne, the whole goddamned city.

A split second before hurling an old sports trophy through a window, he halted and froze. Then, overcome with shame and sadness, he collapsed on the couch.

My view of reality and theirs is worlds apart, he admitted inwardly. Getting sober hadn't erased his separateness, nor had becoming a teacher. In this moment, his fundamental judgments seemed as strong and absolute as ever. He heaved a sigh of weary exasperation.

Fifteen minutes later, he was still wishing he could cause objects to burst into flames. Then, among the contents that had spilled out of his backpack onto the coffee table, he spotted an envelope. It was a copy of a letter that the principal, Gordon Hooper, had given him earlier in the day. It now occurred to Henry that there had been an odd urgency that he had missed at the time.

Curious and in serious need of a mood shift, he reached for it.

Dear Mr. Hooper,

Greetings! A lot has transpired since I met you and toured your school last November, and I wanted to let you in on a little secret. By the way, thank you so much for sending the packet of student work. I got it just before Christmas, and I have displayed the pieces in my office here in New York. They brighten my day.

As you may be aware, I stepped down as chairman of the Koyne Foundation in order to pursue a new cause. Perhaps I should say the same cause, but with a new approach. You should know that my vision for Vox Stellarum and its singular enterprise known as The Contest grew out of a myriad of influences, some of which were subconscious, some of which were mysterious, but all of which, I truly believe, were divine.

Aegis Academy is in the business of guiding children, and, as occasionally happens, it can even educate some adults along the way. I was one of the lucky ones. I have you to thank for that, as well as my grandnephew Henry. What I realized, as I visited his classroom and toured your campus, was that I had lost touch with the youthful optimism that had always buoyed me up through difficult times.

Self-doubt had been eating away at me for months, even years, prior to my trip to Houston, and I found the atmosphere at your school to be a tonic. The positive outlook of the children, not to mention the teachers, was like fertilizer on the tiny seed of my emerging vision.

I am writing, therefore, to thank you and to warn you of the possibility of a small administrative challenge. Specifically, you may need to start looking for another math teacher. In appreciation for helping to bump me into a new orbit, and because I was very impressed with his style of inspiring children to speak the language of hope and success, I have offered Henry a position with my new foundation. I told him he could begin one week after school is out, for I would not want to upset the present classroom dynamics.

I am hopeful that he will say yes, but Henry is an independent spirit. I believe that deep down we share a vision for the world, but that does not mean he will necessarily want to align himself with my methods. We will see.

Thank you for your leadership.

Best Regards,
  Minerva Bennett

Henry was dumbfounded. He read the letter again, and then stared into space. "Huh," he said aloud, "New York better have some decent Mexican food."

Chapter 19

"IT LOOKS LIKE a gumdrop," said Lisbeth Needham, pointing at the setting sun. She was perched on top of a jungle gym that stood next to an old-fashioned swing-set, the kind with a metal slide.

"Or an orange puffer fish," countered Dylan, her cousin, who hung upside down on the same contraption.

"Have you ever seen one?" she asked, impressed.

"No, but I've seen a barracuda!"

"Was it scary?" she asked.

"A little," he said. With a minor grunt, he turned right-side-up and bared his teeth, pointing at them dramatically. "It had a hundred razor sharp teeth!"

"Whoa," whispered Lisbeth.

The other members of Team 603, officially located on the island of Maui, were milling about on the lawn, also admiring the setting sun. Everybody was aware that this sunset would mark the beginning of spring; it was the vernal equinox. Neighboring islands could be seen in the hazy distance—Lanai to the south, Molokai to the north.

The vantage point from Sara and Tony Carminati's house in the foothills of the West Maui volcano, which had been extinct for millions of years, offered a beautiful montage of earth, sun, and sky. The crimson disc approached and then kissed the Pacific Ocean. A minute later, the Earth's silent eastward spin left the sun behind and over the horizon.

The diverse group slowly made its way over to the open-air pavilion that dominated the back of the property. Sara and her daughter Francesca taught yoga there, along with ecstatic dance, qi gong, and meditation. The structure, with its open rafters, wind chimes, and hanging baskets of flowers, had an oriental feel. Patio furniture had been placed in the center of the large, breezy space, along with large pillows made for sitting or kneeling.

The two children were called to join the rest of the group, and everyone settled into a moment of silence. Pualani Kahike, the eldest member, said a prayer.

"Mother Earth and Heavenly Father, angels and spirits, we ask that you guide and empower us on this auspicious occasion. Align our hearts and bodies for the task that is before us. Help us summon our best efforts so that our passion and insight come together in a good way to ... bring about a new age of beauty, harmony, and prosperity."

"That was lovely," said Sara, marveling at the woman's vitality. Pualani, or Mama Lani, as many in the neighborhood called her, was ninety-four. She was known for her old-world remedies and recipes, as well as an eclectic mix of new-age ideas. Stu Monroe, the organizer, had grudgingly included her. He knew she could shift from lucid elder to wild-eyed mystic in a heartbeat. The old woman, great-grandmother of two male team members, had been the only woman in the community able and willing to fill the highest age bracket as stated in the rules.

"Yes. Thank you, Mrs. Kahike," said Stu. "I want to welcome those members that missed our first meeting last week." He looked around and nodded at the new faces, testing himself silently with their names and ages.

"This evening, we have three main items on our agenda. 1—introduce ourselves; 2—decide on a team strategy; 3—pick the key issues that we will address. We'll also review the calendar to make sure we're clear on dates and deadlines."

Their hostess volunteered to go first.

"Hi, everybody. I'm Sara Carminati, in case you don't know me yet. I'm fifty-eight years young, and I feel *good*. I'm *so* excited! I've been thinking about this all week." She beamed. She was that rare type of person who actually becomes more active and more physically fit after the usual peak in one's mid-twenties, and perhaps a little too willing to share her story with anybody and everybody. "Tony and I, and Francesca," she motioned to her daughter, sitting on the other side of the circle, "are proud to have the team meetings here. We want you to consider our house as your second home.

"And I know I'm preaching to the choir when I say that physical and mental health are fundamental to solving bigger issues, but that's my most basic truth and perspective. Through my meditation practice, I've learned to look around and notice what is, and to learn the lessons that nature offers us." She paused at the "what is," holding her hands outstretched, palms up, the way some people will do when they're trying to emphasize some esoteric truth of reality.

"This evening, I've been made aware of beauty, generosity, open-mindedness, and mutual respect. Oh, and balance! So, here we are, between day and night, land and sea, east and west. I feel we ought to use this theme in our team approach."

"Great start, Sara," remarked Stu, and his eyes moved to her left.

"Hi, everybody. My name is Tommy Choy. As most of you know, I'm a carpenter and handyman. I like to surf and fish. My approach to life is pretty simple. If something's broken, fix it or replace it with something better. I think people should keep their belongings limited to what they use on a regular basis and that they ought to care for their belongings with respect."

The twenty-eight-year-old sat back in his spot on the couch. Haley Look nudged her son, who was next. "Go ahead ... it's your turn."

"*Hi!* I'm Dylan. I'm nine years old, and I'm gonna be in the fourth grade. I think we need more time to play. I'm good at school 'cause I like to read. I like to swim and explore. If there were more playgrounds and parks, old people could have more fun, and everybody would be happier." He looked at his mother and beamed. She reached over and ruffled his hair playfully.

"Very good, Dylan," said Haley, thirty-four, grinning at his mischievous look. "Good evening, everybody. I like what I've heard so far, even from my own son. If we approach the issues with a simple attitude, we can't go wrong. Fix it. Clean it up. Restore balance."

Stu Monroe, the manager of the West Maui Airport by day, freelance writer by night, went next, and the rest of the members followed suit. Next, he reminded them of their main objective: choose an approach for the tasks that the contest organizers would soon begin to distribute.

"Stu, can you give an example?" asked Ross Hamilton, the eldest male at seventy-two.

"Sure, but I don't want to put words in anybody's mouth. A general approach could be emphasizing Christian doctrine. It could be emphasizing the scientific method. It could be emphasizing the profit motive." Quick glances shot back and forth. "Hey, these are just examples. We're going to hear from everybody."

"I think we need to be flexible," said Hiapa'i'ole Kahike, or Hap, as most people called him. He was eighteen, one of more than a dozen great-grandchildren of Mama Lani Kahike.

"Whatever we come up with has gotta work for lots of different cultures, because everybody's different. We're supposedly a Christian nation, but there's millions of non-Christians. And of the non-Christians, there's Jews, Muslims, Hindus, Buddhists ... but then, you know, there's people like me. I don't fit *any* of those categories. So, I think our approach has to include all those groups without making anybody feel wrong."

Makani, a soft-spoken Hawaiian girl, went next. "What I've been thinking about is the types of leaders we have and the types of leaders we need. I know we can't go back in time, but, according to our tribal legends, things were much better before the Europeans and Americans invaded our islands. The government put us down and treated us like children, and we're still struggling for respect. We need leaders who will admit their mistakes and speak the truth."

Several of the older members were taken aback but impressed too. Stu Monroe went next.

"Thank you, Makani. It's pretty obvious that you and the other young members have already contributed in a big way. If the rest of us can match your common sense and your courage, then I'd say we have a good chance of going the distance in this contest." She inclined her head humbly and then stole a glance at Hap, who smiled at her.

"The approach I bring to this effort," continued Stu, "is the same one I have for life in general, which, by the way, I borrow from Aristotle. 'Happiness is the meaning and the purpose of life, the whole aim and end of human existence.' I don't make a habit of memorizing quotes, but this one really resonates for me. It helps me keep things in perspective. We can debate about the nature of happiness, of course, but I like the way it keeps me looking within. It helps me realize that my gut, believe it or not, knows how I'm doing.

"Even listening to myself right this second is critical. It feels good to be honest about what I think is important and to communicate clearly. That's what first attracted me to The Contest. This is a chance for us to take part in a grand reality check—to speak honestly about what we like about ourselves and what we don't like.

"I guess what I see is that too many people are short-sighted. Too many people do things to receive a short-term benefit, but the long-term cost is greater than the benefit. This is my definition for selfish.

"I'd like to see us raise awareness about how we as a society need to be patient enough to enjoy the benefits of thoughtful investment."

Haley looked at Stu, her boyfriend going on three years now, as if he were speaking Greek. Her glazed-over expression caused him to refocus his point, so that the others might follow him.

"What I mean is that, when I look around, I ask myself if I like the way things are going. I make an assumption that most of us think alike and that we want the same basic values. I ask myself why we've allowed certain problems to persist, like pollution, and poverty, and discrimination. We complain, but we don't look far enough into the future to see what the results of our solutions will be. We sit by while big business and big government make things even worse.

"We need a more thoughtful approach to our problems. We need to use logic and restraint before we launch another trillion-dollar fix—which will probably just add to the national debt anyway, and make matters even worse." He finally sat back, annoyed. He had said too much.

Hap's brother, 'Akau Kahike, was next.

"We need to be much more committed to protecting the environment than we have been. As most of you know, I'm a commercial fisherman. I've been going offshore since I was sixteen, and I even remember a few trips from when I was twelve. The fish are disappearing. The ocean is dying. There are dead zones where nothing can survive, and it's getting worse every year. I think it might be the same on the land. It's crazy."

The twenty-year-old 'Akau had brought a sudden sobriety to the discussion by reminding them of the purpose for which they were gathered. It was a world-wide quest for, not just high-minded ideals but, real solutions to profound global threats.

After several more shared, they moved to the next item on the agenda. Ross Hamilton, a wealthy retiree who spent his time fishing and flying his rebuilt biplane, distributed a one-page handout. It was the official list of global problems published on the Vox website: *Dangers Confronting Mankind.* The rules stated that each team must address at least eight of the twenty-four issues from the list, as well as one issue *not* on the list.

Religious Extremism	Overpopulation	Human Rights Abuses
Toxicity & Industrial Waste	Accelerating Species Loss	Eroding Property Rights
Anthropogenic Climate Change	Diminishing Fresh Water Supplies	Erratic Economic Cycles
Nuclear & Biological Weapons	War & Terrorism	Political Corruption
Death Penalty, Abortion & Suicide	Deforestation	Illiteracy

Genetic Engineering	Global Economic Uncertainty	Shortage of Clean Energy
Sex & Gender Discrimination	Breakdown of Nuclear Family	Media Censorship
Drug Addiction	Dying Oceans	Rise of Random Violence

Hamilton suggested, "I think we should each circle our top eight, and then we can determine which ones are the most popular."

"Is this the full list?" asked Mama Lani.

"Yes, I printed it off the website this morning," he said.

"I can't imagine why they didn't include *Animal Rights Abuses*," she said with obvious contempt. "*Human Rights* made the list, but what of our fellow animals?"

"Good observation," noted Stu, quickly adding, "That would be an excellent choice for our unlisted issue." He wondered if she were about to launch into one of her trance-channeling stories that he had heard about, but she seemed satisfied for the moment.

The tallying process yielded an extremely broad selection, with only a few obvious winners. They needed to have a runoff vote but decided to eat first.

As the team members milled about the dining room, Francesca looked at her plate of food—she had taken a little bit of everything.

"Hey, I have an idea! What if, instead of having a runoff and narrowing our choices, we decide to address every issue on the list?" She spun around, showing her overflowing plate as proof of concept.

"Can we do that?" asked Dylan, intrigued by the thought that his team might choose to intentionally break a rule.

"Sure," said Stu, who was seated next to Dylan and his mother. "The rules say to pick at least eight, so we can pick more if we want."

Hamilton, who, despite being a retired entrepreneur, was a bit of an ex-hippie. He liked the idea of approaching things in an unorthodox way. But he had a pragmatic streak, as well.

"Francesca, that's an interesting idea, but that'll spread us pretty thin. If we make it past the first several stages of elimina—"

"Of *course*, we're going to make it. *Keep it positive!*" interrupted Sara, flashing her New Age smile in his direction. Ross Hamilton grinned.

"Yes—*when* we make it to the later rounds—the contest administrators are gonna challenge us to flesh out our solutions. We're gonna have to give specifics on how we think each of our stated issues can be handled."

"That's true," added Stu, who narrowed his eyes with a sudden look of excitement, "but if we base our strategy on basic principles, and we demonstrate how every problem results from the rejection of these principles, then we can effectively handle *all* the issues!"

Chapter 20

"THE CALL ENDED abruptly," said Catherine Myers into the speaker phone. She looked at James Ruhle, who was seated on the other side of her desk.

"What was the last thing he said?" Minerva asked.

"It was muffled, but it sounded like 'Gotta go.'"

"Just before we lost contact, we heard voices in the background," said James, "and a car door slamming."

"Did you try to call him back?"

"Yes. We waited about ten minutes—got a recording. That's when we called you."

"So, you're concerned."

Catherine couldn't tell whether it was a question or a statement, but she looked at James and they nodded at each other.

"I am. Something's not right," she said, leaning toward the speaker.

For two weeks, Malcolm Conroy had been checking in daily by satellite phone. Things had gone without a hitch since he had begun his recruiting mission, until now. Catherine and James waited amidst the silence.

"What do you think we should do?" asked Catherine.

More silence ... James was about to say something when Minerva spoke.

"I don't know," she said with irritation. "Where in the hell is Burkina Faso?"

"It's near the west coast of Africa," said James.

"There's probably an American embassy," said Catherine. "Shall I check?"

"Yes, but wait 'til we're done here," said Minerva. "Before he hung up, did he have any news for us? When was his last report?"

"Yesterday he sent in a profile on number eight, which I forwarded to you. He's a professor at the University of Cairo, a man named Mahmoud Azzam. This current visit is to sign up number nine."

"Did he give you a name?" Minerva asked. "And what was he doing there? Catherine, you told me last night his next destination was going to be Liberia."

"It was. Early this morning they landed in Monrovia, the capital, and they were given an escort to the government offices. Conroy met with the President, a woman who received the Nobel Peace Prize in 2004."

"What happened?"

"He wasn't able to sign her," said James.

"Why not?" snapped Minerva.

"According to Conroy, her term of office won't be up for another year and a half, and she doesn't want anyone to accuse her of a conflict of interest."

"That's admirable, I suppose." Minerva sighed. "So, he must've had a good reason to go to Oowa-dogo ... whatever it's called. How far is that from Liberia?"

"He said it was only a one-hour flight ... to *Ouagadougou*," said James, immediately regretting his impulse to correct Minerva Bennett.

"And he arrived there at what time?"

"12:30 PM local. He said it took them two hours to clear customs and would have taken longer had he not 'greased the treads,' as he put it."

"A bribe?" asked Minerva.

"Several," said Catherine. "He and Sean, the copilot, left the airport with a driver to meet with somebody recommended by the Liberian president."

"You mean she wasn't even on his list?"

"No."

"It must have been quite a recommendation to inspire him to make a spontaneous flight into the middle of nowhere." Silence, then in a mocking afterthought, "*Ouagadougou* ... good grief!"

"Um-hmm," agreed James.

"And we don't know the woman's name?" Minerva asked. "It doesn't matter. Number nine, you say? If this is the second spot to fill for Africa ... shouldn't it be an even number ... He must have missed one somewhere." Her nervous chatter hung in the air for several seconds before either Catherine or James could think of anything to say.

"Yes," said James, "a couple of days ago he signed a Frenchman. His female prospect for Europe was away on business, and Conroy said he plans on circling back to meet with her before returning to North America on Tuesday."

Catherine looked at some scribbled names on her note pad. "He said something about 'Somay,' but it wasn't clear whether it's a person or a place."

Minerva said, "Okay, here's what I want. James, call Aaron Newsome. He's the pilot. If Conroy took Sean with him, Aaron probably stayed with the airplane. Find out if he knows anything. And, I want you to try the satellite phone every 30 minutes, just in case he comes back on line.

"Catherine, call the Liberian President. Maybe she can give us a heads-up, at least a name, so we know where to begin. And see if you can get somebody at the US Embassy or the State Department. If none of that works, I may have to pull strings higher up the food chain.

⋆⊷◉ ◉⊶⋆

The Ford station wagon was parked under a shea tree, one of several on the dusty property. The original color of light blue was long-since faded to gray, and the faux wood paneling was sun-bleached to a dull white. The driver, having delivered the Americans to the compound, leaned indifferently against the passenger door and lit another cigarette. His superiors had told him to wait there until further notice, a task which came natural to him.

Inside the house, a squat concrete and mud affair, it was surprisingly cool. A rotating fan that sat on a short stack of cinder blocks jerkily switched directions every few seconds; the worn gears caused stuttering clicks before each transit. An exposed low-wattage light bulb, hanging from the ceiling, and a terracotta lamp in the corner supplied the only light.

Malcolm Conroy sat on a high-backed wooden chair with a straw seat. Now that his eyes had adjusted to the relative dimness, he studied the room and its contents. He marveled at the ability of third-world residents to piece together discarded furniture, recycled appliances, and fifth-hand knick-knacks to create a modicum of comfort. He'd seen much worse.

Sean Thompson, the other "guest," sat on the end of a low couch, the kind that looked as if it had been the centerpiece in one too many fraternity parties. Conroy studied his interaction with their hosts and was pleased to see the co-pilot handling this little detour with humor.

Hovering just behind the awkward request for their patience and forbearance as they were led to this "waiting" room, Conroy could smell fear and envy in the place. The distance between the local squalor and the visitors' wealth was great enough to trigger desperate actions. He would need to play his hand carefully.

Maurice, the man who had greeted them so smoothly and politely at the airport, had ordered a stocky, muscular thug to relieve them of their "distracting" satellite phone and to watch them. Maurice had then exited, presumably to report to his superior.

Conroy wondered about the identity of the man behind their detention. It was now obvious that Maurice's promise to help the Americans set up a rendezvous had a price well beyond taxi fare, and the former diplomat passed the time by playing a mental game of Guess the Ransom.

A guard stood by the door, but the label that came to Conroy was "expendable." *How many more expendables are waiting outside? How many have guns?* he asked himself as he glanced at the blank-faced man.

This must be a spontaneous venture, Conroy decided, inspired no doubt by the sight of a gleaming private jet. *But what if it's not?*

As he balanced speculation against facts, he took an inventory of their assets. Sitting up a little taller in his chair, he could feel the reassuring pressure of the Glock .40 caliber pistol tucked into a holster centered on his lower back, hidden by his blazer. He turned to his co-pilot and wondered if he, too, were thinking of contingencies. Thompson was of modest height, but he was stocky and athletic. Conroy knew he was carrying a Sig Sauer 9mm in an ankle holster and was impressed that he couldn't detect it.

The fact that nobody had frisked them yet was surprising. This was either sloppiness or a subtle demonstration of tactical superiority. Conroy wondered how physical he could afford to get, if things came down to a fight. Despite his own military training and excellent physical fitness, he knew he was well beyond his prime.

The sound of voices interrupted his thoughts. Seconds later, Maurice and two others entered the room and maneuvered to the corner with the lamp.

"Good afternoon, gentlemen," greeted a dark black man of a significantly rougher cut than Maurice. Perhaps in his mid-forties, he had the build of a street fighter. He spoke English in a thick tribal accent.

"You must be Mr. Conroy," he said, "and you must be Mr. Thompson." He looked back and forth at the Americans with mild contempt. He sat down in a chair and angled it mostly toward Conroy. Maurice and the other man, apparently a bodyguard, remained standing.

"My name is Kuma. Welcome to my country." Conroy inclined his head faintly, but said nothing.

"As you Americans like to say, let us get down to business." He looked back and forth, perhaps hoping to elicit a smile, but his guests remained stoic. "Very well. I am told that you have come in search of a local citizen. For what purpose?" Conroy showed no sign of answering, so Kuma continued. "I take an interest in all that goes on in this city. When outsiders arrive, they usually do so with my blessing. But you have come unannounced and have not obtained permission."

"We are here on a private errand," said Conroy. "We have no intention of interfering with you or your business interests."

"When men such as you, flying expensive airplanes, come to our country, it is never an innocent meeting. You come to profit from our land, take our minerals, exploit our people ... it is *never* an innocent purpose."

Conroy smiled. He had to admit the man had a point.

"I understand your concern, but I assure you—we're here on a humanitarian mission. Beyond that, I dare say it's none of your business."

"This is not the United States. We do things different here. It *is* my business. So, tell me. Why have you come to meet this person—a *woman?*" Conroy knew that challenging the man's chauvinism would get him nowhere, and he ignored the slur.

"And if I tell you, are you going to let us go? Will your driver deliver us as promised?"

"That depends," said Kuma. He smiled faintly, for the conversation had now entered his favorite phase: negotiation. Conroy knew that there was no point in stressing constitutional rights or any other vagaries in a land where might still apparently prevailed over right. He sighed.

"Okay. We're here to meet with a woman named Sobonfu Somé. Have you heard of her?"

Kuma glanced at Maurice and cocked his head, as if to say: *Are they serious?!*

"Yes. She is from the Dagara Tribe. She writes books and talks about *spirit.*" His emphasis on the word was almost as derogatory as his pronunciation of "woman."

"I know this person travels a great deal. What makes you believe she is here?"

"I have contacts in Liberia who assured me I would find her here."

"You have an address?" Kuma asked.

"Yes."

"How important is this meeting?"

"Do you mean how much am I willing to pay you to take us to her?"

Kuma laughed. "You catch on quickly, Mr. Conroy."

"My organization is interested in hiring Ms. Somé. If we do, I might be open to a finder's fee."

"I like the sound of that. But what I like even better is a *seeking* fee." He looked quickly to Maurice and then back. His look was confident, as if to say: *This is how it's done.* He continued, "That way, you pay me even if the woman is *not* to your liking."

Conroy stared at the man. For someone about to make a concession, his look was surprisingly direct. "Mr. Kuma, I think we can agree to that. When can we leave?"

"Soon, but there is the matter of the amount." His mouth was actually watering.

"Very well," said Conroy. He leaned forward casually, his elbows on his knees. He looked at Thompson and winked, as if to say: *No, this is how it's done!*

"In my country, we call organizations such as yours a protection racket. It's bullshit, and everybody knows it. People pay though, because they're scared. What you need to know about me is that I'm not. If I offer you any money at all, the amount will be non-negotiable. You'll take it because I will hold you responsible for the actual task of protecting my assets, whoever and wherever they are."

Kuma flinched, as if he'd been slapped. Conroy continued.

"If you help us find the woman, *and* we come to an agreement with her, I will pay you ten thousand dollars. This will obligate you to me and my organization until further notice. Your job will be to protect her from harm of any sort."

"That is a good joke, Mr. Conroy," Kuma said with derisive laughter. "I was thinking of at least ten times that amount."

"I don't joke about money," said Conroy as he slowly straightened up, maintaining direct eye contact. "You have two options. Either kill us now, or accept my terms."

"Mr. Conroy, you seem to have overlooked the fact that you are in my custody. You are in no position to make demands, and nobody tells—"

"That you are holding us is obvious," interrupted Conroy, "but you've bitten off more than you could possibly know. Let me enlighten you, Mr. Kuma. If you decide to kill us, or even detain us for too much longer, my friends in Washington will initiate an extraction. Within two hours, they will access infrared satellite images to determine your numbers and positions. They already know our location by the way. My satellite phone has a passive beacon—it can be tracked even when it's turned off.

"If we're not seen exiting by sundown, you can expect an unwanted visitor later tonight—a laser-guided Hellfire air-to-surface missile. By the time the delivery drone is ordered back to the USS Harry Truman, stationed in the Gulf of Guinea, this entire compound will be little more than scorched rubble."

Something about his specific knowledge and facile use of combat jargon unsettled the African, though he wasn't a man to lose his composure too easily.

"Come, come ... serious corporate backing I can believe, but a military strike? You must come up with a better bluff than that!" He glanced around the room and laughed, a little too nervously. His darting eyes stopped on Conroy's relaxed face; there was no smile, no sign of fear. This simple fact seemed to burrow into Kuma's grip on the situation and unravel it. Like a hyena who suddenly decides that a porcupine is not worth the trouble, he stood up with an odd look on his face.

"I think you people are not worth any more of my trouble," Kuma announced to the room at large. "I accept your offer." He looked at Conroy and grinned. It was a look of respect, if not admiration, one adversary to another. He turned to Maurice.

"We are done here. Deliver the gentlemen to the address they gave you. See that they are returned to the airport at the conclusion of their business."

◦╍◉ ◉╍◦

The clock in Minerva's office showed 5:15 PM. *No wonder I'm exhausted,* she thought, *but I hate to leave when everybody is still working so hard.*

It was the end of a frantic Wednesday, just days before Task One would be published to 1000 teams. And it was twenty-four hours after their internal deadline for assembling the panel of judges, still incomplete. She was nervous, worrying more about the last two positions than the first ten.

She certainly could not accuse Malcolm Conroy of loafing. By any standard, he had been busy, having logged over 30,000 miles in eighteen days. *But he's not done!*

He had interrupted a staff meeting just an hour earlier, making a quiet back-door entrance into Minerva's office, and had requested twenty minutes of her time. Minerva had signaled Libby and Catherine to accompany her for the impromptu meeting.

Conroy appeared haggard but retained the glint in his eyes. He presented them the resumé of his latest acquisition, a woman by the name of

Kim Campbell. A former prime minister of Canada, she was an attorney and author with a mix of conservative values and a flare for speaking her mind.

"Excellent," Libby had commented enthusiastically as she scanned the woman's curriculum vitae. "Your choices are as impressive as they are improbable."

Conroy received the compliment with the mildest of nods. Though he declined to give any hints as to his prospects for the remaining positions, he shared a few details of his recent trips, including a brief description of the detour in west Africa.

"We had a chance to meet some of the locals, and I was inspired to *lubricate* the economy with a small offering. Then I met with Somé, a delightful woman, surprisingly well educated. I was impressed with the level of support she has throughout central Africa, not to mention Europe and North America. She showed me a video clip of a TED talk she delivered on spirituality, which I trust you will find captivating."

He informed the women that his appointment with the other North American candidate would be first thing in the morning. "I'd better get going if I expect to be successful." He then added, "Assuming that goes well, I'll depart immediately for eastern Europe to secure the last judge and wrap up my assignment."

When Minerva asked what had gone wrong with his previous choice, he had replied, "The Spanish woman—who appeared on paper to have a flattering resemblance to you—turned out to be all icing and no cake."

The last thing he mentioned, before exiting as quietly as he had entered, was that security needed to be tightened.

"Do you see a problem?" asked Catherine.

"For one thing, on my next visit I expect to be inconvenienced by a security check. All visitors should be ID'd and searched. If I'm able to walk in the back door, undesirables can do the same. I recommend armed security guards be stationed at the street, in the garage, and at both entrances to this office. Undercover agents would also be a good idea."

"Do you have reason to believe a threat is imminent?" asked Libby.

"Threats don't need reasons."

⊷⊨◉ ◉⊨⊶

As Minerva ordered her driver to bring the car around, she perked up. She and Gladys Atchley had tickets to a Broadway show, and she looked forward to treating her friend to some big city culture that she knew her new roommate had not enjoyed in many years.

The doorman spotted her car pulling up to the curb and ushered her out of the lobby. A cool spring breeze greeted and refreshed her as she stepped into the black Mercedes. *I've got no reason to worry,* she thought. *Everything is falling into place.* But something nagged at her.

"Good afternoon, Mrs. Bennett," greeted Carson, making eye contact with her in the rearview mirror. He accelerated into traffic, and she felt herself pressed into the leather seat. *Everything will be fine,* she thought. *Conroy will round up the last two judges, and Task One will go off without a hitch.*

They merged into the stream of taxi cabs, executive town cars, and city buses as they made their way towards her apartment. Minerva liked seeing businessmen, so sharply dressed, peppering the stream of pedestrians. People moved casually along the broad sidewalks, obviously delighting in the mild evening. Even the joggers seemed to be in low gear, sightseeing and enjoying the weather.

Like a ticklish sensation that turned into an itch, then a bothersome irritation, something Conroy had said rose to the surface of her thoughts. *What was he picking up on? What are these threats that "don't need reasons?"*

Her dark speculations were fleeting; they disappeared as quickly as they surfaced. She peered out the windows at the shops and people. She loved this route. It offered her a daily connection to the pulse of the city, but from the safe isolation of the back seat of her car.

⊷⊨◉ ◉⊨⊶

The men in the gray sedan, three cars back, didn't need to see in the tinted windows to know that Minerva Bennett was the sole occupant of the limousine. They'd been watching her for some time.

"We've got the old lady in our sights," said the man in the passenger seat, speaking through his lapel-mounted microphone and listening via an earbud. "She's leaving her office and heading toward her apartment."

"Good," said his boss. "Keep your distance."

Chapter 21

"LADIES AND GENTLEMEN of the press, teams, friends, followers, and supporters," said Libby Armstrong, "*welcome* to the Vox Stellarum Headquarters in New York City! We are the proud hosts and administrators of the broadest and most inclusive global initiative in history, and today is a big day for us.

"Two hours ago, at 8:00 AM local time, Task One was published and assigned to 1000 teams around the world. This marks the real beginning of 'A Global Contest to Create and Present an Integrated Set of Solutions to the Problems Confronting Humanity.' Most of you refer to it simply as *The Contest*. So do we."

Laughter in the small audience relieved some of the tension in Libby, who felt as tightly wound as she had ever been. She had called her doctor that morning, hoping for an excuse to bow out of the responsibility of speaking to an international audience so big she didn't even want to think about it. "I'm a nervous wreck! Can my anxiety harm my baby?" The doctor told her not to worry, but that didn't help. She was glad to have the support of Minerva, Catherine Myers, Stewart Maxwell, and Sam Minton, all of whom were seated nearby on the dais.

The audience inside the newly leased space on the ground floor of their headquarters was comprised of about thirty staff members, dozens of reporters, and several elected officials, including the mayor, a senator, and three city council members. Seated in an array of folding chairs set up in the middle of the large room, the audience seemed good-natured and forgiving.

An hour before the press conference began, the police department had closed the street for one city block due to the media invasion that had overwhelmed traffic. Television crews had clogged both sides of the street with vans and trucks, most of them equipped with telescoping transmission antennas. Barricades had been brought in to keep the growing pedestrian crowd from spilling into the headquarters. When even this had appeared to be insufficient, a half dozen mounted police had been dispatched.

Libby tried not to think about the broadcasts fed by the cameras and microphones that seemed to come at her from every direction. Every network she had ever heard of was there, along with quite a few she had not. Seeing one reporter from the *BBC* settled her down for some reason, but when she realized that the logo emblazoned on the jacket of another reporter was in Arabic script, and that it was *Al Jazeera*, she almost fainted.

Focus, she told herself, *and breathe!*

She continued with the bullet points of the script that Catherine had taped to the podium, hidden behind the bristle of microphones.

"My name is Libby Armstrong, and I'm the president of Vox Stellarum. Before I introduce some other members of our foundation, I'm going to give you some facts about the task that our contestants received a short time ago.

"All official communication surrounding the competition is Internet-based. Teams, each of which consists of twelve participants, must log on to their designated pages within The Contest website and enter special serial numbers and passwords. Although the task itself will be public knowledge shortly, all team responses must be submitted confidentially. These responses will only be visible to a small set of designated personnel—a panel of judges that has been assembled by an impartial third party. No responses will be made public until the judges have cast their votes and eliminated the teams that failed to qualify and advance.

"In three weeks, Task One responses will be due, although teams are welcome to submit them early. Each judge will be assigned a random assortment of one twelfth of the responses, and he or she will have two weeks to eliminate half of them. That means that, in this first round, 83 or 84 teams will be considered by each judge, and only half of those will be allowed to proceed to the second round.

"The criteria on which the judges will base their decisions are listed on our website. Not even the senior staff members on this stage will be privy to the selections of the judges until they are announced to the public five weeks from today.

"Those of you who have visited our website and read the rules and guidelines may have seen that the panel of judges is to be a 12-member body, two from each of the six populated continents. And, just as with the teams, the panel will be gender-balanced. We did, of course, forego the requirement to include children, which we hope you will appreciate." More laughter.

"Minerva Bennett, our founder, will reveal the names of the judges in a little while. First, though, let me introduce the Vice President of Vox Stellarum. She will read the exact text of Task One. Please welcome Catherine Myers."

Catherine walked to the podium, donned her reading glasses, and began to read.

"Task One ... Consider these questions as you prepare your response.

1. "What inspired you and your teammates to enter The Contest?
2. "In reference to the list of *Dangers Confronting Mankind*, published on the Vox Stellarum website, which issues will you address and presumably solve? Explain your approach. Also, identify at least one important issue—*not* listed—that you will include in your solution set.
3. "How will the age, gender, and residence requirements for eligibility in The Contest affect your team's ability to arrive at effective solutions to the referenced list of issues?

"Answers to these questions should be contained in a single, comprehensive statement or essay, not to exceed 2500 words (in standard English). Your response must be submitted through your unique log-on combination on the Vox Stellarum website by 6:00 AM GMT on Monday, May 2.

"Sharing your response with outsiders (e.g. family members, friends, teachers, reporters) will result in disqualification. Responses will be made public once the panel of judges rates them and posts the results on Monday, May 16.

"The 500 teams that survive Round One will be eligible to receive Task Two, which will be immediately published in similar fashion: Monday, May 16."

Then she looked up. "Questions?"

There was a hum of activity in the audience as a few cameras flashed. Several reporters waved their hands, and Catherine nodded at one.

"The length of this essay seems quite brief. Will that really be enough for your judges to go on?" asked a *CNN* reporter.

"We designed the tasks to begin simply, with each one increasing in difficulty and complexity. If you've ever tried to write a 2500-word essay, especially one covering such a wide range of topics, you will recall how difficult it is. We know that one of the primary challenges is going to be the cooperation within each team. Combining twelve different perspectives, within a broad age range, and coordinating these in a well-written, creative fashion is a tall order." She nodded at another reporter.

"Granted that the essays will be a challenge, why have you allotted three weeks? And will all the tasks last this long?"

"Our curriculum experts put a great deal of thought into this question. We know that giving the contestants this long to perform a pretty straightforward task is going to apply pressure. We imagine there will be lots of editing, revising, and rewriting before the teams are satisfied." She turned to another reporter, but then added. "Oh, regarding the time allowed for the tasks ahead, they will actually be a bit longer—anywhere from four to six weeks."

A reporter with a Russian accent asked, "Many teams do not speak English. Is not this a serious disadvantage?" Several audience members nodded sympathetically.

"This is a very good point. Again, it's something we have spent a great deal of time working out. In fact, one of the biggest areas of our budget is language translation. We don't expect our contestants to speak or write English, nor do we expect the judges to. We have a serious contingent of linguists, many of whom work for the United Nations, and many of whom are university language specialists from all over. These people receive the essays in the teams' native languages, interpret them, and translate them into English, as well as the preferred language of the judge for that round. This is part of the reason for the two-week grading period."

There were only a few more questions. Apparently, the crowd was underwhelmed by the simplicity of Task One. Catherine motioned to Minerva, hoping the disclosure of the judges would recharge the enthusiasm of the audience. Leaning into the microphones slightly, she said, "Please welcome Minerva Bennett, founder and driving force behind Vox Stellarum and The Contest."

Minerva walked to the podium amidst healthy applause and shook Catherine's hand. She whispered, "Well done."

She wore a navy blue outfit with only a single piece of jewelry—an exquisite brooch with a circle of twelve jewels, alternating diamonds and pink sapphires set in white gold with a ruby in the center.

She stood for a moment and looked out on the immediate gathering, but seeming to also take in the millions who were watching on distant televisions. She took a deep breath and smiled as cameras flashed.

"Good morning, ladies and gentlemen, boys and girls, viewers of all ages and nationalities. My name is Minerva Bennett. I suppose you have me to blame for this wild-eyed stunt that we call The Contest." Laughter and applause.

Good, thought Libby. *I knew Minerva would bring them around.*

"We have been blessed with enthusiasm and encouragement from so many of you, and I am honored by your support and interest. Since making our announcement approximately six weeks ago, I have had the opportunity to appear on several talk shows and hold numerous interviews. It's quite natural—people want to know what we're trying to accomplish. People want to know if this contest can actually change anything?

"My basic response to these questions has remained constant. We can accomplish more than we can imagine, and we have already changed a great deal.

"What I'm here to talk about today is what we've done to ensure that the contest is fair and equitable. One of the key decisions had to do with how we will judge the results. Some of our critics imagined that The Contest would be nothing more than a puppet show—a small circle of hand-chosen friends putting their stamps of approval on my pet ideas. I was surprised, frankly, that some would have such a cynical view, that they would ascribe to me such a limited vision. Nevertheless, I took this skepticism seriously. I made it my highest priority to place two degrees of separation between me and the judges.

"My team and I underwent a search for independent agents who, we imagined, would be able to assemble a team of prominent leaders, activists, and visionaries who could sit in fair judgment of the contestants ... of the solutions they create and present. I stepped out of the decision process completely. My staff independently chose the agent with the best qualifications, and that agent was charged with the job of building a panel of judges who would be immune to political sway. We are proud of the results, and we think you will approve.

"One more thing before I read the list. As Libby and Catherine indicated earlier, the judges have been directed to act independently and to disregard all influences beyond their best and highest sense of virtue. Even if I wanted to get involved, I have no access to the encrypted channels of communication between the teams and the judges. When the judges return the results of the various tasks, I will get the news at the same time as the rest of you.

"Okay, now that *that* is settled, here are the names ..."

⋅→⊨◉ ◉⊨←⋅

Six weeks earlier, within hours of reading the first full-page ad in *De Telegraaf*, Margrit Hoowij informed her husband, Joost, that she wanted to enter The Contest. That evening, as they ate dinner with their daughter, they decided to make it a family commitment and immediately made a list of friends and colleagues they wanted to approach in order to build a team.

When her mother logged on to the Vox website and read the eligibility rules aloud, Pem was disappointed that they would not be able to include her best friend, since they were both twelve. Not until the next morning did the two girls, out of frustration, read the fine print. They were ecstatic when they saw that the cut-off date was at the end of the month, and that Kat would turn thirteen two weeks before that date.

By the following evening, Pem's parents had rounded up eight more members, and they officially registered.

Now, on April 11, the members of Team 233 were gathered in a corner of a warehouse, situated in the Leidseplein district near central Amsterdam. Johannes Driessen had offered the space for its roominess and, after some considerable modifications, comfort. He had two of his employees cordon off a section of the main floor and arrange couches, chairs, and desks centered on a huge carpet.

Klaas Waterman, a seventeen-year-old student and video gamer, was their designated audio-visual tech. Logged on to the website with his laptop, he projected the recording of the press conference announcing Task One onto a large monitor that Driessen had bought for the team. They read and discussed the published task and then watched the recording again to make sure they had not missed any nuances.

"It's pretty straightforward," commented Lodewijk Koning, the oldest member of the team at seventy-six. A former government official who had worked for three decades in the Delta Works project as a senior hydrologist, he was a friend of Joost's parents. Although the team had selected Driessen to be their designated spokesman, Koning had already demonstrated his tendency to speak his mind. "Our biggest challenge will be to write an essay that reads as if it were written by one author, rather than twelve."

"I agree," said Regina Hendriks, a shopkeeper in her mid-fifties. "I have sat on various boards and committees over the years, and these tend to produce rambling publications. We must be careful to answer the questions concisely. I think we should get started at once."

"Let's get to it then," said Johannes Driessen. "We have allowed ourselves three hours this evening, which should be plenty of time to come up with a rough outline. Joost and I were talking earlier, and we have an idea of how we might proceed.

"What if those of us who consider ourselves decent writers each have a go at writing a draft? We will brainstorm as a team, of course, and then create an outline. Let's say half of us write up something at, say, 1500 words—that would be six approaches to compare. We can come to a consensus as to which is the best one."

"And even if we decide to combine sections from several of them," added Joost, "we will at least have a basis for our essay. Then we can fine tune from there."

"How long should we spend on this drafting process?" asked Bregitta Van Houten, the eldest female member at seventy-three. She was the only member unassociated with any of the others, but her reputation as a patroness of the arts was well established. Margrit had seen her name on numerous letterheads and had met her once at one of the dance company's fundraisers. She had been excited when the woman accepted their invitation to join.

"We were thinking one week. Then we could take a full week to read them, come up with our favorites, and offer revisions."

"Leaving us the third and final week to make the actual changes," said Koning. "That's a good plan, but I would like us to limit the editing and revising phase to three days. It's always a good idea to finish with time to spare, especially when the stakes are so high. There is no margin for error. If we submit one minute late, we will be disqualified."

Pem listened quietly, wondering if and when she and Kat would have something valuable to add to the proceedings. For all her fanciful ideas, Pem had doubts about her inclusion on the team. Her parents would certainly be key players; they were super smart and established in their professions at a high level. *But I'm just a twelve-year-old*, she thought. She loved the concept of the project. She thought it was great that Minerva Bennett, the American philanthropist, had come up with a new way to deal with the problems that she had been borne into. *I'm pretty good at a couple of things, and I know how to have a good time. But what am I doing here?!*

Pem was popular. She knew how to get along with practically everybody, but she wondered if she could measure up. Even the other child member, Daan Bomgaars, who was ten years old, seemed to have self-confidence that far surpassed hers. He was smart and articulate for his age. Furthermore, he was a promising speed skater, which, in the Netherlands, was a symbol of all-encompassing virtue.

She had no doubts about Kat; she was the smartest kid in their class. She played piano like a prodigy and could speak twice as many languages as the rest of their peers. It seemed to Pem that her friend was more on par with Klaas, the seventeen-year-old, than with her.

She felt very small, like a token passenger on a train that was going to a land where she might not belong. The one ray of hope she had, as she sat listening to the discussion, was a quote she had read on the website. Minerva Bennett had stated: "My original inspiration for the idea was a group of school children who, unaware that they were much too young to make a difference in the world, proceeded to treat the biggest problems with the simple faith and self-evident logic that moves mountains."

Pem clung to this nugget of truth more tightly than anything she had ever known, for she knew this about herself. *Most of the time the world makes no sense, but I know how things could be. And sometimes, I see how to get there.*

Klaas started a new document: Task One—Outline. Then he brought up the official Task One statement, which listed the three items to be addressed.

"I'd like to start, if I may," said Carlos Rivera, an employee of Driessen Imports and Exports in his mid-twenties. His family was Spanish, but he had grown up in the Netherlands and considered himself thoroughly Dutch. "We could easily list twelve different responses to the first item: what inspired us, but I think we will probably find that we hold two or three obvious reasons in common. And we can list these."

"That's true, but if we want to stand out, we should also include something unusual ... something that is not obvious," added Bregitta Van Houten.

"Good point," continued Rivera. "So, I joined because the guy I work for seemed to think it was a good idea." He smiled at Driessen, his boss. "Seriously, I joined because I'm tired of all the mess I see on the news. This contest is precisely the kind of collaborative effort that I've always wanted to be a part of. Sure, the prizes are attractive, but the best prize would be knowing that I helped to create something that could put things back on track."

Several others shared similar points, and Driessen signaled that they should move on. Pem, who had still said nothing, raised her hand.

"I heard about The Contest at school. Some teachers were saying something about this crazy ad in the newspaper ... something about a rich lady who wanted to solve global problems. That's all I heard, but I suddenly felt like there was finally a reason to even bother. School is just a place we have to go, but most of the time I don't really see the point. What's it all for?

"When I got home and my parents were talking about this lady and her contest, I was so excited. I don't even care about the money. I just need to know things can get better." She stopped and wondered why they were all looking at her so strangely.

"Did I say something wrong?"

"No, dear," said her mother softly. "You said exactly what we were all thinking. It was perfect." Pem's face was flush, and when she smiled it brought a warmth to the whole gathering.

Johannes Driessen nodded. "*That* is the tone we must stay with: simple, authentic, hopeful. Okay ... on to item two: Dangers Confronting Mankind. We have already come up with our list, but now we need specifics. I suggest that we list at least three statements or directives for each of our chosen issues. Of course, these should imply *solutions*."

Geertje Snellen, Kat's twenty-one-year-old cousin, raised her hand. A graduate student at the University of Amsterdam, she had an impressive grasp of international affairs. "I know we already talked about which issues to highlight, and I'm not really proposing we change them. But, I think we should classify them in terms of their initial causes and work from there.

"For instance, religious extremism is a matter of philosophical dogma. The problems associated with toxicity and industrial waste, however, are matters of economic necessity and scientific or technological limitation. Dying oceans is, on the surface, a scientific problem, but this could also be approached by property rights and governmental policy."

For the next twenty minutes, they debated. As opinions flew and judgments were cast, several factions emerged.

"This is precisely what the people running this thing knew would happen," said Bregitta Van Houten in a loud shrill voice. "Excuse me for raising my voice."

Everybody stopped and turned.

"The real challenge we have before us, before we can even begin to address these issues, is to make peace with ourselves and with each other. Every team is having this same debate, and most of them—perhaps all of them—are arguing and talking over one another precisely as we are. We must stand taller than this. We must accept that our answers will not be perfect, but that they will represent our best efforts.

"This is why Joost and Johannes have a good plan. Because we each have our own ideas of how to prioritize these issues and how to approach them, we must see words on paper. And then we will see who comes up with the best angle. Together, we can come up with basic points—and Geertje has shown us a very good analytical tool—but a single mind must sit down and compose something that flows.

"The creators of this contest have delivered Pandora's Box, and we must be careful not to open it too widely."

Chapter 22

THE NEXT MORNING, the *New York Times* reported on the much-anticipated official start of The Contest. The tone was lukewarm.

The front-page article described the press conference, giving as much space to the attendance by various government officials and the traffic barricades as to the content of the Vox Stellarum representatives' statements. The foundation leadership, the writer said, was "clear and straightforward in its delivery of the simple task." The article included the list of the international panel of judges.

In a separate article in the "Fashion & Style" section, high marks were given to Minerva Bennett's choice of outfits, maintaining that she was still among the best-dressed women in the world. There was a close-up of her diamond, ruby, and sapphire pin, with a gushing review of Tazio, the designer.

In the "Editorials" section, a staff writer with a more critical stance of The Contest stated: "With no results due for five weeks, the excitement surrounding this global scheme will certainly wane in the days ahead. Those who see Minerva Bennett as a beacon of hope in troubling times will need to be patient; the promise of her philanthropic vision, as enticing as it is, has little chance against the rolling tide of dangers it purports to stem.

"As the campaign season kicks in, don't expect fresh solutions from the politicians either. Efforts in Congress will be stifled by over-the-top presidential campaigns—on both sides of the ticket. We predict record-breaking levels of money raised, promises made, and issues dodged."

Even his one positive remark was underscored by doubt: "Vox Stellarum is to be commended for the venerable panel it has assembled to serve as judges. Unfortunately, their task, not to mention the objective of The Contest itself, is too utopian to offer any real hope."

In "Letters to the Editor," two brief submissions were positive, while a longer one was rambling and vitriolic. "As long as we fixate on the caprice of the wealthy, we will continue to see the lot of the majority decay further. This contest is just the latest ruse of the power elite to distract us from the ongoing trampling of our rights by the Wall Street/Beltway alliance. It doesn't matter which teams end up in the winner's circle, the vast majority of us will have wasted our time pinning our hopes on kitchen table philosophers who, if they win, will be obliged to suffer the same frustration of the legion of do-gooders who preceded them."

In Manhattan, the Vox Stellarum triumvirate convened in Minerva's office for their usual mid-morning meeting, each seated in her favorite spot in the informal sitting area. Laptops, purses, cell phones, and newspapers blanketed the large coffee table and adjacent cushions. Coffee mugs, imprinted with various shades of lipstick, sat empty.

Libby Armstrong tossed the unflattering editorial to the floor in disgust and whispered, "That son of a bitch." Catherine Myers, scanning status reports from the executive staff, managed a sympathetic "Mm-hmm." She had already read the article. Minerva was on the phone with her son.

"Hello, Mother."

"Julian, what a nice surprise. Are you in town?"

"No, but I'm driving in tomorrow morning for some meetings."

"And how are things going?"

"Now that I think about it—a little dull, actually. How are you? We haven't talked in a while, and I've been meaning to call you since yesterday, but I figured you'd be swamped after your big press release."

"It's been strangely quiet. Libby and Catherine and I were just talking about that—hoping that it isn't just the calm before some new storm."

"I seriously doubt that. I think it's a tribute to how well you and your team have handled this ... this adventure, and to how well you've organized everything. I'm not surprised. I know firsthand how well you manage things."

"Well, that's—"

"So, I just wanted to say well done, Mother. *Congratulations.*" Julian's voice had been strong and matter-of-fact, but he spoke this last word softly, almost inaudibly.

Minerva didn't respond right away. She could sense the incongruity in her son's words, and yet she was impressed by his humble gesture. An echo of his earlier antagonism reverberated in her mind, almost as if she had heard him add: "I didn't think you could do it." But, he hadn't said it, and she nodded faintly, the phone pressed to her ear.

"Thank you, Julian."

They talked idly for a few more minutes, and then she said good bye.

"Julian sends his compliments and congratulations."

"That's sweet," said Libby. "At least *somebody* has something nice to say."

"Come on, Libby, don't let one sourpuss reporter spoil your day," said Catherine.

"Catherine's right," said Minerva. "We've received plenty of compliments since yesterday, and we can't expect everybody to jump on our bandwagon. Esposito is a mouthpiece for the unions ... been that way for twenty years. It's interesting how liberals always seem to be critical of anything that involves liberation. Some people just can't handle choices."

"Or real dialogue," added Catherine.

"Okay, okay." Libby shifted her body awkwardly, sidling forward to reach for the next report on her pile of papers.

"How are you holding up?" asked Minerva with motherly interest. "Remind me of your due date?"

"July 15th," she said, holding her tummy unconsciously. "My doctor says everything looks good. I should be fine ... up to then."

"That's about what I recalled. I was looking at the schedule, and it looks like you'll be out of commission and on leave just before Task Three is published."

"Yes."

"Have you put any thought into your plans after that—besides taking care of the baby, of course?"

"Do you mean, when do I think I should be able to return to work?"

Minerva nodded.

"Gosh, I haven't projected that far ahead. It was only a week ago that my doctor told me that I appear to be well past the tricky part ... twice before—"

"Libby, dear, I don't mean to put any pressure on you. You've been blessed with a healthy pregnancy, and that's more important than anything else on our agenda. I just wanted to be clear about your departure date, so that we can plan ahead and assign the right people to take over your responsibilities."

"You're right," Libby said. She looked to Catherine and then back at Minerva. "Do you have any suggestions? Do you think we should bring somebody else in, or try to spread my duties around?"

"I'm not sure. How's Rowan doing?" asked Minerva. "Would you say she's up to speed on things by now?"

"Yes, she's been a great help. You're not considering moving her up, are you?"

"Of course not, but a competent secretary can facilitate whatever we decide to do. I just wanted to make sure she's solid."

"I think the obvious person to consider is Catherine."

"I agree," said Minerva. "However, that means we must find somebody to fill her shoes, which is just as tough. Frankly, I'm inclined to keep Catherine precisely where she is, because she not only knows the organization as well as either of us, but she knows how to deal with me." Minerva smiled wryly. "Let's think about this and meet next week. One thing I don't want to do is overburden you, Catherine. Your plate is full already. Maybe too full."

"That's true," commented Libby, "but she's managed to scrape out a *little* free time." She turned to Catherine with a mischievous look. "Did you tell Minerva about your new *friend?*"

"*Oh?*" Minerva's eyes lit up.

"It's way too early to say," said Catherine, "but we've had several dates. He's the first man I've met in a long time that's held my interest."

"What's his name? Where'd you meet him?"

"Anthony Parrish. He's a partner of a small wealth management firm ... mid-fifties, handsome."

"That's wonderful," Minerva said. "Maybe we haven't been giving you *enough* to do!" She couldn't keep a straight face and laughed.

"He's pretty busy too, but we seem to have some chemistry. We'll see ..."

◦◦▸▰▰◉ ◉▰▰◂◦◦

"Come on in," Cade Tompkins said to his assistant. Abby Mitchell crossed the room and sat across from him, laptop in hand.

"How did it go?" she asked. "Mr. Vogel seemed to be in a good mood."

"He's pleased with our accounts. He wanted to know the specifics of the Vox corporate sponsors—what our chances are of leveraging those relationships into new campaigns."

"What'd you say?"

"I told him the truth: I have no idea." Tompkins grabbed a manila folder off his side table and opened it. "He isn't as pushy as the other partners, but he wants me to be more aggressive."

"Was he disappointed about Apple?" she asked.

"Not really. He knew they weren't going to sign. Their proposal for an exclusive platform violated the rules of the contest, and even if it didn't, Microsoft would have dropped out."

"We still ended up with four, and they're all huge," Abby said.

"That's true, but they're not our accounts. Vogel wants us to come up with a way to attract them directly. What I told him was that if we just do our job and convey how we're looking after them, as well as Vox, we'll earn their trust. So, if Vogel asks, tell him we're pushing for more. Between you and me, though, we're going to simply stay in touch and make sure they don't forget our names."

"Got it."

"The partners love the profiles we're running, and they want that to continue." Abby smiled. These had been her idea. Tompkins continued. "With the confidentiality requirement now in play, the participants aren't going to be able to give us any specifics about team solutions, so we'll just focus on back story."

"Family history, education, personal beliefs, and such?"

"Yes, but we need to be careful about personal beliefs. I think it's fine if they disclose how they were raised, what beliefs were important, but we can't publish anything about how they intend to weave these into their team responses."

"Okay." She typed a note into her laptop and then asked, "How international do we want to get with these profiles? What kind of budget do we have?"

"Good question. So far, we've covered a couple of American teams and one Canadian, but we could certainly spice it up by highlighting one or two from each continent."

"That could get expensive, unless we just fall back on teleconferencing," Abby said.

"I'll ask Libby about that. Up to this point, it's been easy, really, to stay on track with our objective. There's no doubt The Contest has been cast in a positive light, but I wonder how much, if any, is due to our work. Minerva Bennett is a one-woman franchise.

"But, even if she stays healthy—which is a big if—and continues to draw the kind of sympathetic media attention that she's enjoyed thus far, our real work hasn't even begun. As several forecasters have indicated, public interest is bound to fall off."

"I was wondering about that," Abby cut in. "What if that happens? What if people just sort of lose interest? Not that I want that to happen, of course, but ... well, ultimately, wouldn't The Contest survive just fine without us? I mean, they're self-funded—Vox Stellarum isn't selling anything. In fact, they're giving everything away!"

"That's the elephant in the room. Our job is to make sure that we add value, and that we take up the slack before the public has a chance to forget."

"I understand," said Abby. "By the way, I presume you heard ... another wait-listed team was added."

"The Moroccans? Yeah, I'll bet they're feeling pretty lucky."

"No, there was a *third* one added—just a few hours before the deadline. They didn't even realize it until Vox notified them yesterday afternoon."

"You're kidding! Where'd you hear this?"

"I logged onto the website this morning to check the activity. There was a small notice about the teams drawn from the Reserve List."

"You know, *that* would make a good story. Abby, what do think about targeting one of these teams for a profile?"

"I like it, but that's part of the reason I was asking about our budget. The last team—the one that just found out—is Chinese. We would need translators."

"We've got 'em," said Tompkins. "Vox won't need their staff of linguists until teams start submitting responses, and I'm pretty sure we'll be granted full access to these resources."

"Excellent."

"The other reason I called you in was to see what you think about doing something with the tax protests."

"Tax protests? What do you mean?" she asked.

"Friday is April 15th ... you know, Tax Day. There's talk of a big protest mounting—not just for the Post Office, but City Hall and Times Square. Remember Occupy Wall Street?"

Abby nodded. "Vaguely."

"Some of the papers, including *The Post*, *The Wall Street Journal*, and *The Daily News*, are hinting at numbers approaching the Occupy crowd, but with more focus. It's an election year, and people across the political spectrum are speaking up. Washington has shown no ability to control spending and, after the recent tax hikes, people are pissed.

"Anyway, we could tap into some of these demonstrators and get their take on The Contest. I've been scanning some pretty colorful memes on Abitibi and Snapchat, and there's already a hundred different threads on Twitter."

"Wouldn't that be getting involved in policy?" Abby asked.

"I'm not talking about taking sides. I was just thinking it would be terrible to waste such enthusiasm. I think we can assume that anybody who's willing to stand out on the curb all day, shouting and holding up posters, is politically active and has strong opinions ... which they will no doubt be willing to share. We just need to harness that somehow and start a conversation. Lots of conversations."

"O-kaaay."

"You're skeptical. Tell me why."

"I don't know. I guess it sounds like such a fringe crowd," said Abby. "Do we really want to tap into that? How would that even look? And besides, I don't think taxes are even mentioned in the list of issues."

"Good point," acknowledged Tompkins. "But that could be our angle. Why *isn't* taxation mentioned? Was this an oversight? Was it intentional?

"By the way, even if we grant that it really is a secondary issue, we can easily relate it to several items on the list: diminishing property rights, crazy economic cycles, world-wide economic uncertainty. I grant that it's a stretch, but this kind of spontaneous protest is precisely the kind of energy which has driven The Contest thus far.

"The question is: will it keep the pot boiling for the next eighteen months?"

Chapter 23

TUCKED INTO A jumble of apartments in the suburb of Shangtangzhen, people gathered in the Chen family home. It was crowded by western standards, but normal for the dozen teammates overjoyed that they'd been included, at the last minute, in Task One. Three members of a Rumanian team had been involved in an automobile accident and were critically injured; unable to find replacements, they had officially withdrawn.

Brothers Liu and Yang Chen had sought to form a team shortly after the Vox Stellarum website had gone live, but two days later their world was rocked by a magnitude 6.1 earthquake in the South China Sea, just east of Taiwan. The entire region suffered power outages and widespread damage. In Wenzhou, a prefecture-level city, there were dozens of fatalities. When the dust settled several days later, the Chens hustled to register only to discover they had missed the cut. And when notified that they had been placed on the Reserve List by a brief form letter on the Vox website, they neglected to follow the ongoing proceedings out of disappointment.

One month later, the original excitement and anticipation around The Contest had long since given way to the realities of daily life amidst the post-quake cleanup. Utterly lacking in sentimentality, neither of the Chen brothers had bothered to follow the press release announcing the first task.

Not until the next afternoon did Liu, the named representative on the original registration form, happen across an e-mail informing him that Team "Alt-3" had been added to the active list and that Task One awaited them on their encrypted page. As he ran to his scooter parked outside the small office of the family business, Liu's father witnessed a rare event—a spontaneous shout of joy from his son.

The elder brother at 32, Liu was the official spokesman, but he deferred to Yang, 28, whom he acknowledged would be the better task master. Yang had won nearly every academic competition in his youth, and he graduated first in his class at university. He applied for and received an international scholarship to MIT, and in three years he earned a Ph.D. in information technology. He returned to China and was invited to join the faculty at his alma mater, Wenzhou University. In the five years since joining, he had become a full professor and had impressed the academic community with his data mining algorithms. In a society that held the wisdom of their elders in such high regard, it was notable that the other members assented to his leadership.

Team Alt-3 quickly shifted to address the questions posted on the website. Bo Liang, one of Yang's graduate students, had her laptop open, ready to take notes. The group listened to Yang as he methodically laid out an agenda on a dry-erase white board.

"We are starting almost two days after many of the other teams, but this will not matter. We have a good team, and we will do what we must. First, we need to choose our issues. I suggest we do this immediately."

Their mother, Rou Chen, a teacher at the Yongjia Experimental Primary School, distributed paper and pens. One of the two youngest members, Ye Lingyun, was one of her students, while several others, including Ye's sister Jia, had been former students. It took the team only thirty minutes to arrive at a consensus on the issues they would address.

"Good. Now, we must identify an issue that is *not* listed."

Gu Buqing, a neighbor who owned a garment business, raised his hand first. "This may be more of an approach than a suggested topic, but I would like us to highlight the need for local authority and freedom to produce and trade. For many decades, we have pursued our own economic and cultural choices, ignoring the central authorities, sometimes at considerable risk. We have gained the respect of Beijing by looking after ourselves, so much so that they have sent envoys here in recent years to find out how we do things.

This is something the rest of the world seems to have forgotten—even the Americans."

"Very good," said Liu Chen. He scribbled the gist of the idea on the board.

"I would like to see education included," said Zhu Hsiung, a friend and colleague of Mrs. Chen, "not just because I am a teacher and have watched so many of you blossom through your studies, but because this is the seed from which all else unfolds."

"Can you be more specific?" asked Yang. "The judges might see this as too closely related to the *Growing Illiteracy* item, which we haven't selected."

"Yes. It is related, but I see an issue far beyond diminishing literacy, which usually refers to reading and writing. I teach music, as some of you know, and it is just one of several disciplines that serve to connect and reinforce all the other subjects, like the mortar which holds the building blocks of accepted subjects together and allows for a stronger foundation on which to build understanding."

Rou Chen nodded earnestly. "If Zhu had not suggested this, I would have, for I agree wholeheartedly. Several of you are testaments to this philosophy, and you have been blessed with a much more comprehensive approach to education than most.

"We hear about schools everywhere that are cutting back on the courses they offer. Our history reveals a record of failed attempts, usually by the government, to impose a simple curriculum on our children, designed to create workers, technicians, soldiers, and bureaucrats. Zhu and I are very fortunate to work in a school that condemns this view. We take a holistic approach, and we are honored to see that our efforts have fostered the success of hundreds, even thousands, of our young people."

Zheng Shipeng, the eldest male team member, spoke. "In my service on the Community Council, I have heard this theme again and again, and I must point out that it seems to always come down to money. The tuition at your school is higher, and you can afford to hire better teachers and to provide a richer education."

"That is only partially true," countered Rou Chen. "Our cost per student is about thirty percent more, on average, than state schools. But this is not a significant difference given our results. Our students have a far greater acceptance rate in universities. They have more options when they graduate and seek jobs. They are more diligent ... more responsible.

"The Europeans had the right idea centuries ago, beginning with the Greeks, and eventually the Ital—" Yang walked over to his mother and touched her on the shoulder gently.

"Those are excellent points, but we need to move on. Let's include this suggestion," Yang said, nodding to his brother. "Are there other ideas?"

Meiying Wong, the eldest female, raised her hand politely. In the relatively forward-thinking, westernized mentality of the Wenzhou region, she was a throwback to earlier times. From a long line of healers and herbalists, she practiced acupuncture—a traditional practice that involves far more than inserting needles into energy meridians. Yang nodded at her respectfully.

"There is an issue with which we have grappled for many years, and I believe the effects have been devastating. What I am talking about is the government's one-child policy, and the resulting practice of female infanticide. Even though this policy was recently amended, it is still a problem."

Yang, who had suspected for years that his parents had been heavily penalized because of his own birth, nodded grimly at his brother. "Add that to our list." He turned to Meiying.

"Thank you."

Her point had sliced through the levity that had permeated the room until then. Because every person present had been affected by this policy, there was a sobering effect as each reflected on his or her own fortune, wondering at the ultimate cost suffered by those not present.

After a moment, Yang broke the silence.

"Liu and I spoke earlier about an issue we might want to highlight or to acknowledge and then avoid. It is the fact that our government is a regime that can be brutal to those who share dissenting points of view." His point, as obvious as it was welcome, helped to dissipate the shame and taboo of the previous topic, and to replace it with a righteous anger and contempt toward the distant authorities.

"I, too, was wondering if this might be something we would want to address," said Zheng Shipeng, "and it worries me." The elder members nodded vigorously, for they had all lived through many regime changes and seen the heavy hand of the state come down in ugly ways. "On the one hand, it seems that Beijing has extended a hand to certain organizations, Vox Stellarum being the latest. But I have heard that the Politburo is prepared to shut down the website if any teams become too critical of those in power."

"I heard the same thing from one of my public policy professors," said Bo Liang, pausing from her note-taking. "He is a small-minded man who enjoys name dropping. He would like us to think he knows half the members of the Communist Party, but I must admit that he seems to have an insider's view. I have made a point to remain as anonymous as I can in his classroom."

Stepping away from the white board, Liu clicked the cap on the marker.

"I think we must proceed very carefully in this regard. Even our children know the consequences of being too critical of government authority. We are only one of about thirty Chinese teams, so it is not as if all eyes are on us. However, any one of us could ruin this opportunity for the others if we are not careful."

Yang motioned toward his brother and spoke, "We propose that we concentrate our efforts on surviving the first several tasks by distinguishing ourselves with strong responses to the list of issues. If we succeed, and it looks as if we have a chance to go all the way to the finals, we can decide then whether we want to risk voicing a pro-democracy stance. Until then, we must be content with the exposure and the privilege of being in The Contest at all."

Rou Chen looked at her sons and smiled faintly, her expression a mixture of sadness and pride. She knew how difficult this restraint was for them, especially her elder. As stoic as Liu was, he had never been able to fully hide his contempt for the Communist Party.

The other team members gave their silent assent to his suggestion, and the meeting continued.

·▸▬◉ ◉▬◂·

Just after six o'clock on a Sunday morning, Minerva sat in her chair in the sunroom, preparing to navigate her way through newspapers and correspondence, most of which were stacked on the ottoman. She had just begun with the Sunday edition of the *New York Times* when a distant point of light caught her eye. She lay the paper on her lap and reached for her coffee.

She loved witnessing the sun's first rays strike the buildings across Fifth Avenue and beyond Central Park, especially after a storm had moved through. The city awakened as the crowns of the buildings seemed to catch fire; in a matter of minutes, the golden light spread to the lower floors and then to the canopy of trees below. The morning sun cast a surreal glow on the distant skyscrapers, somehow magnifying them—like the full moon as it hovers on the horizon. It was a mystery how, even with her gradually failing eyesight, she was able to make out the details of their embroidery, brought into sharp relief as daylight penetrated the streets.

She was captivated by the scene and held her coffee mug tightly in front of her. The colors of the buildings and the flowers in the park, most of which were now in full bloom, were gloriously offset by the pale pink and blue spring sky above, washed clean from the rain. She imagined that she, too, had been washed clean from the spring showers.

When she picked up the newspaper again, she moved from international to national news, and then to the local news in the metro section, practicing a detachment that would, she hoped, help her to hold on to the magic of the dawn. She glanced at the headlines without bothering to dip into the actual articles; she saw mention of European strikes, civil unrest in Brazil, mudslides in California, and tax protests. She sifted her way toward the editorials and op-eds and drew the paper closer, adjusting her reading glasses.

The Contest had moved away from center stage, since the teams were only one week into the first task, and she didn't expect to see much of anything relating directly to her foundation. Then she noticed an article, "A Contest and A Protest," which she couldn't resist reading.

The passionate and aggressive rhetoric from Friday's Tax Day protests is still reverberating two days after huge crowds converged in cities across the nation. Conservative estimates of the crowd that filled the Mall in Washington, D.C. put the number of protesters at one million—a number only surpassed twice in history. The anti-tax, anti-IRS, anti-government sentiments could not go unnoticed as traffic was brought to a standstill in the hubs of nearly every major city.

Political scientists and media pundits believe Friday's crowds were summoned by a perfect storm of discontent arising from stubbornly persistent economic hardships across a broad mix of demographics, a caustic presidential primary season, and the heightened social consciousness inspired by *The Contest*, a global assault launched by the Vox Stellarum foundation to address "Dangers Confronting Mankind." The official due date of American taxpayer remittances to the Internal Revenue Service was merely the excuse to unleash all this pent-up frustration.

The last time such a broad swell of dissent was felt was when the Tea Party, a loose amalgam of conservative and grassroots supporters of a smaller and more accountable federal government, sprang onto the national political stage. The Tea Party's lackluster results spelled its demise, many thought, and that belief seemed to be confirmed when only a few sponsored candidates gained seats in the subsequent elections.

This is why Friday's protests caught so many by surprise. Social media clearly had a primary role in the formation of the organic and seemingly spontaneous gatherings. One reporter likened the Wall Street and Times Square crowds to "flash mobs on steroids." Carefully worded posters and banners seemed to unfurl with uncanny timing; telescoping poles and sticks, on which many of the better produced signs were mounted, materialized out of storefronts, taxi cabs, and backpacks. National media agencies reported similar choreography in Houston, San Francisco, Chicago, Pittsburgh, Denver, and Miami.

Fortunately, only minor incidents were reported. The crowds were vocal and insistent, but mostly peaceful. Petitioning and protesting are, some say, as American as apple pie, but there is a dark side to such phenomena, especially when, as the Chief of Police of New York put it, "We were blindsided—caught totally off guard. Thank God, nobody got hurt." He went on to say that, in the future, city and state officials should strongly consider overseeing the communication networks utilized by activists. When asked if that meant tapping phones, monitoring e-mails and text messages, and even infiltrating Facebook and Twitter accounts, he responded: "Yes, whatever it takes."

As she read on, Minerva felt ambivalent about the mention of her pet project. Proud of the role The Contest was presumably playing, she was suddenly overcome with hopelessness that such protests would lead to any lasting change. *Is my vision nothing more than fuel for discontent, doomed to be a flash in the news, and then to quickly fade from memory?*

She heard a faint creak on the hardwood floor in the dining room and looked up to see her friend padding toward her. Gladys Atchley wore an oversized pink bathrobe.

"Good morning! What a surprise to see you up this early." Her new roommate was not the early bird she was, rarely surfacing before nine o'clock. "I love the slippers."

"Thank you. I found that I couldn't sleep, and I noticed what a beautiful morning it was." She took the chair closest to Minerva. "What a view ... how *grand!*"

Minerva watched her friend settle in and reflected how easily she had adjusted to her new life here in New York. It was a testament to how gentle and easygoing she was. Minerva smiled at her own good fortune that she now had a roommate to share her space and join her in activities from time to time.

"Would you like some coffee?"

"Oh, that's okay," Gladys said, still taking in the view.

"No bother—I'm ready for a refill anyway." She clicked the intercom: "Felix, would you please bring in some more coffee, and a cup for Gladys?"

"Which section would you like?" asked Minerva, motioning toward the newspapers. She leaned forward and nudged the ottoman a few inches toward her friend.

"Thank you, my dear ... in a little while. The news can be a bit much first thing in the morning."

"I guess I'm used to it."

"Have I missed anything?"

Minerva looked out on the distant buildings and frowned. "I suppose not." Gladys peered at her friend but said nothing. "For some reason, I feel compelled to dive right in, get connected to the world out—"

"Good morning, Mrs. Atchley ... Mrs. Bennett," Felix carried in a tray, poured coffee for the ladies, and then retreated.

Minerva held her cup with both hands and continued. "It's too easy for me to float along ... up here. The news keeps me grounded." She sipped her coffee, and they both remained silent for a few minutes.

"When the sun came up a while ago, I felt all warm inside ... content."

"That's lovely," said Gladys.

"Yes, though it might do me good to follow your lead. I tried to confine myself to scanning the headlines, but I got pulled in. Then I came across an editorial that annoyed me."

"What was it about?"

"Mostly rubbish. But it seems that a few reporters delight in misrepresenting our efforts." She paused, wondering whether to dwell on the topic, but added. "It makes me angry."

"If I were in your shoes, I suppose I'd feel the same way." Gladys's reassurance did little to soothe her friend.

"What really bothers me is the way good deeds can invite dark reactions. Why do some people always seem to look for a fight? They make it sound as if any good that a person does must be the exception, that the deep nature of man is to resort to deception and aggression ... and violence."

"Perhaps you're paying too much attention to your critics and not enough to your fans," said Gladys.

"Unfortunately, the critics are the ones that people seem to listen to. They have the ability, and evidently the desire, to spread the view that we are ultimately just a warring species, that we can't be satisfied by working together, that we must deal with challenges by striking out and conquering.

"For instance, this one reporter, even while paying our organization a compliment, chose to label The Contest as an *assault* on the dangers we face." She saw Gladys look at her with mild reproach. "Yes, I know, it's just a colorful word, but that sets the tone for how people see this whole thing. It's like a virus that eats away at any example of positive action."

"Mmm ... well, it seems to me you're doing your part in combatting these dark—" Minerva looked up at Gladys's choice of words. "Oops— sorry! Even *I* resort to forceful language, and I'm one of your most ardent supporters." She laughed lightly. "What I mean is that you must have faith ... faith in your own best efforts. I believe God will judge you on that basis. Let *Him* handle the critics!"

"You're right, Gladys. Thank you."

⊷⊷⊷ ⊷⊷⊷

A steady rain had been falling all night and all morning. Stewart Maxwell and his guest waited for the doorman, who wielded an oversized black umbrella, to come forward before opening the door of the taxi. The men brushed stray raindrops from their overcoats and entered the building.

"You've been here before, haven't you, Bob?" asked Maxwell.

"Several years ago. I think that's when I first met Sam." Bob Godfrey had come to town and had requested a lunch meeting with him and Sam Minton. He had neglected to mention his agenda, but he obviously had one.

They walked down the hall toward the polished oak doors, through which only members and guests were allowed. The hostess took their overcoats, and then the maitre d' directed them to a recessed booth. Minton stood as they approached.

They greeted one another, sat down, and exchanged small talk until the waiter took their orders.

"I guess you're wondering why I asked you to lunch," Godfrey began. "I'm here on a fact-finding mission and, believe it or not, to ask advice. I could have handled some of this over the phone, but I needed to come to New York anyway. I figured it'd be better to meet face to face. Let's see ... where to begin?

"As you may imagine, Koyne Foundation business is the primary reason I wanted to meet. But there're a couple of related issues, one of which will be a personal favor. I'll get to that later.

"What I say next may come as a surprise, maybe not, but the Foundation lost money in the last two quarters. Not a lot, mind you, but any decline in valuation is serious. We're going to have to cut our distributions by five percent this year. My concern with the foundation's assets has stirred up fears regarding my own personal holdings, too. I guess I'm looking for a new approach. The tried and true methods we've used are no longer sufficient.

"The fundamental problem is that the economy is still in the shitter, and we're scrambling to find investments that haven't been affected. It's the Great Recession all over again, but I'm afraid it could take us even lower."

He paused to see if Minton, whose financial judgment he respected, might comment. But he said nothing. He remained quietly attentive, periodically making minute adjustments to the placement of his wristwatch, which he had positioned parallel to his knife.

Godfrey continued. "As you probably know, Mecom resigned a few weeks ago. We think we've found a man to replace him; that's the reason I'm in town—to interview him. Whether we hire him or not, the rules have changed. Holding onto investment capital is a real challenge."

Their food came, and for a minute or two nobody said anything. Maxwell took a few bites of his sandwich and then broke the silence.

"Bob, about two weeks ago, Sam gave us a pretty gloomy forecast, right over there." He pointed toward the far corner of the dining room. "Here *you* are, saying basically the same thing. I don't know the markets as well as you two do. But if what you've both said is true—that climate change has hit the economy too, we're in for some tough times."

Minton cleared his throat.

"I hate to say it, Bob, but you're right. Let me give you a little of my perspective ... you, me, Stewart, our people ... we're going to be okay. We'll survive. Will we be riding as high as we used to? No—nobody will. What worries me is the average folks, the ones who live paycheck to paycheck. Those who barely managed to make it through the last cycle are going to get buried this time. And there's bound to be blow-back ... maybe even some ugliness like we've seen recently in Central and South America. At some point, that could affect us too."

"That's my point: it's *already* affecting us." Godfrey looked grim.

Minton continued. "And you're right about the rules—they *have* changed. The tax code, despite the claim it's been simplified, has grown by 20% in the last two years. Businesses have to contend with more red tape than ever, more taxes, fewer deductions, fewer allowances. Add to that the insanity of the Fed's policies." He shook his head, and his voice was tinged with anger.

"That's why we're all drowning. As Stew said, the picture I painted for them was dark. Unfortunately, I haven't seen anything to brighten my outlook.

"Bob, the only thing we can do—we, who know how economies work, who know how to produce and to manage assets, who know it's impossible to spend what we don't have—is stay a few steps ahead of the crowd. Now it's just a matter of protecting what we've got and keeping the government's claws out of it. It's defensive, of course ... and it's exhausting.

"You know, it used to be relatively easy to identify a good idea, invest, make a decent return, stay a couple of moves ahead. But Congress has removed so many assurances and legal protections that risk on any sizable investment has gone through the roof. Return on investment, meanwhile, has gone flat.

"Goddamn politicians. They have no *fucking* idea."

Maxwell shot a glance at his friend—shocked, not by the profanity but at the fact that he had never heard Minton lapse into hopelessness before. He saw the intensity that he'd always admired in his friend, an intensity that had always been so positively focussed. But this small breach was different; it was darker, more ominous.

"Sorry," said Minton, "but it looks like we're in the same boat." He sighed.

"I'm curious," said Godfrey. "Would you be willing to share any of your defensive strategies?"

"Sure," he answered. "Why not."

For the next fifteen minutes, the two businessmen spoke high finance as Maxwell did his best to follow them.

During a brief pause, Maxwell said, "Gentlemen, I don't know about you, but I think I need a drink." He signaled the waiter. "This friendly banter is getting to me."

"Now *that's* a good idea," said Minton.

"Yes," agreed Godfrey, "sound investment advice if there ever was any."

Two martinis and a scotch on the rocks later, the mood had improved. The friends ordered another round, and conversation flowed from business to sports to hunting to travel. At one point, Maxwell asked Godfrey about the personal favor he mentioned earlier.

"As you may know," said Godfrey, "my son Henry will be moving to New York in about six weeks ... at my Aunt Minerva's invitation.

"I don't know what he'll be doing, and, apparently, neither does he. In fact, I don't know if he has the remotest idea what he's gotten himself into, but he's accepted her offer. He won't tell me how much he's going to be making, and I suppose it's none of my business. He's gonna get a wake-up call, though, when he has to pay three times the rent he's used to. I was hoping that, if he runs into trouble, you might make yourselves available to help him out."

"I'd be happy to, Bob," said Maxwell.

"Of course. I'll help your boy any way I can," added Minton.

"It won't do me any good to get too critical about this Vox Stellarum business, especially since you knuckleheads are part of it too." They laughed. "But at least you guys are financially responsible, and you've got a lifetime of experience to help you stay grounded in the midst of Minerva's little experiment. Henry, on the other hand, is a full-fledged idealist. Between you and me, he's always had a tough time with practical things. His priorities don't necessarily line up with generally established practices.

"Somehow, he gets by, but that's because he still lives and works in Houston, which is totally familiar. I'm worried about what'll happen when he gets here. Manhattan may just chew him up and spit him out."

Chapter 24

In Queensland, Australia, members of Team 25 were seated around a circle of desks in a classroom at the local high school. Being Saturday morning, the place was quiet. Team leader Harry Fanning, a history teacher, had obtained permission to conduct their meetings on the campus.

Evelyn Belmont, a teacher at a nearby elementary school, had distributed copies of what they hoped would be the final draft of their response to Task One, and everybody was quietly reviewing it.

After fifteen minutes, most of them had finished and were idly looking about the room. On a table near the window was a large standard globe, and next to it was a smaller one with the "down under" orientation popular in Australia. It showed the South Pole on top, the North Pole on the bottom.

The two youngest members, Matilda Smythe and Timothy Birchell, were still busy, and the others waited a few more minutes for them to finish. Several minutes later, they too looked up, and Harry Fanning spoke.

"It looks like everybody's had a chance to read through our response. I saw at least a few of you make notes, so we may need to make some final adjustments. Before we get into specific points, I want to thank Evelyn, Christian, and Lucy for their work. The four of us met several times over the past week to combine all our ideas and create this draft.

"One more thing. It's imperative that the language be comprehensible even to our youngest members. Mattie, Timothy, are there any words or passages that you didn't understand?" They nodded.

"There's a couple I didn't know," said Mattie.

"Me too," agreed Timothy.

"Did you circle them? Can you tell us which ones gave you trouble?"

Timothy said, "*Paternalistic.*"

"And *dictatorial,*" added Mattie.

"That's the passage about indigenous peoples," said Lucy Blair, a 50-year-old artist and freelance writer.

"And *that* one," said Mattie, "*... indigenous.*"

"Very well," said Fanning. He turned to Lucy, who, besides being the team co-leader, was also his wife. He asked, "You want to have a go with this one?"

"Sure," she said. "As I think you children remember, we need to include an important issue that isn't on the Vox Stellarum list. Right? So, we chose to make the point that aboriginal people here in Australia, as well as in other parts of the world, need to receive a great deal more respect and protection than they presently receive—from the government, but also the broader culture. *Aboriginal*, which may also have been one of your words, is a describing word for a person who is descended from people that were here long before the British or the Europeans colonized this land.

"When the whites got here, they were often disrespectful of the natives they encountered. These people were dressed very primitively, they were dark-skinned, and they had strange customs—from the perspective of European settlers. The same thing happened in the Americas, when Europeans first began to settle those continents.

"*Indigenous* basically means the same as aboriginal—somebody or something, for it could also apply to plants and animals, whose ancestors have been here through recorded history.

"In that section of our response, we are basically saying that government, and people on an individual basis, ought not treat these people as children, as if we were parents, as if we were superior. That's what *paternalistic* means—acting like a father to a child. *Dictatorial* is a bit stronger. It means acting like a dictator, like an absolute ruler over subjects, as if they were property.

"Does that help?"

Connor Birchell saw puzzlement in his little brother's eyes, and he raised his hand. "Can I say something?"

"Of course," said Lucy.

"You know my friends Warren and Mallana?" Connor asked his brother, who then nodded. "They're aborigines, at least partially, meaning they have parents or grandparents who follow the ways of their tribe. They've told me stories about how they sometimes get mistreated—not by me or my friends, but others who don't really bother to get to know them. For instance, when their parents applied for certain jobs, they got turned down ... because they look and sound different. A lot of people don't trust them."

"That's not fair," said Timothy.

"You're exactly right," said Fanning, "and that's why we've included this among the issues we hope to solve."

A half an hour and a few minor changes later, they were satisfied. Zachary Nuttall, the eldest male and a member of the Chamber of Commerce, spoke next.

"Do we have a word count?"

Lucy Blair, who had been entering the changes on her laptop, responded.

"2160 words—well under the limit."

"I think our response is damn near perfect," said Nuttall, winking at Connor and Timothy, his grandchildren. "I think we're done."

Mattie Smythe raised her hand. "Mr. Fanning, can I ask another question?"

"Of course."

"Do we know who will be grading this?"

"What do you mean?" asked Fanning, intrigued.

"Miss Belmont taught us that when we write a letter we should begin with 'Dear Madam' or 'Dear Sir.' Do we need to add that?"

"Mattie, because this is an essay, I don't think that applies," said Evelyn, smiling at her star pupil. "Very thoughtful though. Great question!" Mattie beamed.

Ten minutes later, Team 25 voted to accept the response as final. Fanning logged on to the Vox website and entered their encrypted user name and password.

"Well, here goes," he said. "Let's hope this is the first of many!"

⋅⟩═◉ ◉═⟨⋅

Ground fog blanketed the valley at dawn. Now at nine o'clock, it had dissipated, yielding a beautiful clear morning sky. Four men stood in the San Miguel River, two near the bank, the other two were twenty yards away, water past their knees. It was a fly fishing scene out of a Rocky Mountain vacation brochure.

Protected from the icy waters by rubber hip waders and several layers of wool and fleece, the men moved deliberately, still getting used to the slippery rocks. Malcolm Conroy, though an experienced fly fisherman, concentrated on finding his rhythm. He hadn't been in several years. He noticed that Sean Thompson, the co-pilot, was surprisingly proficient, and he found himself admiring the man's technique.

"Where'd you learn to cast like that?" Conroy asked, raising his voice above the rush of the current.

"My grandfather, I suppose."

"You suppose?"

"He only gave me a few lessons, but they stayed with me. He died when I was ten. He was strict ... scared the hell outta me. But when it came to fishing or hunting, he'd mellow out and actually explain things." Thompson continued casting as he spoke, never taking his eye off his target. "He was really good. My father said he could out-fish anybody in the county."

"It must have rubbed off. You have a nice touch."

"Thanks."

Conroy's line lay on the water. The delicate lure, caught in the current, was pressed against a large boulder. But he was oblivious—caught up instead in an old wound that Thompson's story had reopened. Like the swirling eddies that could trap a leaf or a stick indefinitely, Conroy was fixated on a memory he couldn't, or wouldn't, shake.

"Hey, Malcolm. Fishing for *rock* trout?" asked Thompson.

"Huh?" he grunted. "Oh, yeah," he said, still staring downstream, into the distance. He reeled in his line slowly, obviously preoccupied. He needed to change the fly, which had become misshapen. After a few minutes, he was ready to cast again. He shifted his position and put a little more distance between himself and the others. He wasn't quite ready to release the line of thought that still tugged at him.

Conroy was thinking of his eight-year-old grandson. As he began to let out his line toward a promising spot, he imagined taking the boy fishing and hunting, introducing him to his dogs, teaching him about—

But suddenly a stab of guilt. He hadn't laid eyes on his grandson in five years. He realized he couldn't even remember what the boy looked like.

Now that he had chastised himself for this breach of duty, he blinked and shook his head, trying to snap out of the funk that had come out of nowhere. He maneuvered into deeper water and felt the added pressure against his waders. *It serves me right,* he told himself.

The head pilot, Aaron Newsome, and their fishing guide joined them in the deeper water. Newsome had the motion down and was looking solid. The hush of the water was the only sound but for the occasional automobile whisking by on the two-lane highway that ran parallel to the river.

Each fisherman let his fly land as lightly as possible, hoping to create an illusion that would summon a trout. Whipping their rods to and fro, paying out the translucent line a little more on each pass, they settled into the flow of the river. At some point, the clutter in Conroy's mind released its hold.

That evening, Thompson cooked the main dish, grilled rainbow trout, while Newsome prepared the salad and the rolls. Conroy tended bar, but mostly he looked around. The Owl's Nest Ranch was way too big for his liking, but he approved of the style. His examination confirmed what he already knew: Minerva had excellent taste, and she knew how to entertain.

After dinner, they moved to the fire pit on the terrace, and Conroy loaded his pipe.

"A man could get used to this," he said. For a while, nobody said anything else. The licking of the fire and the twinkling of the stars above were all the conversation they needed. It was utterly quiet in the vast expanse of the alpine meadow.

"So, gentlemen, what would you be doing if you weren't out here on vacation?" Conroy asked.

"I'd be at home with my wife and kids," said Newsome. "It's a school night, and my girls would be doing homework or texting their friends ... or both. Teri and I would probably be watching TV."

"What do you watch? The news? Sports?"

"Definitely not the news. Teri likes to watch CSI: Las Vegas or Seattle, whatever damn city they're on these days. I can tolerate that for a while, but I prefer the History Channel."

"Nothing wrong with being domestic."

"Nope." Newsome sipped his brandy.

"The funny thing is," said Conroy, "we aren't doing too much different here. Sure, we caught dinner, instead of buying it in the super market. But beyond that, we ate dinner, rinsed off the dishes, and now we're relaxing. Instead of TV, we're watching the fire."

"Maybe so," said Thompson, "but those little differences add up. I mean, look at this place! We're on a beautiful ranch, out in the middle of nowhere. I don't know about you, but if I built a fire on my back patio, one of my neighbors would call the cops. No, I'd say this is a whole different experience."

Conroy relit his pipe. The orange glow in the bowl was the same color as the embers under the logs in the fire pit.

"How about you, Malcolm?" asked Newsome. "What would you be doing?"

"I'd be sitting on my porch with my dogs."

"In Virginia? At your cabin?"

"Yeah."

"Don't you get lonely out there?" asked Thompson.

"Sometimes, but it suits me—the solitude, that is."

"You have any family?" asked Newsome.

"No," he answered quietly, "not anymore."

During their travels to round up the judges, Conroy had kept his relationship with these men at arm's length. He hadn't wanted to give any details, to anybody, ever again. But the campfire and the liquor, and a sense of camaraderie he hadn't felt in years led him to relax his guard and finally open up.

"I've told you guys a few stories about my work with the government. The last position I held was with the Commerce Department as Under Secretary. I was fed up with politics and chose not to pursue any more official positions, not that any came my way at the time. I think Washington was as tired of me as I was of it.

"I was preparing to return to private practice as an attorney—this is six years ago—but I wanted to first round out an inquiry that I had initiated, sort of a task force investigation. My wife Miriam was looking forward to having me around again on a regular basis, and we were considering moving to Arlington, to be close to our daughter Delany and her family.

"Things were coming together, and we decided to go on a skiing trip to celebrate our decision. The morning of, I got a call from one of my associates—his wife, actually. He had acute appendicitis. She took him to the emergency room, and he obviously couldn't handle the deposition we had scheduled. It was part of the wrap-up of our investigation, so I offered to do it. I chartered a jet for the others since they were ready and waiting, and my plan was to fly my own plane out that afternoon, or the next day." Conroy paused. His pipe had gone out, but he made no effort to relight it.

"As I left the meeting ... it was late afternoon by then ... my secretary walked up and handed me a note. I'll never forget the look on her face. It was an official FAA release—the charter had gone missing.

"I was up most of the night trying to get details, wondering what to do. The authorities weren't going to be able to send out a search party 'til sunrise the next day. At eight o'clock the next morning, I took off in my Learjet to help look for—"

Conroy was choked up. After a moment, he continued.

"I got word, in midflight, that the rescue team had found the plane. There were no survivors."

"Jesus," said Thompson, under his breath.

The pilots stared at Conroy as he looked out over the dark meadow. The fire settled, and sparks rose into the darkness. After a while, Newsome broke the silence.

"Were they able to determine a cause? Was it weather-related?"

"The weather was fine—visibility was unlimited. Investigators determined it was a malfunction of the hydraulic system. The black box wasn't much help."

Conroy's voice got softer and softer as he recounted his experience, and the other men strained to hear his words.

"I was supposed to be on that plane. I shouldn't be here."

What he didn't share was how close he had been to taking himself out. Emotionally exhausted and mildly hung over, he had been in no condition to pilot anything. When he heard that no survivors had been found, he held on, irrationally, to some buried hope that it was just speculation. And when he approached the area where the wreckage had been found, he scoured the range until he saw it for himself.

He tried to imagine what the final moments must have been like. He racked his brain, wishing he could somehow undo everything, blaming himself for not making them wait, blaming himself for filling in for his colleague. Blaming himself for everything.

On his third flyby, he had been close enough to the ruptured fuselage to see several search and rescue personnel sifting through the debris. He only discovered the dark impulse to join his family when he pulled up, at the last second.

Now, sitting and staring at the fire, he replayed that moment again, as he had a thousand times before. After a few minutes of awkward silence, he stood up.

"I need a refill."

The others joined him inside, glad to shake the morbid tone of Conroy's disclosure. When they returned to the fire pit, it took several more minutes for anybody to speak. Conroy reloaded his pipe, and Thompson lit a cigarette.

"I can't imagine how hard that must have been," ventured Newsome, "... to live through that. What did ... How did you manage?"

"With this," he answered, holding up his drink. "And my dogs. It was hard ... It still is.

"I stayed drunk for about two years. I don't know how I finally snapped out of it, but it probably had something to do with my decision to isolate even more. I withdrew to our property in Virginia and started renovating the cabin. It's interesting how physical effort and daily progress can heal. As depressed as I was, I began to have a few good days.

"I met a breeder in Virginia whose bitch—a beautiful purebred German shepherd—had just had a litter. I hadn't had a dog in years, and I was surprised as anybody when I found myself going home with *three* of them." Conroy looked up and smiled. "Except for that first night, when there was shit all over the cabin, I never regretted it. My dogs saved me."

→⊱═◉ ◉═⊰←

Dorottya Szilagyi was the last panelist to be hired by Conroy but the first to post her results regarding Task One. She lived on the outskirts of Budapest, in a modest apartment with her husband and two children.

She found her way onto Conroy's radar as one of a handful of members of the *Lehet Más a Politika* party (the LMP) that joined the Hungarian National Assembly via the parliamentary election. In his search for independent-minded judges who were willing to take a stand against the establishment, this group caught his eye. In English, the name translates roughly as "Politics Can Be Different." Borne of a non-governmental social initiative bent on reforming Hungarian politics by directly opposing the current political elite, it had "renegade" written all over it.

From the moment she was elected to her four-year term, Szilagyi was the most outspoken of her party. Her blog was an inspirational focal point for the group. Popular among her comrades, she chose not to run again, but instead to build the organization with the goal of doubling their seats, which she did.

After being hired to judge The Contest, Szilagyi had recruited two of her party colleagues as staff, and they helped her sift through the 84 entries. Three days of collaboration had produced three categories: winners, losers, and a middle pile of maybes. The first group, with just over thirty essays, fell short of the forty-two she would pass, and thus advance to Round Two.

She induced her husband to sit with her as she reconsidered her approach, doing her best to represent a given entry by the brief summary she had scribbled in red ink in the margins. She picked one up from the middle pile.

"This one is thick with Christian sentiment, not very open to the prospect of sharing a world with other faiths. Nicely written, but I can't give it a pass.

"Here's one I liked until I read it more closely. The tone is modern: technocratic. I don't think they put much faith in anything except machines and laboratories. Science is fine, but the politics is a mixture of state programs and strong-armed leaders." She added it to the growing pile of rejects.

"At this rate," her husband had commented the night before, "you will only approve a handful. Maybe you need to relax your expectations?"

"Perhaps. Okay, here is one I set aside earlier. It's very simplistic, but I like the friendly tone. According to their opening statement, the members live in a favela of Rio de Janeiro, which I understand is a sort of illegitimate shanty town. Somehow, they have avoided demonizing the wealthy and, in fact, seem to admire them. They emphasize that if they were to be allowed a fair chance to join the mainstream economy, instead of being partitioned and ignored, they would be able to create businesses and clean up their neighborhoods ... even reduce drug addiction and crime."

Szilagyi placed the response on the pile of winners.

⋆⇥▩ ▩⇤⋆

Few judges were well known to the average citizen, though most were known and generally respected in academia and among a broad spectrum of non-governmental organizations. Conroy had assembled twelve figures that had either avoided the decay of public scrutiny or weathered it gracefully.

One of the more colorful was the Asian judge Garry Kasparov. He had been the World Chess Champion for fifteen years, and many experts considered him the greatest chess player of all time. When the Wall came down, he left the Communist Party and took part in the formation of the Democratic Party of Russia. And when he retired from chess, he reentered the political arena to create the *United Civil Front*, an organization created to preserve electoral democracy in Russia. An outspoken critic of Vladimir Putin, Kasparov entered the Russian presidential campaign. He was forced to withdraw, however, due to a technicality created by Putin's operatives.

It was his defiant and vocal opposition to Putin that endeared Kasparov to Conroy, not to mention his brilliance at chess.

Kasparov's approach to his share of the Task One submissions was slow and methodical, and solitary. He declined to hire any assistants. He requested that the entries be translated into English, rather than his native Russian. Calling on his superlative visualization and memorization skills, he proceeded to read every essay without taking any notes. Then, he read them again, this time making only brief, cryptic symbols in the margins. By the time he scanned them the third time, he had already mentally sifted and ranked them, and it was easy for him to place them in two piles: *Approve* and *Reject*.

·⊷≡◎ ◎≡⊶·

Dr. Helen Caldicott processed her Task One submissions in an entirely different manner. The eldest female panelist, she gathered a support staff of half a dozen loyal assistants and graduate students, some of whom had worked with her for many years. One of the leading voices in Australian politics for decades, she was a renowned scholar and activist. A true collaborator, she welcomed feedback from every member of her staff regarding her critiques of the team responses.

Caldicott had been Conroy's first recruit.

"We've got a problem," she announced to her staff, only twenty-four hours before she needed to submit her list of winners. "We have ten entries too many."

Her tolerant and inclusive approach had always suited her, but now she was faced with an absolute quota. It took the rest of the day, but they finally reached the target of only forty-one advancing teams.

Thirty minutes before her own deadline, Caldicott double checked the team codes, and clicked SUBMIT.

Chapter 25

MIKE, VINCE, AND TJ occupied a circular booth in the corner of the Big T Truck Stop, a few miles west of Hays, Kansas on Interstate 70. As long-haul truckers, they had each crisscrossed the continent countless times. They liked to rendezvous with their buddies whenever overlapping schedules made that possible. The three considered themselves brothers, even though none of them had ever met their friends' wives or children. Stories told again and again had proven long ago that they were all from the same place: America.

They would meet three or four times a year, sometimes with others from their small band of adopted highway brothers. They would stretch their agendas and sometimes feign a minor breakdown so they could linger while a friend would put pedal to the metal to arrive in time for company.

"What is *that?*" asked TJ with a scowl, looking at the large salad sitting in front of Mike. He looked back and forth, from his own chicken fried steak to the unappealing mound of greens, as if his buddy had broken a basic rule of the road warrior's handbook.

"It sure as hell ain't no steak," admitted Mike. "The wife sent me to the doctor when I was home last week. He said my cholesterol level had went from bad to worse, and I have to eat this rabbit food until further notice—at least 'til my next appointment. I don't even git to have any bacon in the mornin' with my eggs, and I'm not supposed to eat them neither!"

Mike's giant gut hid the rodeo-style belt buckle that he wore for good luck.

"Damn!" was all Vince could say as he cut into a T-bone steak. Tall, skinny, and leather-skinned, he turned the bill of his faded John Deere cap backwards while he ate.

"What's that yer readin'?" asked Mike, nodding toward a section of a newspaper.

"It's an article 'bout The Contest," said TJ.

"Contest?" asked Vince as he spread a large pat of butter on his dinner roll.

"You know ... The *Contest*—run by those charity people in New York."

"Oh yeah, I heard about that," said Vince with his mouth full. "What does it say?"

"Well, I've kinda been followin' it 'cause I got a niece in Portland who's on a team."

"No shit," said Mike.

"Is she in the article?" asked Vince.

"No," answered TJ, "but the article's about how they're gonna announce the first round of winners tomorrow. I'm hopin' her team'll make it to the next round."

Mike said, "I followed it for the first coupla days, back when that blue hair first announced it, but I haven't heard much since. Does her team stand a chance?"

"I have no idea, but she's real smart. Goin' to college, takin' all kinds of fancy classes—computers, international policy ... shit like that."

"Go on then ... tell us about it," urged Vince. "What kinda stuff are they doin'? What's the point of this thing?"

"Hell, Vince, it was in every damn newspaper on earth. Didn't you pay no attention?"

Vince shook his head and took another bite of his steak.

TJ continued. "They got a thousand teams from all over—the whole *world*, I mean—and they're tryin' to solve all kinds of problems. This is just the first round, so they're introducin' their approaches—you know, their philosophies. Tomorrow, the judges are gonna cut half the teams and then give 'em another round of questions."

"Sounds like a circle jerk to me," said Vince. "What do they get if they win this thing?"

"Vince, what rock you been hidin' under?" asked Mike. "Even I know that. The top teams'll win somethin' like a billion dollars each."

"A *billion* dollars!" exclaimed Vince, nearly choking on his food. "For just talkin' about a bunch of problems. Holy shit!"

"So, what does the article say?" Mike asked, nodding sympathetically at Vince's point.

"Let's see ... the main point is the judges don't have to answer to nobody. They get to pick whichever teams they like best. Once the teams get cut, that's it. They're out. Move on."

"Well how will anybody know what they did wrong?" asked Vince.

"Good question," answered TJ. "I was kinda wonderin' the same thing. I guess it's like a teacher gradin' a bunch of tests, but there ain't no report cards or grades or nothin'. It's just pass or fail." He applied another shot of A1 sauce to his chicken fried steak.

"*Damn* ... I'd be mad as hell if some professor type flunked my ass," said Vince. "I'd be wantin' to know what I did wrong."

"You're in good company. That's one of this guy's main points. There's gonna be a lot of pissed off teams that're suddenly out of the running ... for a *shitload* of money."

"What kinda problems are these teams trying to fix?" Vince asked, a little embarrassed by his ignorance.

"The website lists a whole bunch of problems—*dangers* they call them."

"Yeah," chimed in Mike, "dangers ... *confronting Mankind.*" He held up his hands, fingers spread dramatically.

"Like what?" asked Vince, now intrigued.

"Mostly obvious stuff like over-population, terrorism, pollution," said TJ. "You know, global warming ... shit like that."

"Global warming, my ass!" exclaimed Vince. "Those sons of bitches don't have to drive Interstate 80 in February. We just had the coldest damn winter I've experienced in 22 years on the road."

"Yeah, well ... some of the so-called problems are questionable, but most of 'em seem to make sense," TJ said, a little defensively. "I like it that each team gets to pick the topics they want, but they gotta come up with specific solutions."

"Like shippin' rates and diesel prices? And taxes?" Vince asked.

"I don't think any of those are listed," said Mike.

"What the hell! Who got to decide what's important?"

"Just hold on," said TJ, unfolding his paper, "I think there's a list here somewhere." He scanned the page. "Here you go."

He nudged the paper toward Vince, who grabbed his reading glasses.

"Religious extremism ... okay. Those fuckin' towel-heads need to be put in their place. Check. Toxicity and industrial waste? Well duh! Anthropo-somethin' climate change? Genetic engineering? Sex and gender discrimination?

"This sounds like a bunch of pansy-ass complainers from Washington. And what's this about nuclear families? Like we need fallout shelters or some-thin'?!" Vince handed the paper back to TJ.

"Jesus, Vince!" exclaimed TJ. "*Nuclear family* means a traditional family. This has to do with how we got way too many single mothers out there ... and too many gays and lesbians raisin' kids ... shit like that."

"Okay, but what can the players do about that? Even if they come up with good ideas, how will that change anything?"

"Good question," said Mike, who was enjoying watching his friends spar. He found himself sitting uncomfortably on the fence between some of TJ's points and Vince's objections. "You know, this reminds me of one of those reality TV shows. Kinda like *American Idol*, but a helluva lot bigger."

Something puzzled Vince. "Who's payin' for all this? Where's all the priz-es gonna come from?"

"If you'd been payin' attention, you'd know it was that rich lady from New York. She's payin' for the whole damn thing outta her own pocket."

"No shit," said Vince. "She must be rich."

"She's a billionaire, you dumb ass!" said Mike, trying to wrap his own brain around that kind of money.

"I wonder what *her* nuclear family thinks about that," said Vince, "... givin' away all that money to a bunch of do-gooders, scattered all over. I'd be pissed!"

"I heard that," said TJ, nodding.

⊷╞═◉ ◉═╡⊷

At the Fanfare Hotel and Casino in Las Vegas, Nevada, a boisterous crowd was gathered at the betting gallery. A row of monitors displayed odds on the usual mix of spring sporting events as well as the upcoming Olympics. Recently, a new screen had been installed and was drawing lots of attention. It was devoted to The Contest.

In a world in which insurance companies will insure a pianist's fingers, protection from alien abductions, and even a celebrity's chest hair and mustache, the world of syndicated betting is even more elaborate and inventive. Bookies will seize on any opportunity to capitalize on outcomes invested with public interest. Within days of the announcement of The Contest, bookmakers from all over the globe rushed to arrange a portfolio of betting opportunities, and the more established houses assigned their best statisticians to the task of setting the odds.

On-line activity tapped into a global hunger for millions of bettors. The odds on obvious bets like which teams might advance to the next round had long since stabilized, but there was a complete lack of new information since team processes were required to be confidential and secret. This didn't keep the betting world totally at bay. Bookies everywhere were busy coming up with fresh twists on ways to place wagers on the biggest batch of uncertainty since the invention of roulette.

The Olympics, always a boon to the gambling houses and bookmaking syndicates, was taking a back seat to Minerva Bennett's global competition. So were the presidential primaries. Even revenue on the Powerball lottery in North America slumped as betting on Round One became the hot new item.

With no historical data available, the odds for and against were set and adjusted by the cumulative whims of millions of spectators and, no doubt, a few participants. The fifty favorite teams were listed on the left side of the new monitor. Below these were the ten long-shots—the teams assumed by the aggregate of bettors to have virtually no chance in making it to Round Two.

A separate set of wagers was posted that was drawing equally heavy interest ... Which teams will make it all the way to the Final Round? What will be the top three *Dangers Confronting Mankind*? Which nation will boast the highest number of finalists? And there were several unofficial wagers that were rumored to exist, but were not officially listed ... Will Minerva Bennett live to see The Contest resolved? How many pages long will the winning entry be? Will any governments fall due to the advancing of revolutionary ideas published in a manifesto?

Six of the top ten favorites were from the USA, two from Europe, one from Asia, and one from Australia. Pride and arrogance, no doubt, were factors in the heavily skewed distribution of odds in Las Vegas.

The long-shots were all from Africa, Asia, and South America. The "Slum Dogs" of Rio de Janeiro, their nickname given by a Hollywood reporter, were listed at 50,000 to 1; a Palestinian team from the West Bank was listed at 15,000 to 1.

⋅⊷═◉ ◉═⊶⋅

Libby Armstrong called a special staff meeting for Sunday afternoon. The Vox Stellarum offices had been buzzing with activity for days, coming off several weeks of low activity.

As the judges submitted their lists of teams that would advance, only two people had access to the master list: Bobby Jabari and Wanda Freeman. But even they would be unable to make sense of the responses, for not until the press release the following day would an auto-decryption program render the entries legible.

Since the Vox website first made its debut, numerous attempts had been made by the hacking community to disrupt and compromise the foundation and its endeavors. Data security and steady performance were ever on Jabari's mind as he monitored the servers and maintained the fire walls.

To aid him in this effort, he brought in several *grey hats*, programmers occupying that blurry region between freedom of information and the sanctity of intellectual property. They raised eyebrows with their edgy attire, questionable hygiene, and loose manners, but nobody could knock their work ethic. Camped out in the server room, lights low, they stared at monitors filled with code for twelve to fifteen hours a day.

"Settle down, people," said Libby from the head of the conference table, her iPad open to a checklist of to-dos. "I don't want to keep you any longer than I have to. I'm going to read through tomorrow's agenda. Let's see if we've missed anything." She was near the end of her pregnancy and was looking rosy and surprisingly relaxed.

"As you all know, we're back on the front page. If you're a fan of *Saturday Night Live*, you know what I'm talking about. The sketch last night was ... well, I can't say that I could really follow it."

"It was awesome!" said James Ruhle. "A brilliant spoof of '24' ... *The Dangers Confronting Jack Bauer.*"

"Maybe it's a guy thing, but I never watched that show," said Libby.

"Not necessarily," ventured Catherine. "I love Jack Bauer." She smiled at James, and several others nodded sympathetically. Egged on, Ruhle elaborated.

"Yeah, so ... Kiefer Sutherland was the host, not quite as buff as he used to be, but still pretty bad-ass. As Bauer, he had only one hour to solve each of our 24 world problems, and then he'd have to check in with CTU, which looked remarkably like our offices here. They had the digital clock counting down, way faster than normal of course, with that ominous sound. His backup units were contest teams, none of whom spoke English, and he'd get all frustrated and have to just handle everything himself."

"Yeah, well, fun and games aside," said Libby, doing her best to roll with the humor, "let's see where we stand for tomorrow's press release. Wanda, have all the judges reported in?"

"Yep. Got the last one a few hours ago."

Libby checked off that item. "Okay, let's talk security for a minute. We're sitting on information that is, in a word, *valuable*. Speculation on the results of

Task One have driven a surge in betting, not just in Las Vegas and Atlantic City, but all over the world. I think we're going to have a huge audience tomorrow, so we need to be prepared.

"Catherine, can you talk about the press conference?"

"Sure," said Catherine. "While we don't expect the kind of media circus we had when we announced the task, we think TV and Internet audiences will be huge. Everybody wants to know which teams will advance and how their responses will read. The release to the print media outlets will include the full list of advancing teams, as well as a brief note of congratulations from Minerva.

"We think the bulk of the reaction will take a day or two. People will need time to go on-line, scan the list, and read the responses."

Bindiya raised her hand. "Once people have time to read some of the essays, I think we can expect questions regarding the judging process. Do we have a prepared statement? Teams will want to know why they were cut?"

Libby decided to respond. "This is one of the issues we've been side stepping, frankly. There's nothing we can do about it at this point. In fact, this is why we're announcing Task Two immediately instead of scheduling a break, which is what we'd originally planned. We hope this will limit the press's ability to dwell on discontent or to scrutinize the judging process."

James cleared his throat. "Going straight from one task to the next will help, but we're still going to have at least a handful who come looking for recourse ... some kind of second chance."

"That's the one thing we can't allow," said Libby stridently. "We're just not set up for it. That could bring down the whole structure of confidence we've built up." She sat back and rubbed her temples, no longer looking so refreshed.

"Cade Tompkins brought up this very point a month ago, and he questioned our policy of allowing the judges to issue their opinions in a pass/fail format. He and his staff have prepared a generic script that we might use if things get ugly. Our strategy will be to deflect anger back at disgruntled teams and invoke good sportsmanship. In the registration process, each team agreed to the terms, including the judging criteria.

"Even if we had the judges submit their logs and scoresheets to us, we'd be crazy to divulge them. That would open us up to a global bitching session that could never be resolved."

Nobody could deny Libby's point. For a moment, they just looked at one another, and the only sound was the faint hum of the air conditioner and distant traffic sounds.

"Libby's right," said Catherine. "We have to stand firm on this. And regarding your question, Bindiya, I'll forward the statement Cade offered. It basically states that the Vox Stellarum staff members are staying out of it. We designed The Contest to run as smoothly and fairly as we know how. The panel of judges is solid, and we trust them.

"If a team wants to lodge a complaint, it'll have to be against the entire panel, and ultimately against the communities they represent ... pretty much the entire population."

⋅◦⊨◉ ◉⊨◦⋅

Malcolm Conroy and the pilots cut their getaway in Colorado one day short and returned to New York on Friday, ahead of a late spring storm that precluded their last day of fishing. He had planned to fly back to Virginia, but Minerva intervened with a dinner invitation and offered to put him up for the weekend. He accepted the dinner invite but opted to stay at a hotel.

Having just been a guest at her ranch, Conroy resisted another dose of her hospitality out of a deep reflex to maintain his independence. Suspicious of too many kind gestures, he tended to assume an agenda lurked below even the most benign offerings.

Conroy rode the elevator down to the lobby and walked out the hotel entrance. He looked forward to a brisk walk through the park before heading to his dinner engagement. He glanced at a bellman, busy extracting an inordinate number of monogrammed suitcases from the trunk of a limousine. He noticed the line of polished luggage carts, the crisp uniforms of the concierge and the valets, all standing in formation, ready to pounce on the next guests, hopes of hefty tips thinly disguised as enthusiasm. This simple scene, with its elaborate subtext, triggered a current of memories as he made his way to the crosswalk.

It reminded him of a book he had read many years earlier—*Steppenwolf*, written by Herman Hesse. He identified with the hero's dilemma, which was having to navigate two worlds while belonging to neither. Like the protagonist Harry Haller, he condemned society for its decadence. In his dark moods, he saw the trappings of polite civilization as an elaborate package of lies. Conroy felt a sudden urge to avoid the dinner engagement and just go on a walkabout.

After thirty minutes of exploring Central Park, he realized that keeping his word outweighed his desire for solitude. He turned toward Minerva's building.

The concierge ushered him onto the elevator and punched in the top floor. He had fifteen seconds to banish the scowl on his face, as well as the underlying melancholy.

"Good evening, Malcolm. Come in, come in," said Minerva, who rose to meet him as he stepped from the foyer into the living room.

He quickly scanned the small gathering, wondering what sort of guests Minerva had brought together for the evening. Until he saw her elegant figure standing across the room, he didn't realize that the one person he had hoped to see was Catherine Myers. When their eyes met, and he saw her smile, his lingering regret at having accepted the invitation dissolved.

Minerva introduced him to Gladys Atchley and then Louisa Tourangeau, visiting from Switzerland. He bowed toward both women, then followed his hostess to meet the other guests.

"You know Libby, of course, and this is her husband Scott." Conroy smiled at Libby and shook hands with her husband, who, he was pleased to see, was a normal Midwestern type—not one of those overly groomed metrosexuals for whom he had only contempt.

Minerva then maneuvered toward Catherine Myers. When Conroy realized the man next to her was her date, he felt a stab of jealousy. He shook her hand and smiled, holding it a little longer than he probably should have, then turned to meet her escort.

"This is Anthony Parrish, her ... *friend*," said Minerva awkwardly, barely avoiding the term "boyfriend," which Catherine had thus far denied.

Shaking hands with Parrish, Conroy tried to convince himself that his jealousy was based on a fatherly concern for his favorite Vox Stellarum employee, but his glare belied this fabrication.

He welcomed the distraction of greeting the remaining guests: Doris and Stewart Maxwell, Trish and Sam Minton. A half an hour later they all moved to the dining room.

"Mr. Conroy, Minerva has piqued our interest in you," said Louisa, "and I'm intrigued. The fact that you rounded up your panel on such short notice is nothing short of miraculous."

"Thank you." He inclined his head.

"Would you be willing to entertain us with a story or two? I found your choices fascinating. Did you know any of them?"

"I had met two of them during my tenure with the State Department, but neither one remembered me. I believe it was Minerva's reputation that paved the way. *She* gets the credit for getting me in the door."

He took a bite, but noticed they were all still looking at him expectantly.

"Oh, a story ... okay ... Let me tell you about my meeting with my third recruit. My conversation with her was unique." Except for the sound of forks and knives, the room was quiet. Conroy sipped his wine and then continued.

"I began my search in Australia, and I signed the first two judges easily. From there, we flew to southeast Asia: Yangon, Myanmar. Some of you may know it by its former name—Rangoon, Burma.

"Asia is huge. I was rather daunted, I must admit, by the prospect of finding one man and one woman to represent it. Of course, that could be said about the other continents too, but Asia was the most challenging due to its extreme cultural diversity. One woman, Aung San Suu Kyi, was at the top of my list—recent controversy around the Rohingya refugees notwithstanding. She was awarded the Nobel Peace Prize over twenty years ago.

"I knew little about her other than that she had to endure decades of hardship and that she had always maintained a strictly peaceful stance. I liked what I'd heard about this woman, and because she had just left the Parliament, I thought she might be open to serving on our panel.

"Well, I was in for a surprise. This woman, petite and elegant, turned out to be one of the hardest negotiators I've ever met. It had nothing to do with raising her voice or pounding her fist. She was soft-spoken, very articulate, an Oxford graduate, worldly ... tough as nails.

"'Mr. Conroy,' she said, 'tell me why you are here.' I recited a stock introduction I'd composed, stating my position as an envoy for Vox Stellarum ... very straightforward.

"'But why are you here?' she asked. I restated what I'd just said, but she was unimpressed. I asked her if she had heard of The Contest. I stated that Minerva Bennett's vision would inspire much needed change to the whole world, and that I believed her record of activism qualified her to serve on our panel. I heaped praise as thick as I could.

"Still, she looked at me—looked *through* me. 'Why are you here?' she asked again. I didn't know what to say.

"'You are typical of the western mindset,' she said. 'Something is created and put in a box, packaged for general consumption. You are given this box and told to sell it. You don't really know what's in the box, but you think that's not important. Your job is to find a buyer.'

"She was accusing me of being a traveling salesman! It was the damnedest thing. She let me squirm as I tried to figure out her angle, and I kept having to remind myself that I was speaking to a sort of female cross between Nelson Mandela and the Dalai Lama.

"'You come as a messenger, but you don't understand the message.' She glared at me. 'Why should I listen to you if you don't believe in the message?'

"I explained how I'd been approached, how I'd been skeptical, but had in fact been won over. I told her of my former diplomatic positions in various branches of the government. I made some general comments about the value to society, but she interrupted me.

"'Yes, but you still don't believe in this cause. You are here to do a job and collect your fee. You will go back to your life and nothing will change. *You* will not change.'

"We just looked at each other, in silence—the most awkward minute of my life.

"'You're right,' I said eventually. "I don't know how you know this about me, but you're right. I see it, but I don't feel it. I'm trying to feel it. No, that's not right ... I'm hoping that I'll learn to feel it, learn to believe it—believe in it—The Contest, I mean. I'm not an idealist, but I'm trying to open myself to the possibility that people can change, including me.'

"I went on for a few minutes, and she listened very respectfully. I guess at some point, I began to relax and speak to her like ... like I used to speak to my wife Miriam.

"'So,' she said finally, "are you here to *sell a product?* Or to *serve a cause?*'

"I'll be damned if I didn't suddenly get her point. I didn't realize I was just going through the motions, but, on some level, I was.

"'I'm here to serve a cause,' I told her.

"'Okay, then,' was all she said ... and she signed the agreement."

Conroy looked down to take another bite, hoping to hide the fact that he'd suddenly gotten emotional.

"I think you're a romantic at heart," said Louisa Tourangeau. "Lovely story. Thank you."

Plates were cleared shortly thereafter, and conversation broke out around the table. While Louisa told stories of some of her adventures with Minerva, Conroy listened with polite, yet detached, attention. His gaze kept gravitating toward Catherine.

Mildly chastising himself for thoughts unbecoming of a gentleman, he endeavored to limit his glances, and to keep them as discreet as possible. When he saw that she and Libby, both sitting at the far end of the table, had launched into a colorful account of their trip to his cabin, Conroy was happy he could stare at her without pretense. He grinned at several memorable points in their story, including the dramatic way she described his gorgeous, yet lethal, "attack dogs" ... how he was able to communicate with them "as if by telepathy."

The dinner party transitioned to dessert and coffee, and then Minerva led them to the living room. Shortly, Conroy was coaxed into another story.

"I had to brace myself for one of my last encounters—the second North American judge, Stewart Brand. As the founder and publisher of *The Whole Earth Catalog*, I expected him to be a tough customer. In my research, I found out Steve Jobs declared the Catalog to be the Google search engine of its day, but in paperback form. It was one of the bibles of his generation.

"I came across one of his most recent works a couple of years ago. It's called *Whole Earth Discipline: An Ecopragmatist Manifesto.* Talk about attitude. Here's a guy who talks pragmatism, but who approaches life as an idealist.

"When I arrived at his home in northern California, I found him hospitable and polite. I could see the intensity in his eyes from the moment I shook his hand. For someone who had overseen dozens of projects and written hundreds of articles, he spoke in a very measured fashion. Once he got warmed up, he was like a talking encyclopedia.

"At one point, Brand asked me, 'What do you know about critical path?'

"Since I had no idea what he was talking about, he explained that *Critical Path* was Buckminster Fuller's magnum opus. In the book, Fuller described the history and pre-history of mankind, and he speculated about several possible futures. He declared that if we are to survive as a species, without poisoning or incinerating ourselves, we must design a critical path—a blueprint—and diligently, cooperatively, intentionally follow it.

"I remember him looking at me oddly, as if to say: *Get it?* Then he said, 'By the way, I'd add *immediately* to Fuller's list of adverbs, because our time is running out.'

"This was quite a statement from a man who co-chairs the Long Now Foundation, an organization that promotes long-term thinking and responsible action on the order of ten thousand years. This guy even writes the date with five digits."

Conroy noticed that Minton grinned and nodded.

"Sam, you know what I'm talking about?"

"I do. I've read most of his work. For instance, instead of writing two-zero-one-eight for 2018, Brand and his colleagues insert a leading zero. To emphasize that we humans are still in the very early stages of what we all hope will be a long stay on Earth, they write *zero*-two-zero-one-eight."

"Exactly," said Conroy. "Well ... then he asked me if I knew the significance of *vox stellarum*. I did, of course, but he must have thought my Latin translation missed some deeper meaning. He could tell I had no idea what he was getting at. Of course, this gave him another opportunity to connect the dots for me—yeah, he's a bit of a show-off.

"He spoke of Minerva's desire to tap into the collective consciousness of the planet, and how her contest is a way to survey and document the ideas of the global village. He stated that, in order to accept the role of judge, he needed to determine that it was congruent with his own approach to the same issues. His biggest concern seemed to be that the competition builds up to a dynamic climax, but then it culminates too abruptly—with insufficient accountability.

"'But *then* what?!' he cried.

"I was doing my damnedest to keep up with him at that point, and I resorted to using his own invented word. You see, I knew Brand was a biologist, and that he'd made a critical study of genetically modified plants. I used the analogy of contestants acting like bees—attracted by the fragrance of prize money—pollinating and cross-pollinating the seeds, which were their ideas, their solutions. I explained how a thousand seeds had been planted and that each team was like a pod with yet more seeds ... and that the judges would decide on the most potent and *ecopragmatic* strains.

"That did the trick. Two minutes later, he signed."

Chapter 26

CNN News Flash: "We take you now to Jill Putnam, New York correspondent, on location in Manhattan at Park East Synagogue, headquarters of Team 981, one of 500 teams who have just learned they are to advance to Round Two in The Contest."

"I'm standing here with Beate Sirota Gordon, the eldest member of this urban group of would-be political scientists, and a half dozen of her colleagues. We find them in a celebratory mood—they're still in the running in this high-stakes global competition.

"Ms. Gordon, would you tell us what's going through your mind right now?"

"I'm very excited," she replied. "We put our heads together and came up with some very good ideas, and I'm proud of our work. The judges must think that we're on the right track."

Putnam asked, "Now that the results are in, can you tell us about some of the ideas you presented?"

"I suppose I could, but here's someone better suited." She motioned to a man in his fifties to step forward. "This is David Greenberg, our team leader." Gordon, who reentered the limelight after the *New York Times* interview with her and Minerva Bennett, stepped aside, almost off-camera, catching the reporter off guard.

"Very well ... um, Mr. Greenberg. Congratulations! Your team has advanced to Round Two. Can you tell us what's on your mind? What do think the judges liked about your essay?"

"Thank you. First, I want to thank Ms. Gordon. Her wisdom and experience in world affairs was a huge help as we crafted our approach. I also want to thank the rest of our team. Even our two youngest members, both of whom attend school here, made important contributions.

"Perhaps that's what the judges first noticed about our approach. We decided to start with the third question of the assignment, which had to do with the eligibility requirements, and we spoke to the strengths of these restrictions. Our intention was not so much to compliment the foundation for coming up with an interesting set of conditions, but to demonstrate that we embraced the structure. We showed that any problem, large or small, could be better handled by a variety of perspectives, especially across the age spectrum."

"Mr. Greenberg, I see you're wearing a yarmulke, which is not unusual in a synagogue, but let me ask this. Can you honestly present yourselves as a group that can propose broad solutions to world problems given that your team is predominantly Jewish?"

"Thank you for this question, Ms. Putnam," he said. "It's very central to our response, in fact. We acknowledged that no single person, or small group like ours, can ever hope to relate perfectly to the whole of humanity, or to attempt to represent it. But what we can do is advocate open-mindedness, tolerance, and patience. We can strive to listen to cultures that do things differently than we do. And if, individually, we make a practice of expanding our awareness, we'll tend to arrive at answers that suit more people.

"By the way, only half our team is Jewish. We have three Christians, one Muslim, one Buddhist, and one agnostic."

"Thank you, Mr. Greenberg. Best of luck to your team as you go into Round Two."

Putnam turned to the camera. "And now, we take you six thousand miles eastward—half a world away—to another advancing team."

Five seconds of silence accompanied a white screen, but then a night-time scene came into focus as a voice-over redirect from the CNN headquarters in Atlanta.

◦→▷◉ ◉◁←◦

"We are live from Atyrau, Kazakhstan, an industrial city near the mouth of the Ural River on the northern end of the Caspian Sea." The following interview was conducted in Russian, but through an English translator.

"My name is Ramazan Esergepov, and I am with members of Team 8 in The Contest." He addressed the eldest male, a man in his mid-seventies. "Congratulations, sir. Would you please introduce yourself?"

"I am Akmetzhan Musabayev, senior member, but not the official team leader. I am happy to be part of this group. We are proud to advance to the next round." Esergepov thanked him and moved to the man standing next to him.

"Good evening. Would you like to introduce yourself?"

"Yes. My name is Takhir Burkitbayev. Immediately after hearing about The Contest, both my wife Umit and I wanted to form a team. It took us less than a day to gather these good people, including our son, Serik, and daughter, Luba. We are like a big family, and we are very proud to be representing Kazakhstan in this event."

"And what do you think your chances are of advancing to Round Three, and even beyond?" asked the reporter as he glanced toward the rest of the team members standing beside him. At a nearby table sat two officials, stone-faced, apparently unimpressed by the hoopla in the patio of the lively cafe.

"I think our chances are good. We are smart. We are committed. We have extensive cultural history to draw upon as we respond to the questions posed by the organizers."

"Very few of us have had the opportunity yet to read any of the actual team responses," said the reporter. "Can you tell our audience what your main approach was?"

"I can do better than that—I will show you." Burkitbayev waved his wife over, and then his two children. The reporter looked at him curiously. When the man said nothing more, but nodded at his wife, Esergepov reluctantly held his microphone in front of her.

"Thank you, Takhir," she said. She was holding her teenage children's hands, and she gave each of them a noticeable squeeze. "My husband just demonstrated the approach we took with Task One. While still respecting old traditions, we suggested new ways to tackle the big problems we face. Sometimes it is an embedded hierarchy or bureaucracy that needs to just open itself to some fresh ideas ... and then long-existing problems can be handled."

The two men sitting at the adjacent table, their overcoats buttoned up uniformly, leaned forward as they listened for any hint of unauthorized speech, prepared to intervene on this special exception to the limited press policy of President Nazarbayev's regime. They had been sent by Nur Otan, the largest and most influential political party in Kazakhstan, with deep ideological ties to the Communist Party in Russia. Their tactics had softened in recent years, but their grip on political and cultural conversations was still a daily fact of life.

After Umit's response, two other team members spoke to the reporter, careful to follow the guidelines the team had discussed earlier in private: give only vague generalities, and when possible speak in proud nationalistic terms. "Otherwise," Takhir Burkitbayev had warned, "we risk being censored by the government, and even barred from the competition."

The CNN programming staff soon realized that the bromides coming from the Kazakhstani affiliate were less than exciting, and they switched to the next location for their whirlwind sampling of teams.

"One more live interview before we begin our in-depth analysis of team responses—some that made the cut, some that did not. We move six thousand miles southward ...."

⋅≻⟩═⊚ ⊚═⟨≺⋅

"Good evening. I am Sophie Hendrikz, coming to you live from Durban, South Africa. We're gathered in the home of Dr. Florence Pass, a professor at the College of Humanities at the University of KwaZulu-Natal. She's the spokesperson for Team 765, one of 500 who now advance to the next round."

Dining room chairs had been arranged in a gentle curve where several other team members were seated alongside Dr. Pass, just beyond the glare of the powerful halogen lamps brought in by the lighting assistant. The reporter had obviously selected her subjects to highlight the ethnic diversity from the post-apartheid nation, including both black members of the predominantly white team. Steven Pace had been included, too, perhaps because of his military background.

"Our focus in this task was to acknowledge that we're a society in transition," said Dr. Pass. "We see many changes that need to be made, yet we know these can't come about overnight ... nor should they."

"Could you explain what you mean—that change should *not* happen overnight?"

"Yes. We think it's a trap to try to force change, for that often brings about undesirable consequences that are sometimes worse than the original problem. For instance, my colleagues and I sought out a variety of participants when we first decided to register a team, but we knew we were up against the clock. If we had taken only an extra day or two, trying to recruit more blacks, and perhaps more religious diversity, we would have missed the deadline."

"Besides the undesirable consequence of missing out on registration, I take it you're pointing to larger issues. Can you speak to that?"

"Yes. One standard technique for correcting inequities, especially racial ones, is to implement a quota. But there have been numerous studies from all over the world that have shown that these quotas often backfire. Our essay describes ideal final outcomes, but with realistic intermediate goals, achieved voluntarily and organically.

"As South Africa has struggled to navigate life after apartheid, we still see embedded racism and segregation. Yet, there are several fine examples of voluntary integration that have occurred spontaneously. As a team, we stated that these are cornerstones on which racial and ethnic desegregation ought to be built. We drew on examples in the worlds of entertainment and sports ... how these arenas contain precursors of a wider cultural shift. Blacks and whites have always come together more readily, and more genuinely, when there are clear sets of rules, and when there are clear incentives for doing so.

"Even in the financial world, to limit a business to just one homogenous population is a recipe for failure."

The reporter moved to the two blacks, who were seated together.

"Would either of you care to comment?" she asked, holding the microphone in their direction.

Ode Sangweni, a former world cup soccer player, raised her hand. "Although I was born into apartheid, I was fortunate that it ended when I was still young. I remember my tenth birthday, in 1994, the whole country celebrated the formation of a new government. Mandela and the ANC took over, and things began to improve noticeably. We're still a young country in terms of racial equality. It's not perfect, but I agree with Dr. Pass that reform must be peaceful and attractive."

"Where were you born?" asked Hendrikz.

"In Transkei, near the border of Lesotho. It was one of the *bantustans* where my people were forced to live. We had separate passports—we weren't even considered to be South Africans. Because of the strict isolation forced on us by the former government, our standard of living was third-world."

"How did you manage to maintain hope growing up in such conditions?"

"My family was very poor, but my parents believed in education. We had books, and my brothers and I learned to read at a young age. Besides reading, and staying out of trouble, my parents encouraged us to play sports and to never quit. I'm grateful to them for my competitive attitude."

"And you?" She aimed the microphone at Thabo Khune, a seventeen-year-old boy.

"I'm still in high school ... most of these changes happened before I was even born. We're learning about apartheid in school, buy it's hard to imagine how difficult it was for my parents. I'm only beginning to appreciate the courage it took to endure those times. I want to help our country keep moving towards freedom. I want to show that we all deserve the opportunity to live happy and productive lives."

"Well put," said Hendrikz. "If I may, let me ask a tough question. What would you say are the challenges to being black on a mostly white team?"

"I think my age has been more challenging than the color of my skin. But I think they're both an advantage too. I can see issues without the memory of how things used to be. I just speak about what I want for my future, and what I want for my friends and family. I think we all want the same thing really."

Steven Pace sat on the couch between Jessie Schumacher, who recruited him, and Andries Smit, a semi-pro rugby player. He wondered if they were squirming in the same way he was. He had nothing against his black teammates, but his background was steeped in a racism that he dared not admit. He had struggled with it for much of his adult life.

Listening to the reporter's questions regarding race and class struggle put him on edge. He recalled the slurs that he and his recce buddies used to throw around routinely, and he wondered if he could reconcile this with the fact that he genuinely liked Ode and Thabo.

Jessie noticed the tension in his body and nudged him with her elbow. He had been holding his breath, and his jaw was set.

"You okay?"

"Yeah," he lied.

When the interview was over, he retreated to the far corner of the room to reflect on one of his first missions, forcing himself to face what had occurred several years earlier.

His special ops unit had been dispatched to Zimbabwe, part of an anti-terrorist task force to quell the instability in the neighboring country. The official objective was to help stabilize civil unrest. Hyperinflation and heavy corruption in its mining industry had taken a heavy toll. But as every member of Pace's unit knew, they were really there to gather intelligence for a subsequent coup, co-signed by the commander of the South African National Defense Force. This branch of the military was notoriously old school and had resisted official mandates to integrate non-whites. They considered such missions a waste of time and that saving the *kaffirs* was futile.

Pace wondered if he could leave that part of himself behind.

⋅⊶⊜ ⊜⊷⋅

"Libby, what's your assessment?" asked Minerva. It was their daily meeting, and Catherine and Libby sat in their usual places, legs crossed, laptops open.

"As far as I can tell, we're looking pretty good," said Libby. "The editorials are focusing on the responses with only incidental mention of the teams that were cut." The floor was littered with newspapers.

"Good." Minerva turned. "Catherine?"

"I agree ... mostly neutral tone from the articles I've read. Lots of little summaries, a couple of feel-good quotes. Except for the fact that pretty much everybody is looking forward to more in-depth responses in Task Two, they seem to agree that we advanced some decent teams.

"Several articles touched on what the judges had to deal with, and they speculate on the challenge of whittling down the next batch. More than one reporter zeroed in on the variety of wild card topics the teams managed to come up with."

"It's an impressive list," said Minerva. "I found myself thinking that a few of them could have been included on our list."

"Uh-huh," said Libby. "I hate to admit it, but James was right. He predicted that would happen."

"Speaking of James, he approached me first thing this morning. He's already worried about our next task. He and Irina were talking about some of the on-line feedback, and they think the critics are going to come down on us unless we can keep the tension. He thinks we ought to spice it up somehow. What do you girls think?" asked Minerva.

"I think it's premature," said Catherine. "I don't know where he's getting that. Nobody expects the down and dirty answers yet. We need to build slowly."

"I agree, although if there is a weak link, it's Task Three," said Libby. "Since we're having them focus on their top three issues in this one, I suppose having them pick two more, and digging a little deeper ... it could end up sounding like a bit of a rehash."

Minerva nodded. "The teams will bring the drama, but we can do better. Let's work up some alternatives. I may even give my nephew a call—Henry, I mean. He's a very creative teacher, and he may have some ideas."

When they left Minerva's office, Catherine and Libby heard laughter down the hall. Bill Finch and Bobby Jabari stood behind Wanda Freeman at her desk in the social media room, watching a *YouTube* video. They were so engrossed that they barely looked up as the women joined them.

The scene was of a roomful of people, speaking in English, but with thick eastern European accents. They were in an animated debate about something, but none of them could identify what the issue was. One person was accused of being too emotional; another was accused of being too callous. The camera panned to a white board; it was filled with ominous, if not absurd, political pronouncements.

The actors seemed to hover in pairs: a man and a woman, a boy and a girl. As the camera panned again, there were even two dogs. Off camera, somebody called out, "Attention—time for roll call. Find your seats!"

The actors stopped their arguing and yelling momentarily, and they shuffled toward two portable picnic tables placed end to end, men and boys on one side, women and girls on the other. They were obviously enjoying themselves in the farce. The "old man" was just a twenty-something wearing a wispy gray beard; he was using an old-fashioned ear horn and couldn't stop snickering.

The players had exaggerated the age groups on the young side too. There were two "teenagers" and two "infants," played by more twenty-somethings. The infants were wheeled over in baby carriages and were dressed in swaddling clothes and diapers. They held sippy cups and gurgled. In mock seriousness, the leader pointed at each member and counted. There were only eight, so he called to the dogs and whistled. They trotted over, one in a blue bandana, one in a pink bow.

"Wait a second ... that's only ten. *Who is missing?!*" he asked frantically, glancing directly at the camera. Somebody off camera called out, "Here they are!"

The scene cut to a large cage with two white mice, and laughter is heard off camera.

"Oh, no! They've destroyed our outline. We have to start all over!"

The camera zoomed in through the stainless-steel mesh of the cage, and we see that the mice were nibbling on a tattered page of text. The title was just legible: *The Most Important Ideas in the World!*

Libby grinned. Just under the title of the video, which was "The Protest: Task Two," she noticed it had been viewed over forty million times.

"Good grief! I had no idea this sort of thing was so popular."

Wanda turned, startled. She was still smiling. "You should see the others. They're even funnier. These people have a serious following."

To the room at large, Catherine asked, "What effect do these have? Should we be concerned?"

"They're just having fun," said Jabari.

"In fact, they're probably helping our cause," said Wanda. "Satire usually increases interest in source material."

"Do we know how many groups out there are referencing our contest?"

"No idea," replied Jabari. "Hundreds ... maybe thousands."

"Some people have *way* too much time on their hands," said Libby as she and Catherine turned to go.

"Libby, wait a second," said Wanda. Her smile faded. "Several hours ago, we received a report from Bangladesh that riots have broken out in Dhaka, the capital."

"What does that have to do with us?" asked Libby.

"Not exactly sure yet, but we've been monitoring the story and waiting for more details. We were just taking a little break when you came in. A crowd has gathered to protest poor conditions and low wages, which we've seen many times before, but some of the banners are clearly anti-American. And at least one mentions Vox Stellarum."

"*What?!*" exclaimed Catherine.

"According to the BBC," said Finch, "a crowd of a hundred protesters grew to a mob of twenty thousand in just a few hours. Two multi-national companies made back-to-back announcements that they planned on shutting down their operations and relocating. And when word spread that both Bangladeshi teams had been cut, that added insult to injury and things got ugly."

"Shit!" said Libby, not quite under her breath. She wheeled and headed back to Minerva's office.

Chapter 27

"As-salamu 'alaykum," greeted Khaled Hammad, leader of Team 872, in a neighborhood just north of Hebron in the occupied West Bank.

"Wa 'alaykum as-salam," responded the other members as one.

"I am sorry this auspicious occasion has been tainted by violence. Many of us knew and loved Jihan Bahour. That she is no longer here to brighten our days with her warm smile is a tragedy. This is exactly why our work here is so important. This is the type of persecution that we must confront, but we must do it peacefully."

"I agree," said Farooq Husseini. "I wonder if it would be good to attend the memorial as a team—a show of solidarity?" Several nodded.

"That would be a mistake," interjected Ibrahim Massad, the eldest member. As a hafiz, a scholar of the Qu'ran, he commanded great respect. "We must mourn this loss, but we must do so privately. Any public displays as a group, especially one that could be viewed as a political statement against the Israeli government, could mark us for future reprisals."

The team had planned to gather in the Hammad family's home on Monday evening, immediately after the team results were announced. But the elder members had considered it too dangerous—an Israeli patrol had just carried out an eviction in a neighboring street. The authorities claimed that a restaurant and attached market, both of which had been there for over three years, were unlicensed. The scene became tense, and a security patrol was dispatched. Tempers rose quickly, harsh words turned to rocks and sticks, and then gunshots put a swift end to the clash. The wife of the owner had died, and one of the sons had been seriously injured.

Now, two days later, it was clear that the team had indeed advanced to Round Two; the team finally managed to assemble. They were encouraged to enter the home, a second story flat, as discreetly as possible. Though the mood was still muted, due to the lingering presence of Israeli security forces, they were looking forward to a little celebration.

The recent eviction was part of a larger action to make way for a new settlement. It was a fact of life to all who lived in the West Bank that the basic agreements of the 1993 Oslo Accords had ceased to offer any legal protection to the Palestinian people. This latest incursion was just that—the latest. It was the third such incident in six months, and that was just within their village of Halhul, separated from Hebron by a narrow band of Area B, and otherwise surrounded by Area C. These were designations that the state of Israel obviously interpreted as permission to oust the second-class Muslim population, block by block. Such insertions occurred almost weekly in the West Bank.

Through the open windows, the cool evening air was redolent of almond blossoms from a small orchard down the hill.

"Khaled, if I may?" asked Dhakirah, his wife. She carried a tray of cups filled with *tamar hind*, a beverage for special occasions. When everybody had been served, Khaled lifted his cup.

"May Jihan find eternal peace in Allah." They each repeated this softly. Then Khaled raised his cup a second time. "Praise Allah for our humble victory. We are one step closer to spreading the wisdom of our people." This evoked a more spirited response, and everyone took a sip.

Amani and Faris, the youngest members, looked coyly at one another and then to the bowls of treats, obviously wondering if they were fair game. Dhakirah noticed her son's glance and nodded toward him. "Go ahead children. Faris, let Amani go first. She is our guest."

This simple gesture broke the tension in the room. Likewise, several others moved to the table to fill plates with nuts, dried apricots, and cookies.

The team members had gathered a dozen times since Khaled was first approached by his daughter Wadha, a precocious teenager who had raised eyebrows since she was a young girl, not so much for her looks but for her boldness. In a traditionally patriarchal society, her behavior was seen by the men, especially the elders, as immodest, even sinful. She had learned the hard way to keep her modern notions to herself, but, in this setting, she had gradually allowed herself to relax and speak more freely.

Wadha had been the one to tell her parents about The Contest. Half expecting to be punished for even bringing it up, since many believed it was a trick by Zionist forces in the United States to undermine Islamic culture, Wadha had been surprised when her mother agreed to bring it to her father's attention.

Despite a lifetime of adherence to the basic traditions of Islam, Khaled Hammad had come to adopt a relatively liberal perspective regarding the Mohammedan path. Perhaps because he was, at forty-one years of age, neither old nor young, he was able to resist the call of orthodoxy on the one hand and heresy on the other. In his personal life, as well as his family life, he sought to apply the *sunnah*, the "clear and well-trodden path" described in the scriptures.

"The judges have blessed us with a vote of confidence. Our objective tonight is to review our first response and then examine the next assignment. Then we can open up for discussion," said Khaled. "Farooq, would you please distribute the documents?" Farooq, who managed an appliance repair business, passed around copies of the team's Task One response, as well as a copy of Task Two, which was published concurrently with the list of advancing teams.

The leader continued, "Before we consider the new task, let us scan our first response and refresh our memories ... it has been several weeks."

Ten minutes later, he nodded to Muhammad Husseini, a young man nearing his thirtieth birthday. "Muhammad, would you read our next assignment?"

"Yes." He read as the others followed along. For a construction worker and laborer, he was surprisingly articulate and soft-spoken. His Arabic was lyrical.

"Thank you, Muhammad. Okay, who would like to begin?"

Nadia Dajani raised her hand. She was forty-nine but looked older, for she had been through many ordeals as a community organizer. She was known for working tirelessly all over the village, as well as in other parts of the West Bank.

"When I reread our response, I felt proud. I love the way we crafted our position. We made religious and cultural tolerance central to our approach, and, given our status here in the West Bank, this takes on a special emphasis. I believe that must have been on the judge's mind, and I think we should continue in this vein."

"Absolutely," said Ibrahim Massad. "We are obligated to keep our allegiance to Allah at the forefront of all our actions, and that includes this competition. I think Nadia is correct. The judges will know that we speak with authority on these matters, not just because we reside in the Holy Land, but because we carry on in spite of all our hardships."

"Very good, Sir. I don't think we'll have any disagreement there," said Khaled. "I believe we must be careful, however, not to overstate our Islamic position. While not hiding or denying it, we must not draw the enmity of the Jews or the Christians ... or the Hindus and pagans for that matter." Wadha, Khaled's daughter, raised her hand, but the men appeared to ignore her.

"Perhaps you are right, Khaled. Allah will judge the infidels for their mistakes. Since our position is stated so plainly, we must move forward. I think we can continue to root each of our points solidly within the scripture, but we can offer plenty of earthly evidence for the unenlightened. In the long run, this will attract more to our way of being." The others nodded agreement.

Only then did Khaled turn and acknowledge his daughter. "Go ahead."

"Since the assignment is to pick the three issues we think are the most urgent, excluding our wild card, I have a feeling they are going to ask us to focus on that in a later round."

"And?" urged her father.

"That means we can't mention the One-State Solution. And since we really emphasized that when we talked about war and terrorism, I think we should shift away from all that, even though it was one of our top choices from the published list."

Nasmah al-Qasim, the eldest female member, smiled and nodded. "The girl makes a good point. In the introductory response, we made our basic stance very clear. The judges are well informed; they know what we deal with on a daily basis. Now we have a chance to show that we can think globally too. We must apply our precepts to problems that affect everybody."

Not to be outdone by his sister, twelve-year-old Faris Hammad raised his hand.

"I looked on-line at the statistics. There were certain issues that almost every team picked, including us. Maybe we should avoid these in our next response. The judges will probably get sick of hearing about them."

"Which ones were so popular?" asked Farooq.

"Climate Change, Human Rights, Religious Extremism, and War & Terrorism."

"Hmm ... that's four out of our eight," he acknowledged.

"Just because we chose issues that are universally popular is not a strike against us," said the hafiz. "There are several possible interpretations. One is that these are truly the most pressing problems the world faces, and failing to select these could have knocked us out of the advancing group. But think about it. Nobody knew what the statistics were until all the results were in. The judges couldn't have taken that into account, but going forward ... that is a different story. Therefore, I am inclined to agree with the boy. It is important for us to distinguish ourselves from the rest of the field."

Khaled and Dhakirah glanced at one another, sharing a brief moment of pride in their children.

Fadiyah al-Khatib, a woman in her mid-twenties, raised her hand. Normally demure, she rarely contributed. Dhakirah had spoken with her privately, urging her to take more chances. She knew her to be intuitive and thoughtful.

"Even though this task restricts us to three topics, we can relate these to several others by implication. That way, we appear to cover more ground than we have been allowed to cover."

"What do you mean?" asked Khaled.

"For instance, if we pick religious extremism, we show how this often leads to war and terrorism, and also how it involves human rights abuses. We can't go into too much detail on those consequences, because then we would be seen as breaking the rules. But, if we mention them in passing, we look clever."

"Very devious!" exclaimed Nadia. Blushing, Fadiyah continued.

"If we choose diminishing fresh water, we can speak about toxicity and industrial waste and dying oceans, and those weren't even among our selections. Our third choice could be global economic uncertainty, and, if we wanted to, we could tie this to at least four or five other problems on the master list."

Khaled spoke. "I like your suggestion, Fadiyah. It's logical to tap into the essential causes of one problem and to demonstrate that they lead to other related problems. We must be sparing in this approach, though, for as you said the judges will see through this ploy and eliminate us for ignoring the discipline of the stated task."

Nasmah smiled at Fadiyah, who reminded her of one of her own granddaughters. "I, too, like your idea. I move that we adopt this approach and that we use those specific examples. We will drive home a powerful message."

Ibrahim said, "Praise Allah! Let it be so. This is an auspicious start."

◦•═◍ ◍═•◦

Amid camera flashes and applause, a woman walked to the podium in the center of the stage. She wore a tailored chartreuse suit that fit just a little too tight. Her smile, also, was a little too tight. The master of ceremonies, a gentleman in a pinstripe suit, shook her hand as he presented her the Whitney P. Baxter Service Award, an engraved crystal plaque which bore the profile of the man for whom the award was named.

Representatives for the principal sponsors of the annual luncheon flanked the MC. Stepping forward in turn, they each shook the honoree's hand. The applause ended abruptly as they took their seats on the edge of the stage, and the audience in the Camden Hotel ballroom turned its full attention to Brenda Koyne-Hollingsworth.

Seated near the stage at one of the tables reserved for past recipients of the award were Minerva Bennett and her friends Gladys Atchley and Louisa Tourangeau. Minerva wore a simple dress, white gloves, and a hat. During the lunch, she had chatted animatedly with her friends and the others at the table, but now, as she turned her chair toward the stage, her expression hardened.

The Whitney P. Baxter Service Award was given each year to the man or woman who, by singular commitment and cooperation, raised awareness in the humanitarian community of one or more important causes or critical issues. Brenda Koyne-Hollingsworth had had her eye on this prize for a long time. She was sixty-five.

She looked out on the audience and drank in the smiles and nods of approval. Her gaze settled momentarily on her aunt.

Minerva looked directly at her, thinking back on their recent conversation. Brenda had called her in an attempt to break the ice that had formed since the pivotal Koyne Foundation Board meeting during which Minerva resigned as Chair. Brenda had apologized for her lack of tact during the meeting and then praised her aunt for her success with Vox Stellarum and The Contest. The tension mellowed, and they chatted for several minutes. The next day, Brenda had an invitation hand-delivered to her aunt's apartment. It included a personal note stating how honored she would be to have her "dear aunt" in attendance.

Despite the fact that Minerva had already received an invitation, as she had for decades, directly from the chairman of the event, and despite the fact that she had immediately seen through her niece's ruse, she decided to reconsider her decision not to attend. Ultimately, it was Gladys who convinced her to put aside her judgments and just allow herself to attend, neither to align herself with the status quo of the humanitarian world nor to endorse her disingenuous niece. Attending the luncheon, her friend suggested, would simply demonstrate that Minerva Bennett is someone who rises above such petty allegiances.

Brenda began her address, glancing occasionally at her notes. Typically glib, she enjoyed being the center of attention. She spoke about the privilege of position and the importance of a grand vision. She spoke about the need for commitment and the discipline of sacrifice, her studied gestures punctuating and highlighting her key points.

Alas, her speech—one part Sunday sermon, one part used-car pitch—bored the audience. A few nodded here and there at references to safety nets, to giving back, to *noblesse oblige*, but most sat with expressions of endurance.

Genuine empathy was something that Brenda Koyne-Hollingsworth had never inherited or acquired. She droned on, confusing polite indifference for rapt attention. During various strategic pauses, her eyes moved from one tableful of notable faces to the next.

Minerva turned her gaze inward, recalling her own presentation at a similar podium, thirty years earlier. With the stinging clarity of 20/20 hindsight, she saw the selfish pride and reflected glory in which she had indulged during her early days in this arena. She shuddered. *Was I this pretentious?* she asked herself. *This patronizing?* She felt a wicked impulse to jump up and walk out.

She glanced at the raffle tickets sprinkled among the place settings, the abundance of which made them impossible to ignore. These were the standard way to squeeze a little more out of attendees that had already paid $500 a seat, many of whom had written checks for thousands more. Like the roulette wheels in Las Vegas, here was a way to buy another chance to win the jackpot and, presumably, to feel good about it even if you didn't. The colorful script printed on each one stated the justification: "To Benefit the Fight Against Cancer."

Benefit? Minerva asked herself doubtfully. The word seemed oddly tainted to her now, somehow a counterfeit of the standard to which she had devoted much of her life.

She turned to watch her friends' reactions to the spectacle. They looked politely ahead, Gladys with earnest attention, Louisa with faint amusement. She shifted uneasily in her chair, sitting up even straighter in the hope of fending off the shame that had settled on her like an itchy blanket. Gladys turned and placed her hand on Minerva's forearm.

"Are you okay?" she whispered. "You're perspiring." She handed Minerva a tissue.

Minerva patted her forehead and cheeks, then closed her eyes and took several deep breaths.

When the speech was over, the crowd responded with measured applause. Minerva rose and walked directly to the exit, and Louisa and Gladys followed. They were joined by one of Minerva's bodyguards, who had remained standing to the side of the crowd. He alerted the driver that they were on their way down.

"My apologies," Minerva said, looking at her friends. "I'm feeling a bit lightheaded, and I didn't think I could handle the receiving line." Once the car pulled into traffic, she added, "Carson, please take us home."

As they approached Central Park, Louisa turned to Minerva.

"Minerva, my dear, I know what you need. How about a stroll in the park?"

"I don't think—"

"Oh, come on. Some fresh air will do you good. It will clear away some of that stuffiness from the luncheon."

Gladys smiled conspiratorially at Louisa and nodded. "I think that's a marvelous idea. It's such a gorgeous day."

Because she felt guilty for dragging her friends to the luncheon and then yanking them away so abruptly, Minerva acquiesced. Upon pulling up to the curb on 5th Avenue at East 76th, Gladys and Louisa giggled as they exited the car.

After asking the bodyguard to follow at a distance, Minerva turned to catch up to her friends, both of whom were obviously anxious to explore.

"I haven't been down here in far too long," she said, "but if I remember correctly, right through those trees is something I think you two will like."

They soon came upon a bronze statue that was surrounded by several dozen people.

"It's a girl ... she looks familiar," said Gladys.

"I'll give you a hint. She's a character in a children's story."

"*Alice in Wonderland*?"

"That's right. Isn't she great?" said Minerva. "One of my heroes!"

"Oh, and why's that?" asked Louisa.

"Besides being a clever girl, she was very independent ... she was always ready for an adventure," said Minerva.

"I liked the book too," said Louisa. "Did you know the author—Lewis Carroll—taught mathematics at Oxford? Yet he was a deacon in the church who played with puzzles and logic."

"Maybe that's why I loved the dialogue," said Minerva. "I recall one quote in particular, although I can't remember the scene. Alice said, 'I try to believe in as many as six impossible things before breakfast.'"

"I like that," said Gladys. "And what a fitting declaration for someone in your position."

"What do you mean?" asked Minerva defensively, wondering how her friend had picked up on her smoldering shame related to Brenda's speech. Indeed, it *did* seem impossible to tolerate, much less accept, her niece.

"Vox Stellarum, of course. You dreamed up the most ambitious social experiment of all time, and yet you remain so calm in the face of what, to me, looks impossible."

Minerva breathed a sigh of relief. "Thank you, Gladys. What a nice compli—"

"Oh, look!" shouted Louisa. "Is that where people sail their little boats?"

Sure enough, on the far side of the nearby pond, there were several remote-controlled sailboats gliding about, with a sizable crowd of onlookers.

"I've seen this on the *Travel Channel*!"

The women lingered at the pond for several minutes and then walked on. While Gladys watched a horse-drawn carriage in the distance, Louisa became absorbed in a sidewalk drawing that several children were creating with colored chalk. Minerva walked ahead and stood at the edge of an expansive lawn, dotted with picnickers and kite flyers.

Louisa caught up to her. "You're looking better. Is everything okay?"

"Yes, thank you. This was a good idea."

"Something got under your skin. Care to talk about it?"

"I don't know. But if I did know, I wouldn't know where to begin." Minerva turned and looked at Louisa. "There was a moment there, at the luncheon, when I was caught up in some old memories ... some of them, I'm afraid, were rather ugly.

"I'm ashamed to admit it, but I detest my niece. What she was presuming to stand for up on that stage, and the way she was carrying on, I was ..." She sighed and shook her head in exasperation. "That was bad enough, but what really bothered me was that I recalled my own acceptance speech for that award. Nothing exact, of course, but the general ideas, and I couldn't help but think that I must have appeared just as insincere and self-righteous.

"I'm not sure anymore. I don't know whether I've really changed, or if I've just put on a new face, a new mask. Maybe I'm peddling the same rubbish we were subjected to today."

Gladys had joined them, and she exchanged a look with Louisa: *Do we say anything, or just listen?* They waited. Minerva turned away again, looking toward some old men playing chess. She reached up and adjusted her hat, and sighed again, this time with a touch of resolve. She continued.

"I don't really want to talk about it, but if I don't, it will continue to eat away at me."

"We're here for you, my dear," said Gladys. Louisa crossed her arms and nodded.

"It's just that ... my niece demonstrated, quite vividly, how a good thing can be turned upside down and inside out. Good ideas, positive words, somehow strung together to become meaningless and lifeless. I couldn't help but judge every word coming out of her mouth. It was all a—" She shook her head in frustration, unable to find the right word.

"May I share a thought?" asked Louisa.

"Of course."

"There's obviously a great deal that has transpired between you and your niece over the years, but she probably wasn't as bad as you've painted her. Yes, she came off as artificial, maybe a little arrogant, but I didn't sense anything mean. She's just not a very effective speaker. Her words fell flat.

"By the way, you might not have been as mature thirty years ago as you are now, but you've always impressed me as a genuine, caring person. I can't imagine you ever coming across like your poor niece did today."

Minerva smiled faintly.

"My turn," said Gladys. "I agree with Louisa. You and Brenda may be related, but you come from different worlds, and it's not just because you're from different generations. There are other issues, I'm sure, but it doesn't matter.

"Here's what I know about you. You have integrity, commitment, passion ... honesty. Unfortunately, your niece comes up short in a couple of these. It's as if she's trying to live a dream that isn't even hers. She has followed examples—perhaps yours primarily, but she mimics without actually understanding. Following somebody else's lead is hard work. It takes discipline.

"You, on the other hand, are focused and intentional. And what makes you special is that you have the humility to question the nature of one mission and to create a new one. Now, *that* is something that's, that's ... terribly unique." Gladys, suddenly infused with emotion, reached into her purse and pulled out a tissue. Minerva did the same.

"Thank you," she whispered.

The three women composed themselves and continued their walk, the sun-dappled trees forming an arch over their heads. Most of the park benches they passed were occupied, some by couples, some by nannies and children, a few by solitary bag ladies busy feeding pigeons.

A man, dressed in stained, ill-fitting clothes and reeking strongly, emerged from the bushes. It was not clear whether he had been sleeping or relieving himself, but he made a beeline toward the three ladies, no doubt attracted by their opulence and a chance for a handout.

They weren't aware of the homeless man until their bodyguard strode past them and stood five yards ahead. He created a subtle, but absolute, barrier between the man and the women. They paused and watched. Although they could only see the bodyguard's back, they could tell the panhandler was being sent a very clear, if silent, message. Utterly outmatched, the homeless man, whose wild expressions hinted at mental illness, shuffled away as he grumbled obscenities.

The bodyguard turned and nodded at Minerva, as if to indicate all clear.

"Thank you, Mitch," she said, and the three friends continued onward. They were just a few blocks from her apartment.

"Will your contest change any of this?" Louisa suddenly asked.

"What do you mean? Homelessness?" asked Minerva.

"Not just homelessness ... *hope*lessness," said Louisa emphatically. "There seem to be so many people living in their own worlds, disconnected from the rest." She gestured abstractly at the people all around them, toward the park and then toward the busy street on the other side of the rows of shrubs and flowers. "Everyone clings to his own possessions, his own identity, as if that's all he has, and is. People just seem so ... so overwhelmed."

"Don't we do that too?" Gladys asked. "Maybe in nicer clothes, and shinier cars, but we cling to what we have, to what is familiar. And we shudder at the thought of losing it."

Amazed to hear her friends talking on such a level, Minerva recalled bits of their earlier conversation. She grasped at a thread which offered her a ray of hope.

"I've begun to see everybody in a new light," she said, glancing at Gladys and Louisa, but also looking beyond, taking in at least some of the people Louisa had included in her gesture. "I don't know if The Contest will change all this, but it's changing me. Maybe that's enough."

Chapter 28

"HUNTER, YOU AND Madison come on down. We're getting ready to start," yelled Chase Madden.

"Aww, Dad. We haven't seen any whales yet."

"Don't worry, buddy. You'll get a chance. By the time we're finished with our meeting, we'll be on the other side of Catalina. If they're around, that's where we'll see 'em."

The kids reluctantly left their vantage point on the flying bridge of the *Cha-Ching*, a 90' motor yacht owned by Hunter's grandfather. They descended the ladder to the top deck and then joined the group in the main salon.

"Okay, let's get started," said Madden, leader of Team 121. First, I want to thank my dad for hosting us. This is a pretty sweet way to mix a little work and a little play."

Chase Madden loved the fact that the media were making a big deal about there being three generations of Maddens on the team, especially now that they had made it into the fourth round. This played directly into his plan of using registration in The Contest as a marketing stunt. "The bigger the splash, the greater the cash!" he liked to say.

Growing up in and around Los Angeles, fluent in Hollywood spin and Century City slick, he knew that being nominated for an Academy Award was, in terms of box office receipts, almost as good as winning. He applied this logic to Team 121 and its over-the-top social media presence. Regardless of how well the judges liked them, he was hell-bent on leveraging their publicity, *his* publicity, while the time was ripe.

His father had been highly skeptical when Chase first approached him about joining the team. Jack Madden was among the dwindling breed of west coast arch-conservatives, and he condemned the big giveaway offhand as a ridiculous gesture of left-wing insanity. Chase assuaged his old man's doubts by telling him his real intentions. This softened him up, but the kicker was when he said, "Think what it'll do for Hunter's resume ... 'a family devoted to world change.' There's not a single university that'll turn him down when he graduates high school!"

After recruiting his father and his son, Chase added his girlfriend Heather Wild to the roster—a runway model who had appeared in several national campaigns. For obvious reasons, he liked having her around, and he knew she would go along with his agenda. He then signed up Pamela Knight, his of-fice manager and bookkeeper. He didn't give her a choice—he simply added participation in The Contest to her job description. The rest of the members were approached in rapid fire fashion, and he was able to field one of the earlier teams.

"Did everybody get the notes from our last meeting?" he asked as the boat changed heading, causing everybody to lean in order to regain their balance.

"Assuming that everybody reviewed the list of wild-card topics, what do you think?"

They all looked at him but said nothing. They were already used to his autocratic style. Chase had an annoying habit of asking questions and then telling you the answer.

He had e-mailed the agenda several days earlier, at which time he an-nounced they would be meeting on Sunday, even though it was Labor Day Weekend. Nobody complained too much when they heard they were going to meet on his father's boat. It was one of the biggest fishing yachts in the marina.

"Come on, don't be shy. Let's hear from somebody. Should we consider switching?"

Ashley Martin, a twenty-three-year-old waitress and Twitter addict, raised her hand. Besides being good-looking, she had been recruited for her amaz-ing knack of always knowing what the new thing is. She had friends from Manhattan Beach to Malibu, and even hung out with some industry geeks in

East Los Angeles. She wasn't necessarily knowledgeable about world affairs, but she was a natural-born barometer of fashion and popularity.

"I've been monitoring tweets about gun violence and gun control for the last week, and the posts have lost their edge. I think it's a fading concern." Proliferation of guns and the violence they cause was Team 121's choice for a wild-card issue.

Frank Pearson, Jack Madden's mentor and co-investor in numerous ventures, looked at Ashley and scowled. "I don't know about that Twitter business, but everyone I know is hot under the collar about the new gun registration laws. As usual, the California Legislature has its head up its ass. I don't know how in hell they expect to enforce 'em. I, for one, don't think it's a fading issue. Limiting the number of guns a man can own is a sure-fire way to piss off a good chunk of the population."

Jack Madden nodded and took another sip of his scotch.

"I agree," said Chase, "but we're probably in the minority on this. Even if we're not, we want to focus on the issue that packs the biggest punch. Who else?"

Ethel Hudson, sporting a Dramamine patch for motion sickness, raised her hand.

"I studied the list, and there are several that I like: Animal Rights, the Living Wage, the Gender Equity Act—for wages, that is—and the Green Space Initiative."

"Okay. Good list. Anybody else have a feel for any of these?" asked Madden.

Dominic, Pamela Knight's son, raised his hand. "I like the Green Space Initiative too, although I'm not sure how it would work. But I also like the one about colonialism."

"I don't see that one," said Ethel.

"Do you mean the one about imperialism?" Pamela asked her son.

"Oh, yeah. Sorry. It's about how certain governments try to control what's going on in other parts of the world, and how that leads to all kinds of problems."

"That ain't gonna change, son," said Frank Pearson, matter-of-factly.

Nicole Morgan, Dominic's classmate at Venice High School, decided to weigh in. "I liked that one, too. Even if the odds are against us, it's controversial. It's pretty much the reason for the wars we're still fighting, and that means pretty much everybody would, you know, have an interest."

"What are you gettin' at?" asked Jack Madden, adjusting his recliner forward. "We're at war because a bunch of goddamn terrorists decided they don't like *who* we are or *how* we choose to live our lives. If we don't take the fight over there, we'll have hell to pay over here."

"I disagree," said Nicole. "A lot of people believe that the Muslim world, for instance, has targeted the United States because of our military occupations. We've had troops sta—"

"I've heard that argument before," he interrupted. "Blowback they call it. Well, I call it bullshit. Those sons of bitches can't stand to see us prosper. They hate freedom, and they're sworn to wipe out our way of life. If you believe in pulling our troops back and letting those people do what they want, you're more naïve than I thought."

"Okay, Dad, you've made your point." Chase looked at Nicole sympathetically. "Even if you disagree with what they're saying," he continued, pointing at Dominic and Nicole, "they've hit on a hot topic. Remember, we don't actually have to *solve* the problems of the world, we just need to come off sounding reasonably intelligent. And in this task, I think we need to pick what the majority believe is the most relevant topic."

"I think I could get behind this one," said Ethel, earnestly. "Listening to you two go at it makes me aware of how mixed my own beliefs are. If we can demonstrate valid points on both sides, I think the judges will be impressed."

"I'm glad I won't be around too much longer," said Frank Pearson. His melodramatic statement startled the others, and they all turned. "The government is doin' its damnedest to disarm its own citizens, and now a bunch of folks are trying to put us on the defensive in terms of the military. They're tryin' to get us to turn tail and withdraw from fights that we depend on if we're to maintain our standard of living. Hell, when a man can't defend himself and his country *won't* defend itself, we're gonna go the way of the dinosaurs."

Chase glanced at Madison and Hunter, classmates in their second week of fourth grade, and realized they were blissfully tuned out of the discussion. They sipped sodas and ate chocolate chip cookies in glad detachment, apparently enjoying the view—out the starboard windows—of Santa Catalina Island. Satisfied that they were heeding his instructions to behave themselves and stay out of the way, he turned back to the others.

Since nobody else offered any other significant options, they voted to switch to the new wild-card topic. Chase urged them into the next phase of their meeting by throwing a bone to the NRA contingent.

"Part of the objective is to explain why we think this issue is more important than our original choice, and that will give us a chance to restate why we chose that one in the first place." He looked back and forth to Pearson and his father as he spoke. "I don't think we'll need to dwell on it, but we can communicate those concerns that Frank brought up. I like the way he tied the two issues together: individuals and their firearms compared to nations and their armies.

"I guess the ultimate issue is security, and that will be how we connect this back to our emphasis on property and maintaining our standard of living."

⋅⋗▣◉ ◉▣◁⋅

Henry Godfrey looked wearily out the backseat window of the taxi, thankful for his sunglasses. His fellow scout Tamara Johnson, fresher and more rested, reached for her overstuffed handbag to access her iPad. As she pulled up Google Maps, she chatted with the driver in Spanish, one of several languages she spoke fluently. Henry only understood half of what they were talking about and made no effort to follow along. He had a hangover. As the taxi exited the terminal of the Escobedo International Airport in Monterrey, Mexico and headed south toward downtown, he closed his eyes.

They were in their fourth straight week of travel, having already visited fifteen teams. For Henry, the cities, the teams, and the faces were a blur. To help counteract this inevitability, James Ruhle had directed each pair of scouts to keep a log book along with all receipts. They were expected to write up a trip report within three days of returning to New York.

Tamara embraced this mandate and took it a step further; she kept detailed notes and supplemented them with photos. At first Henry was intimidated by her type A approach, but he was happy to refer to her notes when his were lacking.

They had plenty to process at the end of each day, and they would usually meet for dinner to debrief. It reminded Henry of how he and his fellow teachers would discuss their students, comparing impressions and making predictions. None of the scouts' opinions were official. Speculation was strictly forbidden in the official reports, and they were instructed to detail only objective observations. Vox Stellarum could ill afford any trace of favoritism. Unofficially, though, that's practically all they talked about—how this team seemed on the ball, how that team couldn't possibly make it to the next round and so forth.

They had each been paired with other scouts during Task Three, which is when the scouts were first sent into the field. Tamara had been in Europe with Katsuo Kuroki, of Japan; Henry had been in South America with Patricia Bencomo, of Venezuela. The mixing and matching of scouts and regions, while designed to send a message of gender-balanced multiculturalism, did not always go smoothly. The office in New York received numerous distress calls, complaints, and requests for replacements in the early stages of Task Three. Mostly, though, the scouts rolled with the punches and remained in their assigned locations.

The roster of scouts had been announced in June, in a relatively minor press release. The male-female partners were touted as reflecting, in a manner similar to the Panel of Judges, diversity. Recruited from the ranks of United Nations operatives, the Peace Corps, and the International Red Cross, they had been chosen on the basis of linguistic fluency, cultural flexibility, and a willingness, if not desire, to log thousands of miles in a short time frame.

With the help of Bill Finch and Bindiya Bhattacharya, Ruhle oversaw the selection and preparation of the scouts. Prior to Task Three, Malcolm Conroy gave the scouts a two-day crash course on the fine art of dealing with customs agents, check points, curfews, government agents, unscrupulous officials, and pickpockets.

The organizational role that Minerva had originally promised Henry never quite worked out. He spent his first five weeks in New York hovering about as an intern, during which time he felt like a glorified gofer. When Minerva was informed that one of the twelve scouts had had to withdraw in mid-task, she instructed Ruhle to send Henry in as his replacement, despite the fact that he spoke only one second language, Spanish, and that only moderately well.

Now, with another dose of aspirin kicking in, Henry sat up slightly and looked forward. He fought back conflicting memories of the romp he and his college roommate had made along San Antonio's River Walk the night before. After a non-stop conversation during dinner, for it had been several years since they'd last seen one another, Henry had foolishly agreed to accompany his friend for some bar hopping. Pent-up desires and the frustration of relentless travel had finally gotten the best of him, and he defiantly accepted a challenge to have a shot of tequila, once again throwing his on-again-off-again sobriety out the window. He had no idea how he had gotten back to his room. He had blacked out.

"It's cooler than I expected," Henry said, sensing that he might just be able to keep his lunch down.

"Yes," said Tamara, an attractive black woman several years older than Henry. She was engaged to an attorney in Vancouver, her home town. "I love the way the mountains cradle the city. It reminds me of Tucson, but greener."

"Uh-huh," was all Henry could manage. He suddenly regretted speaking up. He knew his partner was liable to launch off on one of her impromptu travel dissertations, about Mexico, the city of Monterrey, the Spanish explorers, or perhaps the history of commercial and economic development of the entire region. He usually liked this about her, but he doubted he could carry on a decent conversation in his present state. He just wanted to get to the hotel, pull the shades, and check out.

"According to my map, they're part of the Sierra Madres," she continued. "Oh, and did you know Monterrey is their richest city? Most of the literature describes it as a first-world destination."

"Good," Henry said, "maybe the hotel will be decent."

"What do you take for your headaches?"

"The strongest stuff I can find," he said, immediately regretting the irritation in his voice.

"Shall we stop at a pharmacy?" asked Tamara. "We have time."

"No thanks. I took something just before we landed. I'll be okay." He sat up and drank from his bottled water. She continued her monologue.

"What do you think this team will be like? I mean, they're North American, but also Hispanic. More like the European teams? Or the American teams?"

Henry barely listened, thankful she wasn't pressing him for any responses.

"The Europeans are worldlier than the teams on this assignment, more up to date on global issues. It's strange ... over here we have ready access to so much, yet, when it comes to news, I think other cultures are way ahead of us.

"I think it has to do with the permeability of their borders and the size of their countries. Europeans are surrounded by so many different cultures, and it's normal to speak several languages. Maybe that's why they're more open to what's going on.

"In the US, and to a lesser degree in Canada, we're sort of monolithic and self-contained. Now don't take this too personally, Henry, but I think Americans are the worst ... they're *so* provincial. They think they are the be-all and the end-all. Remember the team from Denver, for instance?" She paused to see if Henry might comment, but he just stared straight ahead. She continued.

"Oh, and the one from Los Angeles—er, Venice. Now *there's* a classic example."

Henry nodded. "I can't believe they've made it this far. You ever read the *New Yorker*?"

"Occasionally. I'm familiar with it."

"There was this cover from ... I don't know, *years* ago. It showed a street scene in New York, but, in the background, it showed the whole rest of the world—all out of whack. Beyond the Hudson River was New Jersey, then the Rocky Mountains, the Pacific Ocean, and a couple of countries in the far distance ... Japan, China, Russia ... as if everything beyond the city was totally irrelevant."

"*Yes!* I know that one. You're right, that's exactly how some of these people come across, whether they're New Yorkers, or Texans, or just Americans in general."

Henry nodded. "Yep ... good ol' 'mericans. We don't care 'bout them damn for'ners!"

Tamara laughed at his sarcasm.

"Did you have a chance to talk with KK?" she asked. "I know you kind of joined mid-stream."

"Who?" Henry asked.

"Oh, sorry—Katsuo. I got in the habit of calling him KK. He's got a great sense of humor, very dry. He grew up in Osaka, but he's lived all over ... Singapore, Hong Kong, Moscow. During our assignment in Europe, he admitted that the Japanese are a bit like that—very proud, very provincial. But it's a different sort, I think. At least theirs is an informed sort of self-centered behavior. The western flavor, at least with Americans, is sort of an 'ignorance is bliss' attitude." She paused and looked off in the distance; then she turned back to Henry abruptly.

"But you're not like that. Thank goodness." She nudged him playfully and then laughed when he cracked a smile. "There's that smile. I thought maybe you left that in San Antonio."

He sighed and glanced at her. It suddenly occurred to him that she knew exactly what his headache and his melancholy were about. They had become decent friends in the course of their travels, and Henry liked her. And he liked her sense of privacy. He knew she wouldn't say anything about his escapades unless he brought it up first, but she was letting him know that she wasn't blind.

Henry shifted in his seat and took another sip of his bottled water. Feeling marginally better, he decided to give his impressions of the South American teams.

"I became a scout a couple of weeks into Task Three, so I only got to meet about half the South American teams. Patricia told me a few stories about the ones I missed, but I saw enough to agree with your point. Most of them were pretty aware of global events. Their knowledge of geography was impressive ... history, too."

"The Europeans were the same way," Tamara interjected.

"The South Americans were proud," Henry continued, "but somehow humble. They pretty much all agreed that if they were to be cut, they wanted another South American team to win. It's like they were part of an organization ... sort of like a National League/American League thing."

Tamara looked puzzled.

"Sorry—baseball analogy. You know, if a major league team loses in the playoffs, they still want their own league to win the World Series." She nodded. "Even though South Americans have this sense of belonging to a group of nationalities, they're still interested to hear about teams from all over ... Europe, Africa, Asia, wherever. But you're right—most Americans seem oblivious, even about other Americans."

"You think there's a correlation between a team's culture and the extent to which we can view them positively?" Tamara asked.

"Maybe, although I can think of an exception."

"The team from Rio?"

"Uh-huh. The favelas were horrible, but those people made us feel right at home. Despite the conditions, they showed off their community, *proudly*, as if it were their private kingdom. They were more grateful for the chance to participate than all the other teams combined."

Overcome with emotion, Henry looked away. In his mind's eye, he was seeing the fierce hope and undaunted determination in the eyes of a ten-year-old boy.

Tamara waited for Henry to continue, but he remained quiet. She said, "I know we're not supposed to have favorites, but I certainly do. I hope they continue to advance."

Chapter 29

"Is everything okay, Señora Carvalho?" asked Jaime Martín, captain of Team 915, based in the foothills of Rio de Janeiro. Carvalho, the eldest female member of the team, was helped to her seat by her nephew Vitor Rocha, with whom she had arrived late.

The other ten members were already present, and they were well into the meeting, two days from the deadline for submission of Task Four responses.

"Vitor's daughter is very ill, with a fever. He had to find her some medicine. I could not make it down the mountain without his help." Everybody looked at Vitor with concern. A tall, skinny man with thick black hair and a distinctive beard, he leaned forward in his chair. His hands clasped with concern.

"Ana will be okay," he said. "She is with her mother."

"That is good," said Laura Vereira. "She is a precious girl." Tiago, the youngest member on the team, nodded. He and his brothers knew her, and he thought she was cute.

"Very good," said Martín. "I will give you a brief summary of what we have done thus far. We have been reading through our draft and have only made minor changes. My wife Gabrielle, Señor Mendes, and Rosa have done a good job of putting our points down clearly. Take a look. I think you will agree. Rosa is making a note of the changes on her copy, and she will enter them when we are done."

He mentioned that they had all agreed that their introduction, in which they explained why the team had decided to switch topics, was still rough and needed revising.

"We still want to include this issue among our examples for the new topic, but it doesn't quite work yet. Our country's overreliance on hydroelectric dams is too specific, too regional, and we need to demonstrate that this is just one of many short-sighted governmental policies that is adding to the economic divide that is tearing our culture apart. I think we can smooth it out after we finish the meeting."

Once they determined that their original choice was not broad enough, it had taken the team a week and a half to come up with a new topic: Increasing Polarization of Economic Classes. Meeting several times a week for the next three weeks, they finally collaborated on a response that they all liked.

As the older members spoke, Tiago and Natalia, the two youngest members, looked at each other. Being street smart was not enough to prepare them for all the big words that were being tossed about. They looked at each other and fidgeted.

Disenfranchisement, equitable access, voluntary transformation, peer pressure—these concepts meant little to them. They struggled to keep up as Gabrielle, Jaime's wife, made one of her gardening analogies. She advocated a political approach akin to composting, the process by which discarded food and organic waste are transformed into rich soil.

She explained. "A society that treats certain groups as untouchables, isolating them and relegating them to illegal zones such as the favelas, will be less effective than one that embraces the entire population. Such a society will become paranoid and less able to adjust to change, eventually becoming sterile.

"It will look exactly like what we have now—whole neighborhoods that breed pestilence, crime, and corruption. This arrangement tends to encourage citizens to barricade themselves into their gated communities and high-security fortresses."

Though her metaphor had made its way into their essay, she wanted to expand on her point. The others, including her husband, argued against it.

"The judges will see your point, Gabby, and they will like it. It's very convincing. But we cannot expand on your point without going over the limit, and we can't afford to trim the other sections."

Raquel Almeida spoke next. She was twenty-one. "I am glad we showed that this problem is bigger than just something we face here in Brazil. This is a problem in every culture, even in the United States. The immigration population there is getting bigger and bigger, and many of them barely have enough to eat. Their bosses are rich. I see some of them in the hotel where I work."

"Thank you, Raquel," said Paco Mendes, the eldest member on the team. "We hope the judges will agree. If we speak only of our own difficulties, we will appear to be nothing but complaining children. They will not take us seriously, and we will be eliminated."

"That would be easy for us to do," said Laura Vereira, "complain, I mean. But I think we know better than most that it does not do us any good. Do you know who demonstrates a positive outlook better than anybody?"

The others turned to her, curious.

"He is sitting right there ... looking a bit bored, I am afraid." Tiago looked up suddenly to see Señora Vereira looking at him. She smiled.

"Tiago and his little club visit me almost every day, and they are always happy. Nobody gives them a special chance, nor do they expect one. They approach life the way we all ought to approach it—innocent, generous, playful. I have never heard him or his friends complain, even when they get cheated and bullied by the older boys.

Tiago blushed, and they all laughed.

"It's funny you should mention that, Laura," said Paco Mendes. "That is exactly the spirit I think we need to finish with. Many Brazilians believe we should propose more state-mandated assistance and social programs, but what we have come up with is quite different. We talk about how we would like to be treated, how we believe we should treat others, but we do not demand anything. We do not claim entitlements. We do not want or expect any special dispensations.

"This is what makes our culture here unique. I think this is why they will listen to us. This is why the judges will advance us to the next round."

⋯⊱❦ ❦⊰⋯

"Gentlemen, we are coming down to some hard decisions. We have one more day to finalize our selections, but it would be nice if we could come to a consensus tonight and then sleep on it."

Mahmoud Azzam and Noel Pearson nodded. Kim Campbell, former Prime Minister of Canada, had tacitly assumed the role of mediator, and the two men had accepted her lead. Besides her diplomatic credentials, she was the eldest by almost ten years.

The three comprised a sub-panel of judges, one of four, that grappled with the same objective of sifting through their allotment of Task Four responses and submitting 16 of the 64 teams that would advance. By this stage, the quality of the contending teams was generally strong, and the essays demanded a high level of discernment for the winnowing process.

Vox Stellarum had set up video conferencing portals specially encrypted for the purpose. Translated copies of team submissions were uploaded to the judges' individual accounts, and they could then discuss specific documents in real time with their fellow panelists. Early in the Task Four judging period, which was four weeks, they had agreed to meet face-to-face for their final decision process, an idea that caught on quickly with the other sub-panels.

Through the first three rounds, each judge had had absolute say over his or her choices. To a degree, the weight of that responsibility was offset by the freedom of not having to answer to any counter arguments. Most of the judges had staffs and assistants, but their individual authority was final. Now, though, each judge had to reach a consensus with two peers who were, by design, from vastly different cultures. It had been a steep learning curve for all of them.

At fifty-one, Noel Pearson was the youngest of the three gathered in the private conference room at the Ritz-Carlton Tokyo. A large, barrel-chested Aboriginal, he was well known in legal and media circles in Australia as a man who would take on the highest authorities on behalf of the indigenous population. He specialized in treaty negotiations for several tribes and was a land rights activist on their behalf. While he contributed bluntly provocative op-ed articles to various Australian publications on a regular basis, he was friendly and jovial in person.

Mahmoud Azzam was a professor at the University of Cairo, with a Ph.D. in information technology. His specialty was cultural and linguistic evolution in the post-Internet world of social media. Besides being a language specialist and a talented programmer, he was the author of two books about cultural integrity in a global economy. He had been at the center of a controversy three years earlier when he proposed that the "flat earth" reality of multinational trade and its influence on homogenization of customs and semantic memes was not necessarily destined to erase the tenets of the mainstream religions or ethnic traditions. His thesis had been that people need not fear the invasion of new ideas, that these would, contrary to the stance of numerous orthodox groups, tend to strengthen and purify the principles of all existing ideologies. The fact that he had stood up to the militant regime in his home country had gained him a cautious respect among his fellow academics, even many fellow Muslims.

Azzam now looked at Kim Campbell. "Madam Prime Minister, when we break for dinner, I propose we consider eating downstairs or in one of the restaurants nearby. As good as it is, I don't know if I can take another round of room service."

"I agree," said Pearson. "I don't know when I'll have a chance to eat real Japanese food again. Though I've never seen such obscene prices, I think we can afford it."

He was referring to the fact that their trip had been endorsed by Minerva Bennett and that all their expenses were being covered. Her decision may have been influenced by the fact that, early on, at least half the judges made headlines by announcing they had donated substantial portions of their Vox Stellarum stipends to pet projects and charities in their home countries. One of them had even donated his entire pay: Noel Pearson.

"Very well. Let's knock out a few more before we head down." Campbell reached toward the stacks of team responses in front of her, straightened them, and picked one up.

Pearson also preferred hard copy—his papers were strewn about the coffee table and the floor in front of him. Azzam, on the other hand, used one of the new iPads, with twice the viewing area as the earlier models. Leaning back in a leather armchair, one leg crossed over his knee, he rested the device on his lap, swiping, pinching, and tapping the screen as the three of them resumed their debate regarding two of the contentious essays.

"As I was saying earlier," said Azzam, "my objection to this next one centers on their main hypothesis. It's too extreme. Advocating for the removal of government oversight of education through privatization is something that runs against my beliefs."

"I agree," said Pearson. "I don't have a problem with their point about eliminating religious indoctrination from state-run curricula, but I'm skeptical about their projections. I just don't think they make a strong enough point."

"I'm not terribly attracted to it either," responded Campbell, "but it's a fresh idea that seems to address several related issues rather elegantly. That's what impressed me most." She picked up the essay submitted by Team 981, from New York City. Though the identities and nationalities of submitting teams had been stripped away, the content sometimes made it obvious. She angled her printout toward her two colleagues and pointed to some highlighted passages. "For instance: 'Disputes around religious practices would become moot if the choice for integrating faith and spiritual topics into the daily lessons were left to the parents, if not the children themselves. A spectrum of choices would naturally arise, from the purely secular to the orthodox religious.' And here: 'Soaring costs have no real basis in pedagogical practices; these are due to entrenched governmental bureaucracy, inefficiency of social programs, and union contracts that steadily outpace the free market in terms of efficient delivery of services.'

"For that last statement alone, I think this team must be considered. It's undeniable. It's not only true in the United States, it's true in Canada and, from what I have read, in multiple countries in Europe, South America, and Australia."

"Madam Prime Minister, this may be one of those cases in which we must agree to disagree," said Pearson. "I don't see it the same way you do. I suggest we turn to the next essay and see if we can come to a consensus."

Azzam nodded. "Mr. Pearson is right, Madam Prime Minister. The more I reflect on this, the firmer my vote to reject this essay."

Kim Campbell struggled to let go of her doubts about Mahmoud Azzam's ability to be neutral, not to mention her own free-market bias. Was his real resistance to the essay due to the team's acknowledgement that half its members were Jewish? If he had allowed his faith to cloud his objectivity, there was nothing she could do about it.

She laid the essay on her "No" stack and sighed. She reached for the next essay from her pile of "Maybes."

The language was idiomatically western—probably from the United States, but the authors had kept personal remarks and regional hints completely out of the text. None of them could know it had been submitted by Team 489 from Tulsa, Oklahoma.

"Where do we stand on this one?" she asked as levelly as she could.

"This one is interesting," began Azzam. "I think this team did a good job of folding its original topic into the broader one of deficit spending, certainly a global issue. I'm intrigued by their claim that a long-term effect of this practice, by government leaders, is that its insidious logic tends to take root in the mindsets of individuals and businesses. People tend to save less and rely more on credit, and citizens connect this to a sense of entitlement ... which is interesting. If there's a weakness, it's the way they condemn the potentially positive results of this policy."

"I had a mixed response to this one," stated Pearson. "I like their critique of central banks and government management of credit markets. No matter what the intentions are, I have seen firsthand the corruption that manipulation of interest rates causes. Bankers, and the government officials they pay off, have the luxury of hiding in their boardrooms and their gated communities, but they are the first people, and often the only ones, who benefit from these manipulations. The vast majority get stuck with higher prices, higher mortgages, higher taxes.

"What concerns me, though, is how the team speaks of unions and entitlement programs. They appear to overlook the value of trade unions and social programs, and repeatedly refer to both as 'entitlements.' They advocated that these be diminished to what amounts to draconian levels. It's easier said than done, and it comes off as simplistic. I found some of their points similar to the language in the previous essay."

It was Campbell's turn to weigh in. She liked this essay, despite some of the over-the-top ideology that underpinned most of their points. She wanted this one to be approved, but she had to be careful not to assume that her colleagues' mildly positive responses would be translated into approvals.

"I have been hearing this anti-central bank argument for thirty years, and I still find it weak. These arguments always have a utopian basis, usually involving the return to a gold standard and a reliance on the free market. While nobody can deny that the free market has fostered countless advances and raised the average standard of living, few would deny that governments must have access to unlimited credit ... in times of financial crisis, preparing for and recovering from natural calamities, and of course in times of war. At least they acknowledge that these scenarios are inevitable, and they make some interesting recommendations to provide buffers and safety valves.

"The thing I like most about this group is that they don't mince their words. They acknowledge that they're coming at this issue from a very idealistic perspective, and they make some startling predictions if nothing changes. I particularly liked this line, found in their summary: 'There is ultimately no logical reason to assume that nations can practice with impunity that which *always* renders individuals, families, and businesses bankrupt and insolvent.'"

"I thought that—" Azzam halted in mid-sentence.

All of their cell phones buzzed and beeped simultaneously. Startled by the coincidence, they looked at one another, perhaps wondering whether to break their agreement to ignore calls.

"That's strange," said Pearson. "I just received two e-mails, one from Catherine Myers, one from James Ruhle. It's 5:00 AM in New York—something's going on."

They all reached for their cell phones. A group text said: <Turn on the news!>

Campbell reached for the TV remote, but it took her a minute to find an English news channel. They saw live images of the aftermath of a horrific blast site in a crowded city.

"Less than one hour ago," stated a reporter, "two car bombs exploded within seconds of one another in front of a hotel in central Athens.

Sources tell us these were detonated shortly before noon, just as people were making their way to various lunch destinations. One bomb exploded in front of the King George Hotel, the other about 100 meters away, in front of a popular restaurant. Conservative estimates put the casualties at fifty or more.

"No one has claimed responsibility, although unofficial speculation centers on sectarian rebel groups that have been tied to recent assaults in southern Greece. The nation has been on the brink of civil war for many months."

After several minutes, Pearson looked at the others and asked, "Have you read the e-mail from Ruhle?"

"No, what does it say?" said Azzam.

"It says we should stay where we are and to call hotel security. One of the judging panels is staying at the King George."

They looked at one another, in equal states of shock.

"It could be a coincidence."

"What if it isn't?" asked Campbell.

⋅→▐▌◉ ◉▐▌←⋅

"How bad is it?" asked Minerva, looking more distraught than Catherine had ever seen her.

"Our people were in the restaurant where the second bomb went off," said Catherine. "The good news is that they're alive, but two of them have been hospitalized. The third is physically okay, but he sounded disoriented."

"Who was injured?"

"Kasparov and Szilagyi. They both received cuts and bruises, and Kasparov has a broken leg. Ambassador Chiriboga is okay, but he thinks his hearing might have been affected."

"Oh my God," Minerva said. She closed her eyes and hugged herself.

James Ruhle and Rowan Detering sat nearby. Both appeared dazed themselves since fielding the first bits of news in the early morning hours. They were gathered in Minerva's study. It was 9:15 AM in New York.

"What can we ..." Minerva began, "what steps can we take right now to mitigate—I mean, the damage is done, but what—" She stopped abruptly and turned toward the window, tears streaming down her face.

"As bad as this is," Ruhle ventured in a quiet voice, "we think we can still move forward with tomorrow's task. Catherine and I—"

"I don't give a damn about that!" Minerva cried. "I want to know if our people are going to be okay."

He winced, sat back, and looked at the floor. The others were afraid to say anything.

Minerva finally reached for a tissue and wiped her cheeks. She let out a beleaguered sigh.

"I'm sorry, James. I didn't mean to bite your head off. What I meant was, what can be done to assure these three are safe? Furthermore," she said, sitting up straighter, "we need to safeguard the other judges. What if this was not a coincidence? Does anybody have the slightest idea who was behind this attack?"

Catherine said, "James and I have been in contact with at least one representative from each of the other sub-panels, and they're all okay. Anxious, nervous, angry ... but okay. By the way, one group is in Atlanta, one group is in Tokyo, but the fourth group decided to stick with video conferencing.

"The bomb intended for the hotel didn't do as much damage as the other one, and the hotel is staying open until all the guests can be accommodated elsewhere. After the ambassador gave his statement to the police, he spoke to us from the judges' suite, which was unharmed. He intends to remain there until he's certain that his colleagues are okay."

"Señor Chiriboga said the place is swarming with security," added James. "Meanwhile, Rowan was able to get through to the Athens police and arrange for guards to be placed at the hospital and at the hotel."

Minerva turned to Rowan. "Thank you, dear," she whispered.

Catherine continued. "Journalists have descended on the city, and it's all over the TV. It doesn't appear that the media have figured out that our people were among the victims, or even that Vox Stellarum personnel were in the city."

"Yet," interjected James.

"Right," said Catherine, nodding grimly. "The judges had been urged to maintain a low profile, stick to the hotel if possible, and to venture only to quiet places when in public."

"That's probably what saved them," said James. "The ambassador told us they were seated in the back of the restaurant, in a corner booth. It sounds like most of the guests seated near the front were badly injured or killed."

Minerva closed her eyes again and shuddered.

"That brings us to a key point," said Minerva. "What gave them away? How were they targeted? This is just too uncanny to be a coincidence."

"We agree," said Catherine, "but nobody knew their itinerary except for us, here in this room, and presumably their own immediate family members and staffs."

James said, "It's certainly possible that the local paparazzi spotted one of them, perhaps Kasparov, since he's somewhat famous over there. The others aren't really that well known."

"That may be," said Rowan, "but since the panel was announced, all of the judges have become more than minor celebrities."

"What resources do we have?" asked Minerva. "Have we contacted the American Embassy?"

"Not yet," said Catherine.

"Would the CIA be an option, since it's an international incident?" asked Rowan.

"I don't know," said Minerva, "but let's try. I can't remember ... did we ever contact them when Malcolm was detained in Africa?"

"We did, but he resurfaced before they got involved," answered James.

"Well, whoever made that call, let's start with the same agent and get a sense of what can be done. This incident is on an entirely different order. By the way, Malcolm will probably have some ideas about what to do next. Catherine, I want you to call him first."

"Okay."

"Alright, James. Now I'm ready to hear what you were going to say earlier, about the next task."

"As unsettling as all this is, we have to consider the importance of moving forward. Ambassador Chiriboga told us they had identified most of their advancing teams. He said they were five or six short. They had gone to lunch, expecting to process the remainder in the afternoon—yesterday afternoon, that is."

"You spoke to him. Do you think he's in any shape to finish the job? I can't imagine the state of mind he's in."

Catherine responded. "The three of us ran through some options earlier this morning. One is that if Chiriboga is up to it, he can decide on the remaining teams in order to fill their quota. Another is that if Kasparov and Szilagyi are released in time, which is doubtful, they could join him. But even if they're released, we can't imagine they'd be much help. A third option is bringing in some of the other judges, but they will have had no exposure to this particular set of responses, and they would have to start from scratch."

"A fourth option," said Rowan reluctantly, "is waiting for the three judges to heal and clear their heads, and then finish their work. But that would require postponing Task Five."

"I don't like any of these," said Minerva. "I hate to say it, but we've got to keep to our time table if possible. Bringing in some of the other judges at this late hour would be a huge mess ... new translations ... redirecting files ..." She trailed off and looked out the window.

"I think option one is the way to go," ventured James. "It's not optimal, but it's the quickest and safest. We ask Chiriboga to take his best shot and just pick the remaining teams to his best ability. He would be making unilateral decisions, but on the basis of their previous discussions. He's going to have to submit the advancing teams anyway—he's the only one who can at this stage." Rowan and Catherine nodded as they looked to Minerva for agreement.

When she finally turned to face them again, she said, "I agree. As soon as we're done here, I want the three of you to call him. See if he can manage it. Let him know that we trust his judgment absolutely. I'll call Malcolm."

Chapter 30

"GOOD MORNING, EVERYBODY," greeted Catherine Myers in a slightly subdued voice. "Thank you for your continued support and enthusiasm for this grand adventure." She looked out on the reporters gathered in the conference room and sensed anticipation, but also something else—a subtle fear. She couldn't be sure whether it was theirs or her own.

"Before we get to the day's business, I must mention something which is, no doubt, on everybody's mind. Yesterday's attack on innocent and unarmed people in the downtown district of Athens was the latest case of senseless violence to hit our global community, and it affected us here at Vox Stellarum more directly than most of you know.

"Three of our twelve judges had convened in Athens for the weekend to finalize their selections of the Task Four responses. Not only were they staying in the hotel where the first bomb went off, they were seated in the restaurant down the street where, just before noon on Saturday, the second bomb exploded."

The press room suddenly lit up with camera flashes, and Catherine paused briefly before continuing.

"This was a terrible blow for the city of Athens, its citizens, visitors and tourists, and obviously the victims and their families. We are deeply saddened and angered by this cowardly act. Fortunately, our people sustained relatively minor injuries, and they are expected to make full recoveries.

"Dozens of others were not as fortunate. To the other victims and their families, we want to convey our condolences and deepest sympathy."

Catherine paused again, but this time because she was choked up. Flashes illuminated her bowed head. A somber mood settled on the crowd as they realized that a tragedy half a world away had just spilled over in front of them.

Taking a deep breath, she continued. "We hope that the perpetrators will be identified and prosecuted to the fullest extent of the law. In the meanwhile, we ask those of you who are listening to pray for healing and justice."

She looked at James, seated to the side of the stage, and nodded. He made his way to the podium as Catherine walked to her seat. He leaned toward the microphones.

"My name is James Ruhle. I'm in charge of verification logistics.

"It's impossible to fully shake off this sad news, and yet we are here to celebrate the success of our advancing teams. One hundred twenty-five teams entered Round Four, and 64 have advanced, poised to respond to the challenge of Task Five.

"To the teams that did not advance, we wish you the best in your ongoing personal missions. Everything you have done thus far has helped awaken your respective communities, and we know you will continue to work for positive change.

"To the 64 teams who have advanced: *Congratulations!* There are still too many teams to name them all here, but it appears that every continent is still represented. We are at the halfway point—four tasks to go. Here, then, is the text of Task Five:

"There are several reasons why Vox Stellarum required a broad range of age groups for the composition of the teams. In this task, we focus attention on the children, who, according to Minerva Bennett's vision, can offer hope and fresh insight to long-standing debates that have ceased to yield effective solutions to our most critical issues.

"If your youngest team members can grasp the issues and can be conversant regarding the pros and cons of your proposed solutions, then the odds of communicating these ideas—to the nations who might eventually choose to adopt them—are improved. With that in mind, demonstrate and document that your two youngest members are playing more than a superficial role. Even if that has been the case thus far, you now need to produce a video highlighting their involvement, as well as a summary that is clearly written in their words.

"We know that coaching by the adult members is inevitable, but you are encouraged to allow the children to use their own words as they reference their personal hopes and dreams. Of course, their points must be in alignment with all previous responses.

"The written response shall be two separate essays—one by each of your two youngest members, each one not to exceed 1000 words (in standard English). Your video should demonstrate that each child is, in fact, capable of writing the essays that you will submit in their names. The total running time is not to exceed 30 minutes. As usual, sharing your response with outsiders (e.g. family members, friends, teachers, and reporters) will result in disqualification."

James looked up and added, "These responses will be due on November 27, which is four weeks from today. The judges will then have three weeks to cut the number of teams down to thirty-two. And, as I think you know by now, successful responses to Task Four can be found on the website. Any questions?"

Hands went up, but several reporters shouted out questions without waiting to be acknowledged.

"I see that Minerva Bennett is not present. How is she taking the news of the bombing?" asked a *Fox News* reporter.

"Mrs. Bennett was very disturbed by the news, as we all were. She is exhausted by yesterday's drama, and she chose to sit out this press conference. She's in good health, just tired and concerned. She expects to be in the office tomorrow."

"Do you think the judges were the primary targets of the bombings?" asked a correspondent for *Al Jazeera*. "If so, how will this affect the other judges and, for that matter, the contestants?"

They had anticipated that somebody would ask this question, but James suddenly found himself unprepared. He looked at Catherine apprehensively and was relieved to see her approaching the podium.

"It's too early to tell," she said. "The investigation is barely under way, and we don't want to speculate unnecessarily. The nature of our competition is to invite creative ideas and solutions to urgent problems. We are obviously invested in peaceful and respectful inquiry, and it's unfathomable that this could be considered a threat to anybody.

"As to how this affects us going forward, I would have to say that caution and vigilance are key, but we won't let this action cow us into submission or silence. Since early yesterday morning, when we first heard about the incident, we have been in contact with our top staff and our board of trustees. More than one asked Mrs. Bennett if it might be best to call off The Contest. You should know that, while she seriously considered this option, she was adamant that we proceed. There was unanimous agreement.

"That being said, we know that continuing to participate in an enterprise that's potentially threatening is something that each individual must decide on his or her own. If there are teams out there, or judges, who think that their lives are in danger and want to quit their involvement, nobody here will judge them. We're not the ones on the front lines."

Several more questions regarding the extent of the judges' injuries eventually gave way to questions about the new assignment. Ruhle fielded these.

"One of the most controversial aspects of The Contest was the inclusion of children in the makeup of the teams. We have acknowledged from the beginning that this is unprecedented. I think most of you know that, to a degree, this is one of the reasons that the response to Mrs. Bennett's vision was so enthusiastic. By the conclusion of this task, it will be clear just how well our youngest contestants grasp the big issues. And we are just as intrigued as you are to know whether this requirement was an overreach or a stroke of genius."

⋆⇀═◉ ◉═↼⋆

The Watcher sat back in his chair, smoking. The press conference at Vox Stellarum had concluded, and he now watched with amusement, on his array of monitors, the spin applied to the latest twist in The Contest.

CNN was the most brazen in its exploitation of the incident. The graphic that splayed across the giant wall of monitors in its *Headline News* studio read "Judges Targeted in Athens Bombing?" Background music modulated to a minor key to highlight the deliciously ominous possibility. Other media outlets played the story similarly.

The Watcher tapped his console to accept an incoming call.

"Yes, I just switched it off ... Right, pretty predictable response ... No, but we had to try. It sounds like they were close to calling it qui— ... Possibly. If only they'd been sitting closer to the street—they might not have been able to shake this off ... No chance. If Golden Dawn doesn't take the blame, the neo-Nazis will. We're fine ... No, our only connection is wearing a Chicago overcoat in a hundred feet of water, somewhere north of Crete ... Yes, occupational hazard! ... (laughs) ... Another strike? Hmm ... I don't know. We had a pretty unique situation here—crossfire between two separatist groups and a country on the verge of collapse ... No ... No ... Yes, he's got a foot in the door. He said there're hints of a more urgent task still to come, but no specifics ... Okay. We'll see if we can come up with another scenario ... Yeah ... No shit—a bunch of goddamn kids! ... (laughs) ... (laughs) ... Okay ..." Click.

Still smiling, the Watcher reached for another cigarette and then turned his attention back to the international markets, the Chinese incursion in Tajikistan, and the riots in northern Mexico.

⊷⊷● ●⊷⊷

In their apartment in Amsterdam, Pem Hoowij was huddled in a pile of clothes and stuffed animals. She held a pillow to her stomach and lay in the fetal position, sobbing. A desk lamp cast shadows across the far walls in the otherwise dark room. Earlier, she had heated up the dinner her mother left for her, but the plate of half-eaten food now lay on her desk. Both her parents were out—her father in Paris for a concert, her mother at a rehearsal with her dance troupe.

Two hours later, Pem had stopped crying. She was asleep. The sound of the front door opening and closing didn't stir her, nor did the creaking of her own bedroom door as her mother looked in.

"Pem? Pem darling, it's me," Margrit Hoowij called softly. It was ten o'clock.

She sat down next to her daughter and stroked her hair gently, surprised she was already asleep. She watched her for a few minutes and then rose, debating whether to wake her and get her under the covers. She decided to let her be. She picked up the plate, switched off the lamp, and made her way to the door.

"Mommy?"

"Yes."

"I need to talk to you," Pem said in a weak voice.

"What's wrong, darling?" asked Margrit as she set the plate on a chair. "Are you okay?"

"No ... I'm not." She began to cry again, and her mother swiftly moved to her side and reached over to turn the lamp back on.

"What's wrong? Tell me what's going on," her mother said softly.

"I can't ... I can't do it," she said, straining to get the words out between her screwed up face and her tears.

"Do what?"

"... and I'm afraid," she sobbed.

"Pem, *what* is going on?" Margrit looked around the room for evidence of a mishap, something that could be the source of her daughter's distress. Except for the clean clothes on the foot of the bed that hadn't been put away, everything appeared in its normal state of disarray.

"Did something happen to you, Pem? Did you get hurt?"

"Nooo ... not yet," she whimpered.

"Not yet? What do you think is going to happen?" she asked, now with a touch of impatience. "Sit up, dear. Tell me why you're crying. I can't help you unless you talk to me."

Pem released her grip on the pillow and turned toward her mother, her hair in a tangle, tears streaming down her face.

"I don't think I can do the assignment," she said, sniffing to clear her running nose.

"What assignment? For school? Maybe I can help you, or your fath—"

"*No!* The Contest."

"*What?!*"

"I've been trying to come up with something, something good ... so we can keep going. But I can't think of anything. *I'm stupid!*" she exclaimed, anger on top of shame.

"Oh, Pem," said her mother, reaching out to stroke her hair. "No ... no you're not! You're one of the smartest little girls I know. In fact, you're much more than that. You're sensitive ... you're wise."

Margrit Hoowij spoke in this manner for several minutes, and her words gradually calmed her daughter, stemming the tide of tears. She leaned forward and summarized her point with a hug.

Pem wiped her eyes with her sleeve. She sat up and looked almost normal.

"Now, tell me. What's gotten into you?" said her mother. "This morning you were doing fine. What changed?"

"People at school were talking about me. They were making fun of me."

"What were they saying?"

"That it's too bad Kat doesn't get to respond. Then we might have a chance. They said I was the weakest player and that we're going to be eliminated."

"Oh, Pem, I'm sorry." She reached forward and stroked her daughter's hair again, but then sat up abruptly.

"Now listen. That was mean and ignorant. Unfortunately, lots of people fall into those categories ... it's just part of life. You're going to have to learn to accept it. What they say about you—what they *think* about you—is none of your business."

Pem looked at her mother, feeling comforted and supported, but doubting her ability to take the advice.

"But what if they're right? What if—"

"Pem, we've talked about this before. We can second guess ourselves until we're paralyzed with fear, but that does us no good. All anyone can do is ... her best. And one's best is constantly changing. Yours, mine, your father's ..."

"I don't think I can do it," Pem whispered. "I don't want to pretend that ..." She paused, afraid to admit her real fear.

"Go on."

"I don't want to pretend that I know what I'm doing."

"Pem darling, nobody is asking you to pretend. And, by the way, do you think the rest of us know what *we're* doing?! We're just working things out as best we can, and we're somehow still in this thing. "Your job is to say, in your own words, what we've already been talking about. Nobody expects you to come up with anything new or brilliant, though I wouldn't be surprised if you did."

"It's just that people seem to think I don't have what it takes ... and I don't want to let everybody down."

"Listen to me, Pem. You have been a key part of our group from the beginning. You have contributed in ways you don't even understand, and I'm very proud of you." As Margrit spoke, her daughter leaned forward, thirsting for proof that her fears and doubts were unfounded. "*You* are the reason your father and I joined. You may not believe me, but it's true. Your enthusiasm and passion were so powerful that we couldn't stay on the sidelines. If you can remember that sense of hope and talk about the possibilities that suddenly occurred to you when you heard about The Contest, then everything else will make sense."

"But I'm terrible at essays."

"We're going to help you, Pem. The rules allow us to coach you, and that's what we're going to do. I'm sure Daan is going through the same thing right now, and of course we're going to help him too. In fact, all the children, *on every team*, are feeling this pressure right now. This is exactly what the organizers knew would happen. Children aren't usually placed in the spotlight, and it's a big challenge. But that doesn't change the fact that you know what to say. You know. I have absolute confidence in you, Pem. You *know*."

"But a thousand words? That's ... I don't even know ... pages and pages."

"Don't worry about that. That's just the maximum limit. You may only need a hundred words to summarize everything we stand for. In fact, the judges will be grateful when they see a child with the courage to keep it simple.

And that is your best quality. That's what I meant a while ago when I said you were wise. You know how to keep it simple."

Looking deep into her mother's eyes, Pem finally managed to smile.

⋅⊱⊜ ⊜⊰⋅

Listening to the news on satellite radio, Julian Fielding drove in to Manhattan and arrived just before the afternoon rush hour. He found his mother napping in the sunroom. Gladys Atchley sat nearby, reading, but she excused herself to allow them a personal visit.

Several days before, Julian had spoken to his mother about staying with her the night before he would attend his monthly Wednesday meetings at the Koyne Foundation. She hadn't noticed his raised eyebrows when she had interpreted his appearance as a spontaneous visit. This sort of lapse was becoming more common, but he knew it would accomplish nothing to point it out.

When he made an offhand remark regarding the political season, Minerva voiced her disgust with both the Democrats and the Republicans. Not sensing any agreeable perspective in his mother's tone, he switched to the relatively safe topics of family, health, and business. In other words, they exchanged foundation updates.

Julian had to remind Minerva that Brooks Mecom was no longer with the Foundation, that he'd been replaced. While he knew his mother had never expressed a deep interest in the workings of the fund managers and the specifics of their asset portfolio, he was shocked by her apparent ignorance about the latest economic forecasts.

He wondered whether her detachment was intentional or a function of her declining mental acuity. Through the windows, the overcast sky had gone from orange to red to pinkish gray. Now it was dark, and the lights of the buildings across Central Park were obscured by the reflection of the interior apartment lighting.

"Mother, I'm worried about much more than the economy," Julian said. "I'm worried about *you*."

Minerva turned to him with that look he had seen many times before—
Oh, you're just a worrywart.

"Jules, I'm fine ... just a bit tired."

"I'm not talking about your physical health, Mother. I'm talking about
your safety. Sam Minton told me about the investigation by the Athens Police.
They're convinced that it was your people that were targeted, and I'm afraid it
will happen again, maybe a lot closer to home." This gave Minerva pause and
she looked away, unable to dispute his point.

"We've been assured this was an isolated incident. Apparently, it was some
splinter group of a political party in Greece, banned several years ago."

"Yes, I know, but whether it's some wackos from the Golden Dawn, or
Muslim terrorists, or neo-Nazis right here in our midst, the danger is clear. Tell
me the truth. How many of your teams have withdrawn? How many judges?"

He had heard lots of speculation in the media about the reaction of participants in The Contest, but nothing official from Vox Stellarum. His mother
remained silent and looked out the windows. Julian waited.

"To my knowledge, nobody has quit. No teams, that is. Catherine gave me
a report last Friday that several teams informed us of some replacements ... but
why is anybody's guess."

"I think *I* can venture a guess. And what about judges?"

"Two."

"The ones injured in the blast?"

"Actually, no, which surprised me. Cordeiro, one of the South Americans,
told us she had received several threats even before this happened and that
she had ignored them. The bombings in Greece made her reconsider, and her
family pressured her to withdraw. The other was Gillard, a Frenchman. He
had also received some very specific threats."

"Why hasn't this been made public? Are you going to replace them?"

"We've been scrambling to work this out. When we find replacements,
we'll hold a press conference. Our search team is—"

"Look, Mother, maybe you think I'm still being critical of your competition, but that's not why I brought this up. I'm—"

"Why *did* you bring it up? Do you have a better plan?" Her sharp tone cut through her earlier evasiveness and caught Julian by surprise.

"No."

"Do you think we should just quit? Call the whole thing off?!"

"I didn't say that. But there must be something that could ... I don't know, soften the reactions of the people who would do such things."

"What do you think we've been trying to do for the past week?" said Minerva. Julian noticed the pillow his mother was holding in her lap. She was unconsciously twisting the corners with her fingers, and he could tell she was more consumed with anxiety than he had imagined.

"Mother, I grant you that calling off your contest is probably impossible, but I guess what I'm saying is that there has to be a way to increase security."

"Do you want to know what the judges who were injured told me?" she asked. "They said they were more determined than ever to see this thing through. They are not about to quit. Do you want to know how many e-mails our office has received, from contestants, saying basically the same thing? Several hundred."

She finally released her grip on the pillow and set it aside.

"Except for the relative few that have quit, this tragedy has steeled the resolve of most everybody else. It makes me proud ... and at the same time it scares me half to death.

"So, you tell me, Jules. What should we do? What should *I* do?"

He stared out the window, straining to see beyond the distortion of the reflected images. He sighed and turned back to face her.

"I wish I had an answer, Mother. I just want you to know I'm concerned. As much as I criticized your plan when you first described it, I believe it would be a shame to abandon it now. I don't think you should call it off. But it's imperative that you take as many precautions as possible. Security guards, government reinforcements ... I don't know.

"Just be *careful!*"

Chapter 31

"COME ON, TIMMY, quit screwing around! You're such a fruit loop." Connor Birchell, of Team 25, was beginning to regret being asked to join the video session. His brother Timothy, who was ten, was goofing around with a mask he had found on one of Mr. Fanning's bookshelves, trying to get Mattie Smythe to laugh. She was the other junior member of the team, but she resisted his playfulness.

"Hold on, Connor. He'll get it. We've got plenty of time," said Fanning, the team leader. Though a high school teacher, he showed remarkable tact when working with the kids, and he had been able to maintain patience, at least outwardly, in guiding the pair in their Task Five essays and video presentations.

Lucy Blair, Fanning's wife, was in charge of the video, and nobody saw her grin as she kept the camera recording.

Meanwhile, Evelyn Belmont, Mattie's elementary teacher, seemed to take it all in stride.

"Timmy, why don't you show us that mask?" she suggested. "Go ahead, put it on. Would you like to wear it during your piece?" The boy's eyes lit up, but his big brother turned to Ms. Belmont in disbelief.

"Come on! He's not got the full quid today. That'll just make it worse," said Connor as he brusquely grabbed a chair in the far corner of the classroom.

Sienna Walker, assigned to be Mattie's tutor, just as Connor had been for his little brother, sat a few desks away. She grinned at Connor sympathetically, but said nothing.

"Go ahead, Timmy," said Fanning. "I think that's a good idea. Let's see how well we can understand you." The boy picked up the bright red ceremonial mask, made of pith, wood, rattan, dried leaves, and feathers. It covered his entire upper body. He giggled as he tried to find out how to see through the eye slits, obviously designed for an adult.

"Is this from Oz?" Timmy asked, meaning from Australia.

"No. Pretty close though. It's from Papua New Guinea, part of the big island just north of us—north of Queensland. The Sulka tribesmen would make these in secret and wear them to initiate the boys."

"To do *what?*"

"To initiate their boys," Fanning said. He shot glances at Lucy and Evelyn and made a mock grimace. They both nodded and smiled, urging him on in the impromptu lesson.

"What does *that* mean?"

"Hmm ... well, it means that when boys reach a certain age, usually older than you are, Timmy, the elders in the village take them away for a secret ceremony ... and they test them. They want to see if the boys are ready to become men. The boys must demonstrate they're ready to be given responsibility and new challenges."

"Like what?"

"Like hunting and going into battle."

"*I* want to be initiated!" the boy exclaimed.

"You're a little young, Timmy, but the fact that you joined our team is a very good sign that you're ready to take on new challenges. You've been doing a great job so far, and, now that I think about it, this assignment is like a mini-initiation for you. For Mattie, too." Fanning winked at Mattie, and then turned back to Timothy.

"Tell you what—I'll make a deal with you. You can show off the mask in your video and talk about how you like challenges and how you're ready to take on new responsibilities. Maybe you can even challenge other kids your age to do the same. But then, you must put that aside and talk about the ideas that you wrote about in your essay. Does that sound good?"

Timothy nodded. "Okay."

The boy's attitude shifted noticeably, and he was suddenly on task, almost serious. Two hours later, the group gathered their things. The adults, and even the kids, were pleased with their results.

As they walked to their car, Lucy Blair said to Fanning, "Look over there."

Across the parking lot, by the main entrance, Connor and Timothy Birchell were waiting for their ride. Their playful antics indicated that the earlier tension was all but forgotten. The younger boy was beaming, for he held a new treasure under his arm. It was a bright red tribal mask, made in secret by strange men for a purpose that Timmy had now decided was the most important thing in the whole world.

⋅⊷⊨⊙ ⊙⊨⊶⋅

The corner table at the Club was more crowded than usual.

"Good afternoon, gentlemen," said Stewart Maxwell. "I hope you don't mind my bringing a friend along." Half the table turned to see who it was. His casual and slightly rumpled attire brought to mind an archaeologist on a dig.

"This is Malcolm Conroy, one of our secret agents, fresh off a special assignment." Conroy kept a straight face, despite Maxwell's mock introduction.

"Hello, Sam," Conroy said, smiling at Minton, the only other man he recognized.

"What a nice surprise! Good to see you, Malcolm," Minton said. He turned to the others. "You should know that Stew's introduction wasn't too far off the mark. It was Conroy who single-handedly rounded up the judges for The Contest, and he's just helped us fill two vacancies."

Raised eyebrows hinted at the connection the others quickly made as they recalled the muted press release by Vox Stellarum the previous afternoon.

"Nice work," said Ed Nance. "I was impressed by the personalities you brought together. I've been wondering how in the hell you were able to approach all those people in the first place." He went on to introduce himself.

"Yeah, me too," said Greer Johnson. "I wouldn't know where to begin."

Conroy said, "I used to work in the State Department, so I had experience in approaching foreign dignitaries."

"What do you do when you're not flying about for Vox Stellarum?" asked one of the men who had not yet been introduced. "I'm Bob Godfrey, by the way. I'm a guest, too, here in town for a family meet— ... for some business." Conroy peered at him more closely as he made a connection.

"In fact, Malcolm," interjected Minton, "Bob's the one who gave us your name in the first place. I'd forgotten about that."

"Oh? Well then, I guess I have you to blame, and *thank*, for my adventures," said Conroy, grinning. "How did you happen to forward my name, given that we've never met?"

"You were a guest speaker at a luncheon I attended a number of years ago in Houston. It was part of an offshore drilling and exploration conference. You spoke about regime change in the Middle East and in Russia, and what sort of environments the oil companies would have to navigate. I liked what you had to say, and I remembered being impressed with your no-nonsense approach. The other presenters bent over backwards to be politically correct, but you just told it like it was. I guess I filed away your name as somebody who knew how to get things done."

Conroy inclined his head.

Maxwell elaborated. "Now what you don't know, Malcolm, is that Bob was, and perhaps still is, one of the biggest critics of Minerva's vision. He's one of her nephews and sits on the Board at the Koyne Foundation. So, it's a bit ironic that he was the one who put your name in the hat."

"Interesting," said Conroy, looking at Maxwell. He turned to Godfrey. "Are you still critical of your aunt's scheme?"

"I am, although I must admit I've softened a bit. I still consider it a colossal waste of money. I can't imagine it will make any difference, other than giving the media something to distract us with." Conroy nodded.

"Bob, one thing *you* probably don't know," added Minton, "is that Malcolm originally turned us down."

Godfrey looked at Conroy. "Really? What changed your mind?"

"Good question. I'm still asking myself that one. When I first heard about The Contest, I dismissed it as idealistic nonsense. Several weeks later, when I got a phone call from your Aunt Minerva, I was flattered, but still entirely critical. Her offer intrigued me, and the money sounded nice, but I turned her down."

The waiter had brought their food, and while the others ate, Conroy continued. He briefly retold the story of Minerva's envoy, dispatched to negotiate with him directly. How they, too, were refused and sent away. How they had returned and eventually won him over.

"What I've discovered since then, however, is that I still wasn't on board. Yes, I had agreed to play the part of the Pied Piper for the panel of judges, but it wasn't until I was actually presenting the terms of the agreement to a couple of them that the nature of the assignment hit me. I had to decide whether I was really all in, or not.

"When I quit working for the government and retired, I vowed to never again go along with something I didn't fully believe in. Before I knew it, I had drawn my own line in the sand and ... I guess I stepped over it."

As if remembering something, Maxwell turned to his guest.

"Malcolm, I believe you forgot to answer Bob's earlier question: 'What do you do when you're not flying about for Vox Stellarum?'"

"Well, I like to hunt and fish ... and play with my dogs. Mostly, I like to sit on my porch, drink Scotch, and smoke my pipe."

"Damn, that sounds good," said Godfrey. "Want some company?"

"Any time, Bob," said Conroy, glad to establish a connection with a man he imagined was more aligned with him than he cared to admit.

⊷⊷⊜ ⊜⊷⊶

The stream of humanity flowing from "Customs & Immigration" had gone from a trickle to a torrent. People of seemingly every nationality, ethnicity, and age moved through the wide space next to the row of bars and duty-free shops where passengers could await a connection or find a deal on cigarettes and perfume.

Bob Godfrey sat at the edge of a bar on the mezzanine level of the terminal, waiting to catch a glimpse of his son. He had decided to greet Henry and to provide support in what he presumed would be a rough reentry.

Just as the tide of people threatened to overwhelm his ability to keep track of who was moving where, he spotted his son, carrying a duffel bag and a backpack.

Having already cleared his tab, he got up and headed for the escalator. He wondered what his son's reaction would be. Henry was heading for the exit doors toward the taxi and shuttle stand, and his father caught up with him as he was about to set his bags down near a bench.

"Henry!" he called out, catching his son completely off guard. "Hey ... I bet you didn't expect to see me." Henry's mouth was wide open.

"*Dad?!* What are you *doing* here?"

"I haven't seen you in a good while, and I thought it'd be nice to surprise you."

"Yeah. You have. I ... I can't believe you're here." Still holding his duffel, Henry finally set it down and took his bearings.

"How did you know I'd be here? I mean—"

"Sorry to surprise you like this. I didn't have a way to get a hold of you."

Even after the coaching that Stewart Maxwell had given him earlier that afternoon, Godfrey searched for what to say next. At least he knew not to ask about the fresh shiner his son had acquired during his recent escapades.

"I'll tell you all about it once you get settled. First, we need a taxi. Come on." He grabbed his son's duffel, while Henry held on to his backpack.

Ten minutes later they exited JFK International Airport in a Yellow cab, and the driver navigated toward Manhattan. Connecting the dots as to why his father had decided to meet him, Henry faintly wondered if he were about to be whisked away to a rehab. He was relieved that his father deferred to him when the driver asked for a destination.

He began to imagine the scenario, even before his father cleared his throat in that special way that always signaled some heavy pronouncement. He had associated that sound with practically every instance of conversation in which he'd learned of passing relatives, serious mishaps, even stock market news that adversely affected the family's holdings. No doubt his siblings and mother had heard his father clear his throat in that singular way when he'd gone AWOL ten years before. Now, he'd done it again ... sort of.

When had it started? he thought, waiting for his father to broach the subject—amazed that he hadn't done so yet. His father was, he suddenly recalled, capable of super-human, almost sadistic, patience. When he and his brothers were young, their father would hold off, as if he somehow knew that the future delivery of a punishment would be twice as potent by waiting until they practically begged for the spanking, anything to get it over with.

As Henry looked out on the city lights and watched vehicles in the next lane, he flashed back on the course of his relapse, which he was now certain was the reason for his father's presence. As he recalled some of the uglier scenes of his assault on his own sobriety, he became aware of his internal editing. *I'll tell him about this one, maybe that one, but definitely not that. Shit, I'm lucky to be alive.*

"How does it feel to be back in the good ol' USA?" his father asked, jerking Henry back to the present.

"Huh? Oh ... good, I guess." Henry didn't face his father, but instead just looked out the window at the distant skyline. "It'll be good to sleep in my own bed again."

His father let the conversation fade, biding his time—if that was indeed his intention—to allow the anticipation of pain and recourse to become so acute that Henry would beg for help.

Six months before, only two weeks after he had moved to New York, Henry got high with some neighbors from down the hall. He had caught a glimpse of their furniture, their posters, smelled the pungent aroma of marijuana, and decided to introduce himself. Twenty minutes later, he had thrown away six years of sobriety.

In the next weeks, and even months, he had kept his old habits at bay, kept his desire for escape from accelerating beyond his ability to step back, walk home, take a taxi, go to bed. No harm, no foul.

That had changed in Brazil, during the Task Three assignment. He had been transported from one city, New York, that was at least something like Houston, just more of everything, to a city that was of a different world. When the local press realized that he was the grandnephew of the lady who started it all, he was treated like a special ambassador. He received VIP treatment beyond his wildest dreams ... cocaine, alcohol, even prostitutes. How he had managed to keep that from getting out of hand, or in the news, was a miracle.

When Task Four rolled around, and his assignment was back on home turf, North America, Henry vowed to get things under control. He had been successful for a couple of weeks ... but then San Antonio. Even his old room-mate had been concerned.

During his Task Five stint, he was lucky that his ability to communicate, and therefore negotiate, in Africa and the Arabian Peninsula had been muted. This had kept him out of harm's way for the most part. That is, until he got to South Africa.

The night before he was to head off again with his fellow scout to their final location, one of the contestants from Durban invited Henry to join him for a drink. Socializing with team members was his first mistake. It had started innocently enough with a local South African cream liqueur called Amarula, seductively easy to drink. When his new friend headed home, shortly after midnight, Henry was just warming up. Making unwanted passes at several women and belligerently demanding more drinks after being told to leave had led to a fight with a couple of locals, which he summarily lost. At a quarter to four in the morning, Henry landed in jail.

He chose not to call Chanda Subramaniam, his Indian partner, for she was neither sympathetic nor resourceful. Besides, by the time he was clear-headed enough to call anybody, she was on the flight that he had missed. Instead, he called Steven Pace, with whom he had started the evening. While that conversation was mildly humiliating, he was able to at least share a good laugh with the former lieutenant. What still made him cringe, though, was his call to James Ruhle—at six o'clock in the morning, on a Sunday. And when Stewart Maxwell was called in to mitigate the legal damages, Henry lapsed into one of his worst shame spirals ever.

He now realized, as the taxi made its way into his neighborhood, that it was inevitable that his father was notified. *I wonder what Aunt Minerva will do.* He let out a mournful sigh as they pulled up to the entrance of his building.

Since boarding the plane in Johannesburg, Henry had looked forward to entering the sanctuary of his apartment and getting high—the only way he knew to blot out the reality he had brought upon himself. That escape was now out of the question as he unlocked the door and was obliged to invite his father in. He braced himself for the judgments that were sure to follow.

He quickly scanned the apartment for paraphernalia and was relieved to see only a few empty beer bottles on the kitchen counter.

"Have you eaten?" his father asked.

Henry nodded. "Have you?"

"Yes, at the airport."

His father found a spot on the couch and dragged a chair from the desk closer to the coffee table. Then, sure enough, he cleared his throat. Just as he was about to deliver his sermon, Henry spoke.

"Dad, I know why you're here, and I guess I'm grateful." Slumped into the chair, he sat up slightly, trying to summon a modicum of self-respect. "I really fucked up. I was ... I think when I ... It was going to be—"

"Henry," his father said softly. "Relax. I'm not here to chastise you. You've already taken care of that."

"I thought I could handle it," Henry blurted, "but I couldn't ... I didn't. Now it's too late. I don't know what to do. I can't ..." He stared at the floor. "I feel like a total failure."

His father waited. Then he asked, "Would you like some help?"

It was such a simple question, asked in such a genuine tone, so unlike his father, that it took Henry by surprise. He melted.

"That would be nice ... yes," he mumbled, his voice soggy with tears.

"Okay."

His father leaned forward and rested his elbows on his knees, in a pose that somehow disarmed Henry even more.

"The first thing we need to do is assess the damage."

He paused for a second, and Henry nodded.

"We'll get to other considerations in a minute, but first we need to figure out if there's any legal fallout. Other than court costs and fines, and the amount of your bail, is there anything that you need to tell me?"

"No ... well, I missed my flight to Nairobi, so we had to pay a lot more for my flight home."

"Anything else?"

"I don't think so."

"I was hoping you'd say that. The good news, then, is that everything has been taken care of. Stewart Maxwell sent a wire transfer to the Durban Police Department that satisfies all your fines and court costs ... more than enough to keep this off the books. He also paid back the young man who bailed you out.

"Now you're here, safe and sound. It could have been worse—a *lot* worse."

Henry nodded, but his expression was mournful.

"So, the question is where to go from here? What do you want to do?"

Surely there was more to it than that, Henry thought, for he felt as if the ceiling would come crashing down any second. He just stared at his father, unable to see beyond the next moment.

"I don't know," he said. "I suppose I'll move back to Houston and ..." He looked away.

"Don't you want to stay here and resume your duties?"

"I doubt that's possible. I can't imagine Aunt Minerva would forgive me."

"She doesn't know."

"*What?*"

"She doesn't know. She doesn't *need* to know."

A glimmer of hope dawned, and Henry almost smiled.

"Henry, one thing you should know about me is that I'm pretty good at taking care of messy situations. Unless there's something you're not telling me, I think your little escapade has been contained. There's no reason that you can't pick yourself up and continue. Stewart convinced James Ruhle to speak to the other scout—I can't pronounce her name—and she's going to keep this to herself. Nobody else knows about it.

"The only demons you need to worry about are internal."

That comment hit Henry full force.

"It's going to be an uphill struggle, but it may not be as bad as you're imagining. Ruhle was reluctant to give you another chance, but Stewart and I won him over. He likes you, Henry, but he's dealing with a lot of pressure. He can't afford to have any of his people stirring up trouble in faraway places ...

not with the whole world watching. Reputation and integrity have to be maintained. I'm sure you agree." Henry nodded.

"Ruhle assured me that you're welcome to resume your position, but he also made it clear that you won't get another chance. If something like this happens again, you're done."

Henry felt a flood of relief, but a low-level anxiety remained.

"What are you worried about?" his father asked.

"I don't know ... nothing, everything. I know it sounds crazy, but I don't know if I can stay sober. Everything is different here, and when I'm traveling, it's as if there's no balance, nothing to fall back on.

"When I decided to accept Aunt Minerva's offer, I was excited ... but also nervous. I was pretty sure I would contribute to something good, something worth doing. But what I've found out is that my work as a scout, other than being colorful, has been kind of meaningless.

"It's nothing like teaching. In my classroom, I'm the expert. I deliver lessons, in my own style, and I see the results almost immediately. Here, I'm nothing but a glorified referee. Most of the teams resent us, or barely tolerate us, and we don't have any input. In fact, we're forbidden to influence them in any way. We quote rules and regulations, maybe assure them that what they're considering is legal, but not much else."

As Godfrey listened to his son, his gaze softened.

Henry continued, "We're not supposed to have favorites, but of course we all do. I found out a few weeks ago that the one team I was actually rooting for got eliminated. It's a very poor team, and they missed the deadline because their entire community lost power and Internet access for a couple of days. What good is working for an organization if the best people still get screwed?"

"When you're in a depression, Henry, it feels terrible, but it also means you can't see very far. Problems seem exaggerated, and everything seems to conspire against you. Would you like to know what I see?"

"Huh?"

"I see a young man with incredible talent, unshakable integrity, lofty ideals, on the verge of discovering a whole new life ... and he's scared. *You're* scared, and understandably so. The mission you've chosen is the most challenging and dangerous one there—"

His father stopped, suddenly choked up by a truth that he had never fully admitted. Henry sat transfixed, not daring to interrupt.

"You're one of the few people I know who can cast aside what others think. You see what is true, despite what everybody else claims. Even as I've disagreed with you on so many occasions, I've always admired your sense of honor. You can't be bought ... I've tried.

"Unfortunately, you have an Achilles' heel—your addictions. If something doesn't change, you're going to undercut your own success, just when you're on the verge of achieving it."

His father fell silent and sat back, with an odd look of introspection.

"I don't know what to say. It sounds like you think I ought to stay here ... and I'd like to, but I feel like I've sabotaged myself. I guess I could start going to meetings again and get a sponsor."

"As you know, Henry, I love to tell people what they ought to do. That's just my way. I want to avoid that this time. I want you to know I support you, no matter what. If you decide to stay here in New York, you'll do a great job. If you decide to move back to Houston, go back to teaching, whatever, you'll do a great job.

"But I don't think you stand a chance unless you get sober again. Your mother and I will help you in any way we can."

Chapter 32

THE PRESS CONFERENCE to announce the advancing teams was noticeably more buoyant than the previous one. No threats or mishaps had been reported in the prior eight weeks, and the Athens bombing seemed but a distant shadow. The crowd of reporters was thinner than in the early phase of the competition, but it was still a crowd. The previous week saw renewed interest by the media toward The Contest due to the anticipation of viewing the children's input. As a result, influential educators and specialists had requested invitations to the press conference, and the downstairs press room included a diverse spectrum of teachers and professors.

Even the Secretary of Education made the trip. Though he failed in his attempt to be seated next to Minerva Bennett, he, the Mayor of New York, and a Columbia University professor were seated on the opposite side of the platform.

"Good morning! We are pleased to announce, for the first time, the *names* of the teams who will advance to the next task. We're down to only 32 teams. Although we still have ten months to go before the award ceremony, we are approaching the home stretch."

Catherine Myers looked out on the sea of cameras and microphones, and she recognized several reporters and local dignitaries. Looking fit and rested, she had come to feel at ease with being the primary spokesman for The Contest. Minerva Bennett, preferring more and more to stay out of the primary spotlight, sat on the edge of the dais, as did Libby Armstrong, who held her five-month-old on her lap. She was still on maternity leave, but she wanted to be included in the spectacle. James Ruhle and Stewart Maxwell sat close by.

"Today's press release is also unusual in that we won't be announcing the next task immediately, as has been our routine. This is out of deference to the upcoming holidays. We felt that, regardless of faith and spiritual practice, it would be good for all concerned to have some real time off, to relax and be relieved of any pressure to perform. Plenty of time for that when Task Six is announced on January 2nd."

She waited as several muted comments and grumblings passed through the crowd. After thanking the teams who were eliminated, she continued.

"I think it's safe to say that, in this past round, our judges were taxed with some very difficult decisions; they compared and ranked essays composed by our teams' youngest members and then scrutinized the supporting videos. Of course, nobody has seen these yet, but they will be released to the public in one hour, at which time we will all be able to judge for ourselves.

"I don't know about the rest of the staff, but I know I'll be busy for the next several days reading and watching as many as I can. I'm confident they will reveal an untapped reservoir of fresh ideas." She glanced at Minerva and smiled.

"Now, I'd like to invite James Ruhle to come forward. He will read the names of the teams that will be invited to participate in Round Six." She yielded the podium to Ruhle, who held up a sealed envelope and opened it.

"With no further ado," he began, "here are the advancing teams—in registration order. I will include the home city and country, and, if they created one, the team name.

"Team 8—from Atyrau, Kazakhstan ... Team 25, *Over the Top & Down Under*—from Gundiwindi, Queensland, Australia ... Team 121, *Imagine*—from Venice, California, USA ... Team 233, *Binnen de Ring*, which means 'Inside the Loop'—from Amsterdam, Netherlands ... Team 489, *Aequitas*, which is Latin for 'fairness'—from Tulsa, Oklahoma, USA ... Team 603, *Maui Wowie*—from Maui, Hawaii, USA." Laughter in the audience startled Ruhle, who paused and smiled. "Yes, I think that one is self-explanatory."

Minerva rolled her eyes when Libby whispered to her the cultural significance of the name.

"Moving on ... Team 765, *KwaZulu-Natal*, which is a geographical reference—from Durban, South Africa ... Team 872, *Sunnah*, which is an Islamic term meaning 'a clear and well-trodden path'—from the village of Halhul, near Hebron in the West Bank, part of the Palestinian Territories ... and, last but not least, Team Alt-3. They were the third team on our wait list in the registration process, and the last one to officially enter The Contest. This team hails from the city of Wenzhou, in the Zhijiang Province of the People's Republic of China. My notes tell me their team name translates as *Peaceful Industry*. Congratulations to *all* of the advancing teams!

"One more thing before I open it up to questions. At the bottom of my list, I see a break down by region. Of these 32 teams, two are from Australia, three are from Africa, four are from South America, six from Asia, seven from Europe, and ten from North America. Every continent is represented, and this contest is still *global*.

"As Catherine Myers mentioned, the responses will soon become public, and we invite everybody to log on and view as many of these as you can find time for. See for yourselves how these teams impressed the judges." He nodded at Catherine, signaling her to join him for Q & A.

"Okay ... questions?" Numerous hands went up, but as usual several reporters didn't bother waiting for a nod. A *New York Times* reporter got the jump on the others.

"According to your numbers, the majority of advancing teams come from the more-developed regions, with North America and Europe leading the way. Does this concern you? Have your judges been given a quota? Has there been any type of mandate to maintain representation from the other continents?"

Catherine took this one. "First of all, there are no quotas or mandates. We've said this before, but it bears repeating. Vox Stellarum is, of course, completely responsible for the format, the timing, and the objectives of each task. The responses are obviously up to the teams. But the results are up to the judges. We have no influence as to which teams advance.

"That being said, it does appear that the geographical distribution of advancing teams is weighted toward more developed regions, but there are several notable exceptions. We take this as proof that our format is sufficiently accessible and equitable, regardless of cultural, political, or socio-economic backgrounds."

"In fact," added Ruhle, "quite a few teams that were presumed to have an advantage, by virtue of academic degrees and corporate C-level representation, have been eliminated, while several of the advancing teams lack obvious credentials that might have hinted at their success."

After a few more questions about the results, a reporter from the *Associated Press* spoke.

"It appears that the authorities have still been unable to identify the perpetrators in the Athens bombings. Whether they do or not, how has that incident affected the way your judges conduct their business?"

Catherine responded. "We're still hopeful that leads will surface and that those responsible will be apprehended and prosecuted. In the meanwhile, although no credible threats have been made, our panel has been advised to keep travel to a minimum. Their conferencing is now completely on-line, and this has presented no difficulties."

"And what of the judges that were replaced?" another reporter called out.

"They have adjusted very well," said James. "The new judges—Gabriela Ocampo, from Argentina, and Michel Bauwens, from Belgium—have performed admirably."

As fewer and fewer hands went up, Catherine was about to adjourn. A final question from a *Fox News* reporter came: "What about Task Six? Can you give us a hint?"

"I'm sorry," said James. "All I can say is that we're excited about it. It will be the most serious inquiry yet into what the teams are up against ... what we're *all* up against."

⋯⊷▣◉ ◉▣◖⋯

Two German shepherds lay on the porch asleep, their noses inches from each other, their master just a few feet away in his armchair. Malcolm Conroy turned a page of his book and reached for his tea. He liked seeing the cloud of vapor billowing from the cup as he brought it to his lips.

It had been several days since he had ventured off his property, and he was glad to be settling back into the quiet rhythm he had missed for too long. His travels on behalf of Vox Stellarum—the trips to Argentina and Belgium, then New York, and Washington, D.C.—had all gone well. Now, he embraced solitude with a vengeance.

The sky was slate gray with faint bands of darker clouds to the west. The weather was frosty and invigorating. A breeze stirred the top layer of leaves on the ground nearby as snow began to fall. He had positioned his chair near the edge of the porch, his legs extended toward the far end, resting on an ottoman.

Except for the evergreens, the trees were bare, giving the canopy of branches overhead a filigree, like the panels of an ornate bank of stained glass. Conroy loved this time of year for its stark beauty. It was the first snow of the year.

After a while, the flakes became larger and floated down more gracefully. He laid his book down, draped a blanket over his lower body, and reached for his pipe. As he puffed on a freshly packed bowl, he regarded his dogs. They were content, and so was he.

He wore long johns under his denim pants, a wool shirt, and a hunting jacket. Smelling the fire from inside as wind eddies carried the scent of the burning logs from the chimney, he was comforted by the knowledge that he could retreat to the warmth of his cabin at any time. He picked up his book and continued.

Several pages later, both dogs looked up, instantly awake. Their eyes, noses, and ears intently focused on something in the distance, but their bodies remained motionless. They both looked straight into the forest, sensing something that Conroy could neither see nor hear.

"Apollo, what is it?" The dog turned momentarily and then again riveted his attention on something unseen. A half minute later Conroy heard an approaching vehicle. Somebody was coming up the road. The dogs remained still and vigilant.

He stood up and made a low whistle. Both dogs turned and stared, waiting for instructions. With his left hand, he pointed to one side of his property at a stand of trees and thick bushes.

"Mercury, go," he commanded in a low voice. The dog immediately ran to the appointed station, turned, and lay down. With his right hand, he pointed in the opposite direction to another stand of bushes. "Apollo, go."

By the time the vehicle crested the hill and came into view through the trees lining the road, both dogs were invisible and silent. Conroy slipped his Glock into the right-hand pocket of his jacket and mentally prepared himself. Then he sat back down, relit his pipe, and looked up as casually as he could, feigning indifference.

An unfamiliar vehicle turned into his driveway. A lost traveler? An unannounced visitor? He wasn't taking any chances. Though the SUV had tinted windows, Conroy could tell there were at least two men inside. He glanced at his watch. It was ten after three.

Only when they drove all the way up and parked next to his pick-up truck did Conroy set his pipe down and stand up. Three men, all well dressed with wool overcoats, got out and slowly approached.

"Mr. Conroy? Malcolm Conroy?" asked the driver. Conroy said nothing and simply waited on the porch as they came closer.

"May we have a word with you?" he asked. The two passengers lagged several yards behind.

"That's close enough," said Conroy curtly. They all stopped and waited. "You know my name, so you're obviously not lost. What's your business?"

"My name is Jack Carter. We're here to ask you some questions regarding your involvement with Vox Stellarum."

"What business is that of yours? Who sent you?"

"We," said Carter, turning to his associates, "... this is Bill Smith ... this is Ed Jones ... we work for an investment group. We've come down from New York to see if we might—"

"What company?"

"It's a private company. I doubt you—"

"What company?"

"East River Holding Company. Our shareholders are interested in the successful outcome of your contest, and we're here to discuss how we might help insure that ... that this is the case."

Conroy scowled. "First of all, it's not *my* contest. Second, my business with the foundation is complete. Third, there's no indication that they're in need of anybody's help—yours *or* mine."

He sat back down. "Now, if you'll excuse me, I'm busy."

Smith and Jones moved even with Carter, who persisted.

"Mr. Conroy, I understand your annoyance. Nevertheless, I think it would be in your interest to hear us out."

Conroy held his pipe and looked off in the distance. After several seconds, he turned.

"Oh?"

"We have information you may find valuable regarding the security of your colleagues—your former colleagues, that is."

"That sounds like a threat," Conroy said.

"I didn't mean for it to be, I assure you. We have reason to believe that several organizations have been waiting for an opportunity to disrupt the course of The Contest, and that the next task will trigger events that will lead to undesirable disclosures."

"Ignoring for the moment the fact that the content of these tasks is highly confidential, putting the odds of your knowing anything specific about the assignment near zero, what is it that you think you know?" Conroy set his pipe down and put his hands in his pockets. "What are your people worried about?"

"So far," said Carter, "the teams have been laying out general recommendations ... saving this, fixing that. But, in two weeks, they will be instructed to identify specific institutions, even individuals, that are perceived to be standing in the way of change.

"You know how these things work, Mr. Conroy. If somebody were to shine a light on any individuals or groups that prefer to remain anonymous, it could get messy." Despite his past experience in dealing with corrupt negotiators, Conroy was unable to contain his anger.

"Why don't we start with you, Mr. Carter. Let's shine a light on the fact that this 'East River Holding Company,' if it exists at all, is a corporate shell for arms dealers and offshore hedge funds. Your earpieces, your overcoats, your haircuts ... you guys are obviously ex-CIA ... or is it ex-NSA? At any rate, well-dressed thugs.

"You come here, uninvited, with the ruse of warning me against a vague danger. It's obvious that it is *your* people who are afraid of the spotlight. What are they up to? Why in the hell are they worried about a bunch of do-gooders? They can't possibly know anything that could jeopardize your schemes."

"You're wrong, Mr. Conroy. Despite the fact that most people behave more like sheep than men ... and do what they're told, there are some who are taking notice of things that ought to be left alone. They're asking questions; they're expecting answers."

"That's not my problem."

"Not yet," Carter said, losing patience. He turned to his colleagues, straining to remain calm. Jones, older and more weathered than the others, stepped forward.

"Where are your dogs, Mr. Conroy?" he asked.

"*What?*"

"You have two highly trained attack dogs. Where are they?"

Carter at least had charm, artificial though it was, but it was better than the humorless demeanor of his colleague. Jones's eyes were dark brown, almost black, like the blunt staring eyes of a shark.

Conroy stood and moved to the edge of the porch. "That's it. I need you to leave. *Now.*"

"As you wish, Mr. Conroy," said Carter. "May I presume to leave you with one point before we go?" His calm composure convinced Conroy to give him a faint nod.

"In an organization that is ill-suited to handle the storm that is coming, you are the one man who can influence the senior members of Vox Stellarum—to keep things from getting messy. Should you refuse this opportunity, we can't guarantee that it won't become more personal than they, or *you*, would care to see."

"What was that you said earlier ... about not meaning to threaten me?"

Carter's face hardened now that his agenda had been exposed.

"After we leave, and you review your surveillance video, you will find that we don't exist ... that our company doesn't exist. Any steps you take to find us will be wasted. We will return to the shadows, happy to remain there unless undue attention forces us to take defensive measures. And be clear, Mr. Conroy, we don't do defense."

He turned to go. Smith followed him, as did Jones, but only after a parting glance that was ugly, somehow personal.

Conroy remained standing until long after they had driven away. The peace and serenity he had felt only twenty minutes earlier had been displaced by confusion, suspicion, and rage. It now occurred to him that the snow had continued to fall lightly during the encounter and that he had been oblivious to it. He took a deep breath and expelled a giant sigh, which appeared as a cloud of steam.

He felt the cold metal of his pistol in his jacket pocket. He hadn't been aware of it during the conversation, but now he imagined drawing it and placing a bullet in the head of each of the bastards that were driving back toward the highway.

"Apollo, Mercury, come!" Instantly, the dogs sprang up and trotted toward their master, still on alert. Sensing his tension and anger, they remained on guard, ready for their next orders. Conroy stepped off the porch and approached them. Finally, with another deep sigh, he allowed his own guard to relax, and he signaled them to drop theirs. Wagging their tails happily, they moved to Conroy as he kneeled and embraced them. He grabbed first one, then the other, hugging them and allowing them to lick his face, a rare lapse in their protocol.

When Conroy stood up, he turned and inspected his cabin. How had they known about his surveillance cameras? Even he couldn't see them. They were disguised by the paneling and other fixtures. An educated guess? He could only assume that veterans of the intelligence community would know how he might design his own security system.

A dozen questions swirled in his mind, besides the obvious challenge Carter had made about his not being able to find any trace of their existence. If that were so, this was a much more formidable threat than he first imagined. Who had sent them? How had they gained access to confidential information about the next task? How did they know about his dogs?

So much for peace and quiet.

As Conroy entered his cabin, he decided to call their bluff. He issued a stay command to the dogs, and they settled in front of the fireplace. Then he walked into a hallway closet, closed the door, rotated one of the coat hooks 90 degrees counter-clockwise, then 360 degrees clockwise, and the false back wall slid away, revealing steps into a hidden basement. The low lighting automatically switched to active mode as he descended into his safe-room bunker. The monitor of his computer woke up, and the lights of the short-wave radio equipment flickered to life.

He poured himself a scotch from the small bar in one corner of the 12 x 12 room, and he sat down at the desk. Once logged into his computer, he accessed the video file log. With only rudimentary facial recognition software, Conroy's search for the identities of the three men came up blank. So did his search for the so-called 'East River Holding Company.' He would need help in his search, and he sat back, reviewing names of old contacts. He didn't want to move until he had a plan of action.

The basement was Spartan, with only a few personal touches, one being a photograph of his wife and daughter. His eyes landed on their smiles for brief moments, but then he would look away. With this new threat, the pain of that old wound was ripped open yet again. He felt a vague connection between that loss and the present threat, but he knew that was absurd.

The ultimatum the men had just delivered felt like a kick in the stomach. It brought up a host of memories, all of them dark. As a man, and furthermore as a soldier, submitting to some nameless threat was something he could not abide.

They, Miriam and Delany, had been taken from him. He was not about to let this sort of thing happen again. He forced himself to look at the picture, taken twenty years before ... forced himself to look into their eyes ... forced himself to not look away. Gradually, he felt commitment harden into an iron resolve—an oath. *Their blood, not mine.*

He recalled the last thing Carter had said: "... we don't do defense." Finishing his scotch in one gulp, Conroy said aloud, "Neither do I, you son of a bitch!"

He emerged from his safe room with an implacable resolve to find and expose these people. He made four calls—three to New York to set up a meeting the following morning and one to an old friend, a man who was good at picking up a scent where one didn't exist.

Chapter 33

EARLY THE NEXT morning, Conroy flew to New York and made his way to Minerva's apartment.

"Sorry to be so cryptic yesterday. Thanks for meeting on such short notice," said Conroy.

Gathered in the study, Minerva sat in her chair next to the fireplace. Stewart Maxwell and Sam Minton were on the couch. Their looks were grave, matching Conroy's dark mood.

"Yesterday afternoon," he began, "I was visited by three men who claimed to represent some outfit by the name of East River Holding Company. It doesn't exist, and neither do they."

"*What?*" asked Maxwell.

"I'll go into that in a minute, but let me tell you about their agenda first. One man did most of the talking. He implied that they had reason to believe the next task will instruct teams to identify specific organizations and groups, even individuals, that stand in the way of progress. He said I was the only person in a position to convince the staff of Vox Stellarum to modify the assignment, to water it down somehow, so as not to rile any groups that value their privacy.

"And this was followed by a vague, but serious, threat. My inaction, he implied, would force their people to make things 'more personal' than you or I would care to see."

"That's outrageous!" said Minton.

"Yes," agreed Conroy.

"What do you know about these men?" asked Minerva. "Had you ever seen them before?"

"No. Once they left, I viewed my surveillance video footage and was unable to come up with anything."

"You had *video* running at the time?" asked Maxwell.

"Yes. When I built my cabin, I had several safeguards put in place, among them motion sensors and recording devices, including smart video. These men knew that I probably had something of the sort, and they practically dared me to try to find them. I've sent the close-ups to an old friend who's still in the business. He's got connections that I no longer have, and he owes me a favor or two. I'm hoping he'll be able to turn up something.

"I couldn't find anything on their company either. They probably just made up the name in the moment, but they obviously work for someone with considerable resources. This morning, before I took off, I made inquiries at the airport. The men were seen boarding a charter jet with a flight plan naming Baltimore as their destination. No such airplane departed from or arrived in Baltimore yesterday. My friend is going to conduct a more extensive search. I gave him the tail number of the aircraft, but I have a feeling that'll come up blank, too."

"What do you have?" asked Minerva, nervously twisting the corners of a cushion.

"Nothing substantial, I'm afraid. I do, however, have a suspicion, based solely on a hunch."

"Whatever it is, let's have it," said Maxwell. "We've got to start somewhere."

"You're not going to like it, especially if I'm right. That's why I'm going to hold off until I do some digging on my own." The others pressed him, but Conroy held firm. He continued with his threat assessment to the organization.

"What we have, then, is a leak. Assuming that their intel was correct ... and judging by the look Stewart gave you a minute ago," he said, looking at Minerva, "it *was* ... we have a security issue. This is a problem above and beyond the ultimatum they issued." The others nodded.

"Which of you knows the specific contents of Task Six?"

"I do," said Minerva.

"I do as well," said Maxwell.

"Not me," said Minton. "As a board member, I've kept my distance."

"I thought that might be the case," said Conroy. "Minerva, you're obviously beyond suspicion. And so are Sam and Stewart."

"That's true," said Minerva, "but I would include everybody else for that matter. I trust these people more than my own family."

"Nevertheless, who else?"

Counting on her fingers, Minerva called out the others. "Besides Stewart and me, there's Catherine, James Ruhle, Rowan Detering, Bill Finch, Bindiya Bhattacharya, and Bobby Jabari. Eight of us. We're all under strict orders to keep the assignment absolutely confidential until it's made public in January."

"What about Libby?"

"Since she's been on maternity leave, she's been out of the loop."

"Do any of them strike you as having the motivation to share information of this kind?"

Minerva shook her head. "I can't imagine any of them would betray my confidence or do anything that would put this project at risk."

"Isn't it possible that our people aren't the source of the leak?" asked Minton.

"Right ... couldn't it be a hacker or some such thing?" asked Maxwell.

"Yes," Conroy said. "That's a possibility, maybe even a bigger concern. If somebody has gained access to Vox Stellarum internal communications, whether it's through the Internet routing system or through e-mail, or even the cell-tower grid, we need to know.

"Jabari is sharp. He obviously knows about encryption, but I doubt he set up the office network. We probably ought to bring in somebody to do a full analysis and a sweep. I know somebody if you want my help."

"You're right," said Minerva. "It was either Libby or Catherine who handled the office network. I agree, a security check is a must. Stewart, let's make that happen."

Maxwell nodded, but then said, "Regardless, we need to decide whether we alter the task or not. I don't think we can afford to take any chances."

He looked at Minton and then at Minerva, who was staring out the window distractedly.

Tough as she was, Conroy saw that Minerva was struggling. The men waited. After a long silence, she turned.

"This seems somehow worse than the incident in Athens, and I don't know if I could take another ... another blow like that."

Minton spoke. "Malcolm is obviously taking this threat seriously. If we can't identify the source pretty quickly, I think you need to revise the assignment. Since I haven't been involved, I'm not sure what that would look like. It sounds like the focus on specific individuals and groups needs to be removed. If the teams are told to target only institutions and laws, maybe that'll satisfy these people."

"Now that I think about it," said Maxwell, "that might not be such a bad idea. Putting people on the defensive isn't necessarily a great way to change public opinion anyway. We don't want this to become a witch hunt."

Minton said, "I imagine the contestants will still be able to sink their teeth into a scaled-back version, and of course they'll never know the difference."

"Malcolm," asked Maxwell suddenly, "how will these bastards know whether you perform as they hope? It doesn't sound like they left a calling card."

"Hmm. Good question. I hadn't thought of that."

"We could leak a story to the press," suggested Minton.

Conroy nodded. "Whatever their source, we might interrupt it through tightened security. In that case, a leak to the press may be the only way to send the message that we're complying. These people are dangerous ... of *that* I have no doubt. The sooner we respond, the better the odds are that they'll back off."

"It's settled then," said Minerva. "As much as I hate to yield to pressure of this sort, that's what we're going to do. We can't put our people in harm's way."

"I think that's wise," said Conroy, "but know this—I'm taking this personally. I won't stop my investigation until these people are in my crosshairs."

◦•◦▷▤▨◉ ◉▨▤◁◦•◦

In Atyrau, Kazakhstan, Takhir and Umit Burkitbayev hosted the gathering of Team 8 as they primed themselves for Round Six. The 8-hour time difference allowed the group time to meet for dinner and conversation before listening to the Vox Stellarum press conference live from the United States. As their 15-year-old son Serik turned off the television, a lively discussion ensued.

"I like this one!" exclaimed Marat Kriazhev, one of the younger professors at the Atyrau State University. "We can finally make references to things we have only hinted at thus far."

"I agree," said Yana Karimov. She had recently graduated with an engineering degree.

Daniar Teteriuk, Serik's cousin, was in the next room. His uncle had asked him to print the text of the new task. He now brought in several copies and handed them out. Conversation ebbed for a moment as they scanned the official statement.

TASK SIX

Consider the resistance by certain segments of the population to the ideas your team has presented thus far. Even if you have managed to come up with a fresh approach, consider that some of your ideas may have been around for a long time and that they have been ignored, discounted, or rejected. In this context, describe how the solutions that you present might take hold, not just in your local community and your nation, but in the world at large.

And, even if your proposals have been well received by the general public, what are the institutional and cultural impediments that will be the hardest to overcome? Be specific regarding religious and/or spiritual groups, government agencies, constitutional and statutory precedents, commercial practices, and socio-economic indicators. Keep your focus on the authorities that we tend to take for granted and be willing to offer alternatives to these embedded structures. Explain the benefits to adopting your philosophy while showing how maintaining the status quo will continue to deteriorate the standard of living for the vast majority should your solutions fail to be implemented.

"This is enough to get us in trouble if we choose to be courageous," said Akmetzhan Musabayev. He was the eldest member, and his voice carried weight. The others looked at him, puzzled.

"What do you mean?" asked Umit, who was busy picking up plates and glasses.

"This is the opportunity we have been hoping for, but of course there is a risk. We could easily alienate these so-called authorities and invite unwanted scrutiny upon ourselves. And close them off as potential allies. It is okay, but I think we need to discuss how specific we want to be, how critical we can afford to be."

"We've already demonstrated courage, and we've been rewarded for it," said Takhir. "I don't think we should stop now."

"That may be," responded Musabayev, "but chastising the super powers for their ongoing imperialism, as we did in Task Four, is one thing. Naming institutions much closer to home will be another matter. If we confront the officials in Astana, not to mention Beijing and Moscow, we will have government officials breathing down our necks, whether we advance or not.

"We all know that President Nazarbayev is basically a dictator; he can have us all put under house arrest any time he wants. The fact that he has been fairly progressive so far does not offset the fact that he wields tremendous power. We must be very careful not to incur his wrath ... and, yet, I would love to send him a few jabs!"

"You're talking in circles, my dear Akmetzhan," said Aidana Yegorov, the eldest female team member. As a school administrator and nurse, she had a way of bringing conversation back down to earth. "I think what you really mean is that we want to push our views as much as possible, without being censored or rounded up."

The old man laughed. "Yes, that is precisely what I mean."

Takhir sat down in his chair, for he had been helping his wife clean up the room. "Let's get down to business then. Malika, would you please take notes?

Let's make a list. I want everybody to come up with at least one thing that is standing in the way of progress. The children can go first, and let's try not to repeat. Everybody must come up with a fresh idea."

Luba, Serik's 12-year-old sister, raised her hand. "I vote for the principal of my school. He won't let me take the classes I want. The boys get more choices!"

Takhir smiled at his daughter. "Good one! Let's call that school administration policy."

"How about the Church?" suggested Bulat Usenov, an eleven-year-old. He had demonstrated such impressive poise during the previous round that the video portion of his response had gone viral. His teammates had begun to look at him in a new way, and his precocious manner sometimes startled the others.

"What do you mean, Bulat?" asked Takhir.

"The bishop and the priests don't like it when we ask questions. They tell us to read the scripture and to have faith. But when I ask about why we do certain things, they punish me and tell me to know my place."

"I see," said Takhir sympathetically. He vaguely knew that the boy's family attended one of the Russian Orthodox churches in the area. Inwardly, he expressed gratitude that he and his wife had successfully avoided religious entanglements. Both were descended from families for whom the Soviet suppression of religion had produced the desired effect: he was an atheist.

"Put that down as religious suppression," he said to Malika.

As each member gave his or her suggestion, it got more and more difficult. By the time they adjourned, the group was pleased to have agreement on a half dozen weighty indictments. Other than Musabayev's admonition with respect to incurring the wrath of government officials, the team seemed committed to throwing caution to the wind.

⋅⟩═◉ ◉═⟨⋅

Holding a fresh copy of *Tulsa World* in front of them, twelve people smiled for the camera, as they had done dozens of times before. The librarian handed the smart phone back to Rhianna, the team member assigned to upload documents to the Vox website.

"Thanks, Dorothy," said Pete Talley to the librarian. She exited the room to return to the quiet of the main area.

For several months, The M. J. Fowler Library had been abuzz with energy around its status as headquarters for Team 489, or *Aequitas* as the general public now knew them to be called. Talley had noticed the spillover benefit to the library of the team's weekly presence, and he wondered how long the uptick in attendance might last.

Over the weekend, a pair of scouts from Vox Stellarum had shown up and caused a small stir in the community. They asked questions of numerous visitors to the library, even people walking in the neighborhood. They wanted to know anything and everything about the habits of the team members—conversations overheard, books and magazines accessed, computers used. This was for show, of course, since the group never ventured beyond their reserved conference room.

The librarian was among those interviewed, but she too had been unable to report anything beyond the fact that she was the one who took their weekly photos. It became clear that the group followed the rules to the letter, and the scouts had spent the final day of their visit sitting quietly in the back of the meeting room.

The team was reworking its Task Six response. They had included the ACA (Affordable Care Act) as one of their targets, and Rhianna, an intern at Talley's clinic, spoke of how she and her colleagues had experienced firsthand how disruptive the sweeping legislation had been to their business and to the level of care they could offer their patients. She recommended, though, that they modify some of their antagonistic language.

"I agree with Rhianna," said David Butler, the eldest male on the team. "But I have another concern: we've gotta trim this thing. I'm looking at our draft, and we're at about 5000 words. We eventually need to get it below 3500."

"You're right, Dave," said Talley, "but let's keep going. Until we get a thumbs-up or thumbs-down on each issue, we won't necessarily know how much each piece needs to be revised."

Paige Davis raised her hand. In her early sixties, she was well dressed and youthful looking.

"I don't have a problem with any one section, but I'm noticing the order, and I'm wondering if we need to rearrange things. We seem to bounce around. We've got a couple of decent segues, but I think we can do better."

"What do you have in mind?"

"I think we need to stay more focused on our core theme and use it every chance we get. We should open with a stronger statement, sort of like what we did in Task Four. We introduced our wild-card topics only after we made clear how and why we chose our main mix of issues. If we do this again, we can launch into each one and show how they're all just variations on a theme."

"And how would you formulate that theme?" Talley asked.

"Something like: Let the government do what it does best—which is very little—and let the people do everything else."

"But that's part of the problem," said Nick Rogers, a high-school science teacher in his mid-thirties. "I know what you mean, *sort of* ... and that's what the judges are going to think. They kinda sorta know what we're talking about. What we're up against though is that, when we state the actual problems, the inept policies that cause breakdowns in the system, we'll lose sympathy. We'll come off as harsh and unsympathetic.

"Most people love to hear about more freedom and a looser grip in terms of taxes and regulations, but they get turned off as soon as somebody reminds them of the cost—more individual responsibility, more family responsibility, more community responsibility, and so on. And *that's* when things are going smoothly. Given the state of the economy right now, if we lay out this live-and-let-live doctrine, I'm afraid that what they're gonna hear instead is *live and let die*."

"You're right," said Talley. "That's why we need to stay with specific policies and institutions we believe are problematic. As soon as we bring in philosophy, as much as I think that's a good thing, we'll lose our audience.

"So, let's do it—let's tie it all together. But we need to keep it fact-based ... objective. For instance, in the section on the ACA, we give results of a study done by the American Medical Association. It's only one study, but, given the source, I think it adds weight to our point. It spells out the decline in our business and others like it, in patient coverage, and the huge increase in red tape we have to deal with on a daily basis."

"That's true," said Dave Butler, "but what's missing is how we would have things go if the ACA *were* to be repealed. We need to show what should replace it. Even people who hate it don't want to just return to what we had before. We need to make a stronger case for the free market approach."

"But that didn't work," said Nick Rogers.

"That's not true. It wasn't *allowed* to work," argued Talley. "There was a climate of crony capitalism and a hive of special interest groups skewing the whole system. So, look, I can see we need to take a risk here and go farther out on the limb than I originally imagined. We're talking about a wholesale shift, back to what we used to have actually, which is individual freedom to make choices. For instance, if people were to view health care in the same way they look at transportation, we'd be a lot better off."

"What do you mean?" asked Butler.

Talley turned to Tyler Sullivan, a high-school senior and Eagle Scout. "Tyler, what kind of car do you drive?"

"I don't have one ... but I'm saving up."

"Well, how do you get around?"

"My bike ... sometimes the bus. Or I get a ride ..."

"Do you think you deserve a car?"

"*What?*"

"Shouldn't you be given a car? Don't you have the right to a car, just like everybody else? In fact, don't you think you should be given a car like the one I drive—a Mercedes?"

"What's your point, Pete?" asked Paige Davis.

"Don't you see? Here's a hard-working student who knows that driving a car is not an entitlement ... it's a privilege. He knows that he can only have what he can afford, unless somebody gives him a car, of course, which some parents do. But the point is that he doesn't see it as something that he deserves or is entitled to. And the notion that he should be given one similar to mine is crazy."

"I see where you're going, Pete," said Dave Butler, "but it's a stretch to connect these two situations."

Talley turned to the boy. "Tyler, I didn't mean to put you on the spot. By the way, your response was perfect."

He turned back to Butler, and then he looked around the room and continued.

"If we could somehow make the case that *that's* how healthy people look at their options, in all areas of their lives, then we might be able to turn things around. When you get right down to it, it's a matter of personal priorities and affordability. Not just for automobiles, smart phones, and running shoes—but for food, housing, education, *and* health care."

"But what about people who can't afford any of those things?" asked Jenna Cole. "What if somebody doesn't have family to fall back on? What about communities that are so poor that everybody is just barely surviving?"

Everybody turned toward Jenna. A junior at the same high school Tyler attended, she rarely spoke in their discussions. And when she did, she asked questions—the sort that often stop free marketers in their tracks, as they now did Pete Talley. He regarded her for a moment before answering.

"I know there're lots of people in those predicaments, Jenna, and of course they need help. My view—and I know a lot of people won't find any comfort in this—is that that's where charity comes in. This issue is at the heart of the divide. Some believe charity ought to be fully voluntary and private. Others believe it ought to be a function of government. I guess you know which group I'm in."

Elizabeth Fisher got up and walked around the table, something she did from time to time to keep her legs from cramping. As she sat back down, she signaled that it was her turn to speak.

"Peter, I think we're getting bogged down. Jenna's questions put you, quite naturally I'd say, on the defensive. But that's what we want to avoid.

"What if we were to start our response with a series of questions, similar to the ones she just asked? What if we were to acknowledge right off the top how these issues are the very ones that divide this country and even keep the world at war? It's really simple. It's a case of the 'Haves' and the 'Have Nots.'

"What we need to do is make clear that we aren't in either camp. We're the ones who are going to offer an alternative. We're going to explain how misfortune can strike anyone, and of course nobody wants to be a burden. We're going to explain how we value a culture of people who help and support one another. But most importantly, we're going to explain that there are better approaches than putting the government in charge.

"Because you're right, Peter. We used to be a society that took care of our own. The challenge, and it's a big one, is showing that the 'Have Nots' stand a better chance of achieving health and prosperity in a society that maximizes freedom of choice than in a society that is constantly limiting it."

Chapter 34

CATHERINE SMILED AT Malcolm as he stood upon her approach. He had reserved a quiet table in the corner of a bistro, enough off the beaten path that they were unlikely to run into anybody who might recognize her. Despite her growing celebrity, she knew how to dress down, put her hair up, and hide behind large frame sunglasses.

As the waiter seated her, Conroy sat down. "Hello, Catherine. Thanks for coming."

"My pleasure, Malcolm."

"Even in disguise, you look gorgeous." She blushed.

"Thank you. You don't look bad yourself."

They ordered and shared small talk, but she grew impatient.

"Okay, what's this about? As much as I enjoy your wit and charm, I'm sure there's something more dramatic going on."

He gave her that piercing look she recognized from their very first encounter, then grinned, softening the tension in his jaws just enough to put her at ease.

"As you know, several weeks ago I was visited by some men who issued an ultimatum, through me, to you and your colleagues. You were traveling the day I flew in to meet with Minerva, Stewart, and Sam. As vague as it was, we had to take the threat seriously. We had no choice. As a result, the task was modified. Of course, you know all that." He sipped his scotch and peered at her before proceeding.

"But what you may not know is that I intentionally excluded you from that meeting."

She furrowed her brow, straining to see the purpose in his point, and the implication.

"The reason is that you were a suspect." Conroy let that sink in as he watched her closely.

"*What?*"

Satisfied that her reaction was genuine, as he'd hoped, he reached to touch her hand. "You may not like what I'm getting ready to tell you, so bear with me. During that meeting, I told the others I had a hunch about who might have been behind the threat, but I declined to explain until I had a chance to do more investigating on my own. I haven't been successful ... until now.

"I want you to know I've gone to great lengths to disprove a connection that I'm afraid is very much real. Now listen carefully and withhold judgment until I tell you everything I know ... everything I *think* I know." She nodded faintly.

"The men who appeared at my cabin claimed to know something about the next task, which I knew to be a closely guarded secret. That was disconcerting enough. When one of the men asked me about my 'highly trained attack dogs,' I almost snapped. How could they have possibly known that?

"The list of those who knew the task *and* knew about my dogs is very short, I'm afraid." Catherine stared at him.

"While I never, for an instant, suspected you, or Libby, of leaking this information to these people, I did flash on another person who may have had access to this information."

Catherine shook her head slightly and pursed her lips, trying to process something that didn't make sense.

"*Who?!*"

"Catherine, how did you meet Anthony Parrish?"

She suddenly got the connection but rejected it in the same instant. "*No!* He couldn't have done this. He's a great guy, and he—There is *no way!*"

"How did you meet him? Maybe a better question is: *where* did you meet him?"

"What does that matter? How could you ... how could you think that—"

"Calm down. I know this is hard to hear, but it's critical we determine if Parrish is involved or not. Information can be intercepted in any number of ways, especially in this age of micro-cameras and wire taps. But until I determine the information was not leaked, I'm afraid he's a suspect."

"You think Anthony's a *spy?* Come on, Malcolm. You're not serious."

"*If* he's involved, and this is still an if, there are several ways it could have happened."

"What do you mean?"

"It could be what is sometimes called a soft trade, an innocent tip. Parrish could've overheard something from you, insider information so to speak, and he passed it on thinking that nobody would really use it for anything nefarious. That's the most innocent scenario, and he'd be unaware of his role.

"If, on the other hand, he was more conscious of the value of information that he passed on, it would still depend on what his intentions were ... and what the stated purpose was of the people he shared it with. For instance, what if he was under the impression that a colleague, or a friend, wanted to place a bet in Las Vegas. After all, there's an enormous amount of money to be made on such side bets these days. That would still be a fairly innocent motive.

"But, if he knowingly passed on details that he knew would be used as leverage for an ultimatum like the one that was, in fact, delivered, well ..." He saw Catherine's mood darken, and he waited to deliver his fourth scenario.

"There's at least one more possibility. Again, assuming he's involved at all, it's possible that Parrish was recruited under duress."

"What do you mean?"

"He could have been blackmailed—forced to fish for information because he owes a debt. Now, I've met Parrish. A spy he is not ... nor a thief, nor an assassin. But that doesn't mean he's immune to being talked into something that's gone way beyond his understanding."

Catherine was dumbfounded. She stared at her drink. Conroy repeated his question.

"Where did you meet Anthony Parrish?"

⇢⟫═◉ ◉═⟪⇠

Henry Godfrey was back in the United States. He had returned from his Task Six tour in Asia, during which he had been partnered with Salma Farouk, an

Egyptian. Embodying the progress her culture had garnered since the Arab Spring, she had raised eyebrows in several cities, but there had been no incidents to speak of. After scrutinizing all six Asian teams, they hadn't reported any irregularities. And Henry had stayed out of trouble.

He was glad to be back, and, for the first time, he was beginning to feel at home in New York City. Perhaps it was finally time for that new reality to sink in. Perhaps it was his renewed commitment to sobriety and a sense of being grounded for the first time in months. Having embraced his father's advice to recommit to the program, he set out to regain the rhythm he had established prior to his move from Texas.

As far as he could tell, his Aunt Minerva never did find out about the episode in South Africa. And Chanda, his Indian partner, had kept her word; the story had spread no further. Henry even sent her a text with a photo of his 60-day sobriety chip, and he got a row of smiley faces in return.

Meanwhile, a few blips had suddenly appeared on his romantic radar, just when he didn't need any new complications. Not only had he received several long and intimate letters from his old girlfriend, but he had met a girl in the program. Eliza, though a few years younger than Henry, had more sobriety. She was close to getting her nine-month chip.

After a Saturday morning meeting, he and his new friend walked toward a cafe where 12-steppers often gathered. The fact that they were holding hands was auspicious, Henry thought. It was strange too, he thought, that he knew very little about her, other than her first name. And, of course, Eliza knew very little about him.

Back in Houston, he had never bothered to maintain strict anonymity, in or out of meetings. But that had changed. Given his role in The Contest and his relationship to Minerva Bennett, he had kept this part of his life private, strictly off limits for sharing in meetings. So far, only his sponsor knew this part of his background. Now, looking forward to spending time with Eliza, he wondered how much he could afford to tell her.

In his past romances, he had always struggled to prove himself, always made a point to build himself up. He knew this was a bad habit, but he couldn't help it. That's why, given his obvious physical attraction toward her, he was surprised to realize he had no such inclination to put on airs with Eliza.

When they got to the cafe, there was a line out the door.

"What do you say we just keep walking?" Henry suggested. "It's kind of nice out."

"Good idea," Eliza said. "I'll have you to myself." If that wasn't a sign, he didn't know what was.

"So, where are you from originally?" he asked. "You don't have a New York accent."

"Michigan. I moved here a couple of years ago to study acting."

"Why not L.A.?"

"I'm interested in the stage—real acting, not TV or movies. Plus, I had a boyfriend here."

"Oh, *I* see ... What happened?"

"He was a jerk. He works for some Wall Street company. It was fun for a while, but we drifted apart. He didn't really support my dream, never came to any of my performances. He just wanted to have sex ... and someone to do his laundry. After about a year, I moved out." Henry nodded sympathetically.

"How about you?" she asked. "You're from Texas, right?"

"Yeah. Houston. I moved here about six months ago."

"And? Wha'd'ya do?"

Henry was reluctant to say anything more and hesitated. She waited.

"What do you think I do? Take a guess." He immediately regretted his approach. It was phony ... precisely the kind of behavior he was trying to move beyond.

"Well, I know you were just traveling, but I have no idea where ... or why. Sales?" Henry shook his head. "Insurance?"

"Nope."

"Okay, I give up."

"Oh, come on. That was lame. Do I look that dull?"

Eliza rolled her eyes and let go of his hand. She stopped and gave him a look over.

"Okay ... you're a secret agent—for the government. No, wait. You're a high-class gigolo, with clients in a dozen cities."

Henry laughed. "Don't you wish!" He grabbed her hand, and they continued walking.

"Now, I really give up," she said.

"So ... I used to be a teacher."

"That's cool. What age?"

"Middle School ... sixth-grade math."

"But you're not teaching anymore?"

"No, although I may teach again next year. I'm not sure. I'm kind of on a sabbatical."

"Rehab, huh?" she ventured softly.

"What? *No.* No, I did that once, but ... no, I'm just working the program like, you know, regular folks. I know what to do."

"So ... a *sabbatical?*"

"Well, that's not really accurate either. It's more of a special project." Disgusted with the game of cat and mouse he had initiated, Henry decided to tell her. "Have you heard of The Contest?"

"Who hasn't?" She turned. "Are you working for that foundation? *Vox Stellarum?*"

"Uh-huh. I'm a scout."

"A *scout?*"

"Yeah. Have you been following it—the competition, I mean?"

"Not really. I think it's pretty cool, but ... not lately."

"Well, I'm one of the people who travels around to check on the teams to make sure they're following the rules."

"This thing is pretty big, right? I mean, it's global. Where've you gone so far?"

"I just got back from Asia ... five different countries."

"*Whoa!* What a cool job. It sounds to die for."

"I suppose it is, but it's taken a toll. All the travel, the distractions, the isolation ... that's pretty much why I relapsed." Eliza nodded knowingly.

"Well, how'd you get the job in the first place?"

It was too late to hold back the final card. If his objective had been to assure himself that Eliza wasn't cozying up to him because of his family connections, Henry had to admit she'd already passed the test. He answered the question.

"My aunt—my great aunt, actually—is involved. She got me the job."

Eliza halted suddenly and turned.

"Wait a second. Your *great* aunt? Are you *kidding* me? You're related to Minerva Bennett?"

Henry blushed and nodded sheepishly. Eliza's veil of mild indifference regarding The Contest suddenly evaporated.

"... *'involved'?!*" she repeated. "Dreaming up the craziest competition in history and paying for it out of her own pocket ... I'd say that's a little more than *involved!*"

Eliza turned and, for several seconds, just looked off in the distance ... beyond the busy streets, the crowded sidewalks, the flags on top of distant skyscrapers. Shaking her head faintly, she turned to face him again.

"You're not kidding, are you?"

"No."

"I don't know what to say. That's ... that's amazing."

"Does it change anything?" asked Henry. "I mean, does it change your opinion of me?"

"I don't know ... *No!* I don't think so."

"Good," he said. "Then, come on, I'm hungry."

Hand in hand, they walked into the hazy chill, each one privately exploring a landscape of tantalizing possibilities.

⋅⊷⊶⊷ ⊶⊷⊶⋅

Three days later, Henry waited in the reception area of the Vox headquarters when Catherine Myers approached.

"Hi, Henry. Are you ready?"

"I think so."

"Nervous?"

"Yeah."

"Don't be. It's a friendly group. Your aunt is looking forward to seeing you."

They walked into the conference room where a staff meeting was under way. Henry walked over and gave his Aunt Minerva a hug.

"I think most of you know Henry. He's recently returned from his Task Six assignment in Asia, and he's here to give us a sense of what it's like out there on the front lines. He's going to read summaries from the other scouts and then give his report."

As Henry read, a pattern emerged. Each pair of scouts spoke of the intensity of the teams, their guarded behavior, and their aloofness toward the Vox representatives. Not a single group had any infractions to report. The scouts invariably became glorified bystanders, concentrating on enjoying the hospitality, the food, the culture.

His own summary added very little to the picture, and he sensed his report was anticlimactic. Having conveyed the summaries of the other pairs, Henry became even more convinced that the scouts hadn't served a vital role. *After all,* he thought, *what good is being a referee if you never get to throw a yellow flag or send someone to the penalty box?*

Disqualification, in fact, had only happened three times thus far. These occurrences were each very early in the competition—two teams during Task One, one team during Task Three. Henry couldn't help but think of himself and the other scouts as window dressing.

As if reading his thoughts, James Ruhle asked, "Did you get the sense that these teams were just putting on a show of compliance?"

"On this recent assignment, no. In previous tasks, yes. That happened a couple of times. The Asian teams treated us cordially. They seemed to respect our authority, but mostly they seemed to ignore us. They were obviously committed to following the rules. I guess they knew how much they'd stand to lose if they risked cutting corners."

Henry rose to go, but his aunt motioned for him to sit back down.

"Henry, I'd like you to stay. I think you will find our last two topics interesting. Then, you can join us for lunch if you'd like."

Pleased by his aunt's special attention, Henry nevertheless wondered how it might be interpreted. His original doubts flared as he imagined the others were judging him as an object of nepotism, somebody without real credentials. Only when Ruhle said something about altering the scouts' agenda did Henry snap out of his dark tangent.

"As we have suspected for some time, it appears that the benefit of deploying scouts was negligible. As these reports made clear, the teams have been so committed to advancing that they dared not break any rules. They have become self-monitoring. Nevertheless, I believe the threat of disqualification encouraged them to internalize this process.

"This would seem to suggest that we ought to dispense with the scouts for the duration, but we have actually decided to keep them on ... and even expand their responsibilities."

Henry was puzzled.

Ruhle explained, "Recall that team prizes will only be granted to tax-exempt, non-profit organizations. It's time for us to prepare the teams for this eventuality. According to Rule 14, we require the eight finalists to commit to the formation of just such a legal entity prior to the receipt of any team awards. Our scouts will be coached on how to assist the teams in beginning this process, which in some countries may take several months."

He invited Stewart Maxwell to explain the process.

"I saw that look," said Maxwell as he stood up. He was smiling at Henry. "You were thinking: *Who me?!*" The others laughed.

"Several of us have been working on a script that the scouts will deliver to the teams on their Task Seven assignments. In one week, we will be down to sixteen teams. James believes we ought to trim the deployment to only four pairs of scouts, and it will be they who guide the teams through this check list.

"Don't worry. They won't be giving any legal advice. They will merely support the contestants as they approach their local government agencies to navigate the red tape. And, of course, they will continue to scrutinize task-related activities." Henry gave a sigh of relief.

After a few other minor agenda items, Minerva rose.

"We have one more important topic to discuss: the location of the Award Ceremony. Since the early planning stages, it was presumed that this would be a local affair. Two considerations, however, have brought this into question. One is security, one is cost.

"Without going into all the reasons why we think it's too risky to hold the ceremony here in New York, I will simply point out that with the population density, the draw of possible terrorist threats, the revisiting of old fears and so forth, we have decided to look elsewhere. We have three possible alternatives, all of which are promising. I should point out that, with only seven months to go, we must decide soon. Any metropolitan area that would host such an event must be allowed at least that much time to plan and prepare.

"We're considering Miami, San Francisco, and Houston. Each of these cities has the infrastructure, the hotel accommodations, and the international airports to handle our needs. Once we decide on the venue, we will immediately look into special-use permits for the stadium, the convention center, parade routes, etc."

Catherine called up a slide that showed three columns, one for each city. Green check marks indicated the availability of the various facilities which Minerva had just mentioned, along with several other considerations including long-term weather forecasts. While all three cities appeared well equipped to handle an event of this size, there were notable differences.

Minerva said, "Stewart, Catherine, Libby, and I have reached a consensus, but we thought it would be wise to let you weigh in before we made our final decision, in case we have overlooked something."

Catherine handed out index cards, and Minerva explained. "Take a moment, consider the information here, and then vote on the city that appears to be the best fit."

After several minutes, the folded cards were collected. Minerva and Libby quickly tabulated the results.

"That was easy," said Minerva, looking at Henry, and smiling. "It appears we'll be heading to the Lone Star State for our grand finale."

Chapter 35

STU MONROE, THE leader of the Hawaiian team, sat up suddenly. Something had woken him up, but now all was quiet. He turned to see if Haley was asleep, but she wasn't in bed. The digital clock displayed 5:15 AM. There it was again—screaming, and this was followed by a high-pitched squeal. He leapt out of bed and ran down the hall.

When he got to the bottom of the stairs, he was immediately relieved. He saw Haley and her son Dylan jumping up and down in the living room, and the TV was on. Just as he was about to ask what the hell was going on, they noticed him.

"We're rich, Stu!" shouted Dylan. "Millionaires!"

"*What?!*"

"We're still in! We've advanced!" said Haley, bubbling with excitement.

Stu stood there in shock. He'd been certain their number was finally up, especially after pulling out the stops on Task Six. As obstacles to progress, they had identified practically every federal agency, all three branches of government, the Pentagon, the UN, the ACLU ... even the Vatican. He glanced at the television. When he saw the Vox Stellarum logo at the back of the stage on which a man was reading something from behind the podium, his head began to clear.

"Really? We advanced?" he asked, not quite believing they had heard the announcement correctly.

Haley put her hands on his shoulders and shook him gently. "We did it. We're still in!"

The phone rang. The caller ID indicated it was their teammate Sara Carminati, and Haley put it on speaker.

"Haley? Stu? It's Sara. Can you believe it! We made it! Isn't it *fantastic?!*"

When Sara finally took a breath long enough to listen, Haley chimed in. Stuart stood there listening and, eventually, believing. He sat down on the couch next to Dylan as they waited for the women to finish their conversation.

"This calls for a celebration," they heard Sara say. "We're going to have the team over tonight, and all the families. Hell, the whole neighborhood! Okay, gotta go. See you tonight!"

Haley turned and grinned. "*Now* do you believe us?"

"I guess I do," he said, still in a daze, "but what was that you said about being rich?"

"Libby Armstrong ... remember, she's the one who had the baby ... anyway, she opened up the press conference," explained Haley. "After she greeted everybody and said how good it was to be back, she announced that the administrators had kept part of the prize structure a secret—to keep the contestants from getting too distracted. She said they had decided since the very beginning to reward individual contestants in the round of sixteen, instead of just the final eight. And *we* are now in the Round of Sixteen!"

"How much are we talking about?" Stu asked, shifting back into disbelief.

"A million dollars," said Haley, looking him right in the eye, waiting for his reaction.

"A million?" he gulped.

"*Each!*" exclaimed Dylan.

⋯⋰◉ ◉⋱⋯

Similar scenes played out in fifteen other communities around the world, most of them with full teams waiting breathlessly by their TVs and computers to find out their fates. No doubt there was disappointment by the sixteen teams that were eliminated, made more bitter by the surprise announcement that Task Seven contestants were to receive individual awards, above and beyond prizes still to come in the last round. Somewhere in all of this, the importance of Task Seven itself, at least among the advancing teams, was relegated to trivial status.

Not until hours later did most of the players come off their clouds of elation to review what, exactly, the people at Vox Stellarum had announced. When the teams replayed the video, they saw Catherine Myers reading to a packed conference room, much more animated than in past press releases. The media were also excited about the earlier than expected awards, and, practically ignoring the details of the new assignment, they asked questions instead about the individual prizes that made the annual Nobel Prizes look like child's play.

Most of the teams had to resort to just reading the new task on-line.

TASK SEVEN

The fact that you have advanced this far demonstrates that your team has excellent ideas and formidable communication skills. Your challenge in this task is to stretch these abilities and to project your vision into the future. So far, certain questions have required you to state what will happen if certain ideas are implemented, but there has not necessarily been a time frame. Now, we want you to take on the role of fortune teller and to describe, as vividly as you can, several future scenarios.

The context of this task is to assume that *your* team has won The Contest, that you have each received your individual prizes, and that your team has been awarded the grand prize—which must be utilized, of course, to establish a non-profit foundation devoted to carrying out your team's blue print of long-term positive change.

How will your families and your neighborhoods be affected? How will your nation change and evolve? How will the course of the world be altered by virtue of learning about the set of solutions outlined in your manifesto? How will you build in the moral accountability required to harness the advantage afforded by fame and fortune? Be as creative as you can in presenting detailed interactions by projecting one year beyond the Final Award Ceremony, three years beyond, five years beyond, and finally ten years beyond.

The objective of this assignment is to sell your vision—to the people, to the media, to the judges—by illustrating that your recommendations are more than just analytical tools and guidelines. These scenarios will illustrate that your team has engaged in dynamic and holistic concepts and that you have addressed cultural, political, environmental, economical, and spiritual facts and necessities. And most importantly, you will describe how you, individually and collectively, will implement your solutions in a world that has, thus far, resisted such transformational ideas.

Your response should be contained in a single, comprehensive story, perhaps separated into four sections pertaining to the four different time frames. Your total response may not exceed 7500 words (in standard English). Again, sharing your response with outsiders (e.g. family members, friends, teachers, reporters) will result in disqualification.

Your response must be submitted through your unique log-on combination on the Vox Stellarum website by 10:00 PM GMT, Sunday, April 16. Responses will be made public once the Panel of Judges rates them and posts the results on Monday, May 29.

⇢⇒◉ ◉⇐⇠

Half a world away, it was five in the afternoon. The Palestinian team was gathered in the Hammad family home, braced for the news, good or bad. When they heard their team was among the winners, apprehension turned to celebration. Stunned by the announcement of individual prize money, their leader urged them to clear their minds and begin their work.

Khaled Hammad said, "Allah be praised! We have been blessed for our devotion to the righteous path ..."

He spoke for a few minutes before pausing, overcome with emotion and disoriented by a bizarre sense of impending fortune. It donned on him that, with three family members on the team besides himself, his family was due to receive four million dollars, whether or not they even bothered to make any further effort. Swirling desires and dreams of conspicuous consumption suddenly overtook his frugal sensibilities.

"Are you okay?" his wife Dhakirah asked.

"I'm finding it difficult to focus. This premature generosity by the administrators has provided an extra obstacle. We must put aside the lure of riches and remember why we are here. We have a job to do."

⋅⊱⋰⊰⋅ ⋅⊱⋱⊰⋅

In the Zhijiang Province, it was 11:00 PM. The members of the only remaining Chinese team, *Peaceful Industry*, was gathered in the Chens' home.

"We do not know how much of this money we will be allowed to keep," stated Liu Chen, the team captain, "and we must stay on task. It is good that we impressed the judges with our response, but I am afraid of the scrutiny that Beijing may be mounting."

"They do not dare stop us now," said Feng Li, who at seventeen years of age had never experienced the wrath of the Central Committee or the severe burdens sometimes imposed by Communist Party officials.

"So far, we have been given extraordinary freedom to speak out," said Rou Chen, mother of Liu and Yang, "but that could change. There is *shuanggui*, of course, and we could be told to disband at any time, even put on trial. The Politburo has the power to shut us down and confiscate our prizes."

Feng dared not challenge his former teacher. He respected her wisdom, and the mention of the disciplinary system usually reserved for corrupt politicians put a damper on his rebellious mood.

"Let's not be hasty," said Zheng Shipeng, the senior member of the team. His calm voice was always a comfort to the others. "It would do the Party no good to come down on us now. The results of this last task are already published to the whole world. Yes, we were critical of much that we are subjected to, but not too much more than is generally acknowledged. We must hope that our success in this contest outweighs the critical nature of our disclosures.

"General Secretary Jinping is no fool. He will see that this task is less caustic than the last one and that we have been instructed to shift into a more visionary mode of communication."

The others looked at him hopefully but weren't fully convinced. Yang Chen, Liu's younger brother and the only one who had ever traveled outside of China, spoke next.

"There's not much we can do about it. I would not be surprised if we are visited by Party officials. If this happens, we must be ready to convince them that our vision of change in China is not as radical as some of them fear. For instance, if we portray a nation that remains guided by the existing powers, but which is more open to change, more open to progressive ideas, we may be perceived as ambassadors of this change, perhaps even endorsed by the Party.

"The critical question is: Would this compromise our integrity? Would this be a surrender of the resolve we had when we first gathered?"

"You are right," said Yang's mother. "There's not much we can do about it. Whether or not that happens, we must remain true to ourselves."

⊷═◉ ◉═⊶

Driving a rental car, Malcolm Conroy pulled up to the porte-cochère of a very large house. A parking attendant gave him a claim ticket, and he slipped it into his coat pocket. He walked toward the lawn as he answered an incoming call—an imaginary one. This ploy gave him a chance to look around without drawing too much attention.

The brick and stone Tudor-style mansion was surrounded by manicured lawns and gardens. He studied the grounds, the walls, the house. *Immaculate.* It all fitted the picture he had of the man he had come to meet: Walter Geier.

Security cameras were positioned throughout the property—on the house, in the trees, at the gates of the broad circular drive and the service entrance. He imagined these were being actively monitored, and he didn't want to risk a more thorough inspection. So, when the next car arrived, he followed the occupants as they walked toward the front door. Conroy had not been invited.

He had waited a long time for this opportunity. The man behind the men, behind the organization, was very private. Well-dressed associates, doubling as body guards, kept him well insulated. This only fed Conroy's suspicion. Whether Geier was the man who had issued the ultimatum prompting the change to Task Six or not, Conroy was already convinced of his guilt.

It had taken several weeks for Lee Fletcher, a former CIA operative, to pick up the trail left by the three men who had paid Conroy a surprise visit on a cold afternoon. Because the car the men had driven that day had been reserved and paid for under an alias, the only real lead he had been able to supply his friend was the tail number of the jet charter. Fletcher quickly determined that the number had been altered. A comprehensive search, however, for similar numbers affixed to that aircraft model—as recalled by the attendant at the airport—produced a short list of potential matches.

In fact, there were only five airplanes that could have been used on that particular day. Two were flying routes on or near the west coast; three were flying in the east, one of which had taken off from St. Louis—presumably bound for Baltimore. Fletcher contacted the charter company and, using a little monetary persuasion, located the pilot.

The pilot recognized the men from the images on Conroy's surveillance video, and he revealed that they never went anywhere near Baltimore. He said that, after they left the airfield in Virginia, he was told to deliver them to Boston and then to return the aircraft to St. Louis.

With the needle dropped in a haystack, Fletcher was prepared to report the trail had gone cold. But the pilot made a minor comment about the license plate of the town car that awaited his passengers. It was personalized and ended in a two-digit number.

There were three limousine companies in Boston with fleets large enough to warrant plates of that variety, and Fletcher was eventually able to identify the chauffeur. The man took Fletcher to the three men's destination—a small office building in Cambridge. With no hint as to which of a dozen organizations these men might be associated with, the trail vanished.

Urged on by Conroy, Fletcher resorted to a stakeout. Ten days later, he saw one of the men, Carter, leave the building in the company of two other men. One was older—more distinguished, and he was giving orders. Fletcher followed them to an expansive house in Newton, a quiet suburb of Boston. When he ran a profile on the owner, he saw evidence of a powerful network.

Armed now with only circumstantial evidence, Conroy was unsure of how to proceed. He was no field agent. What would he say? What would he do?

As he followed the others into the drawing room of the home, he scanned the guests, perhaps sixty in all. Small groups of two and three people stood about chatting. Several hovered near a table of hors d'oeuvres; a few stood at the wet bar. Conroy concluded the guests were oblivious to their host's behind-the-scenes machinations. He was just a wealthy benefactor—a perfect front for a man who conducts corrupt enterprises.

Two women stood near a table with a sign-in book and a placard that stated the reason for the gathering—a fund raiser for a local hospital. Conroy knew how these things worked. Movers and shakers who hosted such gatherings would pull together interested parties, and then committees were formed to put on a much larger campaign.

He stationed himself near a glass enclosure—a free-standing display case for miscellaneous art objects and antique books—where a bronze artifact caught his eye. A neatly typed card explained, in the manner of a museum display, that the object was a cast of a sheep's liver used in ancient Rome for a type of divination that hinged on the interpretation of the entrails of a sacrificial animal. *What the hell!*

His eyes wandered to the books, all of which looked rare and obscure. He cocked his head to read the binding of one of the few that was in English, *The Life of Julius Caesar.*

Why does that seem familiar? As he struggled to make a connection, one of the committee women walked over and introduced herself. The thought faded, and Conroy had to hide his annoyance as he was obliged to shift into cocktail mode. He told the woman that Geier and he were old associates and that he wanted to show his support by sponsoring a table at the fundraiser. After a few minutes, she wandered off.

Soon thereafter, Conroy saw two men exit an adjoining room and enter the main salon. They looked directly at him, briefly, removing any doubt that he had been identified. One of them, Walter Geier, turned away casually and proceeded to greet his guests. Conroy didn't recognize the other man, but he was of the same breed as the men who had come to his property. His suit was tailored, but it seemed a bit snug. *Hmm ... a shoulder holster.*

Conroy decided to let them approach him, but Geier took his time. He moved easily through the crowd, showing no sign of concern for his uninvited guest. Conroy, meanwhile, maneuvered to an alcove that might provide some privacy for whatever conversation that might ensue. A quarter hour passed before the host finally approached.

"Mr. Conroy, so good of you to join us," he said in mock politeness.

"Mr. Geier," said Conroy, bowing slightly. Walter Geier was flanked by two men, Carter and Jones, both of whom Conroy ignored.

"You are interested in charity, I see." Geier spoke with a disarming nonchalance, meeting Conroy's gaze with a dauntless expression. "I'm told you want to sponsor a table at our event. How generous!"

Conroy gave a faint nod. "Excuse my pretense, but I'm sure you understand. Some of your associates—who, interestingly enough, don't exist—paid me a visit a while back. I've been anxious to meet the man who sent them."

"Yes, well ... here I am." Geier gave a faint sigh. "What can I do for you?"

"I'd appreciate five minutes of your time. Alone."

"As you wish." Geier motioned his men to stay put, and he nodded toward two chairs in the corner.

"They're good men. They do what they're told."

Conroy said nothing. They sat down and faced one another.

"Five minutes, Mr. Conroy."

"Okay ... First: Why would you bother to meddle in something that can't possibly affect you? Second: Did you really think I wouldn't come after you?"

Geier regarded Conroy for a moment, but it was as if he were looking through him, seeing somebody or something else.

"We took a calculated risk. Meddling? Perhaps. We like to think of it as adjusting the odds. The Contest is a unique phenomenon—a black swan, if you will. My colleagues and I don't want it to fly too high. Clipping a wing was the best way to keep it close ... *manageable.*

"As for your coming after us, I'm not surprised. I *am* surprised you found us." Conroy ignored the compliment. "Now that you know who I am and where I live, what do you intend to do about it?"

Conroy took a deep breath and sighed. Just as he was about to answer, Geier continued.

"Before you answer, let me say that my colleagues and I are satisfied. We appreciate the role you played and the outcome you effected, and we have no intention of pursuing further action."

"Just like that? Back to your secret agendas? Back to the shadows?"

"In a manner of speaking, yes." Geier held Conroy's gaze.

"How can a man in your position be so casual about a charge of black mail?"

"Even if you have evidence, which I doubt, that would be a mistake. You and I both know that there has ultimately been no harm done. The Contest remains very popular. Only a handful of people know of our little arrangement. Walk away, Mr. Conroy."

"That's not my style."

Geier looked away as he considered his next move, then suddenly grinned at Conroy.

"Name your price."

"I should have seen that coming," Conroy said, smiling derisively and shaking his head. "No ... no, I'm not for sale."

Geier waited, as if he assumed Conroy only needed to let the idea sink in a bit more before changing his mind.

"You are a piece of work," said Conroy. "Is it hard ... being such a hypocritical piece of shit? Just another day, another deal, moving people around like chess pieces, overthrowing governments, fixing stock exchanges, having people disappear?"

"You don't know what you're talking about. We don't—"

"We did a little digging ourselves, Mr. Geier. Yes, *we* ... That's how you like to speak, isn't it? You bastards like to hide in the shadows, behind lawyers ... in the boardrooms of shell corporations. I know about the kinds of deals you like to negotiate.

"No, that's too nice a word. You don't negotiate—you set traps. You fix. You arrange. You cash in on fear and—"

"*Good grief!* You really have gone soft. What happened to the man who used to ride herd for the Pentagon? The man who cut the deal for Halliburton in Iraq? Who landed an acquittal for General Dynamics over falsified testimony?"

"I'm right here," said Conroy weakly, cut to the quick by Geier's indictments.

"Come ... your time is almost up," said Geier, who glanced at his watch. "Why are you really here? Do you intend to reach for your gun? Go ahead. You'll be dead before you get your hand on the grip."

Conroy started. He looked slowly about, wondering just where and how Geier's men could pull off such a feat. He felt intimidated for the first time.

Geier smiled.

"Yes, x-ray scanners have come a long way. That's the kind of technology *we* like to invest in, Mr. Conroy. And, as your research no doubt revealed, we also invest in missile guidance systems, pharmaceuticals, and genetic engineering. If we need to enlist certain influential players, in Washington, London, Tokyo ... or Virginia, we do what we must.

"Now, is that it?" Geier sat forward and prepared to stand. He looked piercingly at Conroy as few others had ever dared.

Conroy was in a precarious position. Whatever bargaining chips he imagined he had were now spent. Just as he was wondering if his physical safety might actually be in jeopardy, he remembered something.

"Tell me about Anthony Parrish."

"*Who?*"

"Anthony Parrish. How did he become one of your pawns?"

"Aah, Tony. Don't worry about him. He's a bit player. He owed me a favor."

"Is he done?" asked Conroy, suddenly recalling the bitter look on Catherine's face at their last meeting.

"That remains to be seen," said Geier dismissively. "Now, I have guests to entertain." He stood, as did Conroy.

"I may have underestimated you," said Conroy, "but I don't want you to make the same mistake. Your men could easily dispose of me, but you should know I've arranged for a few insurance policies, if you know what I mean."

"My men won't visit again, provided your investigation is concluded." Geier raised his eyebrow, turning his statement into a question.

"I'll think about it."

"By the way, we won't hold you to your pledge for the luncheon," added Geier with a smirk. "Good day, Mr. Conroy."

Conroy walked straight to the door and gave the valet his ticket. His car was parked next to several others, in plain sight. It occurred to him that Geier's men could have easily tampered with his brakes or planted a bomb, and he scolded himself for his paranoia. Driving out the front gate, he cursed under his breath.

"That arrogant son of a bitch. *Concluded?* Hell, I'm just getting started."

Chapter 36

IN THE FIFTH week of the judging period for Task Seven, two separate sub-committees, each comprised of six judges, were preparing to bring their choices together for comparison. Though the sources of the responses were encrypted as usual, the teams clearly identified themselves in the text of their submissions. Such was the nature of Task Seven: to present a changed local, national, and global landscape in several different time frames. This presented unforeseen challenges in the subsequent proceedings.

By 3:05 AM GMT, all six judges in one panel had logged in for another round of discussions. From any one point-of-view, the others gazed back from within square cells provided by the video-conferencing platform, part of the Vox Stellarum portal. Three cells on each side of their monitors framed the documents under discussion. Local times were listed under each participant's visage. Convening from six different continents, they rotated the burden of the midnight shift. After ten minutes of small talk, they began in earnest. They were reconsidering a few borderline cases before they would vote on their final choices, which would then be reconciled with the other sub-panel. It had been decided that all twelve judges would weigh in on the selection of the eight finalists.

Gabriela Ocampo, the Argentinian activist and youngest judge on the panel, clicked on the TALK icon; this caused her video feed to become highlighted.

"As much as I like their vision, the Venezuelan team struggles to illustrate the application of their policies. They do a good job in the one-year scenario, but as they extend farther into the future, their program loses focus.

"On the other hand, the Argentinian team adhered to the task beautifully. I particularly like their five- and ten-year projections ... and the way they describe the spread of their policies to neighboring countries, Central America, and eventually North America."

Michel Bauwens, the man who had replaced Laurent Gillard after the Athens incident, clicked in.

"We have already come to a consensus on the team from Venezuela. They fell short of the objective. That does not mean we must now be more generous toward Argentina. I know these are the only remaining teams from South America, but they do not compare to the other submissions." The other judges were still unaccustomed to the Belgian's bluntness, and they waited to see if he would elaborate.

He did. "Yes, the team from Buenos Aires followed the directions exactly, but their program is a mixed bag. I found several contradictory recommendations and did not come away with a sense that they have developed a unified philosophy."

"If I may, Michel," interjected Mahmoud Azzam. "We could all be charged with playing favorites and having personal preferences, and this includes regional and ethnic loyalties.

"Yesterday you spoke on behalf of the English and the Spanish teams, and we have since cut both of them. Perhaps it is a consolation for you that the Dutch response is one of our favorites. Nevertheless, it is difficult to stand above nationality and culture.

"For instance, I am proud that the South African team is in our list of advancing teams. While I do not embrace their vision, I find myself silently cheering them on. After all, we live on the same continent."

Stewart Brand clicked in. "The fact is, we could pick the finalists at random and still be praised for our inspired judgment, such is the quality of the remaining teams. But that's not why we were chosen to sit on this panel. Our job is to subject these competitors to the strictest and highest standards possible. We microwave, we x-ray, we split hairs, we shake and bake, and then we see what's left. We must ignore everything but their ideas. *That* is our job.

"Spanish, Indian, Venezuelan, American ... it doesn't matter. This is a global contest. The winners will represent *all* of us."

Brand unchecked the TALK icon, indicating that he was done, but the others remained silent. Perhaps it was his unique mix of American idioms and emphatic proclamations that required a moment to digest. Perhaps it was the deference the others showed him, for even the most objective among them unconsciously associated him—an *American*—with the foundation that brought them together in the first place.

After a while, Ocampo responded.

"It is true. I have been holding on to the hope that my countrymen would be represented in the final round. It is also true that this is not consistent with our stated purpose and goal. Please excuse my lapse.

"I still support consideration of the Argentinians, but I will, of course, yield to the group's consensus."

⊷⊶⊙ ⊙⊷⊶

The other sub-panel, meanwhile, was finalizing its ranking of the same sixteen teams. Noel Pearson, of Australia, was making a point about the response by Team 121, from Venice, California. He was attracted to their mass-media approach—how social media, flash media, and the Internet were going to continue to catalyze the cultural revolution that The Contest was now turbo-charging. The others were unimpressed. They saw the team's presentation as a slick piece of self-promotion.

"With respect, I am younger than most of you," Pearson stated. "I have seen how this technology has created opportunities for my countrymen, especially ones who were formerly isolated, not just geographically, but culturally. It is the way of the future."

Kim Campbell, the Canadian, clicked in. "I don't think any of us disagree with you on that point. It's the content and the underlying attitude that's the problem. As convincing as this team has been up to this point, it now appears that they were all form and no substance."

"They spent way too much time describing their roles," added Dorottya Szilagyi, the Hungarian, "... their personal roles, how they will be directing a ... what did they call it? A 'cultural engine.' Other teams did much better in showing how specific segments of the population would benefit by their plans. This team seems oblivious to that requirement."

Sobonfu Somé, who rarely commented, clicked in. "I must agree. Even as society modernizes, it is important to maintain rituals and traditions. This group largely ignored that as well. My main objection is that they lack *spirit.*"

After Team 121 was cut, the sub-panel added teams from India, Singapore, and Mexico to the list of teams that would fail to advance. When they adjourned several hours later, they had reached their goal of identifying eight advancing teams.

In the final week of the judging period, the configuration of the portal was expanded to accommodate all twelve judges. It took them the full week to reconcile their lists.

⋅⊁═◉ ◉═⊰⋅

The press room was full to overflowing. Because the media were running on rumors, the excitement around the announcement of the finalists had shoved practically every news item onto the back pages. Except for the imminent Chinese lunar mission and the rioting in Mexico, which was threatening the southern border of California, the buzz was focused on The Contest.

Minerva Bennett took the podium first, something she had not done since the early stages of the competition. Due to broad media speculation regarding her health, Cade Tompkins, still in charge of PR, had urged her to make an appearance to reclaim some of the limelight she had delegated to her staff. She had reluctantly agreed.

She stared out at the sea of reporters and cameras. "Good morning and welcome! The Contest has reached the final stage, and we are down to eight teams. Before we announce the finalists, I want to say a few things about the people who've worked so hard to get us here.

"I want to acknowledge the fantastic work done by every single person at Vox Stellarum. For over a year now, they have been tireless in their support of the real stars, and, by that, I mean the contestants. This has been a monumental effort, and the results are clear. We are on the verge of discovering what a global effort to find lasting solutions can accomplish."

She looked to both sides of the stage and nodded at her senior staff.

"Before we get to the names of the advancing teams, let me give you an update on the nature of our award ceremony. As we bring The Contest to a close, there has been speculation as to the location of the finale. I must say that, early on, this wasn't something we paid too much attention to. And when we did begin to address it, we considered at least a dozen venues.

"Given the global nature of this undertaking, we couldn't confine our thinking to the United States. What about Tokyo? Mumbai? Mexico City? London? Buenos Aires? Cairo? Moscow? Sydney? Or any of a hundred other fine cities?

"There was a strong bias, of course, towards New York City. But then I remembered where I was when I first glimpsed the idea for this competition, and it suddenly occurred to me that *that* should be the location for the final ceremony. And my staff agreed. I'm pleased, therefore, to announce that, from October 16th to the 22nd, Houston, Texas will host ..."

A burst of camera flashes and buzz in the crowd drowned out the rest of her sentence. She retreated to the side of the stage, and then Libby, Catherine, and James approached the podium.

"No doubt you have already guessed the nature of the final assignment," began James Ruhle, "but I will now make it official."

TASK EIGHT

It is time to draw on all of your previous work as you compose a manifesto, the objective of which is to restore hope and optimism in a world beset by dozens of seemingly insurmountable conflicts and challenges.

In a comprehensive manner, present your vision for change and demonstrate that the adoption of your proposed course of action—by governments, communities, businesses, families, and individuals—will remedy a significant number of the so-called "Dangers Confronting Mankind," thus profoundly improving the human condition.

The manifesto may not exceed 100 pages (in standard English). This limit does *not* include the captions on any included visual aids, of which you may include up to twelve. Standards from previous tasks apply. Sharing your response with outsiders (e.g. family members, friends, teachers, reporters) will result in disqualification.

Your response must be submitted through your unique log-on combination on the Vox Stellarum website by 10:00 PM GMT, Sunday, July 23. Responses will be published on Monday, September 4, but the final rankings will not become public until the Awards Ceremony on Saturday, October 21.

"Competition is a force of nature," said Catherine Myers, "and it produces outcomes on many levels. In the first seven stages of this competition, we have seen greater community awareness, improved cooperation among diverse groups, pride in family, community, and country, and a rekindling of hope and faith. And these results have occurred even before the finalists have begun to compose their manifestos!"

She stepped aside as Libby moved to the middle position.

"Before I read the list of advancing teams, I would like to remind you that, as advertised, the contestants are guaranteed team grants as well as individual prizes, above and beyond what they received in Round Seven. The combined prizes and awards will total just over $5 billion."

Someone in the crowd let out a long whistle. Libby smiled and nodded at Minerva.

"Indeed," Libby continued, "we have a very generous person in our midst." Her eyes suddenly filled with tears, and she found herself unable to speak. The reality of how Minerva's generosity, spread so far and wide, had affected her, as well, now overwhelmed her. She grabbed the edges of the podium and looked down, struggling to regain her composure.

Catherine put her arm around her friend and was about to read the list on her behalf, but she too became choked up. James handed Libby his handkerchief and grinned at the crowd.

"Sorry about that," said Libby, her voice husky with emotion. She cleared her throat and turned to James. "Got the list?"

He handed her the sealed envelope.

"Okay, here we go. Congratulations to the winners of Round Seven! I am very proud to present our eight finalists, in order of their original registration numbers.

"From Atyrau, Kazakhstan—Team 8 ... from Gundiwindi, Queensland, Australia—Team 25 ... from Amsterdam, The Netherlands—Team 233 ... from Tulsa, Oklahoma, USA—Team 489 ... from Maui, Hawaii, USA—Team 603 ... from Durban, South Africa—Team 765 ... from Hebron, West Bank, Palestinian Territories—Team 872 ... *and* ... from Wenzhou, Zhijiang Province, People's Republic of China—Team Alt-3!"

⋙⋙◉ ◉⋘⋘

It was mid-August when Lee Fletcher invited Conroy on a fishing trip to North Carolina. Conroy knew Lee didn't like to fish, but he maintained the charade, sensing that a security breach had compromised their usual lines of communication. Sitting in a small boat, anchored in a cove of Mountain Island Lake near Charlotte, North Carolina, the old friends reviewed the dossier Fletcher had prepared. It contained the results of his investigation of Walter Geier.

As he flipped through Fletcher's notes and surveillance photos, Conroy paused on a copy of the flight charter contract of the men who had visited him at his cabin. He squinted at the details, but nothing came to him. He placed the file back in Fletcher's bag.

"Malcolm, this guy's in bed with all kinds of nasty people. You can probably guess the usual suspects, but he has some unusual connections, too. Before

I get to that, I need to tell you about an incident that does not bode well for us. Remember the driver I tracked down—the one that gave me the lead on the location of Geier's office?" Conroy nodded.

"He's dead."

"How?"

"It appears to have been an accident. The police report states that he probably fell asleep at the wheel. There was evidence that he made a sudden turn and ran, head on, into a concrete support of an overpass."

"You met him. Does that fit?"

Fletcher shook his head. "No. I think Geier's men got to him. They could have drugged him, but it's also possible they took control of his vehicle, remotely, by hacking into the onboard computer. It's a new technique these people may have acquired from the Russians ... difficult to detect or trace."

"Why would they do that? Before I left his house, Geier offered me a truce."

"That may be, but then you asked me to keep digging. And his people got wind of it. If I'm correct—that they *were* behind this 'accident,' it's a clear sign to back off. The man was single. He had no family to speak of ... nobody to push for an investigation. In their playbook, he represents only minor collateral damage."

"That's crazy."

"Uh-huh, but that's the way these scumbags operate ... with measured intimidation."

"More like overkill," muttered Conroy, looking out over the water.

"Not necessarily."

"Huh?"

Fletcher said, "I may have come across something that, at least from their perspective, could have warranted such a move. I don't know how you did it, Malcolm, but your hunch about this guy being involved in the bomb threat last year is looking more and more plausible. I gotta tell you, I was skeptical ... linking Geier to these so-called 'Liberators' because of some dusty artifact and a book on Roman history. It was quite a stretch."

"What did you find?"

"Phone records showed that the call to Vox Stellarum last March was a blocked call, untraceable. However, the time stamp showed the exact time the call was placed, as well as the duration—43 seconds. I guess I had nothing better to do last week, so I had a contact do a search for all outgoing calls in the Boston area at that time, for that duration. There was one. The call came from Geier's house."

"You're shitting me."

Fletcher shook his head. "No."

"Can they be linked? Would that stick ... legally?"

"No, it's purely circumstantial. But it's enough for us ... and I think that's why they're playing hardball."

Both men stared out over the lake. A ski boat approached and passed fairly close. The wake caused them to pitch and roll, but they were too distracted to yell at the teenager who was driving the boat.

"What about the Athens bombings? You think Geier had a hand in that?" asked Conroy.

"I wouldn't be surprised," said Fletcher, "but determining that would require significantly more resources than we've used thus far."

Conroy nodded.

"I want to *get* this asshole," Fletcher added.

"You know I do," Conroy said, staring at the floor, "but if we keep digging, they won't hold back. We'll both be targeted. Plus, snooping around in international jurisdictions will up the ante considerably. Are you up to it?" Even as he asked his friend, Conroy wondered if he himself was prepared to go the distance.

"Just say the word," said Fletcher.

Conroy's eyes wandered back to Fletcher's bag, to the tip of the folder he had reviewed earlier. He suddenly reached for it and withdrew the jet charter contract; the letterhead listed the company name as Sky High Charters. *Is it possible?* he thought, staring at the piece of paper. *Could these bastards be the ones who ...?*

He stood up abruptly and looked at his friend, his heart beating so rapidly that he was momentarily lightheaded. "Listen, Lee. I think I just made a connection that makes this far more personal than it already is." Conroy spoke with an intensity Fletcher had never seen. "I need to verify it, but this would change everything."

⇢⟫⊛ ⊛⟪⇠

Conroy departed from the small airfield in his Cessna and flew back to Virginia. When he turned on to the state park access road to his cabin, it was still light out, but the sun was just dipping behind the mountains.

He had been anxious to the point of distraction since leaving Fletcher two hours earlier, and now the evening shadows added to his brooding mood. In fact, the more he dwelt on the dark possibility he had glimpsed, the more his head spun.

Calm down, he told himself. *You're imagining things that can't possibly be true.* But even as he tried to talk himself out of it, he became more and more convinced that he was right. And that scared the hell out of him, for he was not at all confident that he could contain his rage ... or his impulse to kill.

He pulled into his driveway, parked his truck, and proceeded directly to his safe room bunker. As if in response to his agenda, he nodded grimly at the portrait of his wife and daughter, and then directed his attention at his filing cabinet. It took him just a few minutes to find the file, and then the document, that supplied the connection—if not the proof—to his darkest suspicions.

But now what?!

Conroy mounted the stairs and exited the safe room in a daze. What had, until then, only been an investigation into a threat to The Contest was now somehow a larger conspiracy, or, at the very least, a reentry into the same network of evil.

Using the land line, he dialed up the head of security at the Vox headquarters ... visions of the vague, but impending, threat pushing all his other thoughts aside. He didn't want to spread rumors and fear, but he felt compelled to put the detachment on a heightened alert.

His thoughts turned to his dogs. Their loyalty and devotion would be the perfect salve on the old wound that had just been ripped open by virtue of his unexpected discovery. *That's strange*, he thought. They hadn't greeted him, as they usually do, when he pulled into the driveway.

He walked out in the middle of the yard and called.

"Apollo, Mercury, come!" Nothing. His stomach tightened.

He went back inside, grabbed his rifle, and returned to the yard. He called his dogs again. Still nothing.

Their bowls were empty, and, except for their absence, nothing appeared out of the ordinary. He circled the cabin in a widening spiral pattern, scanning the thickets. At first, he held his gun at the ready, but after a while he slung it over his shoulder. *One of them might be snake-bit*, he thought, *but both?*

An hour later, the sun had set; it was getting dark. He reached the fence line of his property and turned left toward the road. That's when he saw them. They lay motionless under a small stand of trees. He ran to them and dropped to the ground. He shook them and felt their noses. Apollo was cool and rigid. Dead.

Mercury was breathing, barely. His nose was dry, eyes milky. He gave out a faint moan but was otherwise lifeless.

Conroy left his gun and ran twenty yards to the road and then sprinted uphill, back toward the entrance to the cabin. Five minutes later, he was in his truck, spraying gravel as he tore out of the driveway onto the road. He placed Apollo in the bed of the truck, but lay Mercury on the passenger seat. Emergency blinkers flashing, he drove as fast as he could without careening off the side of the mountain. When he got to the highway and finally got a signal, he called Ray Lewis, the veterinarian, whom he knew well.

Thirty minutes later, he carried his dog into the animal hospital. It was almost midnight when the vet informed Conroy that Mercury was in stable condition—that he had a decent chance of pulling through.

"You look like hell, Malcolm," Lewis said. "Go home and get some sleep. Come back in the morning."

⊷⊨◉ ◉⊨⊶

"I'm disappointed as well. Two days ago, our man reported that he was close to breaching the firewall ... Well, it's too late now ... Yes ... I've glanced at a few.

I figure it'll take me a week ... Conroy? Yeah, he got our message ... It's impossible to know for sure, but I think he called off his man ... Of course. I'll keep them in position, just in case ..."

The Watcher tapped his keyboard to end the call, and for a moment he just sat back and closed his eyes. He massaged his eyes and, despite the fact that they burned from staring at his monitors for three hours straight, lit another cigarette.

The Internet was humming with a million conversations centered on the manifestos, published that morning—two weeks early. It was a move that took the entire world by surprise. While a few journalists set about to determine the reason for the early release, most of them immediately began polling the public about which team had produced the best entry. Of course, no one had had a chance to read them yet, but that did not prevent the pundits from acting as if they had.

Several minutes later, the Watcher stubbed out his cigarette and logged back on to the Vox website. After all the effort that he and his confederates had invested in trying to sabotage The Contest and block the dissemination of the contestants' treatises, it was humiliating that he now felt obliged to read the damn things. He consoled himself by reasoning that if there were, in fact, any useful ideas, anything to be leveraged by his cohorts, he would find them.

With a sigh of resignation, he opened another document and continued reading.

Chapter 37

HENRY GODFREY STRODE past the elevators and bounded up the stairs to the second-floor offices of Vox Stellarum. Though he was among half the remaining scouts that had been relieved of their duties, since only two pairs were needed for the final round, he had been asked to remain on the staff for the duration. Libby had suggested that he play an ambassadorial role in Houston, and Minerva embraced the idea.

He was early for the staff meeting and decided to visit Bobby Jabari, with whom he had developed a friendly rapport over the preceding weeks. He and the webmaster had a common interest in music and math, and Henry liked to try to follow at least some of what Jabari did. He had shown Henry how number theory played a role in the modified RSA encryption algorithm he had devised, part of which was based on the prime factorizations of extremely large numbers.

"Hey, Bobby," greeted Henry.

As usual, Jabari was perched in front of his monitors. He was busy running diagnostics and checking obscure parameters that only he understood. Henry walked over to admire the graphs and the code splayed across the screens.

"Good morning, Henry. What brings you in?"

"Staff meeting ... I'm being retooled."

"How's that?"

"I'm gonna be part of the public relations team in Houston."

"That's your home town, isn't it?"

"Yeah." Henry looked about the room, marveling at the stacks of equipment and enjoying the light show of red, green, and yellow LED indicators. His attention moved back to the two most prominent monitors. One had a world map overlaid with highlighted data; it reminded him of a weather forecast.

"What's goin' on here? What does all the color-coding mean?" he asked, pointing.

"It helps me keep track of peak usage. And, it's fun to see which teams are attracting the most attention. The shading indicates aggregate traffic levels to each site."

"Your program?"

"Yes."

"That's intense," said Henry. "So, those regions represent the finalists?"

"At this point, yes, but the data base still draws from the entire field. Some of the fainter images reflect social media traffic related to teams that have been eliminated. They probably still have significant local interest ... friends and fans."

"Cool."

Henry was in awe of the information at Jabari's fingertips. This was precisely the kind of computational ingenuity he encouraged in his students regarding the power of numbers.

"Huh, look at that," he said, pointing to the map. "You suppose that's related to people viewing footage of the World Cup?" He was looking at Brazil.

Jabari turned and squinted at the spot where Henry was pointing.

"That's strange. This map is rendered from data directly related to The Contest. I don't think I tagged any sporting events."

Wanda Freeman walked in. "There you are, Henry. We're about to start ... Come on!"

"Later, Bobby!" Henry jumped up and followed Wanda to the conference room.

->]=◉ ◉=[<-

Bobby Jabari was intrigued. Once Henry exited, he looked more closely at the monitor they had just been discussing. He counted the most prominent zones of web traffic, and of course there were eight. Besides these, there were several amorphous areas, paler in color, representing lighter traffic. Activity related to the two recently eliminated South American teams, for instance, had fallen considerably, and they appeared in yellow and light green. The highlighted region in Brazil had no business being there.

He soon found the source of the traffic: a team from Rio de Janeiro. Since launching the web site, he had paid minimal attention to which teams advanced, which teams were cut. Only in the last round had he begun to consider details of the advancing teams.

He sifted through on-line comments to find out why discussion surrounding an eliminated team would be so active. According to a thread initiated by the team leader months before, the group had completed its response to Task Four, but, just prior to submitting it, a power outage had shut down half the city. The blackout had been blamed on a small group of angry protesters that had briefly taken over a hydroelectric power station. When the team was finally able to submit its response, it was too late. Without appreciating the reason, the Vox staff had made the decision to deny the team's request for an extension.

Subsequently filtered out of the published list of contenders by the mainstream media, the team's response had nevertheless appeared on its official contest page. In fact, all previously eliminated teams still had active pages.

Jabari scanned the documents and was astonished to see that the Brazilian team's folders for Tasks Five, Six, Seven, and Eight were also complete. They had even continued to send in weekly time-stamped photos.

"I'll be damned," he said under his breath. "These people are still playing."

As he expanded his search to include related tags, a bigger story began to emerge, not the least of which was that Team 915 had developed something of a cult following.

At first, it was just in and around Rio de Janeiro. Then, word began to spread of the tenacious favelados who ignored the fact that they had been eliminated. Word of the group of underdogs spread to San Paulo and Brasilia, then to neighboring countries. Jabari read fan mail submitted from as far as India, Australia, Sweden, and Canada. Most of it was addressed to the whole team, but someone named Tiago was obviously quite popular.

An hour later, Jabari logged off and rubbed his eyes. He peered at the map. There were eight circular regions ranging from violet to dark red to light red ... and one that was bright orange.

I need to show this to Minerva.

After a six-month break, Minerva Bennett was again a much sought-after guest for TV talk shows and radio interviews. Before accepting her third invitation to appear on The Late Show, she requested that Libby Armstrong and Catherine Myers be allowed to accompany her. The network happily agreed.

Tucker Middleton, the host, welcomed the three women on stage, giving each of them a hug and a kiss. The APPLAUSE prompt was unnecessary as the audience cheered enthusiastically, beginning the broadcast with a rare standing ovation.

"It's been a while since you graced this stage, Minerva. It's good to have you back."

"Thank you, Tucker. It's good to be back." She smiled and waved to the audience.

Upon their introduction, Libby Armstrong and Catherine Myers received almost as much applause as their boss, and the cameras zoomed in on their blushing faces.

"Tonight, we're devoting the entire hour to this delegation of hope and salvation. We've got a lot to cover, so let's get to it." Middleton grinned.

"I think it's safe to say that everybody watching knows what your foundation has accomplished over the past year. You have the entire world talking about change, and just this last week we finally got a chance to see the full results.

"What do you think?" he asked, turning to the audience. Applause and whistles.

Middleton continued. "For those of you who've been under a rock ... or perhaps in solitary confinement, Vox Stellarum recently released the full manifestos of the eight finalists. How many of you have read these?" Silence.

"Uh-huh ... thought so. Ladies, these are thick documents. Most of them weigh in at, what, about 100 pages?"

The guests nodded.

"So," he said, "are we going to be able to fix this mess? Does the Human Race stand a chance? Have the answers that we've all been looking for finally been delivered?"

"If you recall, Tucker," replied Minerva, "on my first visit over a year ago, I stated that my objective was to raise the level of conversation and place important issues on the front burner of human awareness. I think we have accomplished that.

"From what I've read so far, our finalists have demonstrated a commitment to cut through the political stalemate that plagues us. Whether governments and communities adopt any of these solutions remains to be seen, but these viewpoints come from the people. The Contest is the ultimate in grass roots politicking."

Libby spoke next. "The real question is: what will *we the people* decide to do about it? This is the era of social media. The power of the Internet to convey ideas to millions, even billions, is undeniable. As people take the time to read these manifestos, they're bound to resonate with at least some of the ideas. At that point, local groups will take their grievances to the powers that be and make a case for change. We've kick-started the exchange, but individuals must be the driving force if these are to make the difference we believe they can make."

"Fair enough," Middleton said.

After a commercial break, the cameras zoomed back in on the guests.

"Ladies and gentlemen, we have the executive staff of Vox Stellarum with us tonight, and we're now going to take a look at some examples of the recently published manifestos. We're going to show you three excerpts. Then we'll see if you can guess which teams presented them."

On the screen behind Middleton's desk, highlighted text appeared as an offstage announcer read aloud.

We recommend that government intrusion be scaled back, especially at the national level. In practically every nation, we are drowning in a sea of over-regulation and micro-management. Individuals are rarely trusted to do the right thing, rarely allowed to create relationships or conduct business without first having to plead from a central authority for the permission to do so. This is not only wasteful and time-consuming, but it serves to weaken the creative drive of citizens while strengthening already entrenched state-run bureaucracies. It is practically a universal truth that most laws are too difficult to understand. Politicians, most of whom are obligated to special interest groups and lobbyists, create these, not for the good of society but, for self-serving objectives. With their behind-the-scenes deals, they guarantee themselves control in public matters while forcing the vast majority of people to navigate an ever-growing jungle of fees, licenses, regulations, and taxes.

"Okay, here's the next one." Middleton nodded off-stage, and the second example was displayed.

It has been conceded in most scientific communities that anthropogenic climate change is a fact. While this usually refers to global warming, we believe that this conclusion may be premature. However, the real issue is not so much rising (or even falling) average temperatures as it is the irreversible contamination of our atmosphere and our water sources. The *tragedy of the commons* is nowhere more obvious— and critical—than in regard to our oceans and our atmosphere. We can no longer abide any one nation's ignorance regarding industrial and agricultural practices that negatively impact neighboring nations. It behooves us to arrive at a much stricter approach for ensuring the quality of the biosphere. The Kyoto Protocol was a worthy first attempt, but we believe it did not go far enough, for it focused only on the emission of so-called "greenhouse gases." We propose a much more comprehensive approach, one that targets all non-biodegradable waste and emissions that have been proven to have detrimental effects on lakes, rivers, water tables, seas, and oceans. This should include airborne compounds beyond the presently targeted sources of industrial carbon dioxide emissions, chlorofluorocarbons, and tropospheric ozone.

"And ... one more," said Middleton, nodding off-stage.

One of the most corrosive forces we continue to see is imperialism. If there were ever an appropriate time for empire, its time has passed. Yet, several world powers continue to practice this archaic form of statecraft. The United States, Russia, and China are obvious examples, but more moderate examples exist, too. Rather than allowing individuals and groups of individuals to forge effective relationships, armies of soldiers, advisors, ambassadors, and bureaucrats are deployed to meddle in the affairs of people they rarely, if ever, understand. They ply their way with promises of aid and a guaranteed boost in the standard of living, but this almost always backfires and inevitably results in resentment and revolution. While many assume that occupying armies and navies help stabilize whole regions of the globe, we believe that this is the primary cause of terrorism and ongoing civil wars in nations whose citizens want to be left alone and trusted to sort out their own issues.

Middleton raised his eyebrows and loosened his tie, as if to demonstrate things were heating up. He took a sip of his water.

"These examples were picked, no doubt, for dramatic effect," he said, addressing the audience. "Pretty provocative, huh?" He adjusted his glasses and flashed his toothy smile.

"By the way," he added, "these may have been written in languages other than English, so don't be too quick to assume you know the nationality of the authors."

He turned to the guests. "Would one of you like to take a shot at which teams wrote which?"

"Can we see the choices?" said Catherine.

"Oh ... yes! Put up the list," he said, waving his arm and turning to the screen. When the eight teams were shown, he turned back toward the audience. "You try this too. I think you will be surprised."

"I'm a little reluctant to comment," Libby said, looking at Minerva. "The judges have had a one-month jump on the rest of us, but they're still in the process of ranking the teams."

"Go ahead, Libby. It's okay," said Minerva. "God knows the pundits have been busy with their own rankings."

"Hmm ... okay," Libby began. "Because they're all in English, it'd be easy to assume they were written by the Americans or the Australians, so therefore I'm guessing this is *not* the case."

Middleton smiled. "Were you ever on *Let's Make a Deal?*"

"I think one belongs to the Dutch ... and one to the Chinese. I'm not sure which exactly."

"O-kaaaay." He turned to Minerva. "Care to guess?"

"I haven't the faintest!" said Minerva. The audience laughed. "I liked all of them, but I couldn't detect any national bias. These could have been written by anybody."

"Really? *Anybody?* Doesn't that, you know, sort of repudiate the premise of your contest?"

"What do you mean?"

"Well if *anybody* could have written these, why should we pay special attention to these teams?"

Minerva frowned briefly but then explained. "What I meant was that these ideas have surfaced organically ... from all over the globe. These are universal sentiments, not that everyone will agree with them, of course.

"I see several common elements—conviction, passion, discernment. These were written in simple clear language. You don't need to hold public office or to have a college diploma to understand their points. These teams are speaking the language of the common man."

The audience burst into applause.

Chapter 38

HER STAFF THREW Minerva a birthday party at lunch on a Friday, one day before she would turn 89. The foyer and main room were decked out with clusters of helium balloons and banners draped from the railings. Rowan, Libby, and Wanda had some of the benchmark achievements of Vox Stellarum, captured in newspaper headlines, printed on large poster boards, and these were prominently displayed. This was Stewart Maxwell's and Sam Minton's idea. They figured that her birthday was the perfect occasion to celebrate her vision and its realization.

Anybody and everybody who had been a part of the grand adventure was invited, and the office was crowded. Besides all the regular employees and trustees, there were several scouts and a dozen UN interpreters in attendance. Cade Tompkins and Abby Mitchell were there. So were her son Julian Fielding and nephew Bob Godfrey.

The party was also a good excuse for the staff to cut loose before they would brace themselves for the final crunch. In three weeks, half of them would relocate to Houston to oversee preparations for a dozen major events, including the award ceremony.

With a large spread of food and an open bar, the mood was buoyant. One guest, however, stood brooding on the mezzanine.

"Hi, Malcolm," said Catherine Myers. She moved to his side and placed her hands on the railing next to his. "You don't look so good."

He turned and smiled briefly, but then his grim expression returned. His jaw was clenched. Catherine waited for him to speak, but he only looked down on the gathering. When he turned again to face her, his gray-blue eyes were tinged with sadness.

"What's going on?" she asked gently. "Can you talk about it?"

"I don't know."

His mood was palpable, and Catherine could feel his sense of dread. She grabbed his hand and gently loosened his grip. "Follow me."

She led him around the corner to her office and motioned for him to sit down. She had never seen him like this—the wind gone from his sails, strangely docile.

She pulled her chair close to his.

"Talk to me. What's going on?"

"My dogs were poisoned." He could barely finish the sentence; his eyes were dark storms of emotion. Catherine was so stunned by the vision of Conroy in pain that it took her a moment to process what he had said.

She gasped. "*What?!*" She reached for his hands. "Tell me what happened."

"Mercury is okay, but Apollo is dead. I found them lying in the woods, motionless ... poisoned." He stared at the floor.

"Oh ... *no*," was all she could say, barely getting the words out before she too was choked up. She held his hands, massaging them with her thumbs. They sat like that for a moment as Conroy allowed himself to re-experience his loss.

Eventually he sat up, blinked his tears away, and faced Catherine.

"Tell me what happened," she said. "When did you find them?"

"Three weeks ago."

"*What?!*" she said, straightening abruptly. "How could— ... Have you told anybody else?"

"A friend." Looking into her eyes again, he added, "You don't know him."

"I just can't believe ... How can ... Do you know who did it?"

"I think so, but I can't prove it." His melancholy was gone, and his expression began to harden again.

"Why would anybody do that? It doesn't make sense." She tried to read his face for a hint as to what was going on, what drama might have precipitated this cruelty. When he didn't answer, she tried a different angle. "Is there any-thing I can do?"

He closed his eyes and let out a mournful sigh. When he turned to Catherine some seconds later, his composure had largely returned.

"I'm glad you approached me, Catherine. I appreciate your kindness. You're the only one who …" He paused. "I need to ask you something. It's probably none of my business, but I'll explain why in a minute."

She drew back, suddenly uncomfortable.

"Are you still seeing Anthony Parrish?" he asked.

"You're right," she said, glaring at him, "I don't see how that's any of your business."

He looked at her calmly and waited. Her expression softened. "No," she said finally.

"May I ask what happened?"

"After you spoke to me about how he might have been involved with those men, I thought about just asking him point blank, but I couldn't. I didn't have the nerve. I began to doubt his feelings for me though, and … I don't know … he just seemed to lose interest in me.

"Within a few weeks, we were done." She tried to remain stoic, but she sensed Conroy could see the hurt underneath.

"I'm sorry," he said softly. "Maybe it was for the best … because he *was* involved."

Catherine stared at him, her eyes narrowed.

"Through my friend, an investigator, I found the man who put him up to it. Anthony was just a pawn … he owed this man a debt. I don't know what it was, but he was blackmailed."

Catherine bit her lip and looked away.

Before he spoke again, Conroy leaned closer and squeezed her hands, whether to give or to get reassurance, Catherine couldn't be sure.

"The man who was behind the threat sent the men to my cabin. I believe it was they who poisoned my dogs."

This snapped Catherine back to the present.

"You can't let them get away with it," she said, her sudden anger surprising Conroy. "It's not right. You have to *do* something!"

"Yes. I do."

⊷⊨⊙ ⊙⊨⊷

Minerva and Gladys sipped coffee in the study of her apartment, the sun not quite up yet. Along with millions around the world, they sat in front of a television in order to watch the launch of the Chinese manned mission to the moon.

They listened to the BBC reporters as they described the site in central China: the Xichang Satellite Launch Center in the Sichuan Province. Halfway around the world, it was 6:00 PM—five minutes before the countdown.

"Do you remember watching the launches at the Cape?" Minerva asked.

"I do," answered Gladys. "It's been a long time, but I somehow remember the early ones the best. When John Glenn orbited the earth, it was marvelous!"

"I actually remember the first one. It was Alan's ninth or tenth birthday: May 5th. He was so excited to learn that he shared his name with the first American astronaut: Alan Shepard. He seemed to think the launch was scheduled especially for him."

Gladys saw her friend's wistful smile. She rarely heard Minerva speak of her first son.

"You know," she said, "I had a crush on Neil Armstrong. I remember watching a ticker tape parade on television and imagining that I was sitting next to him, waving at the crowds."

"Gladys!" They giggled.

They turned to watch the countdown as the announcers began to sound more urgent. It was two minutes and counting. The Chinese rocket was as big as the Apollo Saturn V booster, but it had a different profile.

At t-minus 53 seconds, the countdown was paused.

"Ladies and gentlemen," said one of the reporters, "we have just learned that a system malfunction has led Mission Control to halt the launch sequence. We will stand by to see if the countdown resumes."

"Ohhh ... that's too bad," said Gladys. "I wonder if they'll be able to continue."

Fifteen minutes later it was announced that the launch had been scrubbed and would be rescheduled. Disappointed, Minerva turned off the TV.

"Better to be safe than sorry, I suppose," said Gladys.

"True," agreed Minerva. "I can't imagine how complex those things are. It's a wonder they get off the ground at all."

"Speaking of things with lots of moving parts, how are the preparations coming for the Award Ceremony?"

"According to Libby, we're on schedule. Barely. And you're right ... lots of moving parts ... lots of people. I had no idea what was involved in putting on such an event." She sipped her coffee and then added, "If I had known, I think I might have canceled the whole thing."

"You don't mean that!" Gladys said with mild reproach.

"No ... I guess not." Minerva felt tired suddenly, as if it were the end of her day, and not the beginning.

"Is everything okay? You look anxious."

"I'm nervous. So much has to be done, and we're only five weeks away."

"Your staff is very capable, Minnie. I'm sure it will all be worked out. By the way, have you been keeping up with the editorials? These manifestos have stirred up quite a bit of debate."

"Actually, I've done my best to ignore them. I figured I'd better finish reading them before I sift through what others are saying. I still have one to go."

"What do you think?" asked Gladys. "Do you like what you've read so far?"

"I suppose I do. It's still a little unreal. There's so much to digest, and my head is spinning from trying to keep track of all the specific recommendations. I have a whole new appreciation for what the judges have had to deal with."

"I know what you mean. I tried to read one of them, but I only made it half way through. I'm afraid politics is not my strong suit."

Minerva nodded. "Between you and me, it's not mine either. These teams have worked so hard on their ideas, but now I wonder who will bother to read them, much less *act* on them."

"You said it yourself, Minnie. The goal was to reset the conversation, and you've done that ... regardless of what happens next."

"I keep thinking about the children," said Minerva. "They seem to have been lost in the shuffle."

"What do you mean?"

"Except for the task where they put things into their own language, the rest of the responses have been written at a pretty high level. I was naive to think the toughest problems could be solved by simple means."

"Don't be so hard on yourself," said Gladys. "Even if the language is more complex than you imagined, these teams have put things in far simpler language than has ever been done. If the same thing were attempted by politicians, it would have required a thousand pages. Of course, most of them don't bother to tell the truth in the first place!

"That's what makes this such a tremendous accomplishment. People from all over the world have named the problems, explained the causes, and offered solutions. You should be proud."

"Thank you, Gladys. You're sweet. *That's* why I want you to be there in Houston ... to keep me from borrowing trouble."

Minerva was about to get up to see about breakfast, but she remembered something. "You know how I said I have one more of these things to read? Well, there's actually one more after that, but it's an unofficial entry."

"What do you mean?" asked Gladys.

"Several weeks ago, it was brought to my attention that a team that was eliminated at Task Four continued to submit responses and post them on their official page. They have completely ignored the fact that they're out of the competition."

"That's incredible," said Gladys.

"They're from Brazil, and they live in a wretched hillside shanty town. They have a huge following on the Internet, but since they're not in the running, the media have largely ignored them."

"That doesn't seem fair."

"No," said Minerva, looking at the first rays of the sun on the distant buildings, "it doesn't."

⋄⊨⊙⊜⊫⋄

Besides the premium he placed on anonymity and deniability, Walter Geier now recalled a much more mundane reason he had only allowed one previous visit for the guest who now sat in his study. He detested tobacco. Barely hiding his contempt of the habit, he said nothing when the man reached for yet another cigarette. His most valuable and loyal associate had, after all, agreed to a risky face-to-face meeting. Geier bit his tongue.

The Watcher, as the core members of their cadre called him, stared into the distance, distracted, oblivious for the moment of his associate's annoyance. His body was pale from lack of exposure to sunlight, and the fingertips of his right hand were permanently stained from nicotine. Behind this façade of gray frailty, however, lurked an uncanny mental ability to tap into and predict economic and cultural trends. His efforts had proven invaluable for their consortium of investors. His name was Hayden Moss.

The only other man in attendance was Carter. He sat motionless and tense, for he would be responsible for implementing whatever agenda resulted from their conversation.

"As I was saying," said Moss, "I'm not convinced that we need to make another play. What good would it do? The manifestos have been published. Not only would we put our network at considerable risk, we would pretty much guarantee widespread sympathy for their cause."

"You're right," said Geier soberly, "however ..." He shot a critical glance at Carter and then turned back to Moss and continued. "We have a security problem. Only time will tell how serious the breach is, but inaction could be catastrophic."

"Go on," said Moss, exhaling a cloud of smoke.

"I don't know how he did it, but Conroy's man stumbled onto some evidence that could expose our role in Athens. We could just take him out of course ... both of them, for that matter. But that would trigger an even broader investigation."

"That may be," said Moss, "but if they won't back off, we have to do *something.*"

Geier nodded but remained silent. Holding fingertips to fingertips, he sighed.

"When he crashed my little party a couple of months ago, he mentioned insurance. That's what we have to get around. If we knew where he was keeping these 'policies,' we could approach this surgically."

"But since we *don't?*" asked Carter. Geier shot a glance of disapproval at his lieutenant. The impertinence of his interjection was outweighed by the fact that it was true.

Moss looked at Carter, too, but nodded thoughtfully. "Since we don't," he said, as if to reinforce the point, "we have to be more creative. And we might have to cast a wider net."

"Perhaps, but that might make this even messier. What we need," said Geier, pausing for dramatic effect, "... is to include a little misdirection."

"What do you have in mind?" asked Moss.

"A hit—multiple hits actually—against the core members of Vox Stellarum. The agenda in Houston will actually make it convenient. And, of course, we'll have somebody take the fall."

"Are you *serious?!*" asked Moss as he stubbed out his cigarette. "Security will be extreme. Getting a man in position with anything bigger than a pocket knife will be next to impossible ... and we're only three weeks out."

"That's true ... but I have an idea."

⋅⇥▪⊙ ⊙▪⇤⋅

When Henry Godfrey landed at the airport, his brother Blake met him at the passenger pickup. Between cussing at the Houston traffic and rambling on about a cocktail party he felt obliged to attend, Blake managed to ask Henry only a few general questions about his adventures. Surprised by his brother's lack of interest, Henry shrugged it off as stress.

Because his condominium was still being leased, he'd arranged to stay with his parents for a few days prior to checking into the hotel with the other staff members. By the time they got to the house, it was dark, and there were only a few lights on inside. Disappointed at the low-key reception, Henry was nevertheless grateful to be back on home turf.

They walked in the front door, and Henry called out, "Hello! Anybody here?"

No answer. Blake nudged the living room door open.

"Huh ... look at that," he said casually. When Henry poked his head in, the lights went on and he saw the entire family grinning at him amid streamers and balloons. Henry looked up to see a big sign that read "Welcome Home!"

"Surprise!"

He slugged his brother playfully. "You son of a bitch!"

In contrast to the loneliness of the preceding fifteen months, it was a genuine homecoming. They barraged him with questions as they moved toward the dining room for dinner.

"Are you aware that you're a celebrity?" asked his father.

Henry was puzzled. In New York, his public connection to Minerva Bennett had remained muted, and he certainly didn't consider himself famous.

His mother said, "It's true, Henry. *The Chronicle* has dubbed you Houston's most eligible bachelor."

"You're kidding," he said.

"No, she's not," said his sister Marian. "There was a big article the other day about Aegis Academy and your work there as a teacher. They got a hold of some pictures of you teaching, and they interviewed some of your students ... even some parents."

"Why in the world would they do that?"

"Don't be so modest, Henry," said his mother. "Everybody remembers how Minerva described her visit to the school, how you and the kids inspired her. People kind of forgot about it, but when she announced that Houston would host the awards, the press went crazy."

Henry was dumbstruck. As much as he secretly loved attention, the prospect of having his picture all over the papers terrified him.

"It's no joke, Hen. Mom saved the article," said Blake. "I think you should take advantage of this. Think of all the women who're gonna want to meet you!"

That's when he told them about Eliza.

Chapter 39

IT WAS MONDAY afternoon, five days before the Award Ceremony, and the media had taken over the city. The paparazzi that had besieged the airports now descended on the teams' hotels. They staked out the Museum District, the Galleria, Greenway Plaza, and most of downtown.

A large platform had been constructed on the Discovery Green, adjacent to the George R. Brown Convention Center. It was surrounded by bleachers and VIP seating areas, press tents, and food courts. The stage was set for the first press conference. The place was packed.

After general opening remarks, the mayor of Houston welcomed Minerva Bennett and her staff, and then she made a broader welcome to the teams, though they were not yet physically present. The president of the Chamber of Commerce spoke next. He talked about the infusion of diversity, of culture, of ideas—how the dynamic blend would benefit not just the commercial interests of Houston and Texas, but the whole darn hemisphere.

They got healthy applause, but when Minerva was introduced, the flash of cameras and cheers made it clear who the real star attraction was.

"Thank you, Houston. And to those of you watching at a distance, thank you. We are delighted to be here. The city has welcomed us with open arms. This is Texas, after all, a land where generosity and hospitality are second nature.

"There are several other prominent members of this community who will speak shortly, and I intend to keep my remarks brief.

"The contestants aren't here before us just yet. They're getting settled and fending off jet lag, but I want to convey a warm welcome to the finalists, especially the six foreign teams. We're proud of them for going the distance and making the trip—to the United States, to Texas, to Houston.

"Maybe you have noticed the flags displayed practically everywhere in the city. I doubt anybody has actually taken the trouble to count them, but there are *one thousand*. The city is flying the national flag of every single team that entered The Contest. We want all the contestants out there, with their families, their loved ones, their loyal fans, to know that we have not forgotten them. We will honor them through the week in various ways.

"If you look around this green, you will see the flags of the finalists flown a little more prominently. Before somebody tells me that we made a mistake, I have a confession to make."

People began looking around, craning their heads to see what she was talking about. Some counted the flags, puzzled to see nine.

"That's right," Minerva continued, "that one over there is the flag of Brazil. They do *not* have a team in the final round of The Contest. However, a few of you Internet savvy individuals out there may be aware that there's a group from Rio de Janeiro, Team 915, that was eliminated after failing to turn in its Task Four response before the deadline. And, you may also be aware, they have continued to participate anyway.

"Yes, you heard me. This team has turned in every task and every assignment, including the manifesto. They did this with the full knowledge that they were officially out of the competition.

"When my staff first brought this to my attention, I didn't believe it. But I've seen the evidence ... it's been there all along, on their team page, just as the pages for all eliminated teams still display their work.

"The fact is, I tried to overrule my trustees and reinstate them after the fact, so that they'd be eligible for the prizes and awards on par with the other eight teams. To their credit, my people convinced me that that would've been taking advantage of my position. And it would have been unfair to the other teams that have since been eliminated. Ultimately, I agreed."

Cameras flashed, but otherwise the crowd was very quiet.

"So, I want to make it very clear that, when you meet the members of Team 915, they are here on a purely unofficial basis. They are here as my personal guests. I hope you will welcome them as warmly as the actual finalists."

⋄⊶⊷⋄

After the press conference, Conroy summoned a small contingent of the Vox staff to Minerva's suite at The Four Seasons. Libby, Catherine, and James were chatting idly when Stewart Maxwell and Sam Minton joined the group. An undercurrent of tension caused the gathering to speak in hushed voices.

Minerva and Conroy could be heard talking at a low volume in an adjoining room. When they walked in a few minutes later, all eyes turned to them. Minerva sat down, her face grim. Conroy remained standing.

"You're all aware of the security breach that affected us prior to Task Six, but, until recently—for lack of evidence—I've withheld some disturbing developments. It's clear to me now that I need to bring these to your attention.

"I believe the men who delivered the ultimatum have had a hand in two other incidents. I've suspected they were behind the bomb threat, just before Task One was announced, but now I have reason to believe they were also responsible for the car bombs in Athens.

"One of my former colleagues, who is ex-CIA, has gathered evidence that links these people to two separate underground networks—one in Albania, one in Greece. Some of these characters are relatively harmless, mostly involving themselves in civil protests and organized crime, but some of them have been known to deal arms with terrorist groups in the eastern Mediterranean and North Africa. We believe a cell from one of these groups built and detonated the bombs."

Even the few who already knew of Conroy's suspicions now looked at him with dread.

"Let me cut to the chase. These people, led by a man named Walter Geier, have gone out of their way to sabotage and derail The Contest. They've tried three times. They may try again."

Stewart Maxwell saw that Minerva was beside herself and in no condition to lead a discussion, so he asked the obvious question.

"Does this mean we need to call off the ceremony?"

Despite the gravity of Conroy's revelations, the idea of actually canceling the final event of the eighteen-month project was so unreal and unthinkable that the others could only stare at him, as if waiting for a translation of what he had just shared.

"I don't know," replied Conroy, looking at Maxwell and then turning to Minerva. Nobody knew what to say.

"Malcolm," said Catherine, breaking the silence, "Do the others know about your dogs?" He flinched at the recollection.

"No." He turned to the others. "These men have made two attempts to thwart my investigation. They killed a man in Boston, who was one of our informants, and they poisoned my dogs. Fortunately, one survived."

James and Libby looked at each other, stunned.

"I considered backing off, but, when I became aware of their potential connection to the incident in Athens, I realized there was no going back."

"What about the authorities?" asked Maxwell. "Surely they can do something."

"Geier is a master at manipulation—from a distance. And he's slippery. It's almost as if he has diplomatic immunity. Who knows how many people he's paid off. So far, our suspicions have been ignored.

"I called you together to let you know that, despite the lack of proof, we need to be on high alert. Our security is already tight, but I want you to know," he said, looking directly at Minerva, "that if you decide to proceed, I'm going to turn it up three notches beyond that."

◦•▸◉ ◉◂•◦

Having committed herself to meeting each team of finalists, Minerva braced herself for a whirlwind tour of the greater Houston area. The destinations varied according to a menu of attractions chosen by the teams themselves; some were well off the beaten path.

Henry's job was to accompany his Aunt Minerva in the role of ambassador and guide. His reluctance was tempered by the fact that they would be shuttled about in a helicopter, to make sure they wouldn't get mired in traffic.

Tuesday morning, they began at the Houston Ship Channel with the Kazakh team. Then they joined the American team from Tulsa at the San Jacinto Monument. Henry impressed the visitors with his knowledge of the local landmarks.

Distracted by the gravity of Conroy's security briefing, Minerva took a while to loosen up. By the time they met the Dutch team in the Houston Medical Center, that afternoon, she was noticeably more relaxed.

They continued their tour bright and early on Wednesday. Hoping to see oil wells and cowboys, the Palestinian team members were disappointed when they were told these were not on the menu. When a helicopter landed next to the caravan of limousines that delivered them to the main entrance of the giant ExxonMobil complex north of Houston, however, they were delighted to see Minerva and her grandnephew step out to join them on their private tour.

The last introductory meeting with the finalists was on Thursday morning. After red tape and stalling gave way to high-level intervention, Team Alt-3 arrived—*two days* after all the others. Negotiations by the U.S. Ambassador to China and the Secretary of State finally convinced the humorless officials from the Politburo to grant visas to their star contestants.

Though they were jet-lagged and exhausted, the Chinese delegation rebounded once they learned that they would be accompanied by Mrs. Bennett on a rare behind-the-scenes tour of NASA. The members of *Peaceful Industry* swelled with pride as they sat in Mission Control and watched the American scientists prepare to monitor the rescheduled launch of the Chinese moon shot ... slated to blast off minutes after midnight.

After all these official rendezvous had been handled, Minerva was exhausted. She wanted to retreat to her suite at the hotel, but she forced herself to rally for one more meeting ... with the Brazilians.

"Henry, did you speak to Señor Martín, the team leader?" asked Minerva. "What would they like to see?"

"Believe it or not, they want to visit my school."

"*Really?* How do they know about Aegis Academy?"

"Well, you have kinda talked it up. But the real reason is that, during Task Three, I told them about it."

"You *scouted* them?"

He nodded. "They were my favorite team."

She gasped. "Why didn't you ... Why ... Did you *know* about them? I mean, did you know they continued to participate?"

"I had no idea. When I didn't see their number on the Task Five roster, I was bummed. But when I heard you announce that—"

He looked away, suddenly emotional. When he turned back, his eyes were moist.

"When I heard that you invited them to be your special guests, that you wanted to honor them, I was ... *Thank you.*"

⇢▸◉ ◉◂⇠

The parade was on Friday. It began on Allen Parkway, the scenic drive connecting River Oaks with downtown. It was a beautiful green expanse along which bleachers and viewing areas had been prepared. The route would turn left between Sam Houston Park and the Houston Library, then wind its way through several blocks before terminating at a public square adjacent to the Alley Theatre and Jones Hall.

Nobody knew how many people to expect, but due to the legion of celebrities and dignitaries, not to mention the teams themselves, it was expected to be well attended. The Houston Police had called in its full force for the entire week, including a hundred mounted police. Three dozen Texas Rangers and scores of county sheriffs and deputies augmented the security contingent.

There were no floats as such, but the contestants rode in a variety of decorated vehicles: convertibles, pickups, and flatbed trucks. This left them vulnerable to the elements, but the weather gods had cooperated. It was cool and clear.

Minerva's vehicle led the parade, and Henry was assigned to be her escort. Her bodyguards occupied the driver's seat and passenger seat. Next followed a truck with Libby, Catherine, and James, standing and waving at the crowds. Behind their vehicle, eight groups of finalists followed in order of registration, proudly waving their country's flags. The twelve members of the Panel of Judges brought up the rear, riding in pairs according to region.

The feedback in the press had been overwhelmingly positive regarding Minerva's invitation and inclusion of the Brazilian team. They were inserted between the last group of finalists and the first pair of judges.

Special seating in various choice locations was given to members of the contestants' families, representatives from the corporate sponsors, foreign dignitaries, celebrity guests, as well as the remainder of the Vox Stellarum staff.

Notably absent from these arrangements was Malcolm Conroy. He had chosen to remain behind the scenes for the two mass events—the parade and the award presentation—and to embed himself with the security personnel. He had spent the bulk of the week briefing the police, sheriffs, and rangers, especially regarding high-profile participants.

⋯⊳═◉ ◉═◁⋯

"Well, Henry, our big moment is here," said his Aunt Minerva, perched in the sprawling, white leather back seat of an immaculate, fire engine red 1959 Cadillac convertible. Despite the urgency of Conroy's admonitions, his aunt seemed to be enjoying herself. Their car began the slow drive behind the lead marching band.

Riding in the parade was yet another obligatory role that Henry would have preferred to decline. He wanted to view the spectacle with Eliza, but from the anonymity of the bleachers. She was seated with the Godfreys in the VIP booth near the end of the parade route.

Now, as Henry and his aunt passed the first bank of bleachers, he reached for the cowboy hat that Libby had urged him to wear. He thought it was ridiculous and was about to take it off, but his aunt frowned at him.

"Come on, Henry. This is a *parade*. You look very handsome."

She was wearing a full-length mink coat and a tiara, so he could hardly complain about dressing up and showing off.

Nervous and self-conscious, Henry tried a trick he sometimes used when speaking to groups of parents at Back to School Night. To keep from worrying about his own appearance, he would picture the audience in absurd costumes. The men wore togas, and the women ... very little else.

It worked, and even Aunt Minerva noticed him relax.

"What are you grinning about?" she asked.

"Just thinking how bizarre it is to be in a parade."

⊷⊷⊶ ⊛⊷⊷

In an almost empty apartment, a man adjusted the light on his makeshift workbench. He leaned forward to make final adjustments to the device on which his reputation—and his retirement—would soon depend. Though he had tested the custom-designed circuit numerous times, he performed one more check and then placed the batteries in the chargers.

Satisfied, he got up, stretched, and walked to the bedroom window. It faced the parking lot and, one mile to the west, the stadium. Peering through his spotting scope, he observed the activity that, as busy as it was, would increase dramatically the following day.

He counted four security checkpoints and dozens of patrol cars scattered strategically along the perimeter of the grounds, their rooftop strobes of red, white, and blue flashing ominously to anybody with a doubt as to the seriousness of their intention to secure the location.

Impressive, he thought, *but it won't do you any good.*

Chapter 40

THE FINAL DAY had arrived. NRG Stadium began to fill up in earnest as the support crews and entertainment ensembles finished their preparations and rehearsals. The Vox Stellarum staff retreated to its private box for a final break from the gathering crowd and to eat dinner. The pale blue sky, visible through the open roof, turned pinkish-gray as sunset approached.

At 6:45, Minerva and her team took a private elevator down to the field level, and six Texas Rangers escorted them to their seats. Minerva, Libby, Catherine, and James peeled off and ascended the stage from behind. The orchestra, occupying a bank of risers on one side, was warming up the audience with a jazzy overture.

An elderly man with white hair and a ruddy complexion was escorted to the seat next to Minerva. He wore the black suit and clerical collar typical of Catholic priests. He was Father Peter Ellison.

Because he hadn't been able to arrive until that morning, he and Minerva had had only a brief visit—after the reception for the judges. Now, amidst the packed stadium, they strained to hear one another over the band.

"Are you nervous?" she asked.

"Terrified," he said, "but I'll manage."

One minute before seven, the lights dimmed. When it was almost dark, spotlights hit the stage, and an announcer said, "Please rise."

Many of the foreign contestants and their family members, as well as a host of others, were wearing lightweight headsets. Tuned to specific frequencies, depending on the native language, these would deliver a translation of the proceedings.

Father Ellison approached the podium.

"Good evening! I can't tell you how honored I am to be here. I have known Minerva Bennett for many years. When she first spoke to me about her idea to put on a contest, I was intrigued. It was not just the unusual nature of the competition she described, it was the way she presented her plan. She spoke with an eagerness that I hadn't observed in her since the old days.

"I was skeptical, frankly, but I sensed that she was responding to some deep passion that had her in its grip. This new idea, to save the world, well ... what could I say but *Why not!* And here we are tonight. This is the result of putting one's vision and action together.

"We have many faiths represented here tonight ... further proof that The Contest is already a success. If the spirit moves you, consider holding hands with your neighbors. You need not bow your heads, or close your eyes. In fact, I'm going to ask that we turn the lights back up and look around at one another."

As the lights came up, seventy-five thousand people did just that—reached out to their neighbors and held hands.

"Gathered in our highest mission, we ask God, the Great Spirit, the Order of the Universe, to bestow upon us this evening, and on the many days and nights ahead, the courage and the strength to follow through on the wonderful work done by these worthy contestants. Help us to pierce the veil of ignorance and to reach out to one another in the spirit of reconciliation and cooperation.

"Help us be willing to make the difficult decisions that only the most committed can make, that we may fend off the march of fear and resignation. Help ignite within each of us the sparks of hope, and passion, and joy, for these are the ingredients we require for a revival of peace and prosperity. Bless us with the curiosity of our children, the patience of our elders, and the humility of our wise. Amen."

The crowd was slow to drop their hands, but as they did, a few started to clap. Soon there was a thundering ovation. Father Ellison returned to his seat and smiled at Minerva.

The lights dimmed, and the master of ceremonies approached the front of the stage.

"Honored guests, contestants, families, friends, and fans ... *Welcome!* My name is Tucker Middleton, and I am honored to be here tonight as your MC. When Minerva Bennett first appeared as a guest on my 'Late Night' show last year, she won me over. She appeared two more times, and I was impressed with her vision.

"It reminded me of *Charlie and the Chocolate Factory* on steroids, or a nicer version of *The Hunger Games*. But there was a key difference: The Contest would be *real*. Minerva proposed a program of sweeping change that wouldn't require any gimmicks. No fantasy, no futuristic science fiction ... just an ungodly amount of money." Laughter in the audience. "And what's more amazing is that it's *her* money!

"For every critic, there were ten who were inspired. Minerva Bennett may be crazy, but she's no fool. She knew that to get the whole world talking about solutions—real solutions to the 'Dangers Confronting Mankind'—she had to strike at our deepest needs and our highest hopes.

"There's no doubt that some of the teams signed up simply for the money, but it became clear that the vast majority signed up for something much more powerful—a commitment to ideas. They only needed a platform ... a stage, and *that* is what The Contest is.

"So, there you have it, folks. We are here tonight, on that stage. We are here tonight to witness the culmination of The Contest as we listen to and, I hope, seriously consider the truths that these stars have voiced."

When the applause faded, Libby and Catherine replaced him at the podium.

"It's time to meet the teams," said Libby, "and we're going to get a taste of what they went through to get here and what inspired them. In order of registration, we're going to see a short video prepared by each of our finalists. After that, we will meet the Panel of Judges. They will do their thing, which is to remind us that this is, after all, a competition. Four of the teams will be eliminated, and we will be down to the final four."

Besides the massive Mitsubishi Jumbotron mounted high above the stage, several other huge monitors had been erected so that nobody would miss the close-ups of the participants. The videos were conducted in the home language, but these were dubbed with English subtitles. Several teams had impressive editing, but the Chinese team employed some computer graphics that stole the show.

⊷═◉ ◉═◠

While the crowd was engaged in the videos, Malcolm Conroy roamed the stadium. He'd been on edge all day. That morning, he had attended the reception for the judges, briefly reconnecting with those he had personally recruited. His pride and satisfaction were overshadowed, though, by his preoccupation on security.

He had arrived on site at one o'clock to inspect the entire premises, checking in with as many security units as he could.

When he moved inside the stadium, he took a bottom-up approach. He started with a visual inspection of the platform and the stage. Then he checked out the waiting areas, the loading docks, and the concession courts, working his way up one level at a time.

He had to delegate the search of the private boxes, for there were over one hundred fifty. He spoke with the security team at every entrance and eventually found himself walking the parapet high above the field.

Conroy noted with satisfaction that, except for the MetLife blimp several thousand feet up, the sky was clear. News helicopters and commercial air traffic had been rerouted—the FAA had mandated a five-mile radius no-fly zone. The retractable roof had been inspected earlier in the day by the bomb disposal team of the Houston Police.

Shortly before the lights dimmed for the invocation, he had surveyed the entire scene with binoculars. From everything he had seen, the grounds were secure.

Why am I not satisfied? he thought. *What have I missed?*

Even though there was no political reason for them to try once again to intercede, for the manuscripts had been published, Conroy could not shake the sense that Geier and his people hovered in the shadows. *The bastard made it personal*, he thought, *and he's not going to quit until he draws blood.*

⋅►═◉ ◉═◄⋅

When the last video concluded, the crowd was restless. They were ready to find out which teams were to advance.

Middleton called James Ruhle over to introduce the judges. As the twelve members were summoned, each one had a brief bio displayed on the monitors. At Conroy's request, his name was left out of the program. He was merely part of the "delegation that had sought out independent activists, futurists, and statesmen of inviolable moral character."

Once they were assembled on stage, several made brief statements.

Mahmoud Azzam spoke articulately. "I teach information technology at The University of Cairo, and I am constantly urging my students to beware the sirens' call of technology. It is easy to forget that *we* are the programmers. We humans create technology to serve us, and we must not let it be the other way around. Programmers write code, but so do we all. The codes we write are called *values*.

"We must not only pay careful attention as we create them, but we must be painstaking in their implementation. In short, we must practice what we preach. What impressed me most about these contestants is their integrity. They stand behind their ideas, and, for this, I salute them."

Going last, Dr. Helen Caldicott, the Australian, summed it up well.

"I've been committed to healing the planet for fifty years, and I can say unreservedly that my role on this panel is the most far-reaching. These wonderful people ... and I'm now referring to the contestants, individually and collectively ... these wonderful people have worked incredibly hard. They have reached deep within themselves in order to share their elegant solutions. Radical though some of them may seem, this is precisely what is long overdue. These independent teams, following their own moral compasses, have shown us several promising paths toward difficult, yet absolutely achievable, goals. My faith in humanity has been restored."

As they took their seats, Libby and Catherine returned to the podium.

"In all the prior rounds," began Libby, "the judges only needed to pass half of whichever responses they received in their encrypted portals. But when the judges received the finalists' manifestos, they were instructed to place them in order. While even eighth place is guaranteed individual prizes and a substantial team award, there is, nevertheless, a sizable gap between that and the top prize."

"So, before we open this," said Catherine, waving an envelope, "we're going to have each team stand and remain standing as we call out the names of every contestant. Then we will open the envelope and announce the four teams who will advance."

Spotlights pierced the giant space and swirled all around the team delegations. Team by team, all 96 contestants were introduced. The entire section directly in front of the stage was bathed in lights.

"Look around, contestants," encouraged Libby. "Breathe in the glory. You deserve it."

For about two minutes, practically the whole crowd stood and applauded.

"Now," Libby explained, "if we call the name of your team, approach the platform and join us on stage. The four teams not called will be seated, and, we hope, join in congratulating their fellow contestants."

She opened the envelope.

"Team 233, from Amsterdam, in the Netherlands, please come forward." The members jumped and shouted and danced as they made their way up on stage. Catherine showed them where to stand.

"Team 489, from Tulsa, Oklahoma, in the United States of America, please come forward."

Amid the applause, the members of a couple of teams turned to one another in concern, perhaps realizing they were being called in order of registration.

"Team 765, from Durban, South Africa, please come forward." They were jubilant, high fiving each other as they excitedly bounded up the steps to the platform. From his prominent seat on the stage, Henry made eye contact with Steven Pace and smiled. The former lieutenant no longer needed his cane, though he walked with a limp. He was grinning from ear to ear.

The Chinese and Palestinian teams huddled in breathless anticipation. They now realized they were being called in the order of registration.

"And finally, Team Alt-3, from Wenzhou, Zhijiang Province, in the People's Republic of China, please come forward."

The Chinese contestants showed their elation by way of toothy grins and tears, displayed on the Jumbotron and on televisions across the globe. They mounted the stage as one, holding hands as if they were afraid to let go.

In most competitions, there are only two teams. People are familiar with the rules, and they are usually intimately familiar with their favorite players. The Contest was different. Of the 75,139 people in the stadium, fewer than one thousand had read all eight manifestos. And of those, most did not necessarily have a clear sense of whether the judges had chosen well or not. Perhaps it was true what one cynical pundit had proclaimed earlier in the week: "It doesn't really matter who wins The Contest. They're all rich. They're all famous. Only a handful of their ideas have a chance of seeing the light of day."

In this moment, though, none of that seemed to matter. The field of contestants had narrowed. There were now only four teams. After several minutes of guarded celebration among the teams on the stage and mutual consolation among the teams on the floor, all the contestants returned to their seats.

Then, portions of the stage slowly shifted to signal a 20-minute interlude. The crowd was entertained by music and dance from a variety of continental regions.

⋯⟫◎ ◎⟪⋯

When the lights dimmed, Tucker Middleton stepped to the podium.

"We'll begin the second half of our program with the woman who dared to share her vision with us ... I present Minerva Bennett."

She wore a navy blue dress, a shimmering white cloak, white gloves, and a sequined pill box hat. She shook Middleton's hand, and he retreated to the side of the stage amid a standing ovation.

"Good evening!" she said. "Thank you for coming." She shielded her eyes from the spotlights to peer out on the sea of faces.

"I can't quite believe we're all here. This is the day many of us have been looking forward to … for what seems like years but has only been eighteen months. I never really imagined what it would it be like to host such a … such an effort, and it's wonderful to see it all come together. My deepest gratitude goes out to my staff and the Board of Trustees.

"Tonight, the real stars are, of course, the contestants. We are here to celebrate their achievements and their ideas. Before we move on to our next elimination round, I thought it would be nice to honor some of the people who knocked me out of my former orbit—who gave me a new way of looking at things."

Minerva gave a much-abridged version of her visit to Houston, her conversation with Henry, and her subsequent tour of his school. While she described her grandnephew's antics in the classroom, Henry, Gordon Hooper, and several students rose from their seats at the side of the stage and joined her at the podium. Catherine Myers also joined them, holding a tray. Minerva picked up a gold medallion, suspended from a red ribbon, and placed it around Henry's neck.

"Henry, thank you for reminding me of what youth is all about."

She gave one to Gordon Hooper as well, along with an envelope.

"Principal Hooper, thank you for all that you do." He looked questioningly at her. "Open it," she said. "This is a token of my appreciation. I trust that you and your colleagues will put this to good use."

Seeing a check with way too many zeroes, Hooper was dumbfounded.

Minerva then awarded medallions to the children. She placed them around their necks and shook their hands. Two were the sixth graders who had read their essays on the day of her visit. One was a third grader named Helen, a girl who learned that if a pig and a spider could get along, then maybe people could, too.

Henry remained on stage next to James Ruhle as the others returned to their seats. Catherine and Libby joined Minerva at the podium.

"Since The Contest began, I've received hundreds of letters of encouragement. One contained a quote which I rather liked, by Antoine de Saint-Exupéry, author of *The Little Prince*. He said, 'Grown-ups never understand anything by themselves, and it is tiresome for children to be always and forever explaining things to them.'

"How true. Let's sit back now and see how the children on our four remaining teams have explained things to us grown-ups."

For the next twenty minutes, they watched edited versions of Task Five.

When these concluded, the eight children were invited up on stage to take a bow. Minerva shook their hands while Libby placed medallions around their necks. Pem Hoowij, from the Dutch team, stepped forward spontaneously to hug Minerva.

"Thank you, children, for showing us grown-ups that the solutions are simple if we only dare to pay attention."

As the children were escorted back to their seats, Minerva continued.

"Earlier this week, I announced that I had extended a special invitation to a team that had been eliminated in the fourth round. I want to stress that it is not my intention to upstage any of the teams that earned their way into the finals. Think of Team 915, from Rio de Janeiro, as an Honorable Mention."

She turned to Libby. "Can we have them come up?"

"Of course."

As Minerva spoke, Libby and Catherine walked down the steps to the floor of the arena and waved at the Brazilians to follow them back up to the stage.

"You know their story. They were eliminated for their failure to submit their response by the deadline. What was unusual, however, is that, rather than walking away and returning to their former routines, this team decided to continue. They knew, of course, that this was all unofficial, but they did it anyway. It seems that they played for the sake of playing ... they solved for the sake of solving ... they—"

Minerva got choked up as she watched the Brazilians mount the stage. Out came her tissue. The crowd was silent. She finished her thought.

"... they hoped for the sake of hoping ... and for that, I think they deserve a big hand." Thundering applause rocked the stadium.

Catherine brought the tray over to Minerva, laden with twelve more medallions. As each member of Team 915 stepped forward, Libby stood at the podium and announced their names. As she moved from the adults toward the children, Minerva remembered watching the Task Five video of Tiago Díaz and his teammate Natalia Santos. She had been riveted by the joy and enthusiasm that came through in every word they spoke.

Natalia looked up and smiled as Minerva presented her medallion. Finally, she stopped in front of Tiago. He stood so tall and proud, as if he were trying to grow another foot on the spot. Minerva suddenly recalled her late son Alan, for he used to do the same thing. Tiago's eyes sparkled with the unbridled hope she had only glimpsed a few times in her life. It was the purest look of youth and promise she had ever seen.

"Hello, Tiago," she said in a whisper, "I'm so glad you're here." She placed the medallion around his neck, put her hands on his shoulders, and kissed him on his forehead.

Chapter 41

ACROSS NORTH AMERICA and, indeed, around the world, the streets were quiet. Very few cars were on the road. It was like a strange holiday. A billion people had gathered around television sets, computer monitors, or radios, and they were tuned to the Grand Finale of The Contest.

A collective gasp circled the globe when Minerva Bennett suddenly collapsed on stage. Announcers speaking every language on earth immediately went into overdrive as they speculated about the nature and the seriousness of her condition.

It had happened simply, undramatically. She had leaned over to kiss the boy from Brazil, and the next instant she was on the floor. Her senior staff rushed to her side, followed by several security officials, police, and a half dozen doctors, several of whom had leapt to the stage from the contestants' section.

The calm of the crowd was surreal. Nobody moved. There was a hush in the stadium.

⋅→══◉ ◉══←⋅

"Yes, I've seen the whole thing ... No, she just collapsed. Maybe a heart attack ... (laughs) ... Yes, that would've saved us some trouble—just a few months too late ... Briefly—he's standing by, awaiting instructions ... What do you think? ... Hard to say—I don't see them just sending everybody home before the presenta— ... Okay ... Agreed. This changes nothing ..."

With a tap on his keyboard, Hayden Moss—the Watcher—ended the call with Walter Geier. Unmuting his monitor, he listened and watched the broadcast as confusion and anxiety gradually gave way to a somber resolve.

Ten minutes later, as Tucker Middleton stood solicitously beside Libby Armstrong, she announced to the crowd and to the world at large that Minerva had been rushed to the hospital. Emotional, but clear-voiced, she declined to speculate, but she assured everyone that, with one of the best medical centers in the world just minutes away, Minerva was in good hands.

Moss blew smoke rings impatiently as he waited to hear her say the magic words. *Come on, lady, let's get on with it. What's it gonna be?*

Libby looked out on the crowd, took a deep breath and exhaled slowly. "We know what Minerva would want us to do, so let's all sit back and gather our wits. The ceremony will continue."

Moss stubbed out his cigarette and immediately composed a very brief message—an encrypted text.

< Proceed! >

⊷⊨◉ ◉⊨⊶

The sky appeared silvery black through the glare of the ring of spotlights high up near the open roof of the stadium. For three hours, the MetLife Blimp had been maneuvering slowly above, supplying the networks with the occasional long-distance close-up, giving the already vivid presentation an even more dramatic perspective.

Now, the captain of the blimp got the word to gain another thousand feet of altitude, for the pyrotechnics were scheduled to begin shortly. While many of the fireworks would be launched from within the arena, from special stations scattered around the field level, the bulk would be fired from special mounts on the roof, as well as from batteries spread around the perimeter of the stadium grounds.

Minerva loved fireworks, and the Fourth of July was one of her favorite holidays. She had insisted on an unforgettable display. From every seat, from every angle, it was going to be a spectacle worthy of the mission that proposed to change the very course of mankind.

⇥◉ ◉⇤

Conroy, standing on the edge of the stage, scanned the crowd with his binoculars. He was so consumed with anxiety that he barely noticed the results of the next winnowing, as four teams became two. Libby and Catherine, with the help of Tucker Middleton, did their best to keep the tone positive.

To switch things up for the crowd, the four remaining teams were asked to stand. Then, one at a time, the Americans and the South Africans were asked to take their seats. It was now down to the Chinese and the Dutch.

⇥◉ ◉⇤

The man looked up from his laptop and decided it was time. He looked out the window toward the stadium. He could just make out the glow of the lights within. It reminded him of a cauldron.

Yes, it's time to stir things up.

The MC had just announced that each of the two remaining contenders would present a ten-minute video showcasing its team's approach. Then, the first place team would be revealed.

The man would need about ten minutes to get his device into position. Sitting at his workbench, he fine-tuned the focus on his viewing scope and angled a second laptop just so, bringing up a live feed from his drone. When the second video concluded, he pressed a button on the controller, and the contraption lifted off from its hidden perch in the back of a dump truck, which was parked several miles south of the stadium, next to a landfill.

The video feed was sharp, and the GPS beacon blinked steadily as the drone moved northward toward the target. Two rental cars equipped with boosting antennas, parked inconspicuously in neighborhoods bordering the giant parking lot, guaranteed a strong signal.

The assassin hummed merrily as he maneuvered the deadly payload toward the unsuspecting crowd.

⟶▰◉ ◉▰⟵

In his most dramatic and attention-getting voice, Tucker Middleton announced: "Ladies and gentlemen, boys and girls, the time has finally arrived to reveal the *winning entry!*"

Libby, Catherine, and James walked toward the podium as the finalists were asked to stand. One had only to glance at the Jumbotron to observe—in the faces of these two dozen final contestants—that their nerves were stretched to the limit.

"Thank goodness," Libby began, "*we* didn't have to decide which teams would be eliminated, which would advance ... They have *all* been impressive. Once again, thanks to our Panel of Judges for handling this crucial responsibility—for bringing forward the best and brightest voices, the clearest visions, the most promising solutions."

"This is the final step," Catherine added, "in delivering Minerva Bennett's vision, but the first step in implementing lasting change. Resetting the course of human destiny will require that we commit to the realizations so ably presented by all our finalists, but which have been most succinctly and elegantly spelled out by ..."

Catherine paused as James dramatically held up a golden envelope, opened it, and handed her a card that contained only one team.

"... the winners of The Contest. Ladies and gentlemen, please join us in congratulating *Team 233, from Amsterdam—*"

A roar from the crowd drowned out the rest of Catherine's words, and for over a minute, there was only the frenzy of celebration and congratulations, spreading from the other teams to the spectators in the highest row.

James and Catherine descended the steps to the floor and waved to the Dutch team to join them on the stage. Screaming and dancing uncontrollably, Pem and Kat were hugging each other. Joost and Margrit, Pem's parents, were almost as jubilant as they laughed and kissed and then hugged Johannes Driessen and every other member of the team.

When they were finally assembled on the stage, Libby gave the signal to dim the lights. Then, from the center of the field, a lone rocket streaked skyward, through the open roof. For a split second, the crowd was silent. When the rocket exploded in a colorful burst of red, white, and blue, the stadium erupted in another round of cheers. This released a fusillade from all of the heretofore hidden panels and bunkers, and a torrent of rockets and sparks were unleashed as Minerva's fireworks dazzled the crowd.

⊷⊷⊜ ⊝⊨⊰⊷

The air was filled with smoke and fire streaking to the heavens. Conroy observed the tumult with heightened anxiety. Not only did the fireworks remind him of the touch and taste of battle, but this particular display overwhelmed his ability to do his job.

As challenging as it was to scan and identify any gestures or movements of interest, his eye caught a young man waving and pointing at something overhead as he ran toward the stage. He wore the formal uniform and maroon beret of the South African Special Forces.

"Steven!" called Henry Godfrey, who stood nearby. The commotion all but drowned out what the two friends were trying to say to one another, but Conroy's attention was now directed upward.

The air was thick with smoke, and tiny bits of disintegrated fireworks fell like confetti. Though the glare of the explosions made it difficult to focus, Conroy could see that something, about a hundred feet up, was maneuvering ominously toward the front of the stage, descending silently by means of six small rotors. In a flash of insight and dread, he knew what it was and turned to two Texas Rangers standing a few feet away.

"It's a drone!" he yelled. *"Take it out!"*

The Rangers reacted swiftly, aiming their weapons in the same direction as Conroy, who held his pistol skyward in a tactical stance. Instinct took over as the imperative of neutralizing an imminent threat took priority over collateral damage. Stray bullets would be nothing compared to the explosive payload that such a device was, no doubt, designed to deliver.

Everybody on or near the stage froze. Even to the uninitiated, semi-automatic gunfire presented a stark and terrifying contrast to the fireworks exploding high above the field. In less than three seconds, Conroy emptied his clip of .40 caliber hollow points. The simultaneous reports from the Rangers' weapons were enough to stun and then terrify the surrounding crowd. All hell broke loose as people pushed, ran, and leapt to get out of harm's way.

The drone jerked awkwardly as one of its motors was damaged by the gunfire. It had continued its eerie descent, but now, fifty feet above the floor of the arena, it began to spin erratically. From the opposite side of the stage, a SWAT officer opened fire with a 12-gauge shotgun. His third shot was a direct hit, and the device plummeted to the ground only ten feet in front of the first row of contestants.

The entire barrage had taken less than thirty seconds, but the retreat from the malevolent tangle of metal, plastic, and—Conroy assumed—high explosives would take much longer. The lights were still dimmed and, though the firework display had been abruptly halted, it was difficult to see. The crowd was disoriented.

No time to evacuate, he thought. *That thing could go off at any instant.*

Tripping over folding chairs and other guests, the crowd frantically vacated the section in the greatest danger. Bounding down the steps toward the device, Conroy scanned the immediate area for anything that could be used as a shield.

Nothing. Everything, and everybody, was exposed.

Two SWAT officers, clad in body armor and helmets and carrying ballistic shields, approached and stationed themselves between the receding spectators and the mangled drone, but they showed no willingness to approach.

"*What the hell!*" Conroy exclaimed as he saw a man suddenly turn and run toward the wreckage. It was Steven Pace.

Conroy grabbed him by the arm and yanked. "You need to—"

"I worked EOD with the South African Special Forces," Pace yelled without looking up. "I might be able to disarm it!" He was on all fours as he studied the wiring.

"You don't have any tools. *Get back!*"

Conroy scanned the area again, racking his brain for options. The stage might work, he thought, but it was still occupied by at least two dozen people desperately trying to flee.

"*There!*" he yelled over the melee, pointing at an enclosure that was approximately fifty feet away—one of the recessed bunkers from which some of the fireworks had been launched.

Pace turned and looked, immediately grasping Conroy's idea. They picked up the broken tangle of carbon fiber components and explosives, and they gingerly carried it toward what they could only hope would be a relatively safe blast site. A red LED light blinked ominously.

Sensing the plan, the SWAT officers hustled the crowd away as fast as they could.

"You're crazier than I am," Conroy barked at Pace. "What were you thinking?"

"I *wasn't!*"

They reached the enclosure and looked at each other.

"It's not as reinforced as I hoped," yelled Conroy above the din, and Pace nodded grimly. The pyrotechnic crew had designed it to be a fireproof shield and to disguise it from view until the appointed time. There was a recess of maybe three feet below the planks that comprised the entire field level of seating. It would have to do.

"The antenna looks damaged," said Pace, "but it's still armed."

Yielding to the recce's expertise, Conroy said, "Just tell me what to do."

"I don't trust our ability to climb over those panels. We'll have to pitch it in and ... and—"

"Hit the deck?" Conroy asked. Pace nodded.

"On three."

They backed up several feet and then, as smoothly as they could manage, lofted the drone to the far side of the square pit. Each man dove as far as he could, face down.

A blinding flash ripped through the air. The concussion was felt at the far side of the stadium, but the shock wave—viewed by a billion people—circled the globe.

Chapter 42

"Here we are," said Henry. He opened the door wide and gestured proudly.

Eliza squeezed his hand lightheartedly as she entered his place—now *their* place, freshly redone after his former tenants moved out. It had taken her two months to be convinced that Henry's decision to return to Houston and his desire for her to join him there were real. When she finally committed, it took her only three days to tie up loose ends in the City, pack her personal belongings, and get on an airplane.

"What a bachelor pad!" she said, laughing. "I think this place is in serious need of a woman's touch."

"I don't know about that, but *I* am," he said, smiling suggestively.

Henry gave Eliza the tour, which, after an amorous interlude in the bedroom, concluded in the kitchen.

"Let's order in," he said. "I don't think I want to share you with anybody else just yet."

Several hours later, they lay on the couch snuggling. The TV was on, and Henry idly flipped from one channel to another.

"You're such a typical guy," Eliza teased. "Can't you pick one channel and just relax?"

"I'm just trying to see what's go—" He sat up suddenly. "Hey, check this out!"

A red banner with the words "BREAKING NEWS" moved slowly across the bottom of the screen as a CNN reporter announced an important development in the investigation of the bombing of the award ceremony in Houston, Texas.

The huge monitors behind the reporter displayed video images of the closing ceremony of The Contest—footage of the winning team standing on the stage, celebrating amidst applause and cheers and fireworks. The camera then zoomed to a close-up of two men carrying something across the floor of the arena amidst a terrified crowd.

As the reporter reminded the viewers of the context—unnecessarily, for the story had saturated the airwaves for weeks following the event—Henry was thrust into a flashback. He remembered how Steven Pace had run toward the stage, calling his name and shouting ... and pointing at the sky. Those were the only clear images he recalled, the rest was a blur.

Even as the announcer continued her update, Henry relived the madness of the immediate aftermath and then the anxiety of the days that followed. Steven Pace, probably because he had shielded Malcolm Conroy when the two men dove to the ground, had sustained critical injuries. Henry had joined the South African team in an around-the-clock vigil at the hospital that lasted four days, which is how long it took Pace to stabilize in the ICU before being moved to a private room.

Since then, Henry had replayed that stream of memories a hundred times. Like everybody else, he wanted closure. Except for the fact that his friend was eventually released from the hospital with the prognosis of a potentially full recovery and that he had returned to South Africa for a hero's welcome, there had been a conspicuous lack of progress regarding the investigation.

Henry held his breath as he wondered if this were just one more instance of the media stringing them along with more of the same rehashed, but inconclusive, speculation. On the verge of changing the channel or turning the television off altogether, he watched the images shift to a completely different scene, a nighttime aerial view of a very large house situated in an affluent suburb of Boston. The property was unnaturally illuminated by diesel-powered flood lights and helicopter spotlights. As the beams danced about, it became clear that the place had become a virtual parking lot for SWAT vehicles, squad cars, and news vans. Yellow crime-scene ribbons crisscrossed the expansive lawns and gardens.

"... approximately one hour ago," said the reporter, "a joint task force of FBI and state police made a surprise raid on the home of the man who, authorities now believe, was behind the bombing of the award ceremony in Houston's NRG Stadium. We have also learned that this man is alleged to have masterminded the car bombings in Athens ..."

"Son of a bitch," growled Henry, hatred dripping from his voice. Eliza turned and stared. Henry's eyes were riveted on the TV, and his fists were clenched.

"Are you *okay?*" whispered Eliza. She placed her hand on his shoulder.

"Huh?" he blurted, the spell broken. "What?"

"Are you okay?"

"Yes," Henry said. "It looks like—" He stopped abruptly and again pointed at the television.

The view switched to an on-the-scene reporter speaking animatedly from the end of the driveway of the mansion. In the background, a body was being wheeled toward the open doors of an ambulance. It was covered with a blood-stained sheet.

"... belonging to Walter Geier, an influential businessman and community organizer. Shortly after the police gained entrance, his body was found with a gunshot to the head, apparently self-inflicted. He was ..."

Eliza put her arms around Henry, who was still leaning forward—tense, frozen.

"That's good news ... isn't it?" she asked, gently pulling him next to her. "Tell me what you're thinking." She peered into his eyes.

Henry released a sigh that was long overdue. He was thinking of the man who had spent only three days in the hospital, instead of the two weeks recommended by his doctors, so anxious was he to take care of unfinished business.

"What do you plan to do now that it's all over?" Henry had asked Conroy, shortly after he left the hospital.

"Find the men who did this."

Staring at the TV, a faint smile of regret softened Henry's features. *He'll never have the pleasure of killing that motherfucker.*

"Henry," Eliza said softly, "what are you thinking?"

"I was thinking that he got off easy, and ..." Henry said, looking away, "I don't think his partners will be so lucky."

⋯⊨⇒ ⦶⊫⋯

"Any movement?" asked Conroy.

"No," replied Lee Fletcher, peering through his binoculars. "But they're in there. The jeep is still parked next to the gate."

The two men had positioned themselves a half mile from the villa, the main habitation of an old banana plantation in the Pacific lowlands of Nicaragua. Conroy leaned against a nearby tree and caressed his hip. And he wondered if the pain would ever subside completely.

"How long before sunset?"

"Thirty minutes."

"Let's move out in one hour then," said Conroy. He glanced at his watch and noted the date. It was December 21st—two months since the award ceremony and one year to the day since he'd been visited by three men wearing overcoats. A faint smile crept onto his face. The tables had been turned. Now *he* was the one paying the unexpected visit. Two of the three were about to receive a wakeup call, before a permanent sleep.

After determining that his friend would recover, Fletcher had been tireless in his search for the men they knew to be involved in the foiled attack in Houston. While the official police investigation centered on Walter Geier, preventing their direct involvement, Conroy and Fletcher focused on rounding up Geier's bodyguards and lackeys, all of whom had returned to the shadows.

Aided by the profiles he had worked up during his months of surveillance and a bit of luck, Fletcher picked up the trail of the man they knew as Jack Carter, but who they now knew went by several aliases. After a prolonged interrogation, Carter finally acknowledged that Smith and Jones had indeed poisoned Conroy's dogs, and he revealed their probable location. Having extracted what they could, Conroy leveled his gun at Carter's head.

"Wait!" Carter had cried. "What if I give you the name of a man you could never catch otherwise? My life for his?"

"Go on," Conroy had said, his pistol pressed to Carter's forehead.

"Haden Moss. He's a key player in Geier's network—the only other man that I know was tied to all the attacks." As Carter described Geier's associate, he revealed a genuine hatred for the man whom he labeled as a "soulless pig." When he gave the man's address, Conroy slowly holstered his gun.

"If you're lying, I will spend the rest of my life hunting you down."

Forty-eight hours later, Conroy and Fletcher paid a midnight visit to the Watcher in New York City. After a brief, but brutal, interrogation, Moss gave up the identity of the man who had piloted the drone. Only when Conroy was satisfied they had enough information to track him down did he put a bullet through The Watcher's head.

It took them a week to ferret out the assassin, a Serbian. He fled to his home country and then made his way to Croatia, no doubt expecting to while away his days on the blue waters of the Adriatic Sea. Pride and a twisted sense of destiny turned to terror when he was finally forced to admit his part in the conspiracy. Offering half his payment for mercy, then all of it, Conroy and Fletcher regarded him with profound contempt. Barely able to squelch his desire to inflict a slow and painful death, Conroy looked at his friend, received a nod of approval, and then emptied his clip into the man's head.

Now, just north of an extinct Nicaraguan volcano, darkness fell quickly. The two avengers moved carefully through the underbrush until they emerged on an old road. They stashed the bulk of their gear in an old shed, retaining only their weapons. Clad in black suits with body armor, they moved slowly and methodically. They paused at the entrance to the courtyard of the villa. The interior was well illuminated, but there was no sign of movement. Faint conversation confirmed the presence of two men.

Assuming that the men had prepped the place with defensive measures, the plan was to draw them outside. Fletcher placed a small object just outside the courtyard and another on the front seat of the men's jeep. He took up his position near the corner of the outer wall. Receiving a nod from Conroy, who was crouched on the far side of the jeep, Fletcher clicked on a remote control and activated a recording. Immediately a lively conversation, in stereo, emitted from the two wireless speakers.

As he listened to the fabricated conversation between two Nicaraguan hoods they had paid earlier that day to read from a script, Conroy summoned all his wits. The decision to turn vigilante, unsanctioned even by loyal associates in the law enforcement community, had long since failed to bother him. He marveled at his calm acceptance of his role.

Within seconds, one of the men, Smith, appeared at the door, gun drawn.

"Who's there?" And then in Spanish, "Quien está allí?"

Fletcher paused the recording.

"Who the fuck is it?" yelled Jones, sourly.

"I don't know," Smith hissed, without turning his head. Holding his pistol in a two-handed combat grip, he took a few steps and then stopped. Jones appeared in the doorway. He held an assault rifle.

"Go find out. I'll cover you."

Fletcher waited a few more seconds and then clicked PLAY again.

The conversation—rapid-fire colloquial Spanish—turned into a heated argument that made no sense to the occupants of the villa. Just as Smith reached the gate and glanced down at one source of the sounds, Fletcher stood and fired. Simultaneously, Conroy did the same.

By earlier agreement, both targets were only wounded, albeit severely.

Emerging from their hiding places, Conroy and Fletcher stepped swiftly toward the men and kicked their weapons away. Fletcher turned off the sound track and placed the speakers in a small pouch slung around his neck.

Jones was slumped against the door, half in shadow from the interior ceiling light. His right arm hung loosely from his shoulder, nearly severed by Fletcher's rapid burst of hollow point rounds. Smith was splayed on the tile walkway. Conroy's shots had rendered his hands a bloody mess.

"*You!*" gasped Jones, looking at Conroy, who had moved fully into the light.

"Yes," stated Conroy simply.

"What are you waiting for? Finish it. *Pull the trigger!*"

"Not just yet," said Conroy. He dragged a chair across the tiled floor, positioned it near the door, and calmly sat down. He imagined that this simple gesture would not only piss off Jones but amplify his pain as well. Aiming his pistol at the man's heart, he slowly leaned forward.

"First, I need you to clear something up."

Fletcher watched solemnly. He knew the gravity of the admission Conroy hoped to extract from the dying man. Ever since he had made the connection during their meeting in North Carolina, Conroy had been consumed with revenge.

"Tell me about Sky High Charters," ordered Conroy.

"Huh?" said Jones, eyes half closed, grimacing in pain.

"Sky High Charters," Conroy repeated. "Specifically, tell me about the flight that left Washington Dulles Airport on February 15—*eight years* ago—en route to Salt Lake City."

Jones opened his eyes a little wider and somehow managed a mocking smile, despite the fact that Conroy's pistol was now leveled at his face. Conroy's austere manner gradually eroded the man's defiance. After a full minute of silence, Jones spoke.

"We were after you," he said weakly. "The others were just ..."

He shook his head with the faintest hint of regret. He lowered his eyes and looked at the pool of blood that had totally soaked his pants.

"I wanted to finish the job, but my superiors waved us off when you went into seclusion ... unnecessary they said."

His voice was calm, strangely devoid of the hatred he had radiated upon their first meeting at the cabin in Virginia. Conroy wondered if the man was holding on to some thread of hope for mercy. But Conroy, who swore long ago to avenge his wife and daughter, hadn't brought any.

"Who sent you?" Conroy asked. "Geier?"

Jones nodded. He regarded Conroy with a matter-of-fact expression, as if to say, *Now, pull the trigger!*

Lee Fletcher watched as his friend raised the barrel of his gun to the man's forehead. He couldn't know the emotional calculus, though, that was tumbling into place to square accounts breached so irreparably eight years before.

Would Jones's death erase the pain and suffering his friend had experienced? He knew the answer was *No.* So did Conroy.

Nevertheless, the man who had assembled a panel of judges for a contest to save the world now cast his own verdict. He pulled the trigger.

⋯⊷⊷◉ ◉⊷⊷⋯

"The packets were mailed yesterday," said Libby, "and that fulfills our charter."

The few remaining staff members of Vox Stellarum looked on and nodded. They were meeting for the last time in the vacated headquarters of the foundation that had budded, blossomed, and flourished for two years. The last step would be to file a legal declaration that the entity that had sent ripples through the world had ceased to exist.

Because the website was to go inactive at the end of the month, certified copies of the winning manifesto had been translated and dispatched to almost two hundred sovereign nations, principalities, and territories. They had included the summaries of the other seven finalists' treatises, as well as that of the Brazilians.

As the grand prize winner, the Dutch team had received the lion's share of the glory in the press, but the other finalists were enjoying almost as much celebrity and adulation. It was still much too soon, though, to know whether any of their ideas would take root.

"I move that we adjourn." Libby looked at Catherine and then at James. What should have been a time for celebration seemed more like a wake. It had been three months since the award ceremony had ended so unnervingly and catastrophically.

With dozens of injuries, it was a miracle that there hadn't been any fatalities. Except that Minerva was gone. It had been determined that her collapse on stage was the result of a massive stroke. She died twelve hours after being taken to the hospital, and her absence still weighed heavily on her staff.

"Now that that's done," said Stewart Maxwell, "I have something for each of you."

He opened his briefcase, withdrew seven envelopes, and placed them in the middle of the table. Each one had a name written in ink. They all recognized the handwriting.

"Just before we left for Houston, Minerva gave these to me for safekeeping. She asked that I deliver them upon the dissolution of Vox Stellarum."

Libby, Catherine, and James reached for theirs, as did Maxwell.

"When I asked her about them, she told me not to get my hopes up: 'These aren't checks—just sentimental reflections of an old woman.'"

"Should we open them?" asked James.

"That's up to you," said Stewart, "but I think I'll wait and open mine later."

They all agreed.

"I'll give Sam his and mail the others," said Maxwell, reaching for the ones addressed to Henry Godfrey and Malcolm Conroy.

Catherine reached across the table. "Let me take this one," she said.

Libby peered at her friend, at first baffled by the request. Then a knowing smile replaced her look of puzzlement.

◦─◉ ◉─◦

Asleep next to the fireplace, the dog looked up abruptly and went to the window.

"What is it, Mercury?"

Conroy sat up in his chair and saw that an unfamiliar vehicle was about to turn into his driveway. He grabbed his coat and was reaching for a gun when he paused. The mud-caked SUV had only one occupant, a woman.

He moved to the porch and stood, hands in his pockets to greet one of the few people he was happy to see. She pulled up next to his pickup, put the car in park, and stepped into the muck of gravel, snow, and ice. She pulled on her jacket, a hat, and some mittens. It was bitterly cold.

"What in the world are you doing here?" he asked, knowing that he didn't really care what the answer was.

"Hello, Malcolm." Catherine smiled guardedly. "I was hoping I would find you here."

"Come on in," he called. Then he noticed the plume of steam coming from the tailpipe of her car. "You gonna leave it running?"

She hesitated. "I've got some passengers. I don't want them to get cold."

"*Passengers?!* What are you talking about?" There was nobody else in the car.

She waved him over and he stepped slowly off the porch. He walked with a noticeable limp. Peering into the rear window, Conroy saw an arrangement of blankets with two balls of fur snuggled together.

"Puppies," she said.

"What are you doing with— ... What *kind* are they?"

"German shepherds." Her purpose suddenly dawned on him, and he glared at her.

"These are for *me?*"

"Yes."

He wanted to be angry. He wanted to tell her to get back in her car and take her little mission of mercy back to the city. "You came all this way ... to give me some *dogs?*"

"Among other things," she said.

"What other things?"

"A letter, for one."

"You could have mailed it."

He stared into her eyes, doing his best to maintain the barrier he'd taken months to reestablish between himself and the outside world. The resolution he managed to effect through his recent vendettas had done little to diminish his propensity toward isolation.

He turned and looked at the door of his cabin. Mercury stood in the doorway, as if channeling his master's confusion. He was neither in guard mode nor pet mode. He looked at the woman, then at his master, as if to say: *Why don't you invite her in?*

Conroy sighed and grinned, a great cloud of steam slowly dissipating between them.

"I can't promise you anything, but you might as well bring them inside."

Before he could change his mind, Catherine turned the ignition off and popped the rear hatch. She pulled the dog bed gently toward her. As Conroy lifted it and carried it inside, one of the pups woke up and looked at him. He set the bundle down next to the fireplace.

"Will Mercury be a problem?" asked Catherine.

"No," Conroy said. He took her jacket and hung it up next to his, and they settled into the chairs by the fireplace. "Now, tell me what you were thinking. What makes you think I want more dogs? And, by the way, just because they're German shepherds, that doesn't—"

"They're brothers."

"*What?*"

"These two were sired by the same dog as Mercury."

"How could you possibly know that?"

"Two months ago, your vet—Ray Lewis—put me in touch with the breeder. When he told me that a new litter was on the way, I told him I wanted the first two picks."

Conroy watched Mercury sniff at the pups.

"By the way, how's your hip?" Catherine asked. "Have you been—"

"I'm fine," he said stoically, cutting her off. "Let's get back to why you're here. You mentioned a letter."

She pulled the envelope from her vest pocket and handed it to him. "It's from Minerva. She gave it to Stewart Maxwell along with similar letters to the senior staff members, to be delivered once the foundation was dissolved. I figured I would bring it since ... since I knew I'd be in the neighborhood."

He glared at her again. "So, what's this really about? Who put you up to this?"

"Nobody put me up to it. I came because I felt—"

"Felt sorry for me?" he snapped. "I don't need your pity. I don't want your sympathy."

Half expecting her to grab her jacket and retreat, Conroy was surprised at her reaction. Catherine just sat there, holding his gaze.

"Aren't you tired of pretending, Malcolm? Pretending you aren't in pain? Pretending you don't miss your dog?" Then, more quietly, "Pretending you're not lonely?"

He sat up rigidly, unwilling to acknowledge her point.

She continued. "I came because I felt sad. I was sad when you told me about Apollo. I know it wasn't my fault what happened, but I still feel responsible somehow. Giving you some puppies won't replace the one that's gone, but I thought it would make you happy and ... I thought you might be glad to see me."

She looked at Conroy and waited for him to respond. He remained silent—jaw set.

She sighed. "I guess I was wrong. I'll take them back."

He saw the hurt in her eyes and the awkwardness in her motions as she rose from the couch and reached for her jacket.

"A while ago," he said, "when I asked you why you came all this way, you said something about 'other things.' What *other* things?"

Now she glared at him, exasperated and disappointed. "Nothing. It doesn't matter now," she said curtly. She pulled on her jacket and was putting on her hat and mittens when Conroy remembered something. He rose from his chair and walked toward her.

"You have an overnight bag in your car, don't you? Were you ... were you planning on staying *here* tonight?"

Catherine whirled on him, red in the face. "That's *none* of your business!"

Only when he realized she was blushing did Conroy finally put two and two together.

"Because," he said, moving even closer to her, "there's nothing in the world that would make me happier than to have you stay. With *me*."

His confession stunned her. She stood there, speechless, struggling to interpret his expression.

That hair, those eyes ... those lips, he thought, and he could resist no longer.

He grabbed Catherine and kissed her before he could succumb to his fear and doubt. When she didn't pull away, he tore off her hat and jacket. He held her close.

When she melted and pulled his mouth to hers, he felt the masonry of his guarded existence finally crumble. Though it was mid-winter outside, Malcolm Conroy had the uncanny feeling that it was spring.

Epilogue

TIAGO AND HIS cousin Abílio waited at their meeting place for the others. It was a typical summer day in February, perhaps a little hotter and more humid than usual. A storm had raged for three days and soaked the region, and several apartments in their settlement were damaged by mudslides. After helping their neighbors clean up and salvage their belongings, the boys had finally gotten away to make their usual rounds.

"Ronaldo told me he might be late," said Abílio.

"Have you seen João lately?" asked Tiago.

"No. His sister told me he got a job down by the docks. Their family is having a hard time—his father was injured in the shipyard."

"What about Silvio?" asked Tiago.

"He is around somewhere ... He knows we are meeting today."

After twenty minutes, they grew impatient.

"Come on. Let's wait in the tree house."

Once they climbed up, they hoisted the ladder and took the radio out of its protective cellophane bag. Abílio clicked it on, but it was dead.

"Here," said Tiago, holding a packet of batteries.

"Wow! These are brand new. It is nice to be rich, huh?"

"I guess so, but my parents only let me have a few dollars each week. They want me to save the money for my education."

"Are they still thinking of moving into the city?" asked Abílio.

"Uh-huh. Some of the other team members have already moved, but Señor and Señora Martín are going to stay. Our team met a few days ago, and they told us they are using their money to open a school."

"Where?"

"Just down the hill from the cafe where Señora Vereira works. She will be one of the teachers!"

"When will it open?"

"I'm not sure," said Tiago. "Since the end of The Contest, officials from all over—even the capital—have been visiting. Señor Mendes and Señor Martín have been trying to convince them to bring in electricity. Maybe even water."

"Do you think that's possible?" asked Abílio, obviously having a hard time imagining such a thing. Tiago nodded. He sat cross-legged with his back to the trunk of the tree. He was holding his medallion.

"Is it really made of gold?" asked Abílio.

"I think so."

"Aren't you worried you might lose it? You should keep it somewhere safe."

"I do," said Tiago. "I wear it around my neck."

"What do you think of when you look at it?"

"I think of Señora Bennett. She was the nicest lady I ever met. She told us that even though we did not win, we accomplished something even more important."

"What was that?"

"We brought the whole world together by playing for the fun of it."

"I am sorry she died," said Abílio. "I think people have changed, and it was because of her."

Tiago's lips quivered as tears filled his eyes. He nodded faintly.

Both boys remained silent for a long time. After a while, Abílio turned on the radio and found their station. Tiago moved to his favorite perch.

The canopy was lush, almost totally obscuring the view of the Baía de Guanabara and the Jobim International Airport. Tiago adjusted his body so that he could have a view to the south. Through an opening in the leaves, he could just see a patch of the Atlantic as it met the horizon, azure sky on the blue-green of the ocean.

He took off his medallion to study it again. One side depicted a helmeted goddess—a spear in one hand and an owl perched on the other. It was the reverse side, though, that intrigued him more. "VOX STELLARUM" was imprinted across the top in fancy letters; the motto *Remis Velisque* was at the bottom. In the middle was an ancient warship with three banks of oars on each side.

He remembered how Señor Godfrey, Minerva's grandnephew, had sought him out the day after the ceremony, before the group checked out of their hotel to begin the journey home. With Señora Vereira's help as a translator, they were somehow able to console one another. They decided that Minerva had passed away in her happiest moment, surrounded by a whole world that loved her. And it was fortunate, they agreed, that she wasn't there to witness the explosion.

"This is the most special thing anybody ever gave me," Tiago had said, pointing at the medallion. And that is when Señor Godfrey explained to him what the motto means.

"With oars and sails," he had said. "It means making a total effort—giving it all you've got. My Aunt Minerva told me that your team, that *you*, inspired her to have these made."

Now, Tiago's eyes streamed tears of gratitude. He blinked until he could see the medallion clearly, and then he looked out on the ocean. The distant waves called to him in a whole new way.

Acknowledgements

1ˢᵗ EDITION: Two friends were directly responsible for my leap into authorhood. Steve Flynn, shaman and voodoo confessor, helped me tap into my passion to realize what I wanted to be doing with my life. Amelia Ozyck offered me inspiration and support before, during, and after the writing process—she guided me through *The Artist's Way*.

Nick Keene, brother and fellow visionary, was my chief brainstormer and formative editor. Greg Love read every chapter hot off the press and couldn't wait for more. Lucy Chambers, with her considerable experience in the world of editing and publishing, gave me excellent advice and encouragement in the early phases. Brian Moreland did a fine job of professionally editing the first draft; he helped me see that much of my manuscript could fall by the wayside.

Of my friends who read various drafts, Tim Williams, Brooks Bolin, Nancy Gex, Bob Beare, Rory Lewis, June Dyke, Will Coates, and Elizabeth Yerxa were especially helpful. They were loving enough to be critical.

To my immediate family—Dad, Rob, Liza, and Laura, *Thank you!* You encouraged me and supported me in more ways than you will ever know. I will always be grateful.

To my two sons—Sam and Henry, *Thank you* for modeling youth so perfectly. They haven't read *The Contest* yet, but they trust it will become a best seller.

2ⁿᵈ Edition: No matter how well I composed my original manuscript, I felt obligated to make various changes—I kept finding things that needed fixing. Case in point: the cover, which I myself designed, was too specific and, somehow, misleading. I decided to change it. In this edition, you will find a leaner and more direct story.

While some from my original circle of advisory readers helped me, special thanks must go to Gay Wickham. Besides being a scary good copy editor, she offered brilliant input on several key issues. And she introduced me to Cheryl Johnson, who designed the distinctive new cover.

To all my fans—who astound me with their continued encouragement to write—*Thank you!!*

About the Author

 Ben Easton, a former math teacher, now works as a software trainer and a freelance writer. When he's not on the keyboard, he can be found playing golf with his friends, discussing politics and metaphysics with anybody who can stand it, noodling on his guitar, or watching Netflix with a pint of Häagen-Dazs close at hand. He lives in Austin, Texas.

Ben is presently working on his next novel: *The Church of the Open Sky*. Stay tuned …

Visit his website:
www.bennetteaston.com

Made in the USA
Columbia, SC
07 October 2018